11th August, 20

G. V. Simmons,

To Val and Stan in friendship
From George.

.

THE INHERITANCE

GEORGE TIMMONS

Published by

MELROSE BOOKS

An Imprint of Melrose Press Limited
St Thomas Place, Ely
Cambridgeshire
CB7 4GG, UK
www.melrosebooks.com

FIRST EDITION

Cover designed by Bryan Carpenter

ISBN 978 1 906050 05 4

Printed and bound in Great Britain by:
CPI Antony Rowe, Bumpers Farm, Chippenham,
Wiltshire, SN14 6LH, UK

Blessed are the meek for they shall inherit the earth. Matthew 5:5

See also:

Isaiah 58:6-12

Ezekiel 36:26

Chapter I

Several times earlier he had almost woken up, but had felt that something was wrong. He willed himself back to sleep. And yet, even in this semi-conscious state, he knew, or rather sensed, that he could not remain between sleep and reality. He explored his awareness of himself a little more — tentatively. Was he in pain …? Yes, but he also felt sick … No, it was worse — it was that sort of nausea that won't go away. He fled away again, but could not reach oblivion: he hovered in the anteroom to consciousness. Was he dreaming …? Probably … No, he was avoiding something … a hangover? It could be, and yet he feared it was something worse.

"Shall we investigate?" he asked himself. The pain was real enough — but it was not in his head.

"That's odd for a hangover," he said. "Let's investigate further … Ah, the pain's in the legs … No, it's in a leg."

Suddenly, panic flooded over him; he was like Douglas Bader! He'd lost a leg! He knew that he had to find out — immediately! And now the struggle to gain full consciousness was almost as difficult as trying to avoid it. He surfaced as though through a deep, viscous liquid, but found himself looking wide-eyed at a ceiling, not at the sky. There was light, but it was dim. He considered it a while. It was not unpleasant … but why was he thinking of the softness of the light?

"Move!" he told himself, but couldn't. Slowly it came to him: he was bound, restrained. Something held his head and limbs in check. He could move, but only slightly. Momentarily, he forgot the pain as panic struck him.

"Oo-er." That silly word from his childhood leapt from his lips because his fear was primitive, primal, despairing. It was like being buried alive, something that had always filled him with terror.

He became aware of a quiet rustling sound: someone or something, in response to his cry, was moving towards him in this seemingly bare room. Again, his reaction was childish. He screwed his eyes tightly closed as though this would take him back to oblivion. Sensing that he was being looked at, he would not look at his gaoler.

"Don't be silly," he whispered to himself through his clenched teeth.

The presence spoke in reply a word that sounded like "pardon'. He opened his eyes and found himself looking into a beautiful face. He focused and saw a smile of great benignity. She spoke again in a language that sounded like English, though the accent was one he had never heard before. He knew she was asking him how he felt, but the words were not quite right even if they were clearly Anglo-Saxon. It was a patois, which he was surprised to find he understood.

"My leg hurts."

"It's because it is broken."

"But I can't move!"

"Just a moment: I'll release you. We put you in a sonic restrainer when we brought you here from the crash. We didn't want you to do further damage."

He heard the click of a switch and felt the restraint release him very gently.

"But after the examination we thought we'd leave you in case you recovered abruptly."

" The crash?!"

"Yes. Your vehicle came down near here; it's badly damaged, I'm afraid."

"What vehicle?"

"Don't you remember?"

"No. No, I just feel confused."

He tried to think, and gradually some part of who he was began to come back to him.

"I was on my way back to the UK."

"The UK?"

"Yes. To England."

"Oh! Enklant! Ah, nobody's used that term for a very long time!"

Now he was very confused. Where on earth could he be? An even more frightening thought hit him — perhaps he was not on Earth! His anxiety became apparent.

She said, very slowly and carefully, enunciating the words precisely, "Perhaps you have injured your head after all.... But we scanned you very thoroughly and you had only a broken leg ... But "Enklant" and your funny way of talking and your strange antiquated craft ..."

Realising that this made him even more agitated, she smiled even more angelically and continued, "Perhaps it's just the trauma of the crash," and then she added quickly, as though she felt she had been remiss, "Are you in pain?"

"Yes ... my leg, but mostly I'm afraid for my ... I want to know where I am!" he almost shouted.

She looked quite shocked. Then she smiled again and the amiability she exuded calmed him.

"Ssh.... Ssh ... There's no need to get upset. You are in safe hands, and I don't think you are badly hurt ... and you mustn't shout.... Nobody ..."

"But where am I?"

She looked at him kindly but intently, smiled again and said, "To be precise, you are in the emergency ward of the Ironbridge Hospital."

"Ironbridge ...! I don't believe it!"

"You don't believe it? Why not?"

"Such a coincidence.... It's where I was evacuated during the war. Fancy that ..."

Her smile became fixed, her eyes puzzled. She said, "What does it mean, "evacuated"? With an enema? And which war are you talking about?"

She was not so wise as she seemed, he thought, and he could not stifle a laugh, despite his confusion.

"The Third World War, the 2028 one."

Her smile disappeared completely. The seriousness that now clouded her face made her look even more beautiful. She began to speak and then changed her mind. She half turned away and then faced him again, saying, "For the pain."

And she lightly touched his arm with what looked like a small torch. Then she said, "I want you to lie still ...just for a few minutes.... I'll be back very soon.... I want to fetch a colleague to see you."

"Why? Are my injuries worse than you ...?" But she had gone.

The panic began to affect him again. Was he seriously hurt? And what had brought him here? He tried to think of the crash she had mentioned, but all that he felt (rather than thought) was that there was a deep, black hole nearby that he did not want to peer into. However, the pain had gone already, and in spite of himself he felt more relaxed, though even that sent one last tremor through him (what had she given him?) before a slight feeling of euphoria drifted over him. He could trust her, he knew.

Marianne had felt concerned from the beginning. Everything about this man was so strange: the way he had arrived; the ancient clothes and the craft; and the way he talked seemed to fit — from what she remembered of her language studies, he spoke what sounded like old Enklisch, and she could understand him even though it was archaic, like his machine and his garb — and then his claim that he had been alive at the time of that ancient war. She found herself trying to remember who had fought it. Was it the Germans and the Russians or was it the Greeks and the Romans, or maybe one of those that the ancient Americans always seemed to be fighting? Perhaps he is a con man with a detailed and cleverly worked out scheme to claim he had travelled through time. People had said it was possible and had even tried it, but they had never succeeded. Perhaps he *had* travelled through time — two thousand years of it! It was so perplexing ... But Asenath would still be in the common room — she would remember the history. And if Radah were there, he was good at asking questions.

Fortunately, they were both still there, drinking coffee and talking about the man. So once she had explained her fears, they were as intrigued as she, though they thought the situation ridiculous. Even so, they knew that it was better to assume nothing, and certainly that one should avoid jumping to conclusions. Nevertheless, they all three talked animatedly, if quietly, as they made their way back towards the patient. They stopped on the way only to look again at his discarded clothes in the treatment room. Asenath said, "This is definitely some sort of suit for air or space travel, but it's one I've never seen before. It must be very early — but it looks new! And it's got his name on. Look — John More — a very Enklisch name."

Marianne spoke the words that were in Asenath's mind, "Perhaps he has travelled through time!"

Radah snorted, but then said, "Let's go and talk to him."

John More heard them coming along the corridor towards him, but was unconcerned, even relaxed. He smiled when they entered, not only because of the effect of the painkiller, but also because the two newcomers were as handsome as the young woman they accompanied. They smiled too, and the man said, very gently, "We hope that now you are awake you feel well enough to tell us something about yourself ... We know your name — it's on your epaulette — but that is all, so could you tell us where you are from?"

"57, Mere Grove, Everton, Liverpool, 5. How's that?"

"Very precise, but it tells us very little."

"Well, I wouldn't expect you to know about the Grove, but you know Liverpool, surely?"

"Of course," interjected Asenath, but rather too earnestly. The others looked at her nervously.

Radah continued, "How old are you, John More?"

"Thirty-six."

"Your date of birth?" very casually.

"Fifteenth of the first, two thousand and twenty-two."

Despite their effort to appear unconcerned, all three were clearly anxious, even nonplussed.

"Excuse us for a moment, John More," said Radah, "We'll be back in a minute."

Once in the corridor and beyond earshot, they all began to talk at the same time — until their training asserted itself. Then Radah, as the oldest, said, "Marianne, you have had most contact with him. What do you think?"

"Well, at first, I thought he must be part of an elaborate hoax, but if he is, then he is a very skilful actor … I began to wonder if he were deranged, but he's quite lucid given the shock he has had. The craft is badly mangled: he could easily have been killed. Then I thought maybe it's a practical joke that went wrong … a very expensive and dangerous one. And who would want to go to such ridiculous lengths, and for what reason?" She paused and then went on, "No, my feeling about him is that he is genuine … crazy as that seems. And all the evidence is that he is what he says he is."

"And what evidence is that?" said Radah.

" The craft, its re-entry burns, the clothes, his speech, his own claims!"

Then Asenath interrupted animatedly, " I wonder if there's anything on the web? It existed before the catastrophes and wars of the third millennium. There's an outside chance some information on him was preserved by one of those ancient groups like the poustinia."

"How accessible is information about such a distant period?" asked Radah.

"As accessible as any other historical information — if it exists."

"Then perhaps we should look to see if there's anything about him."

"I'll stay with him, then," said Marianne.

When she got to his bedside she found he was sleeping peacefully. So after switching on the monitor, she turned to leave, but on reflection she switched on the restrainer too, and then went to join the others. They were just looking at an index of names, but though there were several John Mores or Moores, none seemed appropriate. Asenath was saying, "Father to Thomas More, the philosopher, politician and martyr. Son to the same. They are too early. As is the next — an Enklisch general — and the few from the second millennium — nothing there."

"Try early moon bases. That's where he says he was before the crash," said Marianne.

Asenath's fingers flashed over the keys as she very quickly rejected several sources of information. Finally, she arrived at what seemed to her a possibility.

"Ah, now we are getting somewhere … Aborted missions, crashes … by years. What would his be?"

"Well, given his claimed date of birth and age … er … look at 2058."

"Look! My goodness! There it is!"

"What does it say?"

"Returning from moon base in 2058… disappeared over the Atlantic … No trace ever found …! There's a little more detail … Was on track for uncomplicated landing … disappeared off radar screens when over sea … three day search … vehicle assumed to be on the sea bed but never found."

"And the name is the same?"

"Yes. Look.… But, oh, that's odd — it says he was a schoolteacher! Some controversy about this afterwards … Should he have gone?"

Radah broke in, "Marianne, supposing he is who he says he is, do you think he knows where he is in time?"

"No, I don't think he does."

"What of his mental, and physical, condition. Could we tell him? Would there be any ill effects?"

"We can't be certain, but he is sedated at the moment so he wouldn't succumb to the shock, I don't think."

"Then let's try him. Come on!"

Chapter II

That had been six weeks ago and, despite the sedation, being told that he had somehow travelled two thousand years forward in time had still come to him as a shock. At first, he was sure it was an elaborate trick played on him by the team of astronauts, his recent companions, who had at best only tolerated him, and chaffingly at that — as though he were a pet animal or kid brother.

Even now as he sat in the pleasant spring sunshine on the east bank of the river he had known as the Severn, he found the notion at one moment terrifying and the next laughable. What was even more ridiculous was that the scene in front of him was not so very different from the one he had remembered as a six-year-old. And yet he knew that this whole valley had been badly scarred during the war by terrorist kamikaze bombers looking for the "secret" (but fictitious) high command bunker supposedly hidden there. This whole episode had been written up after the war as a triumph for counter intelligence, but John had lost childhood friends in the devastation, and when he had returned as a teenager he could not even find the house of the Moran family with whom he had been billeted. It was only by chance he had avoided the crashing planes: his mother had been transferred from a munitions factory in Liverpool to a "safe" one in North Wales and had taken the opportunity to bring the family together again in Beddgelert. Now, here he was in the Severn Gorge once more. Marianne had told him that the valley had been restored to what her people believed it had looked like before the destruction. Funny how he thought of them as "her" people. They were his people too, for God's sake! And he was even becoming proficient in their peculiar English.

But it was not just their language that was funny. He thought of the interminable meetings and the hours of questioning in that room in the hospital. At first he felt angry because they did not seem to believe him about who he was and where he came from: they refused to trust him, try as he might to be honest and convincing. But what frustrated him most was that no matter how angry he became, no matter how much he shouted and raved, they remained calm. They even continued to smile at him indulgently as though he were a naughty child in a tantrum. He now felt rather silly about threatening them with his crutches: that had been childish. Again he thought how grateful he was to Marianne for explaining to him that everyone now learned, while still very young, to be calm, not to shout, not even to raise the voice: loud noise was considered to be so dangerous to the human psyche that it was avoided as much as possible.

He listened to the valley below. She was right: he could hear the breeze in the trees and the singing of the birds and little else. Even the group of children he could see exploring the flora of the floor of the wood beside the restored Incline seemed to communicate in hushed tones, though animatedly and excitedly enough as they compared notes about their findings. Just occasionally their joyous and gentle laughter tinkled across and charmed him. He dearly wanted to go across to talk to them, even to air his knowledge of the local grasses, shrubs, weeds and wild flowers, but Marianne had asked him to speak to nobody until what should be done about him had been decided. And, knowing his impatience, she had once more explained carefully and quietly that no decisions were ever taken hastily. It would necessarily be a long process, because several people with relevant expertise had requested an interview with him and they had to be briefed on why it was better to keep his origins secret. Delay had to be accepted: precipitate moves were dangerous anyway, whatever the circumstances.

"What do you bloody do in a sudden crisis?" he had said, raising his voice.

"Mostly, we don't have them," she had replied calmly.

"But what happens when you do?!" even louder.

She looked nonplussed, even surprised and said, "We deal with them! And I've asked you not to shout."

And for once her eyes did flash — but briefly. Then she regained her control. She did not smile, however. He found her impassivity so disturbing that, angry though he was, he had let the matter drop. He realised that he did not want to annoy her.

The young teacher with the children had brought them out of the wood and they were now sitting in a circle ready to discuss the day's findings. John, leaning heavily on his walking stick, approached a little nearer and one or two of the children looked towards him and smiled. He was encouraged, but before he could get any closer he noticed that the teacher had glanced up and seen not only him but someone behind him. A fleeting look of concern crossed her face and he turned round to see what had disturbed her. A man dressed all in black was standing a little way off. Unexpectedly, the teacher said, "It's becoming a little chilly. Shall we adjourn to Milly's house to share our discoveries? Perhaps her daddy will have the cakes ready, even if we are a little early."

The children seemed surprised, but got up and collected their bits and pieces. They began to talk quietly together as they set off down the hill. The teacher followed once they were all moving, but she turned round again and John could see that she showed just a suspicion of anxiety. Who was causing it, he thought, him or the man in black? He looked around again, but the man was disappearing into the wood.

"Bloody hell! He was spying on me! Hoy!" he shouted, waved his stick and hobbled after him, but by the time he got to the edge of the wood this menacing figure was nowhere to be seen. John stopped and listened intently. He could hear nothing, so the man must have gone along the path because no one could move swiftly through the undergrowth without creating a din; or perhaps he had gone to ground. He could be anywhere. John hurried through the wood and then, with a hopping run, along the towpath, glancing round now and then in case the spy had taken up position behind him. He saw nothing but still had the uncomfortable feeling that he was being watched. By the time he got to the nineteen-forties house, which had been allotted to him in the museum's reconstructed village, his anger had subsided, but he felt both frustrated and lost, even afraid.

He was an exile, marooned in time: an alien who had to be watched. The horror of his locked-in predicament struck him so forcibly that he fell on his knees, covered his face and began to cry the great sobs of a frightened child. In the back of his mind was the thought that this would bring him relief. It didn't. The half forgotten words of a prayer he had learned as a boy came into his mind.

"To thee do we cry, poor banished children of Eve,
To thee do we send up our sighs mourning and weeping,
In this vale of tears …"

He heard a gentle tap at the door and knew Marianne had arrived. He felt a little reassured. He shouted, "Come in," and went quickly into the ancient bathroom so that he could pretend he had been washing his face. When he came out into the living room ready to grill her about today's incident, he immediately realised that he would not be able to: she had her little boy with her.

"Hello, you must be George-Louis," he said as cheerily as he could.

"Yes."

"That's a very important sounding name. Where did you get it?"

"It's from my father and my grandfather," the child said very seriously.

Then he smiled and added, "My father was an astronaut but my grandad makes wine."

The use of the past tense puzzled John and he looked at Marianne. He could not tell whether she had put on that impassive face, which she seemed to use when confronted with difficulty, or whether she was suffering some kind of stress. She put her hand affectionately on her son's head and he looked up at her. Though it was little more than a glance, John caught the strength of the bond between them. She smiled and said, "George-Louis came with me specially to look at your house — to see how people lived long ago."

John nearly said that this house belonged to a period long before even he was born, but the presence of the child stopped him, and though his anger at the thought of being a virtual prisoner was directed partly at Marianne as his mentor, he still did not want to upset her, especially in front of her son. However, what he did say still caused confusion.

"Yes. You see there's no television; and look in the kitchen: there's no fridge."

"He means broadcaster and preserver." Marianne added quickly, but by then George-Louis had skipped into the kitchen and was demanding to be told what that ugly brown thing was.

"It's a gas cooker. I'll show you how it works."

And he struck a match, to the delight of George-Louis, and lit the smallest jet. They inspected several other antiquated (even to John) items, but then came to a chest of drawers, which the child asked if he could open. That was when he came across the biscuit tin full of Lego.

"Wow! These are just like mine," he said, "May I play with them?"

"Of course you can." said John, as he saw this might provide an opportunity to ask Marianne some pertinent questions.

Once the boy had become engrossed in building the bricks in the replica living room, John went to make coffee — forty-first century instant, but just as tasteless unless you put at least two spoonfuls in — and motioned her to follow him. He whispered urgently, "You have said several times that I am not a prisoner; that it's simply expedient to keep my presence a secret, but now I find I am being followed, watched."

She looked indignant and seemed ready to deny his allegation, but he went on, "What kind of a fascist republic is this where innocent people are shadowed by menacing blackshirts?"

Now he saw more than a glint of anger, but she did not respond verbally to this expression, which she had obviously found deeply objectionable. She walked away from him and back into the living room where she spoke quietly to her son. He stood up with barely a murmur and they made their way to the front door. George-Louis said, "I like your house, John More. May I come again, with my friends, to explore and to play with the toys?"

"Yes. Certainly. I shall look forward to that," was the subdued reply.

"I'll be back shortly," said Marianne lightly, but with obvious difficulty.

John went back into the living room and sat on the settee. He wished he had a cigarette, but nobody seemed to smoke either in this bloody saintly world. The "Rule of the Saints', he thought — what a God-awful disaster that was: they almost drove even Cromwell to drink! No. He knew that was not fair: they were nearly all old and unworldly Puritan divines and Cromwell never really wanted them to rule. What about the early Christian church? They also referred to themselves as saints, and held everything in common. That didn't last long, did it? And they were an interfering lot too — all that stuff in St Paul about reprimanding your brother, and if he doesn't reform, casting him out into exterior darkness — or is that from a parable? And then there was Stalin; don't forget him! His thoughts got darker and he began to feel sorry for himself again. Then his fear came back too, but that served to remind him that he had offended Marianne, wonderful Marianne, the one bright spot in his life of exile.

A click disturbed his dreaming: she had come back. He got up and went towards her, but before he could say anything, she made him sit down again and asked him to listen to what she had to say.

"John, I'm sorry. I have to admit that I have not been completely honest with you — not that I have told you any lies. It's that I have kept certain things from you.... No. Let me finish, please. I want to tell you as much as I can ... and, really, you have set the people here some problems ... Well, first of all, persuading you to live in this house was not just so that you would be nearer your own time, as we said, it was also to keep you away from people for as long as we could — and there are good reasons for that if you think about it. Though you did not know it, the museum is not yet open to the public — but that must be apparent to you by now. Also, we have appointed a guardian to keep a watchful eye on you, and apart from today's incident, which he has now seen me about, you have to admit he has been discreet. I'll explain all about guardians later if you give me the chance. "

John did not know if he were angry or alarmed, but his confused emotional state must have been obvious to Marianne and she paused momentarily, then continued, " I am only just beginning to appreciate that what happened today has upset you and I can now see why. If you really did think that the guardian somehow represented fascism, it would be frightening, but he does not. Guardians play quite different roles. They are meant to help people, not threaten them ..."

But she could see that John's agitation was not subsiding, and she found it hard to accept that he was having difficulty believing her — it was so uncommon in her world.

"Look," she said, "there are no prisons or mental hospitals, in fact few hospitals of any kind in Europa — or anywhere in the world, for that matter. The vast majority of people are law abiding and mentally stable. Health is better than it has ever been before. But this is not paradise. Occasionally, individuals, and even more rarely, small groups — and they are usually young — become what used to be called criminal ... Now ... listen to me! Six thousand years of civilisation ... please listen ... have at last taught us that imprisonment does not work, that punishment of any kind is unpredictable in it effects. So instead of people being locked up, each "criminal" has a guardian assigned to him or her and we try to change them through education."

"You mean brainwashing!" he burst in again.

"No, I don't mean brainwashing. Nobody is forced to do anything they don't agree to."

"Ha!"

" I understand why you are having difficulty with this and I'll try to explain further later, but just for now, try to calm down and I'll go on."

She stopped and looked at him. He was wearing his sulking face, which she was now beginning to recognise. She knew he would be quiet but that he would also be determined not to be persuaded of the good sense of anything she said. It was rather like being a guardian, she thought. Still, if they could succeed with their recalcitrants, she had better go on.

"Also, at times people fall ill mentally. In most cases their own families help them, but if the strain is too much, they might move out. Then, merely living with one or sometimes two guardians can help them recover, especially because they are treated so sympathetically. Some are more seriously ill, so there could be times when they have to be restrained. Others, who are more uncontrollable, are at last, but after much patient perseverance, seen as unlikely to recover and there are remote places where they are taken to live — though even some of these return to ordinary life. Drugs are used, but very, very carefully, and they have been monitored over centuries — yes, I mean centuries. However, no drugs are used for most people who suffer in this way and all but a few continue to live in society like everybody else. When people see — very rarely, I might add — someone accompanied by a person dressed in black, they know that person has to be treated sympathetically. The teacher today probably became anxious because the guardian came out of the woods so quickly, and he acted so precipitately because you are such a special case."

"Bloody crackers *and* criminal, I suppose," grunted John.

"Oh, John, don't be so babyish," she wanted to say, but of course she didn't.

To his surprise, she came and stooped in front of him, held his hands in hers, looked intently into his eyes as though she was trying to understand what he was feeling, and said, "John, it's very hard for me to imagine what you are going through. Your situation is so unique. But I do know that you feel you are exiled, almost lost without hope, and that must be awful. I am trying to help you, but there are two thousand years between us, and you as a history teacher must know that you are going to have to learn what has happened in all that time if you are ever to come to terms with the life we lead now. Remember, I know your time, but you don't know mine. Please, please believe me: no one wants to hurt you. We all want to help you."

He could not bear to look any more into those beautiful, brown, now tear-laden eyes. They made him feel such a boor. He understood what she was saying. He leaned forward and put his head on her shoulder, and they remained together for several minutes before he managed to say, "Perhaps it's time for you to go and look after your son for a while instead of this silly man."

But she did not get up straight away. Then, when finally she did and moved towards the door, he said, "Why did you bring George-Louis this afternoon? Was it to ...?" He wanted to say, "deflect my anger," but his voice tailed off. She answered, "It really was because he wanted to come. You'll find when you start to mix more with people — I hope very soon — that children are everywhere, even at work with their parents. Whatever is safe for them is safe for everybody. And he would be safe with you ... I'll see you tomorrow and we'll have to start thinking how to cope with that history. I'll introduce you to the guardian — perhaps we can think of a different way to work with him. I'm not a guardian, remember. It just seemed right that I too should continue to help you, but I still have my work at the hospital."

When John looked up sharply at this last remark she gave him one of her most beatific smiles and said, "Don't be alarmed. We still have people who get poorly, you know, but George-Louis and I will try to spend as much time with you as we can."

When she had gone he sat quietly in the living room, his mind a blank, as though he were exhausted. After a while he realised he was hungry and so made use of the one anachronism in his nineteen-forties house: the microwave. He heated vegetables that he recognised and others he did not. He had worried about the latter at first, but Marianne had assured him that they were genetically safe because they had been developed centuries ago and had never caused anybody any harm.

The evening was balmy, as only they can be in England in late May. After his meal he sat outside for a time, and then said to himself, "Damn it, I'm going for a walk." He did not care whether he was followed or not, though occasionally he looked around as carefully and as surreptitiously as he could; the guardian was nowhere to be seen. Perhaps, thought John, he has the evening off or he is practising his skills more judiciously. This time he went down the Incline to where the village of Coalport used to be. The Memorial Bridge was still there, but when he looked closely at it he saw that it had to be a reconstruction. It was built with a substance he had never seen before: you could not tell if it was metal or plastic and the colour seemed to be part of the material. But it was green as it always had been, and it even shook gently as you walked across. On the other side, in Jackfield, he found that the Boat Inn was still there, but it was really only a facade and the back of the building disappeared into the hill that lay behind. There was no sign of the row of terraced houses that used to be there, but something that might have been a half-size model of Maw's tile factory had been built almost on the site of the old place.

Nobody took any particular notice of him, and though he usually felt conspicuous in the clothes Marianne had got for him, this evening they were like a disguise as they were the same as those of the friendly people he met. He could see what he took to be habitations, but they seemed to be only fronts so you could hardly call them houses. However, there were people going in and out of them and children playing around them. Perhaps, he thought, they live mostly underground, and he remembered that even in his own day such notions had been suggested — for greater insulation against either the cold or the heat.

Looking down towards the Werps, which the bottom end of Jackfield had been unfortunately called, he saw that the area alongside the river had been flattened: the sloping field that had been known as the donkey patch was no longer there. Instead, there was a large area spread out and marked for games. High above it there was a transparent covering held up he knew not how. A group of children, boys and girls aged between about eight and fourteen, was playing a ball game. It looked at first like soccer. It was played with vigour and very fast. Yet it was not rough, and though tackles were forceful, there never seemed to be any ill consequences. Players called to each other in muted tones. They were highly skilled, but obviously the aim was to play together as a team. Suddenly the game switched and appeared more like rugby, and even the shape of the ball changed. Again it was played with great skill and the girls were as good as the boys. Then, unaccountably to John, the game switched back again. This happened several times. Finally he figured it out: the changeover came after a technical infringement, but there was no referee and no whistles and no interruptions. The children followed the rules and seemed to derive great enjoyment from the game. It must have been exhausting. However, children seemed to drop out whenever they wished and were replaced by other eager players. There were few spectators and they all looked either fairly elderly or quite young. Some sat at tables in what looked like a cafe. John joined them and was approached by a waiter, who could have been a sixth-former in the old days. Things don't change, thought John.

"What can I get you, sir?"

"What have you got?"

The young man looked a little surprised, but said, "The usual."

Then, to John's relief, he rattled off a series of strangely named beverages, one of which sounded like beer, so this is what he asked for. While he was waiting for his drink he continued to watch the game with great interest until an oldish man came and sat at his table. John immediately felt wary, but his suspicious look was met with a broad grin.

"Thee'st a stranger here, then?"

"Ar," was John's surly but authentic reply. The man had the same accent as the people John remembered in the valley!

"Whear'st from?"

"Up North — near the Wirral," he added, thinking that if Liverpool no longer existed, perhaps the Wirral did.

"Oh, ar — by Nubreton. I bin there for an 'oliday."

John thought, does he mean New Brighton? And he remembered that he was always surprised that these people went there. It couldn't still be the rather tired seaside resort he knew. But he reflected that even New Brighton could change for the better in two thousand years.

"What's thee doin' 'ere, then?"

"Oh, y' know, just looking around."

"Sort of sabbatical, like?"

"Ar."

"I did the same when I were your age — went to Asie and Inde — interesting, but not like us. You bin there?"

Now John was stuck. What if the conversation went on to reveal his terrible ignorance of the world as it now was? Fortunately, his drink arrived. But the relief was only temporary because he now had to fiddle with the money that Marianne had given him — just to get an idea what it was like. It was plastic but very hard. There were numbers on the coins, but there were other symbols too and he began to panic. Again he was rescued, but this time by the old man who said, "Here, let me get that … Thee'st made a good choice. That's home-brewed. And I'll have one too, please, 'ubert."

"Right ho, Mr Caulfield," said Hubert.

As the youngster went off, Mr Caulfield said, smiling broadly, "He's very polite, young 'ubert. Most people call me Tummy Corfill. What's your name, then?"

"John More."

"Pleased to meet you, John."

"And me you, Tommy."

Just as they were shaking hands they were joined by another person who seemed vaguely familiar to John. He realised why when Tommy said, with a look of pleasure on his face, "Hello, Sanjit. What you doin' 'ere, and where's your black suit tonight?"

It was John's guardian, who, now that he had met him face to face, he saw was Asian.

The resentment that he already felt towards the young man was increased with this knowledge because, though John liked to think he was not prejudiced against other races, when he met any in positions of authority he always had to remind himself forcibly that colour did not matter, and the fact that it obviously did not matter to Tommy, someone who in John's day very probably would have been prejudiced, rankled even more; it was immediately obvious that there was real affection between Tommy and Sanjit.

The latter sensed John's resentment, but not realising there were any racial overtones to it, put it down to their earlier unfortunate experiences of each other. Tommy was unaware of all this.

"This is my good friend Sanjit — and this is John who is on sabbatical here."

They shook hands but neither said anything, and Tommy began to explain to John that he and Sanjit had known each other for a long time. Indeed, Tommy had been his guardian! Sanjit, in his youth, had been something of a rebel and Tommy was then doing his stint as a guardian — many people did at some time or another.

"Made him into a potter, didn't I, Sanjit? That taught him something about self control — when he struggled with the clay and saw how it can misbehave, the penny dropped."

Sanjit grinned and Tommy added, "But we had some good times together, didn't we, lad?"

"We certainly did."

"But John here was just goin' to tell us why he is in this part of the country."

John felt the embarrassment rising again, but stumbled out, "Well, I'm looking at everything really ..."

"Perhaps you're interested in all the cottage industries we have in the valley," broke in Sanjit, " besides the pottery that Tommy mentioned, there's the wall ceramics place just up the road. It's more like a museum, really, and makes things to order for restorations."

"Ar, but why do you want to know all that? You a teacher or somethin'?" asked Tommy.

"Yes," said John without thinking, because that was what he was, but he realised immediately that this could lead to further questions he would not be able to answer: he suspected that teaching was very different in this new age.

Again it was Tommy who, in his naive way, put John on the spot.

"Do you teach children or in a college, then?"

John took a long, slow swig of his beer in the hope that he could think of something to satisfy Tommy, but he had no idea why there should be a distinction between children and college when comparing the two worlds. He was about to plump for the latter when Sanjit came to the rescue again.

"From what you said earlier, I suspect you might teach history, John. So that would be in a college, then?"

"Oh, yes," said John.

And so that Tommy could not break in again, Sanjit added, "And have you got a special period? Something really old like the twentieth or the twenty-first century, I hope."

"Oh ar, all them wars — the beginning of the bad times," added Tommy.

"Er, well, er, not quite." John reflected that he'd be safe on the twentieth century, but he knew less than half of the twenty-first. They would know more than he!

Once again he was saved. This time by a girl aged eight or nine, who ran up to them and scrambled on to Tommy's knee.

"Grandad, can I have a lemonade? Hello, Sanjit."

"Hello, Eunice.... And this is John."

"Hello, John."

"Hello, Eunice."

"Can I, Grandad … Please …?"

"Course you can, sweetheart," and he made a sign to Hubert.

John thought he'd better offer to pay: he hated to appear mean or not able to pay his way.

"Let me get it and another for you and one for Sanjit."

He had put his hand in his pocket and brought out the cash again before he realised that he would have the problem he'd had earlier. He looked at Sanjit, who said, "Have you got enough change, John?" and took money out of his pocket too and quickly took the necessary cash, taking some from John's hand and some from his own.

While they waited for the drinks the talk was all about the game Eunice had been playing in — the one John had watched earlier. What struck him was that nobody mentioned the score, and when he asked who'd won, they all looked at him oddly, Eunice especially. Then she said, "I don't think anybody knows."

Tommy had not had a second drink and Eunice finished hers quickly.

"Right, young lady, I'd best get you home to your mam.... Bye, Sanjit. Bye, John. It's been nice talking to you — no doubt I'll see you about." And he and Eunice went off.

"I suppose I ought to thank you," said John, "I think I'd have been in a mess without you."

"That's OK," grinned Sanjit, and added, "But it was luck. I had promised Marianne not to bother you and only came down here to watch my son in that same game. When I saw Tommy go across to you I thought there might be problems, knowing his propensity to ask questions of everybody he meets."

"Was he really your guardian?"

"Oh yes, and a very good one. I owe him a great deal. But he was just himself and that was what I needed at the time. He was everything a guardian should be — unobtrusive, undemanding and very understanding."

John did not know what to say, so he finished his drink and stood up. He felt that his attitude towards Sanjit had changed, but he could not help hoping that he could rile him a little by saying, "Will I be allowed to find my own way home?"

Sanjit merely smiled and spread out his hands as though to say, "it has nothing to do with me'.

Lying in bed later, John reflected that Marianne was right: he had much to learn if he were to ever merge into this society.

Chapter III

The next day, Marianne arrived early, before John had even finished his breakfast. He had made a pot of coffee; she asked if she could have a cup, which surprised him. They then sat at his little table in the kitchen of his 1940s house, and after a while she said she had something important to discuss with him. Would he let her explain? He was immediately wary because, despite her assurances and even though he was beginning to think he might be in love with her, he still thought he was being manipulated and that the "regime" could not be as wholesome as she, and everyone else, made out. There was something sinister about the way affairs were run. There must be some subtle form of control in operation throughout this valley and this whole land. However, he said nothing about this.

"Please do," he mumbled.

She explained that all his fears and worries were understood by the handful of people so far acquainted with who he really was. No one knew what the effect would be of the knowledge becoming general, but the vast majority of people, after perhaps an initial period of excitement, would accept that he had a life of his own to live, wherever he came from. Nevertheless, there was no real guarantee that he would not be plagued by those who were inordinately inquisitive: they still existed, she said — as though she could hardly credit it. So, it had been suggested that knowledge of John's provenance should remain restricted to just those who already knew. They all could be trusted, she thought, but any one of them could let something slip unintentionally. If his secret was not to come out then he should learn as quickly as possible about the history of the world from his own time up to the present. He should also get some idea of how society worked now. However, these were only suggestions and whatever arrangements were made would be flexible. The final decision was with him and, she added, that included the possibility of returning to his own time. When John looked surprised at this she told him that his machine was now at a research centre and a group of engineers and physicists were trying to figure out how it had brought him through time. Already, one scientist, a certain Dr James, had put forward some notions that had possibilities.

Throughout her explanation she looked everywhere but at him. Now she peered straight into his face and asked what he thought. She seemed concerned because, though her eyes never left him, they moved about nervously as though she were trying to discern his reactions and emotions. He found this disconcerting: it could be something personal to her, but on the other hand, it might mean that to someone of her century his reactions and behaviour were difficult to predict — as though he were some sort of primitive person. Though this thought disturbed him, he also felt concern for Marianne and wanted to please her. What she was suggesting seemed to make sense, and if he were being manipulated, he could not see how. Moreover, he himself had no idea what he preferred to happen next, and after yesterday evening's experience — innocuous though it was — he knew he could not wander about indiscriminately. He smiled as broadly as he could and said, "OK."

"You mean you agree?"

"Yes."

"To all of it?"

"Of course."

"Oh, John, I am glad. That takes a load off my mind."

"Then that pleases me too."

They drank some more of their coffee and he said, "What do you think of this? It's supposed to be 20th century."

"It tastes the same to me. Perhaps there's only one way to make instant coffee — I think you'll find that with lots of things."

"So, when do we start? And who is to be my tutor — you?"

She looked perplexed again. "I don't think so; I'm not equipped to do it; I don't know who it will be or how."

John's first sensation was disappointment, then fear because he would be in the unknown once more. And finally anger because, though he had no grounds for it, he again thought that he was about to be manipulated. He could tell from her reaction that his face showed all this — her eyes fluttered and she frowned and looked afraid. He felt even angrier.

"Well, what *can* you tell me, then?" he blurted loudly.

She now looked shocked

"John, please, please don't shout — try to keep calm."

He glared but said nothing. Then, after a long pause, she went on, "Nothing's been really decided, but we thought you could go and talk to a certain Lien Chou in London."

"What's he? A criminologist? A psychiatrist? Or maybe a spy catcher?" John replied bitterly.

Marianne's face set and she said quietly but firmly, "No, he's many things — historian, philosopher — but he is old and wise. And you, yes, you yourself, might be able to work something out with him."

John surreptitiously breathed deeply to calm his agitation. Once more he had upset her because of his stupid fears. There was silence again. She sat with her hands in her lap, her head bowed and her brown face expressionless. She looked so beautiful that his heart leapt.

"OK, I'm calm now — and I'm very sorry I upset you — that's the last thing I wanted."

She looked relieved and said, "I know, and I'm sorry for my reaction … It upsets me if anyone raises their voice.… It could be that people were more honest and open about their emotions in your day."

"Perhaps," he said, remembering how devious people at home were and also how many of them never even reflected on why they felt how they felt, but just acted precipitately, often to the detriment of others — and even themselves, as he had just shown.

"So, tell me more."

The next day Sanjit arrived in a small, silent electric car to take John to the station. The passenger compartment was nothing more than an air-conditioned bubble and there was little else to the vehicle.

"Where are the batteries, then," John asked.

"There aren't any," was the reply, "this bubble is made of a material which uses light to power the vehicle. Only a complete absence of light will disable it. It can run on the smallest amount of starlight … usually, that is.… I've known them fail just when it's most inconvenient, or convenient, if you get my meaning."

The car did not travel very fast and used the same roads as the pedestrians. John, remembering a holiday he had had in northern Portugal where those on foot used the roads as though there were no cars and yet vehicles travelled at motorway speeds to terrifying effect, said, "Isn't it dangerous to have cars and walkers, and what look like bike-riders, all mixed up?"

"Not really. Nobody is in too much of a hurry and everyone is careful and considerate … mostly.… Youngsters can be a bit forgetful and exuberant."

"I find this all so difficult to believe. Why is everyone so careful?"

"Ah, John, that's the secret of our society: we learn to be aware of the needs of others from our earliest years. It doesn't just happen by chance, you know. And there are people who don't conform."

"And those you set the guardians on to!" John said with some force.

"That's an unfortunate way of putting it — no one is "set upon" like that. In a society such as this where the majority are considerate, it's difficult to be anything else. Anthropological studies from your own day showed that. And you do the guardians an injustice — how many of them have you seen?"

"None, apart from you, I have to admit."

"And that's because they are hardly needed."

It was at this point that John noticed for the first time that Sanjit was not in black, and when he remarked on it, Sanjit said he did not want to draw attention to them. He hoped people would see them as friends.

"Does that mean you trust me?" said John.

"Do you trust me is more to the point." said Sanjit. There was no reply.

Having arrived at the station, they got out of the taxi and left it with several others in a bay where it could be picked up by the next person to need it. To John's surprise, they were outside Maw's factory; there was little evidence of a station on the surface, but once underground he found it was larger than he expected and there were several lines. Sanjit led the way to the appropriate platform and before long a train hissed to a stop and doors opened as on a metro. However, this was the only similarity because the inside of the carriage was wonderfully clean, the seats very comfortable and the air conditioning so efficient that it was not noticed. The doors closed quietly, the train started, picked up speed briefly, then stopped and the doors opened again. John thought there must be a problem but when he looked out of the window he discovered they had arrived at Wolverhampton. Twenty miles! In what, forty seconds? He looked at Sanjit who could not disguise the smugness of his smile.

"How fast does this thing go?"

"About a thousand miles an hour."

"Then what about the g force?"

"That's catered for in the design of the carriage, but you'll have to ask an engineer about that."

"What drives it?"

"A combination of electro-magnetic force — it's called linear induction, I think — and suction."

"Suction?"

"Yes, I believe that part of the system is really ancient."

"You don't mean the system used by Brunel on the old Great Western Railway, do you?"

"It could be. The name sounds familiar and this is Western Rail, but I'm no historian. I do know that when we enter the tube to travel fast we are in a vacuum."

They arrived in London in a matter of minutes because there were few stops. As they rode the escalator to the surface, John began to feel quite excited: he wondered just how much of London would be the same.

Initially, what he saw led him to conclude that the city he had known must have been destroyed. There were no very tall buildings — at least not in the immediate vicinity of the station — but those he could see looked elegant enough.

"Are these hotels or commercial buildings or what?" he asked Sanjit.

"Perhaps some are, but most of London consists of communication centres."

John wanted to know what he meant by this, but Sanjit was striding off very quickly under the trees that lined the avenue. John hobbled after him and shouted, "What's the hurry, and are there no taxis?"

Sanjit, and one or two of the passers-by, stared at him.

"Taxis? But everywhere in the city is within walking distance of the station. The old urban sprawl has not existed for a thousand years. It was destroyed by a huge bomb, and what was left standing was uninhabitable anyway. The St Paul's you can see there to the east is a reconstruction."

John did not know how to reply, so he said, "Well, remember my broken leg is still not right."

"Oh, sorry, I forgot — but we don't have far to go."

They turned a corner and ahead John could see the Houses of Parliament! When he said the name aloud, Sanjit told him that it too was a reconstruction but was a college. It still retained a reminder of the original function because it was called the College of Commoners.

"So where is the government housed now?"

Sanjit looked at him, smiled indulgently and said, "I know you are not going to accept this, but as Marianne and I keep hinting, there is no government."

"No, I don't accept it — it's a barmy idea!"

"Never mind. Maybe you will accept it one day. But let's change the subject. That building to the north, behind you that is, is the Millennium Dome from the year three thousand. It has managed to survive London's chequered history. It's now a favourite with everybody; it houses all the facilities necessary for a full World Conference — not that they happen very often — and it's the largest building anywhere: only the moon settlement is bigger. The fourth ancient building is to the west. You can't see it from here. It's a museum of war. It too is very big and it's meant to remind us of what we are trying to avoid."

The day was warm and John felt hot by the time they had reached the college. Fortunately, as he entered, he felt the cool of the air conditioning. Sanjit suggested that they sit for a while and have a drink: they were early for the appointment. He said he thought it would be better if John found his own way to Lien Chou's room, though he promised to meet them both for lunch. In the meantime, he wanted to collect some replica artefacts, which his daughter needed for an education project. He pointed to a plan of the building as he left, so John was able to find his way to Lien Chou's room easily enough.

He looked very old, but he smiled benignly at John, welcomed him graciously and immediately offered him a cup of tea. John had assumed that he would be meeting someone important, someone powerful: this, he had thought, was the object of today's exercise. He would, at last, come face to face with the reality of this modern world. So he was disappointed: Lien Chou did not exude power. Perhaps, John thought, his humble, almost nondescript appearance was part of an elaborate deception, but the more they talked the more he doubted this. Lien Chou was what he appeared to be — an old and even venerable scholar who seemed to know the history of John's time better than John himself.

After about half an hour of easy conversation, there was a pause. Lien Chou leaned back in his chair, put his hands behind his head and said, "John, do you know what you want?"

"Er ... I'm not sure what that means, but I don't think I do know."

"Back in your own time, what were your ambitions? Did you want to get on? Take your time ... Think."

John looked out of the window at the Thames and wondered if it were cleaner than it used to be. You couldn't tell because of the tide. Perhaps it had a new name. Why wasn't he thinking about the question? Then he saw the answer — he didn't have any great ambitions. He replied, "I was only a part-time university lecturer. I wanted to be full time."

"And yet you became an astronaut."

John laughed, "Oh no, that came about by accident. It was completely out of character — it was like a lottery prize, and even when I'd been invited, I nearly didn't go. I was so scared."

"Well, that's not surprising: it's a risky business even now."

"Yes, but it's not just that — I reckon I'm scared of everything."

"Everything? Isn't that a bit irrational?"

"Maybe, but look. My worst fears have been realised, haven't they? I'm trapped in a time not my own!"

"There's no denying that, and your plight is almost unimaginable; worse than Robinson Crusoe's. But let's get back to your general fearfulness. Do you think there's something in you that makes you that way?"

There was a long pause. John had wondered about himself — his irrational fears and his inclination to react abruptly if he felt threatened — and he had considered what lay behind them but never in an articulated way. He reflected now.

"You know, when I was a child there were wars. We were bombed. At times we were short of food. We moved about a lot and I didn't always know where we were going. I can remember thinking sometimes that we might not even find shelter for the night. I don't suppose it's odd that I easily feel threatened."

"Did you have a supportive family?"

"I suppose it was as loving as most, but the wars meant we were often split up."

"Where are they now — I mean the year 2058?"

"My parents are dead. I haven't seen my sister in years. I do have cousins, but rarely see them either."

"And you are not married?"

"No. I was once engaged, but her career got in the way, and she had religious scruples too."

"Do you have any religion?"

"Not really. I grew up a Catholic — you know about them? But I fell away. I suppose that if I'm honest, there is still some belief there." John smiled crookedly and went on, "If I wake in the night I sometimes panic in case God does exist. And in difficult times I find I'm praying the prayers of my childhood."

"Have you prayed since you have been here?"

"Several times."

"Do you want to stay here?"

Again John thought for a long time. Lien Chou, in his gentle way, seemed to have breached a kind of barrier behind which John usually protected himself from others. Now he found he wanted to be completely honest with this grave old man. Talking with him was like talking to himself — but with more purpose. He answered, "Yes and no."

"I think we ought to explore that reply a little further. First, can you tell me, do you think, what makes you feel you don't want to stay here?"

John gave him a sideways look, then gazed at the floor and said, "The people I've met and those I've seen or have been told about are all too good to be true. You are all so careful, so thoughtful, so considerate of others. I know it sounds churlish to say so, but somehow I find that annoying and I'm not really sure why. Perhaps I don't really believe it. Perhaps I think you are all hypocrites. And there seems to be no room for spontaneity, for joy, for shouting from the rooftops, for expressing yourself freely. Everything seems so calculated," and he found himself getting worked up, "and you are all so bloody calm!"

Lien Chou raised his eyebrows, but he continued to smile genuinely at John, who went on, "You know, I was once friendly with an Italian married couple, and if one of them got upset, the other would immediately put the metaphorical knife in by saying, 'calme, calme'… Well, I feel like the knifed one."

"Does this mean that you think you could not live here happily?"

"I'm not sure about that either — I do appreciate that in many ways this is a wonderful world. It has its attractions."

"Can you elaborate?"

The urge to be completely frank faded a little, but then it surged back and John said, "Do you know about Marianne, the young widow who has been looking after me so well?"

"Yes, I know Marianne."

"I'd stay if I could always be with her."

"Doesn't that depend upon Marianne too?"

"Aye, there's the rub."

"Sorry?"

"It's Shakespeare."

"Ah, so it is. He sometimes seems archaic to me."

"I suppose like Plato and Aristotle to me."

"Except that I feel better acquainted with them than with him ... But tell me, is there anything you like about this time, this place?"

"I'll have to think about that."

"Take your time — as I'm sure you've noticed, nobody rushes here."

"I suppose in a way that's one of the things I like. And I do appreciate the quiet with no one shouting or bellowing or screaming — not even kids. Oh, and I do like the music I've heard — there's no raucousness or wailing covering up the structure of it, so the music is just music with nothing to hide ... and I like the look of the place — the countryside in Shropshire."

"Where?"

"Shropshire, where I live now. It's the name it had in my day. It's now so beautiful and unspoilt. And do you know, the farming uses not only advanced technology — computer controlled greenhouses and fields of plants I've never seen before, worked with wonderfully complex yet amazingly light machinery — but next to them is a field being ploughed with horses!"

"But all technology is useful. When it was introduced should not be significant. If it's still appropriate, we use it."

But John broke in, "And I do like your London. I hated going to the old one — it was so crowded and noisy and exploitative and just too big!"

"Well, there are no large cities anywhere in the world now. There is one a bit larger than the others and deliberately overcrowded: it's called Hong Kong. But we don't need them, and they cause more problems than they solve. Still, I think you'll find that good use has been made of the knowledge we have about how and why cities developed. Hong Kong is sort of experimental. And then, of course, there's the moon base — life is a little confined there. But I'm sure you'll come to all that later. Is there anything else you like or dislike … any other worries or fears …?"

"I must say I do worry and I am afraid. I feel a stranger and that I am so different from everyone else — almost an outcast or a pariah. It may seem an unwarranted and irrational fear, but it's there. However, I'm beginning to think that I would like to see if I can become part of things here. I might know then whether or not I can stay."

He fell silent and stared out of the window once more. Lien said quietly, "Perhaps that's enough for now. What do you say to lunch with Sanjit — on the terrace?"

"That would be nice. I doubt I would ever have eaten there in the old days."

During lunch, Sanjit suggested that he might leave immediately afterwards so that John could find his own way home. It depended, he said, on how John felt. The first reaction was to let Sanjit go, but on reflection (was he beginning to learn?), he thought he would prefer Sanjit's company. He imagined meeting another Tommy somewhere along the way. Anyway, Lien Chou said that the afternoon session should not take too long.

When they had settled in his room again, Lien Chou asked if John would permit him to make some suggestions — with the proviso that if John found them uncongenial, they could continue to explore his situation and feelings a little further. John agreed. Lien Chou then explained that he thought Marianne was right: it seemed that John's mistrust of the present world would remain until he found out not only more about it but also how and why it had come about. However, on the one hand, to leave this process to chance was risky, as John had discovered, and on the other, not to allow it to occur in the real world might not reduce John's fear. Lien Chou therefore put it to John that he might like to spend six months or so in a partly isolated environment, where he could study with people who were very knowledgeable yet entirely trustworthy, and who would respect John's situation confidentially. Then he could spend another six months in the real world, either travelling, if that is what he wanted to do, or living in society — in Shropshire, if he liked — seeing if what he had learned in the first six months rang true. He might be in a position to judge whether he preferred to leave or to stay. It was to be hoped that by then more might be known about time travel, though they had to face the fact that no matter how much he wanted to go back, it might never be possible.

He went on to say that the particular community he was thinking about was a sort of monastery in the west of Erin where the members were learned and not completely unworldly. Indeed, some of the most progressive thinking went on in institutions such as the one he had in mind. However, John's reaction to the notion of six months in a monastery was not good. When Lien Chou probed his thinking about this, the old man helped him to see that this was partly due to his fear of religion, which, since adolescence, he had regarded as an impediment to his freedom of action. He also pointed out that there would be other "guests" there: some would be on retreat, yes, but others would be there just to take the opportunity to study or to reflect, or just simply to be away from things. The point was that John's privacy would be respected. He need speak to nobody but the monks, if that is what he wanted.

Then, Lien Chou asked John directly if his fear about going there was in some way connected with his feelings for Marianne. If so, there was nothing to prevent him from communicating with her on the web — every day, if he wished. Lien Chou sat back and smiled at John, who had been silent for a long time. The old man put his hand gently on John's shoulder, "Think about it. If you were religious I'd ask you to pray about it. Perhaps the next best thing would be to talk to Marianne about it."

John agreed.

Chapter IV

Two weeks later, John went to the station at Maw's, but this time got the train that would take him to Holyhead. Though he knew how fast the train would travel, his prompt arrival at the ferry port took him by surprise. So did the ferry. In fact, he had not realised he had boarded it until it was already out to sea, and then it suddenly dawned on him that it was huge and not like any ferry he had ever been on before. He had assumed that the shops and restaurants and offices he saw about him were part of the port: it was as though a whole chunk of Holyhead itself had floated out to sea. Was it a hovercraft? If so, there must be very big propellers somewhere to drive it forward; he looked for the sort of towers that would be needed to support them, but the only ones he could find were hotels. Indeed, he was booked into one of them as this was an overnight crossing. Did it have huge engines and underwater screws like a conventional ferry? He wandered casually to that part of the vessel still close to the land (there did not seem to be a stern) but could neither see nor hear any evidence of such a form of propulsion. Indeed, the only evidence that they were making progress was that Anglesey was slipping away from them, and he thought he could discern the suggestion of a wake. He wanted to ask someone about this strange ferry, but everyone else he met seemed to be so relaxed and uncurious that he could only assume that they were all well acquainted with vessels like this. He did not wish to draw attention to himself, so discretion quieted his curiosity. However, he dined well and slept in luxury.

Most of the journey across what he still thought of as Ireland was uneventful, because the same rapid form of underground transport was in operation there; that is until he got to Galway. Then, for the next stage he had to ride on what he would have called a coach except that, like the little taxi he had used in the Severn valley, it had no wheels and the same kind of Perspex roof. The ride was very smooth and he liked it better than the train because he could look out of the window. The countryside was even more beautiful than he remembered and there seemed to be fuchsias everywhere, though there was a greater variety of colour than in his day. The bus ran as far as Clifden. As he got off, a smiling Cistercian monk, in the traditional habit, stepped forward to shake his hand and say, "Welcome to Connemara, John More."

John, mistrustful as ever at being addressed by a stranger, frowned at the man, who went on, "I'm brother Michael and have been sent to take you up to St Adrienne's."

His hair was very white and close-cropped but still looked as though it might once have been unruly. He was shorter than John, but his nimbleness belied his age and he swiftly took the luggage and marched off to the rear of the bus station. John, taken by surprise, followed several paces behind, and when he got round the corner was even more surprised to see brother Michael throwing his bags on to a jaunting car, and then leaping up into the driving seat.

"C'mon, let's see if we can beat the rain," he said, glancing up at a heavy sky.

John climbed up and Michael clucked to the horse and they were off at a fair pace. For the first mile the road was as smooth as any John had ever seen, but then they met what could only be described as a track; the ride was much less comfortable, but they did not slow down. Michael's comments — about the weather, the physical shape of the countryside, even the clumps of rock they passed — were quiet and gentle, but when they emerged from a narrow gorge and at last could see the sea he was positively effusive, which made John wonder if perhaps this cheerful, softly spoken monk was taking advantage of a temporary lifting of his vow of silence. Anyhow, he now turned his attention towards John.

"Are you coming to study, or to pray? Or perhaps just to contemplate?" And without waiting for an answer, "Or all three?"

"To study mostly, I think," said John — diplomatically, he thought, as a monk might expect him to pray too, and John had not denied that possibility.

"And what might you be wanting to study, then?"

John considered the question carefully. A thoughtless answer could give too much away and he did not know what they knew about him at the monastery, nor who was privy to his situation. And Michael might be a gossip — even if he were a monk, and despite whatever rules might exist in the institution. Yet even from this very brief acquaintance, John felt he could trust this man because there was about him an air of serenity, and the joy he expressed in the ordinary things around him was disarming.

"History," said John, and immediately the paradoxical nature of his answer occurred to him: it was too brief and yet too wide in its implications. He thought it could only lead to further questions. But Michael's reply was a surprise and a relief.

"Oh well, you'll be wanting Father Ambrose, I expect. He's always saying that after philosophy and mathematics, history is the most important form of study. Though, God knows, I had more than enough of it when I was a youngster."

"You got lots of history at school, then?"

Michael looked at him and laughed, "Oh, I never went to school — as soon as my education finished I came here."

John was nonplussed, but he said nothing in case it made Michael suspicious, but he need not have worried because the monk went on, "But what I've learned here has been better than anything you could get in any of those professional colleges. And anyway, I'd had two great educators — Sean and Bridget O'Malley were wonderful; it was our trip with them to Tibet that made me want to have a try at being a monk."

John hid his confusion and remembered vaguely that he'd had a hint of something about this in the conversation he had had with Tommy, but Michael's next statement shook him even more.

"Of course, the Abbot persuaded me to do a lot of travelling in my early years here, just to make sure, but I've always been in God's pocket and on one of those trips — to Mexico — I met my wife. And even better, she liked the idea of coming here. But that's enough about me. What about you?"

John was still struggling with the idea of married monks and did not know what to say, but suddenly, as they had just come round a headland, he got his first sight of the monastery, and because they were below it at that point, it seemed even more impressive than it actually was. Its high walls and elegant church towers rose up majestically, seemingly out of the cliff on which it was built. The light grey stone glowed almost white in the low beams of silvery afternoon sunshine, which flashed horizontally under the lowering black clouds that in turn framed the building itself. His intake of breath was audible.

"Oh, it is impressive," said Michael, "but those high walls make it exceptional. It's one of the few church buildings to survive the long centuries of trouble, and they were built to try to stop some warlord or another from taking it over. Well, they didn't succeed: more than walls were needed to see those guys off. It was badly knocked about, but rebuilt three hundred years ago — as it had been — to remind us what we are trying to avoid. But you must have reminders at home too."

"Er …yes."

The now winding track took them up a hill and through a gorge seemingly cut through the cliff. They emerged at the back of the monastery, turned abruptly and ran smoothly along a tarmacked road between very green lawns flanked by low hedges of box.

They drew up in front of a set of shallow steps leading to a heavy wooden door beneath a gothic arch. Michael, again carrying most of John's bags, led him through a vestibule and into a pleasant sitting room. He dropped the bags and said, "Make yourself at home and I'll go and get us some tea."

John sat down in an easy chair and looked out of a wide window across another expanse of immaculate lawn to what must have been the north wall of the church. The rain, which had threatened since Michael had picked him up at the bus station, now began to cast its slanting lines across the wide courtyard (or was it a paddock?) in front of him. He heard someone come into the room and turned in his chair expecting to see Michael. It was, however, a tall, middle-aged monk with fair, wispy hair, who smiled as his eyes met John's and said, "Mr. More?"

"Yes."

"I'm Ambrose. I've been asked to welcome you to St Adrienne's. Has Michael gone for tea?"

"Yes."

" Good. I'm glad he's out," he said in a low voice. "It gives me the opportunity to say that I'm the only one here who is fully conversant with your amazing situation. The Abbot knows a little, but only enough to keep him discreet. Now, would you mind," he went on rapidly, "if, after tea, I come with you to your room, because I'm bursting to ask you a whole lot of questions?"

John felt uneasy at the thought of being interrogated yet again, but before he could reply, Michael, pushing backwards through the door, arrived with the tea. It was as John remembered tea in Ireland: almost as strong as in the army, its deep red colour turning orange when the milk was put in. However, the biscuits were large and home made, he was sure. He began to relax and Ambrose and Michael behaved as though John had always lived there

"How's the wife, Michael? I've not seen her around lately."

"No. She's gone to see her mother."

"Everything all right?"

"Oh yes, she's just getting old — a hundred and eleven next birthday."

"A good age, a good age."

"Sure it is, but she wants Pilar about her now, so I'll be a grass widower more and more, I suppose," he said laughing. Then he added, "but thankfully the children are all away now."

"But I thought I saw young Michael only yesterday."

"Oh, he's often across to see me: he's working on that new generator — the tidal thing — south of Galway."

Then a bell rang and Michael gulped his tea and said, "That's the first call for Vespers. We'd best make a move."

John wondered if the "we" included him, but Ambrose put his mind at rest by saying that they'd give it a miss and get John settled in instead. They left the sitting room with Michael, but as he turned towards the church they headed up the stairs. John felt the millennia fall away: the smell of polish, the panelled walls and the long corridors took him back to his childhood, and especially to the Jesuit school he had attended. The immediate effect was to make him feel gloomy because his experiences had contradicted the old adage about school days. However, his room was very comfortable, airy and with a large perpendicular window.

As soon as the bags were in, Ambrose sat astride the chair by the bureau with his arms leaning on the back and said, "Well, John, I'm sure that you're tired after your journey, and want some time to collect your thoughts now that you have arrived. And I'm sure that really I ought to leave you, but there are so many things I want to ask you — one in particular that has cropped up in something I'm working on. It's been nagging at me since I first found out you were coming. Do you mind if I ask you now? Please?"

John could not help but smile at the expression on the man's face and so replied, "No, ask away."

"Was President Simon of the New European Union assassinated or did he die of natural causes?"

"President Simon?"

"Yes, Maurice Simon — at the beginning of the 2028 War."

"Err ... No one knows for sure — there were lots of conflicting versions at the time."

"Damn! Pardon the language, but I was sure you would know, having been there then!"

"But I was only six. I wasn't much interested at the time — I was just scared."

"Of course, silly of me to think you'd know."

"Well, I did teach that period later, but in a very conventional way. It was for a state controlled exam — you taught the official line. I'm sorry to disappoint you."

"Not to worry. It's just that I'm interested in that period as it's the beginning of the real decline."

"Is it? When I left there was peace. Well, more or less."

"Why do you say more or less? Now this is interesting! What was it like living then?"

John now felt decidedly uncomfortable — one part of him thought that he was still living in 2058, and that Ambrose and even Marianne were part of a dream. Suddenly, he *was* almost overwhelmed again by his predicament.

Ambrose was unaware of exactly how his words had sparked off this incipient despair, but he realised that John had somehow been shaken by his questioning.

"Oh, I am sorry. How thoughtless of me! I should have realised you'd be tired. I shouldn't be putting you under pressure. Please forgive me. It's just that as a historian ... You know ..."

"That's OK. I'll be all right in a minute."

"Look. I'll go and let you unpack ... I'll come back in an hour or so and show you were you can eat.... Oh, but before I go I'll just switch on your communicator. You may need it."

He plugged in a slim computer. The usual whirring and whistling filled the room and Ambrose said, "Do you know how to use this ...? As a sight-phone as well as the usual functions?"

"Yes."

"I've set you up with an address but you'll need to put in a password of your own if you want privacy. I've put you a brief list of instructions; you should have no difficulty."

He stood up straight, made for the door, went through and then put his head back into the room, smiled apologetically and said, "Sorry ... I'll ...I'll see you later."

John stood for a moment and looked at his bags. He did not want to begin unpacking; he did not know what he wanted to do and so stood for several minutes staring out of the window without seeing anything. Self-pity, he knew, provided only brief comfort, but he savoured it; thought of Marianne, felt a little ashamed, then sat down at the communicator. He worked quickly through the instructions, which were written in what struck him as an archaic script: it looked like copperplate. He then tapped out Marianne's address. Soon the monitor screen was filled with not only her face but also that of her son. John smiled, thinking that the images he saw were alive, so real were they. But then he heard, "Marianne and George-Louis are not able to answer at the moment but will get back to you as soon as possible."

Disappointment turned to annoyance and he was tempted to switch the machine off without using the correct procedure, but checked himself when he remembered that he might have difficulty setting it up again if he behaved so childishly, and he really did need to speak to her. So, having switched off properly, he unpacked and organised all his things with a slow and almost icy deliberation, though the sense of irritation, which he was at a loss to explain, still smouldered. However, something about the room struck him as odd and at first he wondered what it could be. He sat in the armchair and looked around him: this was not very different from his study at the university — that was it: the room was full of books! And the sort of books he was used to, not the audio and video books he had become familiar with over the last few weeks. He knew that people still had books but until now he'd seen so many all together only in Lien Chou's room. Had Ambrose put them there or was he using somebody else's room? He began to look at them and soon came to the conclusion that Ambrose must be responsible because they seemed to cover every period of history from the nineteenth century onwards. He examined those from his own period more carefully; there was Schama — bit out of date, he thought. But what was this? Bronowski's *The Ascent of Man*. This was wonderful: it was this old book that had inspired him to read history, so he felt cheered. However, there were very many other authors he had never heard of — publication dates showed him why. Then he felt overwhelmed. How could he read all these in six months? There were hundreds of them and only very few of them were familiar. As he let his eyes run along the shelves, his attention rested on one with a long title: *The Rise and Fall of World Empires: America, China and Africa*. Africa, he thought. How is that possible? He looked at the name of the author — Dom Ambrose Ryan. Perhaps he could soon find out. There was a light tap on the door. Ambrose had come to take him to dinner.

As he expected, the meal was simple, the food wholesome and plentiful. They drank water and ate in silence while a young monk read to them from a pulpit situated high in the wall half way down the large refectory. John noticed that there were what he took to be other guests scattered throughout the room, and here and there were women who did not seem to be guests because more often than not they were accompanied by children. He wondered which one was Michael's wife and then remembered that she was away. He felt glad that he did not have to talk to anyone and found himself absorbed in the second of the readings because it was concerned with the doctrine of The Fall and how this could be reconciled with the process of evolution. He was not sure he could follow the argument completely and was surprised to find himself considering the possibility of discussing this with Ambrose.

After the meal, Ambrose took him back to the sitting room were they had first met and where coffee was provided. Other guests were there and some seemed to be accompanied by mentors; conversations were in low tones but John was able to ask Ambrose about his book and no one overheard.

"I'm intrigued by the fact that there has been an African Empire — in the twenty-first century the whole continent was in turmoil, the people very poor and diseased, and the climate becoming steadily more and more inhospitable."

"Ah, but the great days of the African Empire, if you can call them that, came long after your period, when other parts of the world had been devastated, and you'll discover that it was a very cruel dictatorship that dominated most of the world at that time."

"I've obviously got a lot to learn … I looked at the books you put in my room; this is all very daunting!"

"Well, don't get too worried about it. Though people see history as very important nowadays, many of them have only a garbled version of it, and a few have no version at all, so you'll only need an overview … to know where everything fits."

"More easily said than done, perhaps."

"Not at all, not at all. We'll enjoy it. By the way, do you like choral music?"

"Yes, I do…. Quite a lot."

"Then can I suggest that you go to listen to Compline before you retire?"

John's change of expression must have alerted Ambrose because he added quickly, "It's a new piece and very beautiful. I feel safe in recommending it. I'm sure you'll like it … Er … you don't have to see it as worship if you don't wish to."

John managed a twisted smile and thought that in the circumstances it would be diplomatic to go.

In the church, he found that guests did not sit with the monks: they were provided for beyond the chancel, and though he had sight of the altar, he could see very little of the monastic community. He sat impatiently and waited, feeling that he had been conned into attending. However, once he settled down he realised that the setting was wonderful. The church was as astonishing as any of the European cathedrals he was acquainted with. Slender white pillars rose elegantly, seemingly endlessly, until they evolved into beautifully shaped and decorated knots. These in turn broke into several delicate branches, which supported a forest-like canopy of leafy forms that made up the roof. John sat enchanted by the beauty around and above him. Then the singing began. Mellow soprano voices, which seemed to hang in the air beneath the canopy, sang an uncomplicated melody. First they were joined by altos in a simple harmony. Then tenors entered, singing a second melody, the resulting counterpoint on occasion creating a pleasant dissonance that was resolved by the addition of rich basses, who took the line through to end in a sonorous chord. A reading from the New Testament followed. Then there was a short silence after which the choir sang what was a variation on the first two themes, but it was in the form of a fugue which rose and fell, twisted and turned playfully like a children's game until it too was resolved with thrilling mathematical precision. Prayers of intercession came next and seemed to John like the bidding prayers he remembered from his childhood. Then the earlier pattern was repeated. The service was brought to an end by the choir singing a quiet, peaceful hymn with many of his fellow guests joining in.

Calmed by the music and the setting, John made his way back to his room. He felt, for the first time since his crash, untroubled. He sat in his armchair and thought about … nothing. Yet he knew what was in his mind: he was thinking about thinking about nothing! This was odd but he knew he liked it and thought, I must do this more often. He simply stared ahead, but saw nothing. Then slowly he began to feel aware of what was about him: the computer sat in front of him and he thought of Marianne and looked again at Ambrose's instructions.

When her smiling face appeared on the screen, he answered it with a grin.

"John, how are you. How do you find St Adrienne's?"

"I think it's going to be OK. How are you and George-Louis?"

"We are both well, but he was a bit disappointed you did not call earlier: he likes using the communicator."

"Sorry. I did try but you must have been out. What time does he go to bed? I'll try earlier tomorrow."

"About seven. But how are you and how did you find the journey?"

"Very interesting."

And he went on to describe all the things he had found so strange about the day — and especially his encounters with Michael and Ambrose. She looked especially pleased when he told her about how affected he had been by Compline. He went on to say that he was looking forward to working in this lovely place, especially as the monastery seemed much more comfortable than he had expected. She talked about the mundane things she and George-Louis had been doing, and their conversation finished with John saying he missed her and that six months seemed a long time. She reassured him it would pass quickly once he started work. He agreed, but reluctantly because, since childhood, he had disliked being consoled: to be told to look forward to the end of a particular misery was little help while you were enduring it. He tried to make a joke about monks having to get up early and said he would sign off. She wished him success and said she would pray for him. He tried to think of a not too cutting reply, but all his thoughts seemed boorish. He said he would call again tomorrow.

Chapter V

He made his own way to the guests" refectory the next morning. During his breakfast of bread and fruit, Ambrose came in to tell him that they would meet in John's room in about half an hour. In fact, when John returned there he found Ambrose waiting outside accompanied by another monk who looked quizzically at John, but smiled broadly. Ambrose stepped forward.

"John, may I introduce you to Abbot Samuel. Abbot, this is John More."

"Hello, John. How are you finding St Adrienne's?"

"So far, so good, thank you, Abbot."

They went inside and at first stood and looked at each other. John could think of nothing to say; Ambrose seemed to be deferring to his superior; and the Abbot, who had no idea that John had travelled through time but had been told that he had come from a remote place best kept secret, was looking at him as though he half expected him to take on the appearance of a science fiction alien. However, being a man of renowned good sense, he cut short his stare and said, "Let's sit down for a minute and I'll put my position to John." After a short pause he continued, "I have been told very little about you except that your provenance is obscure and should be kept that way — Dr. Lien Chou can be both gently persuasive and disarming. Now, though I find all this intriguing, I think it's sensible that I should know only as much as I do. That way, if I'm asked about you, I can in all honesty say that I am aware that you are here to work with Ambrose and that you have been sent here from the Ironbridge Community in Enklant, but that is all. So, you can rest assured that whatever your reason for keeping it under wraps, your secret, if that is not a too dramatic way of putting it, is safe with me."

"Thank you, Abbot. I do feel more secure knowing your attitude."

"Good. I'm sure the rest of the community here will be no more interested in you than in any other of our guests — many of whom, I might add, come here for quite obscure reasons, Also, Ambrose and I have been good friends for a long time and I know you can trust his discretion."

John looked at Ambrose and said, "I think I felt that from the start."

Ambrose inclined his head in humble acknowledgement and mouthed a smiling thank you. The Abbot too smiled, got up, shook hands with John again and left. Ambrose then said, "I thought it best if you met the Abbot like this so there's no chance of an embarrassing situation arising."

"And he's the boss," said John.

"Ah. Perhaps not so much the boss as you'd think — he's a sort of primus inter pares, a chairman of the chapter. His position is titular rather than real, and though he does represent us to the outside world, we are very serious about our democracy."

John was about to raise the doubts he had about this, but thought better of it and said nothing. He simply raised his eyebrows in a way that could have meant anything.

"Right," said Ambrose, "down to work — but where to start?"

"Well, I'm in your hands."

"Erm, I'm not so sure about that — at least not to begin with. In fact, I wonder if it might be better if you started us off by saying something about the world situation as you last saw it — that way we are beginning with what you already know and we can build on that."

"Wow, that's a tall order! Er … can you let me think about that a bit?"

"Certainly, whatever you like. I've one or two things I ought to see to, so shall I go away and let you get your thoughts in order?"

"Yes, that would probably be best."

"Right, I'll leave you to it and come back … in what, half an hour? Would that be enough?"

"I should think so … that'll make me keep it simple."

Ambrose left and John looked at the word processor, decided not to use it and sat down at the desk with a piece of clean paper. As he sharpened a pencil he reflected.

He thought at first he would have to start with what for him was the most important period of his life and that was what had always been called the Third World War. But in order to begin an explanation of it, he realised he would have to go back to the beginning of the twenty-first century and war in the Middle East. From his reading as a student he remembered that the American and British forces seemed to do pretty well, but the text books had said that though the war went as predicted at first, it rumbled on and was difficult to bring to a clear end: the peace was the real problem and nothing was ever satisfactorily concluded. All Arab countries were in a turmoil, exacerbated by the continuing Israeli-Palestinian conflict; dissident groups proliferated; the oil crisis led to a world economic depression, which in turn led to internal crises in countries that before had been fairly stable; and there was a war between India and Pakistan. South America, he seemed to recall, sank into anarchy, as did Africa, but there the situation was made worse by the further spread of AIDS, and there was little help coming from either Europe — which was divided — or the United States, whose military excesses threatened its resources and led it to reduce its commitments. Around 2020, with the economic rise of Japan-China, something like world peace was briefly re-established, but the underlying problems had not been resolved. For instance, the antipathy between Christianity and Islam remained as bitter as ever. Extremist groups tried to use bio-terror (as it came to be called) to destabilise western democracies. Though these attempts were not very successful, they did add to the sense of malaise. Fifteen years of turmoil meant that the United Nations, even though re-established at Geneva and away from American influence, could do little about the increase in nuclear, chemical and biological weapons, and even less about the spread of arms among terrorist groups.

However, the revival of trade, first in the far east and then in south east Asia, led to a partial recovery in the west, even though internal troubles resulted in calls for firm government, which produced right wing regimes whose fascist leanings led them to develop aggressive foreign policies. Yet they all recognised their own weaknesses and so power blocs began to form. The old European Union was revived, though its members were even more uncomfortable with each other than before. Something like a Russian Federation was established. A fundamentalist government in the United States once more began to take an interest in the Middle East because of the need for oil, and this led to tension with the Russian Federation. In 2026, the European Union, under the auspices of United Nations, called for a conference on the Middle East to try to relieve the pressure, and it was at this point that President Simon (who, John was certain, did not die of natural causes) was assassinated, probably by a rogue group. But such was the tension and distrust that this engendered that undeclared war broke out between the European Union and the Russian Federation as they jockeyed for control of Middle Europe and the Balkans. Accusations and ultimata flew between the two. But when the United States became involved, sets of defence treaties rolled into action as in the First World War. The situation was even worse than before because so many petty warlords had seized power in various parts of the world and terrorist groups of all political and religious shades took advantage of the confusion to bomb and hijack and ambush their supposed enemies. In fact, it was one such group that had obliterated the Severn Gorge.

John found thinking about that war very unpleasant: he remembered the fear he had felt and the misery of being almost permanently hungry. Worse still was the uncertainty: so-called friends and allies changed with kaleidoscopic regularity. He recalled also the hideous effects of chemical, biological and nuclear attack, which he had seen on the intermittent television broadcasts. Few parts of England were directly hit, but life was awful wherever his family went; that is until they settled in Wales and for once found themselves part of a supportive community. The war ended in stalemate in 2034 because the main combatants were exhausted, and once nuclear bombs were used again a serious effort had to be made to avoid total destruction. However, even ten years on, the hardships remained and the peace was uneasy and never complete: skirmishes continued.

Then there was a period of real peace; trade revived, goods appeared to be more plentiful and there was food in the shops. There was even a private consortium set up to exploit the old mines that had been sunk earlier on the moon, but it was a purely commercial enterprise. This was a period of confidence when industry revived, even in Europe.

For John, it was the best time he could remember because he belatedly entered higher education and also he had met Dorothea. Then, when he first began to teach, he enjoyed the work, but before too long the tedium of preparing youngsters, who appeared to him as little more than philistines, to grind their way through state examinations began to tell. He managed to get some part-time teaching in a university, but the attitudes of his students were not much better than his pupils. It was the disappointment of that and the unpleasant end of his relationship with Dorothea that had led him to get into the silly television game, which resulted in him travelling to the moon base. And now look at me, he thought. Damn it!

Ambrose chose that moment to come back.

"My goodness, John. You look as though you've seen a ghost."

"I have. Not one, but many. Too many."

As he recounted his thoughts he remembered much more of the detail as he went along. Ambrose was delighted because this was a period of history that he had written about and of which he thought he knew a fair amount, but to have John's view of it was still very illuminating. Yet, in a way, this seemed to make the historian's task even more daunting, for as he pointed out to John, no matter how cleverly we reconstruct the past, the result is rarely satisfactory. We can never capture completely what it was like for the people who lived through it — not even with virtual reality techniques.

"But then, for me, there is a full stop," said John. "I don't know what happened next. Was peace long-lasting?"

"What do you think?" responded Ambrose.

John thought for a moment and said he suspected that there were further wars, but then added, "Was I, in fact, witnessing the decline in American power? There was much written at the time along those lines."

"Indeed not, she was to become even more powerful for an extended period before real decline set in and she was succeeded by other empires." At this point he reached for his own book, held it up and said, "That is what I tried to work out in this — how the empires followed on from each other and how the chaos worsened."

"Worsened?!"

"Yes, worsened. Let me explain. That revival of world trade which you talked about, the Japan-China axis, was in fact based on the increasing prosperity of the multinational companies, most of which were still American and, to a lesser extent, European based — you must have known this at the time."

"Well, yes, we did, but we all thought they were international, and I remember that everyone seemed to think that individual countries had lost power to them."

"For a while it must have appeared that way, but from reading history backwards — which I know we are supposed to avoid — we can see that because of the collapse of world financial institutions, real economic clout remained with the Americans and their junior partners, the West Europeans. The Japanese were their puppets, and through them the Americans were able to exploit the huge Chinese and South East Asian markets. And remember that information technology was dominated by their companies, as was the armaments industry, pharmaceutical research and so on. But even more important was their cultural dominance, especially of China."

"But what of all the anti-American feeling that I remember?"

"Oh, that was always there, but most people, especially after the hardships of war, wanted the style of life they saw in that early broadcaster propaganda."

"Broadcaster propaganda?"

"Sorry, my slip, an anachronism. I think you called one of the early forms of broadcaster 'television'."

"Oh, TV ads?"

"Probably. But look, we had better move on: we might get bogged down, especially as this is my specialist period and you know so much more of the detail of the earlier part than I do."

He then went on to explain how the Sino-American link led also to the terrible exploitation of the Chinese people, even though it gave them consumer goods in quantities they had never had before. Yet strangely, the situation was also bad for the Americans and the Europeans. Manufacturing industries all but disappeared. Service industries grew ever larger. Yet the jobs within them were as repetitive as any on the old production line. To offset possible discontent, salaries were set higher and higher and the multinationals could afford to pay them because of the gigantic profits made throughout the world. Even so, there was widespread unemployment in the west (for those with lowly qualifications), but because market forces prevailed and social services became ever more skeletal, the poor remained largely unsupported — and a good proportion of them came from ethnic minorities. The concomitant social unrest was dealt with ruthlessly. Yet while life in the west was becoming more and more chaotic and ghettoised (for the rich as well as the poor), in the Far East, where societies were more cohesive and education had created benefits for those with greater social aspirations, companies prospered: control gradually moved eastwards. The companies, working hand in glove with the Chinese government, even managed to take control of the space stations that the American government had built and which, furnished with the latest weaponry, could threaten any opponents.

Ambrose could see from John's reactions that he was not happy with this account and wanted to ask questions. He knew he would have to pause.

"Let's get some coffee and talk as we go."

However, by the time they had reached the refectory they were silent, each taken up with his own thoughts. John felt confused: the process seemed to be moving along too fast. There were so many questions to be asked; so many aspects he felt had not been covered — what was happening to the biosphere given the wars and the deterioration of the environment that always came with armed conflict? He knew there were serious, even frightening, developments taking place during and after the Third World War. Had the seas continued to rise? Was the rainforest still being destroyed? What was happening to the ozone layer? Why was Ambrose concentrating so much on America?

Ambrose suspected that John was formulating such questions and realised that he would have rethink the schedule he had mapped out for himself. Originally, he had planned to spend far more time on the latter part of the fourth millennium — when the story would be a much happier one — than on the disasters, and for the earlier part he had hoped one week would suffice. However, during the morning session it had dawned on him that John was bound to be concerned, almost to the point of obsession, with the events that immediately followed his own time. And because this was a period in which he himself was so interested, the discussion had to be prolonged. He looked across the table at John who happened to look up at the same time. For a moment they stared at each other and then simultaneously they both grinned. Then they began to speak at the same time. Ambrose deferred to John who then explained how he felt about their first session. Ambrose responded by recounting his own thoughts on the matter and then said, "Look, there is only about half an hour till lunch. Let's go and sit in the garden and talk it through. I don't think we have a problem, really."

The heavy showers that had arrived with John at St Adrienne's had given way to sunny weather. The two men sat in the garden under cleverly trimmed ash trees, and John asked if Ambrose could proceed more slowly and perhaps on a wider front — to include more than just the economic power of the west. He explained that his concerns before he set off on his trip to the moon had been with the ecological decline to be seen in many parts of the world.

Ambrose said he thought they had taken the particular line they did because John had raised the question of American power, and that had got him on to the empires of the third millennium, which he found so easy to talk about. He agreed that all those issues like the melting of the ice caps were important, but, he said, the really widespread effects of global warming — hothouse gases and all the other climatic changes — were to be felt much later. He calmed John's fear: they would be dealt with. He also pointed out that he considered economic history and the power struggle that went with it worth concentrating on because they formed the framework within which all the fateful trends were to be understood. Obsession with power was, to his mind, the most important reason why humankind had neglected these serious ecological problems, that is until it was finally nearly overwhelmed by them. As they got to the end of the third millennium, he hoped, they would see all the factors coming together. So he suggested that that afternoon John might like to look through his book on the empires while he, Ambrose, looked up a time chart he had come across which might enable John to feel more comfortable with — less overwhelmed by — two millennia of history. They went for lunch.

Ambrose's book was well organised. John realised fairly quickly that the sub-headings did tell you what each section was about, and because every chapter had a summary, he could skip read and quickly get the gist of the story. The theme of the book was that it was the internal weaknesses of the empires that caused each one in turn to decline. Sectional interests in America were so strong that virtual civil war broke out. The lawlessness meant that the multinational companies, on which everything depended, gradually moved their centres of gravity eastwards (or westwards from California). The armed forces depended on the ethnic minorities for their manpower, and yet these were the most exploited social groups; mutiny became endemic. However, underlying the turmoil, the American myths of freedom and individualism, claimed Ambrose, helped to create the unbearable contradictions that fractured society beyond recovery.

The sheer size of China itself was one of the main causes of its decline. Even during the period when The Party seemed to have monolithic control of every aspect of Chinese society, this was an illusion — despite the severe repression — because of the extent (geographical and in terms of population) of the so-called republic. Moreover, corruption was rife. As China was drawn into the capitalist system, the regime's grip had to be further relaxed, especially as the upper levels of education had to be expanded to cater for the proliferation of economic roles, contingent upon the knowledge-based nature of advanced capitalism. This trend accelerated as overall control of the world economy slipped away from the west towards the east. However, this all occurred in a society that had never experienced democracy even of the limited sort that had existed in the west. Corruption worsened as The Party, the multinational companies, the banks, the finance houses and the media became embroiled in a gigantic web of deception. Though perceptive commentators had already warned it would happen, when collapse came it was swift and its consequences worldwide. The Red Army, which might have seized power, was not the force it had once been, and with all of the general staff implicated in the corruption, it too fragmented and added to the confusion. Civil society broke down as people fled the cities.

In the meantime, very little interest was taken in what was happening in Africa, where most forms of organisation had already collapsed. This was a pity because occurrences there were to be repeated elsewhere. Tribalism dominated by petty dictators was ubiquitous. However, one of the more appealing demagogues, Jean-Pierre Mepembe, who gained control of the various mining interests in the south, rose to prominence, and because his armed forces were better organised and disciplined than his rivals, he was able to consolidate his hold. The Americas, Europe, the former Eastern Bloc and South East Asia were in such disarray that the full extent of Mepembe's power went unrecognised. He was seen as little more than a market for surplus weapons. Moreover, he established a dynasty and his successors were even more ruthless than he and extended their power into North Africa, then the Middle East and finally the Caucasus and beyond, giving them control over large sections of the oil producing areas. By shrewd bargaining with the rogue forces, which held the ramshackle remains of the space stations, they achieved brief world dominance.

John had read all this very quickly but had hardly been aware of the passage of time involved. He looked again at the dates: he had dashed through six hundred years! So, he thought, the process must have been slower than he had imagined. It was as though he had travelled from the Reformation to his own time, the twenty-first century, which meant that Ambrose's book dealt with a great sweep of history — yet it did not seem like those general histories, which, he remembered, he had been obliged to read as a first year history student. It had about it that air of confidence that comes from sound research and a good grasp of the detail. There was something disturbing about this and he began to wonder where Ambrose had got his facts if the sort of chaos that the text described had really ensued. Wouldn't he have faced the sort of problems that historians of the Dark Ages had had to deal with where documentation was sparse and unreliable and archaeology so often ambiguous?

He found himself standing up looking out of the window at the trim lawns and brightly coloured roses beyond. People he took to be other guests were walking up and down the neat gravel paths. They seemed to be avoiding each other. He remembered the retreats that had been held at the beginning of each academic year when he was a senior pupil at that so traditional Jesuit grammar school: in the periods of reflection he and his fellows behaved in a similar way, but they had avoided each other for fear they would burst out laughing should their eyes meet — the Js might be watching. Then the longing to be in his own time overwhelmed him and he felt his throat grow tight and the tears come to his eyes. Just as suddenly, his mood changed as the ludicrousness of his situation hit him. In those days he had read his Oman and his Tout on the Dark Ages, and now he was reading Ambrose Ryan on a similar period. Let's go on retreat, he thought and went out into the garden. With his hands behind his back he mimicked the other guests, his eyes cast down but a juvenile grin on his face. That is until he met Brother Michael tending the roses.

"John More, how nice to see you on this fine day."

"Michael, nice to see you too, and so busy."

"Well now, I'd rather be doing this than anything."

"Isn't it tedious?"

"Glory be to God, no! Why should it be tedious? I'm as fond of this rose garden as Ambrose is of his books — do you know he's obsessed with those ancient things?"

John looked at the roses. They were beautiful and everything was so orderly: the edges of the lawn where it bordered the flower beds were cut with geometric precision, and when he looked more attentively, he discovered that they were lined with metal.

"This must have taken hours and hours of loving labour," he said.

"Now, let me see. Er … I've been twenty-two, twenty-three years on this one and now it has forty-seven different kinds of roses."

He paused and looked lovingly across the garden, then said, "Can you not see my colour scheme?"

John looked and for the first time he saw that there was a gradual shift of shade as the eye moved from bed to bed, and though he had gazed, perhaps distractedly, several times from his window, he had never seen it before.

"Why, yes, of course … I see it now … From deeper to lighter red at this end, through orange and amber to peach and yellow and then to cream and white at the far end. Michael, it's wonderful."

"Well, sinful it may be, but I'm very proud of it."

"And I should think so."

A bell rang. Michael put his tools into his barrow and set off immediately.

"Vespers," he said, "Are you coming?"

"I think I might today."

John stood for a moment admiring the roses and then made for a garden gate he had seen the other guests leave by. The church, when he got there, appeared even more beautiful than he remembered. The singing was entrancing and he even listened carefully to the readings. As before, the experience made him feel very calm, even, he thought, at peace, but he smiled to himself at what seemed to him such a banal notion. Nevertheless, he no longer felt he had to quiz Ambrose immediately about the material in the book. It could wait. So when Ambrose came to his room before dinner, John raised no questions but instead let Ambrose expand upon the time chart he had promised to bring. He had obviously copied it himself: John recognised the handwriting.

It took the history into the fourth millennium, and it came as no surprise to John, at first, that in the column headed "Political" the descent into turmoil continued — as Ambrose had hinted. There was an extended bracket enclosing "The Rise of the Warlords'. He noticed too that the ecological disasters he had half expected also figured prominently, so that by the year 3000 the Horsemen of the Apocalypse were riding unchecked across the face of the Earth. He could see references to cannibalism, slavery and piracy, to new diseases, to the disappearance of whole countries either beneath the sea or to nuclear and biological devastation. Ambrose drew his attention to the fact that the world population had been halved as early as 2900. Even though he thought he was prepared for the horror, the calm he had felt earlier had vanished. He was so shocked that he involuntarily sat down saying, "My God, my God." Ambrose actually put his arm around John's shoulders and said, "If it helps, I know how you feel." He paused for a while and then went on, "It's part of my task not to let people forget all this. So, I'm afraid, John, that during the next few weeks we are going to have to look at the detail of all of it ... But let me point out some other features. Look here, 2600, "the beginnings of the commune movement in South America and Russia', and here, 'only small communities prospered', and look, again, "subsistence farming ... followed by a re-awakening of trade'. You know yourself as a historian that the situation could never be completely disastrous. There were always communities that avoided devastation, and science continued to make progress — and not just in the means of destruction. And maybe the thought has already struck you — how is it we know so much about all this? You see, John, forms of information technology were developed that were virtually indestructible. Since about 2500, very little has been lost. We really know our history as never before, and as for science and technology ..."

But John was unconsoled. He felt completely drained. An inexplicable sense of companionship with all the ordinary people who had suffered in the catastrophes possessed him — not for the first time in his life, but more intensely than ever before. These were his people and they had lived in terror and died in a thousand agonising ways. Horrific images from his wartime childhood crossed his mind and he knew that these had to multiplied a thousand times, and worse still, for nearly a thousand years.

He was glad of the silence at dinner, and though the reader had a pleasant voice and the treatise was not deep, John heard very little of it. Even thinking that had he never moved through time and had lived out his three score and ten in his own century, he would have avoided the horrors of what had befallen the human race made no difference. What had happened had happened to his world and so to him and his kind.

Back in his room he hoped that his conversation with Marianne and George-Louis would dispel the gloom, but even his best efforts to be cheerful for the sake of the boy appeared clumsy. Finally, Marianne sent the lad, protesting, off to bed and asked John what was the matter. When he explained, she obviously understood why he felt as he did, as she was beginning to know him very well, but the depth of his despair surprised even her. He confessed it surprised him too. Then John began to realise that he was concerned for her: why should he burden her with his despondency. And that it was a burden was only too clear, so good was the technology: she was virtually in the room with him.

"Perhaps one day I might appreciate that what you say about your society is true."

She brightened and he continued, "Maybe the only way to avoid the centuries of misery I've discovered today is through this kind of society."

"Oh, John." was all she said, and he went on, "But I feel that humankind, as I know it, stands condemned."

"But, John, we are what you are. People are people and what *we* are is built on what *you* are."

Chapter VI

For the next three weeks John and Ambrose worked intensely together. The experience was exhilarating, but John continued to find it painful too, even though Ambrose tried to include in the programme, whenever he could, any of those signs of improvement that indicated that humanity could lift itself from the pit. Unfortunately, all too often, attempts by enlightened groups to live in peace and harmony were frustrated by others motivated by fear on the one hand or greed and the desire for power on the other. Nor, he discovered, were the catastrophes entirely man-made: the devastation wrought to the already worsening global climate by a single large meteorite was further aggravated by a volcanic eruption, which threw up so much debris into the upper atmosphere that what had once been feared as a nuclear winter almost arrived and resulted in further population decline.

Because of the continued miniaturisation of digital data, information could be presented in a variety of forms, and Ambrose was able to use techniques that the colleges employed with adolescents to help John understand what it was like to live through the worst periods. Now, though John was sure that Ambrose's history was as honest and accurate as he could make it, he still worried about these methods. And he said so.

"Well, there's a proper programme of educational study. It's carefully sequenced and the context is one of serious investigation — and what we call the 'full submersion' techniques come towards the very end."

"I should hope so, because I don't see how you can be so certain of the effects."

"Ah, we can't always be certain — how could we be? But then again, as I've said, all this and the full submersion, which you've yet to try, are only for the older students. One of the things we have learned is that it's dangerous to use this stuff with the younger ones. You cannot do it."

"And I should think not!"

"But, John, you don't seem to appreciate that we have worked very hard over several hundred years to make what we do with children and adolescents educative. Upbringing and education are the key to everything we try to do."

"But some of what I've seen so far could be brainwashing, or at least conditioning."

"No, it's not. It's education, though that might legitimately include conditioning."

"Bah!"

"Look, John, just for now will you bear with me, at least until you go to see how it works?"

"I suppose I'll have to … What choice have I got?"

"Don't put it like that. Remember, I am trying my best not to impose my ideas on you, but to let you discover the history and to experience the feel of it for yourself. But one thing perhaps I should say: there are certain luxuries we can no longer afford — given our past — and one of them is just letting education happen, or, more likely, not happen."

John could not think immediately of what to say but he was aware that all sorts of libertarian arguments were taking shape in his mind. He considered it best not to air them at this point, even though it seemed to him that Ambrose was, for once (and uncharacteristically), a little annoyed with him for wanting to argue. This aroused in John a desire to be even more awkward. However, there flitted across his mind several instances when he had not been able to avoid being curmudgeonly with Marianne and they had made matters worse. Ambrose, he recalled, was proving to be a good mentor: usually he was patient, always prepared to break off what he was doing to explain difficulties, always ready to expand upon areas which John wanted to see developed further. But most importantly, he was always willing to explain again matters which John realised later he had not properly understood or had forgotten. Also, he liked Ambrose. Nevertheless, he knew that he would have to raise certain questions, which, maybe unfairly, he thought Ambrose seemed to be skirting round. One was just how the information had been stored so completely, and the other, related to the first, was the sources of power that had been used. John was no expert on IT, but he knew that there might be various types of software available and easily utilised now, but what had been used 1000 years before? And more problematic still, how had the lines of communication been kept open? They must have been — even in the worst of times. Cable and satellite were both vulnerable, given the virtually unceasing war and the almost total social disruption — and again the question of power loomed. Maybe, what he needed to do, he thought, was, in some lighter moment, to give Ambrose fair warning that he wanted to raise serious doubts about all this.

Opportunity came later that day. After lunch, Ambrose suggested that they give themselves a half-holiday: they had both worked very hard and, more to the point, the weather had remained good. It seemed a pity not to take advantage of it, especially as such long spells of sunshine were not so common in the far west of Erin. Moreover, he said he'd been told that the breakers on to the cliffs a couple of miles away were very impressive just now.

John felt relaxed as they strolled along through meadows, which were about to produce their second crop of hay and where the wild flowers grew in profusion. His memory of country walks in his childhood was none too clear but he was sure that he had never seen such a variety of flowers before. He was certain that this was the case, not just because Ireland's fauna might be different from England's, but because the farming methods now used were meant to preserve as many species as possible. The two men walked together silently, having agreed that they would not continue the work begun that morning. But John could not forget it. He still wanted answers. Perhaps, he thought, he could lull Ambrose into the discussion he wanted if he tried an oblique approach.

"Oh, there's something I've meant to raise with you, right from the first week I was here."

"No shop! We agreed."

"No, it's not shop. It's theology, I think."

Ambrose stopped and looked at John quizzically, "Are you sure now?"

"Sure I'm sure," he responded with a broad grin. He went on, "Do you remember — I think it was the very first one I heard at dinner — a reading about how you can square the notion of original sin with evolution."

"Oh yes, I do remember. It was an article by a Benedictine ... or was it a Dominican?"

"Well, I did think about it at the time, believe it or not, and made a mental note to raise one or two queries with you."

"Yes ...," suspiciously. "What ... exactly?"

"Just let me explain. One part of the article dealt with how we are all inherently self-centred. I think it said that this was because our senses, which developed originally as defence mechanisms, are the only means through which we acquire knowledge, an understanding of the environment — and environment means everything. And I got the impression that the writer meant even things internal to each of us, from tummy ache to feeling murderous ... or whatever."

"Y..e..s ... so?"

"Er. Doesn't this mean that we interpret everything in terms of our own interests? And in turn, that even when we believe we are acting selflessly, we have an ulterior motive? Some geneticists in my day certainly thought this to be the case."

"Maybe," replied Ambrose, "but I seem to remember that the reading also included a section on how human babies are born immature — in comparison with most other primates — so that they can survive and learn to be human only if they are provided for. And we now would say not just provided for, but loved and in such a way that they themselves learn to love."

" Yes, that was in it too — and also, I think, a digression on the Holy Spirit, who is sometimes seen as Love and sometimes as Wisdom, the point being that both of these attributes are somehow closely related, and being truly human means having both of these at once. Yes, I do remember that, but it isn't my problem. Mine is — why do we need to be redeemed?"

"Now, that's a considerable jump. How did we get there?"

"Big jump? Why do you say that? If evolution is the story of how God made us, then he made us selfish. Why should we be punished for this? So why do we need to be saved from punishment?"

"Ah, I see what you mean. But aren't you wanting to have your cake and eat it?"

"How do you mean?"

"Well, you seem to want to take the story of The Fall both literally and figuratively?"

"Do I? How?"

"It's the way you talk about punishment. It seems you are still thinking of Adam and Eve as though they were real individuals who did something awful and had to be punished."

"Well, isn't that the Judaic and the Christian tradition?"

"It may be to some, though I should think very few now. Most people are more likely, I'd say, to take the line the article took."

"Ah, now there's something else I wanted to ask you about. I don't think I understood the later parts. What is it I've missed?"

"It's really about seeing the story of The Fall figuratively: it's telling us about us — that's the way we are and always have been from the time we ceased to be hominid and became fully human. Something occurred during that transformation as we became aware of ourselves. But in a way, you summarised it when you said we have a selfish potential and a love potential. Unfortunately, we tend to follow the first of those. But the whole point about Christ redeeming us is that he took on himself all our wrongdoing and at the same time pointed us towards God, to our love potential. He became the model, the New Man that we can be. Indeed, we already are if we follow Him."

Ambrose now became silent and stared out to sea. He felt he had been preaching at John and knew, from his briefing by Marianne, that this could make him prickly, so he thought that, for the moment, he should say no more until he could see some sort of reaction. John, however, felt perplexed. He'd introduced the topic only so that he could engineer a return to the discussion they had agreed not to have. Now here he was, engaged in the kind of debate he'd always tried to avoid because he was afraid of it, afraid of how it could interfere with his freedom of action. He reflected — what freedom of action? In his predicament? And he laughed heartily; he couldn't help it. Ambrose looked shocked.

"What's so funny?"

"Ah, nothing really. I'd have to explain a long rigmarole of thought for you to see that my laughing has nothing to do with what you said but with my own idiosyncrasies."

Without noticing it they had arrived at a point where the cliffs were quite high. They both now realised that their voices had been getting louder as they had to speak against the increased roaring of the waves crashing below them. It seemed sensible to say nothing for a while. As if in one mind, they crept together towards the rim of the cliff. Then John decided to lie flat to look over the edge because the tufted grass made it difficult to tell exactly where it was. Ambrose joined him. Neither spoke: they were fully engaged watching the sea pound the cliff far below them. They could also see gulls and their nests on the crags and cracks in the rock, but what struck John was how odd it seemed to be above the birds, to look down on them as they glided by effortlessly. Probably for the first time in his life, he began to understand air as having substance: it was the medium in which birds flew, just as water was the medium for fish. Even his experiences in space had not brought home to him as forcibly the fact that we exist in three dimensions — looking down on activities occurring at different levels had an almost exhilarating newness about it. The birds seemed unaware of the heads of the two men peering down at them, which meant that they went about their business in their usual uninhibited way. John smiled as he saw how often they turned their heads this way and that as they flew so easily and economically, the movement of their wings at times being barely perceptible as they adjusted to, and used, the changes in the atmosphere.

He wondered for how many millennia birds had lived in this place. Certainly, they were already well established here in his day, but how had they been affected by the climatic catastrophes of the third millennium? It looked as though, even had their numbers dwindled, they must have revived. He marvelled at how robust they must be. Or perhaps conditions in this part of the world had not been as horrific as elsewhere, so today might not be very different from millions of other days reaching down through time. In which case he could be back in his own day! He tried to remember what Einstein had said about time. Was it that it was elastic? Could stretch and contract? It was intimately connected with space and gravity and the speed of light. It was the fourth dimension. Dimension again: today seemed all to do with dimensions. But what did it all mean?

Despite the vagueness of these notions, he suddenly felt as though he was both in his own time and this time, but it was a sensation, not an understanding — which was disturbing. He wished he'd paid more attention, but so much of what he learned in science classes he had done by rote just so that he could repeat it in examinations and then forget it. Had his attitude been better he might have some inkling of how he got here, of what had happened to him in that space capsule. He knew that when he finally met the Dr James that Marianne had spoken of, he would be bemused by the explanations. Did it matter? Did time matter? It did to him, he said to himself, and yet today, on this cliff, time really did not seem important. Usually such thoughts depressed him and he would begin to hanker after his own era, but not just now. Was there a good reason why he should return to 2058? Did he want to go on teaching? He did, he thought, but not in the examination factories back home. Back home! The thought brought a brief pang. Yes, that was it: everyone needed a home to go back to. But when you considered it seriously there was nothing very special about his home or even his home time. And Marianne was here, now. Well, not here exactly, but in this time. He wanted to be with her in Jackfield, in the Ironbridge Community — and at that moment he wondered if the Jackfield of now could become the place he thought of as home. Ambrose broke the reverie.

"I sometimes think I'm on the edge of the world when I watch the waves breaking here — but I know that's nonsense. But it's a powerful sensation."

"Why do you think you feel that? Is it the vastness of the Atlantic beyond?"

"I suppose it could be that — and the sheer size of the cliffs." Ambrose sighed and then said, "Shall we go back? We could go the long way, round that headland."

"If you like."

They got up and set off. John still had not found a way of asking the questions that bothered him. He wondered if perhaps a direct approach would work. As Ambrose had seemed just as pre-occupied as he when they were staring over the edge, perhaps he'd forgotten the no shop rule for the afternoon. It was worth a try.

"Ambrose, how is it that so little information has been lost, despite the New Dark Age?"

"Ah, now that's a complicated affair. There are several factors involved, including, I suppose, good luck … or … as for me, I'd say, the hand of God."

"Oh."

"Aha, the usual sceptical John. But let me tell you what I can — as a mere historian, not an information expert, nor yet a scientist."

"Well, as I'm in the same boat as you, though even more ignorant, I may be able to follow you."

"That's as maybe. You must have realised that miniaturisation played a big part, because that was already happening in the twenty-first century. Look at this," and he held out his wristwatch, "This is as powerful as the one in your room."

"Then, why is mine so large?"

"Oh, only because it's easier to use that size — as you might want to scan or print or talk to Marianne, and so on."

"But that one," pointing to Ambrose's wrist, "can do the same?"

"Oh yes, no problem."

"So, what happened? How is it managed?"

"I think that in your day you were still using silicon chips, but then there was a move to silicone, which was more flexible. However, though it took a long time — a hundred years or more — they learned how to use individual molecules to contain circuits and then there was virtually no limit to the quantity of information that could be stored."

"Wow. But OK, you can store mind-bending amounts of information, but what about a power source, the batteries?"

"Again, miniaturisation — easy once the nanotube could be used for producing a reliable flow of electrons."

"Now, even I have heard of nanotubes, but I seem to remember that they were not all they were cracked up to be. They just did not have the versatility claimed for them."

"Maybe not in the twenty-first century, but afterwards they did. I'll find more on that for you, if you like."

"Right. But we can put that on one side for now. What about the Internet, the World Wide Web? How did that survive?"

Ambrose explained that by the time the real deterioration in social organisation had come about, the land lines were extensive and the cables carried incredible amounts of information, mostly deep underground where they had been put as the political situation worsened. Often, the only people who understood the networks and how they were laid out were technicians, not the politicians. Also, it was in the interests of the various imperial forces to keep them in existence — just as it was for the dissidents, terrorists and countless subversive groups. Even so, there were occasions when they were disrupted. The same was true for the communication centre that had been established on the moon and the satellites, of which there were thousands; some did deteriorate, others were destroyed, but it was always in the interests of powerful groups to retain most of them, even if they benefited opponents too. So they survived and were even serviced in periods of relative calm. Moreover, Ambrose pointed out, many scientists, technologists and what he referred to as "learned people" formed secret societies and networks expressly for the purpose of preserving and concealing information, though this was dangerous. And there were, of course, traitors to the scientific cause and many people were committed servants to the powerful, but there was also a trahison des clercs, which, by the time of the warlords, was very extensive.

Then John asked about how in the confusion of world social dislocation, sources of power were not completely destroyed, and Ambrose explained that many were, but what mattered most to the question in hand was that very powerful portable generators had been developed, again using nanotechnology, so that the communes and the nomadic groups that were to be so important to the Reawakening (as some people called it) towards the end of the fourth millennium, were able to go on functioning and to keep links with each other. They had also perfected techniques for making and using methane and similarly making electricity from the by-products of refuse. Hydrogen technology was also developed. But it's safer to use a mixture of techniques.

By now they had arrived at the headland, and Ambrose pointed out to sea saying, "Look out there. Can you see that huge platform rising and falling with the swell?"

"Oh yes."

"That produces electricity from the movement of the sea. Now turn round and look behind you."

They were looking at a set of five or six mounds with open fronts facing the sea, which John had not noticed until now. Ambrose explained that they were inlets for air and inside were turbines, which were driven by the prevailing westerly winds of this area.

"We no longer need the giant windmills you used to see along this coast."

"But wouldn't the air need to blow through? There must be outlets."

"There are and we passed them on the way up. They are concealed too."

"But these are sources of power that we have in 2058."

"Oh yes, no technology is rejected. On the other hand, many have been improved, made very efficient and ecologically friendly. The monastery itself is connected to a grid and so might be using power produced out there," pointing towards the platform, "or here behind you, but we also have our own generators that rely on processing our refuse or using all the windows."

"The windows?!"

"Yes, they are constructed in such a way, again using nanotechnology, so that they convert solar energy — or any light really. It's the same technology that we use in most road vehicles. Didn't you come here in a coach with a transparent roof?"

"Yes, and I've been in a taxi with that system."

They had, by this time, walked round the headland and could see the monastery before them, looking quite splendid in the afternoon sunshine. Its colour was different from the striking white, which it had been in the rare conditions of John's arrival. Now it was amber and reminded him of the time he had visited Chambord with Dorothea, early one autumn. That really did seem centuries ago, even in his experience.

"What were we talking about?" mused Ambrose, then went on, "Ah yes, what survived the Dark Times."

"Is there more?"

"Of course, we've talked only about the technologies, haven't we? But I did mention the communes and the nomads — and the poustinia …"

"Poustinia?" interrupted John, "I'm sure I've heard that word before, but I've got no idea what it means."

"It's a misnomer really, because in Russian it means a desert, but then came to mean 'hermit': the sort of person who sought out desert places to be with God. However, when they became a focus for radical groups it came to mean a particular kind of community. There are other groups with strange names all over the world that formed in those difficult times. And they are all important because it was through them that the links were kept. There were attempts to destroy them, but they were resilient and spawned other groups. But this whole area would be better tackled when we discuss the revival of civilisation — and that's our next topic. And this is supposed to be a holiday and we should not be talking shop. It's your fault for asking questions."

"And yours because you can't resist answering them."

That evening when he talked to George-Louis and Marianne, he told them about the huge breakers he had seen crashing against the high cliffs and about the strangeness of seeing the seabirds flying so far below him. George-Louis said that though he had been to the seaside he had never seen high cliffs and would like to visit the place John described. He looked at his mother in the hope that she might agree to take him. John hoped she might too. Marianne smiled, but noncommittally. When the little boy had gone off to bed, John told her of his thoughts on time and how he was beginning to associate Jackfield with the notion of home, but though he almost blurted out that it was her presence there that made this so, he managed to hold back because he was still not sure about her affection for him. Sometimes he wondered if it was only her inherent goodness that made her care *about* him. He still did not know whether or not she could care *for* him, but he had enough common sense not to push the matter. She had never spoken about her husband, except to say that he had been killed in an accident. Perhaps she was still in love with him or felt the kind of continuing loyalty towards him that would not permit her to commit herself to somebody else. She could still be mourning him. On the other hand, perhaps she could not love someone like John. Had he spoilt his chances earlier with his quick temper and impatience? Even though he was learning to be more circumspect, she could not know — nor could he — whether he would revert to his earlier form of behaviour. However, this evening, as on all others, she seemed genuinely concerned about him and obviously glad that the work continued to go well with Ambrose. After they had said goodnight, John sat for a long time considering their relationship. Finally, he told himself that any girl would think twice before getting involved with someone who was two thousand years old.

Next morning he awoke early and could not get back to sleep. He knew that today he and Ambrose would embark upon what was probably the most important part of the work. He was sure there were still horrors to come, but at least, from the hints he had been given, they would now be studying a time when the situation was improving. He wondered if Ambrose's approach would be Whiggish, because all the changes for the good might be presented as though they were leading to the present situation, which would, of course, be seen as the best of all worlds. As he lay listening to the dawn chorus he reflected that at least this was a peaceful world. He compared these thoughts with those he had had on similar occasions in his own century. Then, he had never felt that any happiness he experienced could really be enjoyed untrammelled whilst so many people in the world were suffering — from war, famine, exploitation, political and economic oppression and so on and so on. This did not seem to be the case in the forty-first century. That is unless he was being conned. Perhaps he was the victim of very clever propaganda, as in the novel *1984*. It did not feel like that, and then the propaganda in the novel was not that good, was it? He heard a bell ring and surprised himself by deciding to go to Mass.

Chapter VII

At first he was a little disappointed in the singing: it was Gregorian chant. He supposed he should not be surprised. This was a monastery where such music was wholly appropriate. Yet it was old, three thousand years old, and he had hoped to hear the kind of singing he had heard at Compline, with harmonies of a kind he had not experienced before. Nevertheless, the chant was well done; it swelled and subsided in a way that made it seem that the very church itself was breathing gently. It gave the place an air of serene calm and he wondered if this was what was meant by holiness. He had not thought such thoughts since his late teenage years but now he remembered that he had pondered on the meaning of holiness before, so long ago. He'd even asked one of the Jesuit priests what it meant but had not been impressed with the answer: that it was something very special to do with God; that it was sacred. But what did sacred mean? At this very instant now, though, he felt he was beginning to grasp what holiness might mean, and it was a feeling rather than a thought because what he experienced was an unassailable calm. Yes, unassailable because of the power and might of God, but calm because — of what? And he remembered the story of God coming to Elijah: he was not in the storm, nor in the earthquake, nor yet in the fire, but he was in the gentle breeze.

When John became conscious again of the words of the Mass, they were at the offertory and he recalled that in his youth when he had been committed to all this, it would be at this point that he would try to offer himself and all he was to do to God, knowing that because this bread and wine would become the body and blood of Christ, and then once again be offered to the Father, that he too would be offered; so he and his works would no longer be weak and puny but would be transformed and made acceptable. Had he once believed this? Could he believe it again? He did not know. When his fellow guests went up to receive Communion, he still did not know, but he did envy them.

Because guests had breakfast in their own small dining room, the rule of silence did not apply. On this particular morning John found himself sitting with a middle-aged man and woman whom he took to be married. He was right.

"Good morning, I'm Bernard Pugh and this is my wife, Abigail."

"How do you do. I'm John."

"We've seen you about with Father Ambrose. Are you studying with him?"

"Yes … I'm … er … I'm looking particularly at the period he's an expert in … The Dark Times."

Abigail, who looked as though she might be African, spoke for the first time.

"Are you a history teacher then?"

"Er … of sorts … yes."

She looked at him as though she expected him to say more, but he smiled as engagingly as he could and said — to her, "And why are you staying at St Adrienne's?"

"We are on a kind of retreat. Well, not a retreat really, but a period of recovery and renewal."

"Recovery?"

"Oh, Abbie might be misleading you," broke in Bernard, "We are teachers and we have just finished with our group — after ten years — so we are having a little break and some in-service training."

"Yes," said Abigail, "There's some lovely teaching going on in this area. But we'll be home soon."

"And where's home?"

"The Soar Valley," said Bernard.

"Ah." said John, not knowing where that was but not wishing to sound ignorant.

"Not many people know it, but it's very good for teaching."

"How's that?"

"Oh, it's got everything — from Charnian rock on one side to Jurassic limestone on the other — and something from every period of history — very ancient to very modern, everything. But what is it exactly you're looking at with Father Ambrose?"

"I'm looking at the whole period, really," said John vaguely and then added, because it seemed to give his statement more point, "and I'm very interested in the virtual reality techniques, and especially full submersion."

"Oo, them. I found them very frightening," said Abigail, "and I don't want to go through that again." Bernard smiled at his wife and said, "Nor me. They are useful, though."

"But dangerous?" enquired John.

"I suppose they could be, but I've never heard of anyone suffering ill effects — other than the ones that bothered Abigail. Have you?"

John got up from the table saying, "Can't say I have, but I must go and get on with it."

"I'd rather you than me," said Abigail, and she gave John a beautiful smile as she said it.

"Nice talking to you," said Bernard.

"And to you."

Ambrose began the account of the Reawakening much further back than John expected. Indeed, he claimed that the complete story of humankind, right from pre-history, was relevant, and that the trends that became clearly apparent after the Dark Times, and which resulted in the forms of organisation to be found in 4058, could be discerned from the very beginning. He reminded John of that reading they had listened to, which John had wanted to discuss on the visit to the cliffs because it had claimed that from the very instant when hominid became human there was before us a choice: either to behave selfishly or altruistically. Never, even in the worst periods of human cruelty and degradation, had we chosen to be entirely selfish; altruism too has always been integral to human life. However, it is the very conflict between the two that explains our history. So we have wars on the one hand but also, on the other, hospitals, schools and the attempts to bring order and justice — from the laws of Sargon, Hammurabi and the Pharaohs, through the Torah, the Sermon on the Mount and Magna Carta, on to the Communist Manifesto, the constitution of the United Nations — take whichever set of facts you like — right up to the Declaration of Pachacamac ...

"Pachacamac?!"

"Oh, sorry. Yes. That was not until 3002, so you couldn't have heard of it. It was the work of a confederation of South American communes that set up a headquarters in what had been the shanty towns around Lima, next to the site of a very ancient Inca city. Again, it was very worthy, but had little immediate effect — I say immediate because all such developments have influenced the present."

Ambrose went on to point out that very often the most altruistic developments followed periods of the worst depravity and said you could see this particularly clearly in the time immediately preceding John's birth. The First and Second World Wars both ended with serious attempts to bring not only peace and order, but also justice. John was not sure he could accept this thesis unconditionally. It seemed not only too superficial a judgement but also to distort the history. Both organisations the League of Nations and the United Nations had failed, became talking-shops, more useful for preventing beneficial developments than encouraging them. Ambrose said that though all of this was important, what was more so, in the long run, was the attempt, because it added to the stock of human experience — we knew (virtually all along) why they failed. Moreover, it was the revulsion felt by people against the wickedness and stupidity of the wars, against the death and destruction, but most of all the desire to avoid further suffering, which led them to attempt the reforms; you could see this in almost any period of history. John immediately thought of the Thirty Years War, of which he had been reminded several times during the appalling descriptions of the Dark Times, so he interrupted Ambrose and asked where was the attempt at reform after the treaty of Westphalia in 1648. He thought Ambrose would not be so confident about this period and went straight on to say that one of the more important effects was the rise of Prussian militarism which would later be a contributory factor in the very wars Ambrose had mentioned. He was surprised by the reply — that the rise of Prussia would ultimately lead to the unification of Germany and the first attempt at a welfare state.

"But there you go again! I can see the line you are taking but it's all too simple and leaves out so much. And I don't think you should equate militarism with the welfare state."

"I'm not. What I am saying is that here we can see an attempt at organisation, especially under Frederick II, to avoid the earlier horrors. That organisation becomes more complex and leads another authoritarian, Bismarck, to introduce things like National Insurance, a serious reform."

"Blimey, Ambrose! You know your history."

"Thank you. I have made a serious study of all this and actually I'm glad you have brought this up, because one of the points I will want to make later is that authoritarianism usually creates as many problems as it solves, and that is another lesson we have had to learn."

John felt considerably chastened by this exchange, but he was still not convinced. Nevertheless, he remained silent. Ambrose did concede one point and that was that international organisations that attempted to encourage justice and peace on a global scale had all failed, not only the ones mentioned, but many others that followed. On the other hand, he claimed that our experience of them, i.e. whatever measure of success they might have had *and* their final failure were to be of immense importance later, though he apologised for reading history backwards again. Nevertheless, he returned to his theme that revulsion at cruelty and degradation time and again led humankind to look for forms of organisation, both social and economic, that could avoid brutality and strife. Once more John intervened.

"But look, Ambrose, we've spent the last month discussing how the decline into savagery was almost unstoppable."

"Well yes, but it did stop finally and, pray God, we can avoid it in the future."

"So then … the sixty-four thousand dollar question … What made the difference?"

"Sixty-four thousand dollars? What are you talking about?"

"Sorry, my anachronism this time ... It's from a quiz game. It means the all-important question. So, c'mon, tell me, even if it means cutting it all short."

Ambrose became very thoughtful and John began to wonder if there was no answer, or at least none that Ambrose could find. He also realised that he was hoping that Ambrose had actually got an answer. Maybe it required more thinking about: his face was almost contorted. Finally, he looked at John and said, "It's all a matter of degree. I suppose really what I want to say is that no matter how bad the situation was during the second millennium, and for most of the third, it was never so bad as to convince a majority of people, and especially influential people, that wholesale change was necessary. There were always, well at least until the last two hundred years of the Dark Times, quite large sections of the Earth where there was relative peace and even a measure of prosperity. It was only at the very end that the lessons were really driven home. In the worst period of human history ever there was nowhere to hide: the consequences of inhumanity were experienced everywhere. That, I suppose, was one of the crucial differences."

John felt unsure about this. His mind wandered off: Ambrose's explanation seemed like ratiocination — logical maybe, but an answer clutched at because it could be formulated. He tried to work out why he felt uneasy about it. Was it because he did not really believe that those two hundred years were so much worse than all the others? And even if they were, why should people behave any differently from before? Depravity feasted on depravity. How could the cycle be broken? And anyway, when relatively good times returned, everyone would forget their good resolutions never to let it all happen again. He then remembered how the descriptions of the worst times had upset him — perhaps those times were more dreadful than anything humanity had experienced before, even all those periods of genocide he had learned about. And maybe now, experiencing the horrors vicariously was enough; perhaps the full submersion techniques would show him the answer. He just did not know. Suddenly, he became conscious again of his present reality, and from the way Ambrose peered at him, John could tell that his own face betrayed the fact that he was still not convinced, but Ambrose smiled and went on, "But that's only half the story. The attempts to bring about reform continued and at all sorts of levels from very small to large scale international. And here is the sixty thousand dollar answer ..."

"Sixty-four thousand ..."

"OK, the all important answer ... that the small solutions were the ones that did best."

This statement had about it the same air of unreality as the one about the last two hundred years of the Dark Times, and John blurted out, "But, Ambrose, there were many like that even in my day. Take the Kibbutzim, for example. They looked good in their early years but even they became part of the oppression of others."

"Well, maybe they did, but in what circumstances? I don't know about those you have just named, but there were lots of others like them which grander more powerful groups exploited. But it meant that the small groups had to find ways of retaining their independence, and in the long run they did."

"I find that difficult to believe."

"But the proof of the pudding and all that. Look around you now."

"Ah, now that's one thing I'm not allowed to do."

"Not allowed to? Nobody's stopping you! You have a knack for putting things in the worst possible light."

"Well, that's how it feels to me."

"OK, let's suspend this for a week — go and look for yourself about here. Admittedly, it's more sparsely populated than your part of Europa, but it will give you an idea. Invite Marianne to go with you as a guide."

"As a guide or as a guard?"

"Oh, damn me, there you go again!"

At this John burst out laughing, not only because Ambrose had once again showed annoyance, and enough to make him swear, but also because it made him seem, in John's eyes, more human.

Ambrose, of course, was sorry immediately and apologised, but went on, "You know, a break might not be such a bad thing — and perhaps Marianne would be willing to come. I know you would like to see her."

The idea was becoming more attractive, but John was still apprehensive because of his uncertainty about her attitude towards him. There was also George-Louis to think about. Then it dawned on him that he was already thinking of using the boy as a pawn.

"I'm not sure," he said.

"Well, we'll do no more today. Let's go to lunch. But first I must make a note of where we are. It seems that today we've reached a critical point. I want to be sure we can pick up the threads after your holiday."

John had decided to tell Marianne and George-Louis about Ambrose's proposal that he should take a short holiday but not to mention that he would like them to join him. However, the conversation went even better than he had hoped, because almost immediately George-Louis asked excitedly if John would visit the cliffs again, and once more he looked at his mother hopefully. Her smile was so gentle and indulgent that John changed his mind and was encouraged to say, "I'd like you to visit the cliffs with me," and before Marianne could intervene, added, "and also to look at the Burren."

"The Burren? What's that?"

"Oh, it's a place I visited many years ago and it's a kind of limestone plateau. But what I remember particularly was the number of wild flowers — and there's a strange mixture of Mediterranean and Alpine."

George-Louis looked perplexed but Marianne chuckled and told John that the words he was using were too big. John was about to say that he thought someone George-Louis' age would know them when he realised that perhaps these terms were not used any more, so he said, "Ah, sorry. It's just that some of the flowers there are usually only found in mountains and yet others only by the sea. But the really big thing is that that they are all so pretty and there were lots of them when I went — I suppose it might be different now."

"I'm sure there are lots and I would love to see them."

"Well, can you and Mummy come?"

Marianne looked at George-Louis knowingly but with a broad grin and said she would have to check at the hospital, but really she thought there would be no problem.

"Oh, whoopee!" cried George-Louis. "When can we go? Tomorrow?"

"Maybe not tomorrow, but perhaps the next day."

John felt as excited as the boy looked and he knew that his smile must be much too broad and much too foolish, but he could not help it. However, he watched Marianne keenly and she seemed genuinely pleased too.

Once he knew for certain the day of their arrival, John sought out Michael in his rose garden to see if it was usual for him to fetch visitors from the bus station. What he wanted to know was whether he could accompany Michael on the short journey. Michael was surprised he should even ask and then, when he discovered who they were going to pick up and why, he suggested that they should have an old-fashioned Irish holiday and do it all by jaunting car.

"But what about the unpredictable Irish weather?"

"Ar, we've a cart with a hood."

"And what about the horse? I've never driven a jaunting car and I'm sure Marianne hasn't either."

"Sure, I'll sort you out an animal that can do it all for you."

"Then what about feeding and watering it?"

"The people at the places you stop will do all that for you."

"And that's another thing: where do we stop?"

"This is Erin. I've friends and relations from here to Ballydehob … and so have lots of the community. We can set it all up on the communicator. They'll look after you. You'll be all right."

"I've heard that before."

"Well, in Erin it's true."

John enjoyed the look of surprise from George-Louis and Marianne when they got off the bus and saw the jaunting car. George-Louis ran straight to the front passenger seat and climbed up next to Michael, so John was able to sit with Marianne in the back, and as Michael launched immediately into his guide to Connemara talk, they were able to chat uninterruptedly — but ineffectually.

"Did you have a good journey?"

"Oh yes, and George-Louis has loved everything. He'd been on a train before but never on a ferry. He was amazed at how big it was. And he loved the coach journey too because he could see out of the window."

"And what about you? Did you enjoy it too?"

"Mm, yes, and I do need a break."

"That makes two of us — at least in Ambrose's estimation."

The conversation never became any more serious than this because John was so unsure of himself; he seemed to have reverted to adolescence and Marianne was her usual reserved self. He wanted to hold her and kiss her, and tell her how much he missed her, and how glad he was that she had come, but he was afraid that should he be too demonstrative she would take flight. He remembered the day in his little museum house when he had been first so angry and then so despondent. She had come to him spontaneously and he had rested his head on her shoulder. He wished something like that could happen now — but on that day, had she been showing affection or simply treating him as a sick child? He did not know, and so the old questions continued to tumble through his mind. Had she come just for the sake of her son? Was she being heroic — coming to see him not because she felt any personal affection for him, but because he was lost, marooned, and needed help? Did she feel anything akin to the love he was now certain he felt for her? He did not know what to do or how to turn the conversation so that he could elicit some inkling of what she thought or felt. Her closeness only made him more inept — it seemed much easier with the communicator. So, though he sensed that this meeting was one of the most significant of his new life, he could talk only in commonplaces. They even discussed the weather.

Marianne too had her problems. She was not absolutely certain why she had come, and though she wanted to please George-Louis, she thought that maybe she was using his desire to see the cliffs and the waves as an excuse. She knew he liked John and wondered whether this man might be becoming a father figure for her son. Of one thing she was certain, and that was that he knew nothing of John's origins and saw him just as another man, but one he liked. Could she depend upon the judgement of an eight-year-old? If he seemed certain of John's good character, couldn't she be certain too? She was very wary of John's temper but could not decide how serious it was. It could be a real defect or it could be something "normal" in a person from two thousand years ago. And what did that mean? That he would always be given to sudden outbursts? That he couldn't learn, as they had done, to deal with their angry feelings in a positive way. There was so much that had happened to him in his childhood that now, for today's children, every effort would be made to avoid. She knew she felt sorry for him: his predicament was heartbreaking. This last thought brought with it a shaft of light, a hope. He was dealing with his difficulties very well, all things considered. Didn't this mean he had strength of character? She looked at him. He could be regarded as handsome and the slight crookedness of his teeth made him look boyish when he smiled. Perhaps she was a little in love with him. That thought frightened her. How could she ever love anyone after George? Suddenly, all the heartache of his unexpected death came back to her, pushing John out of her mind. She felt cheated out of the happiness she should have had. She tried to tell herself that she ought to be grateful for the three years they were together, but those very years had promised so many more — and they had gone for ever. The pain might not be as acute, but it was still there. And George was so beautiful! How could John ever compare? She looked at him again, hardly hearing what he was trying to tell her about St Adrienne's. Another disturbing thought struck her: what if she did learn to love him and he went back to his own time? No! No! No! The only way to avoid the pain was not to fall in love with him. Momentarily, she made up her mind on this, but by then they had arrived and John was putting up his hand to help her from the jaunting car. His eyes showed how happy he was that she was with him. Her determination faltered.

They were met by Pilar, who had returned from visiting her mother, and she fussed over George-Louis and Marianne and took them to the married quarters of the monastery where a set of very comfortable rooms had been prepared for them. The boy wanted to see the cliffs straight away, but it was decided that that particular adventure would have to wait until the next day.

John wondered how George-Louis would react to the evening meal because, as this was the only occasion when the whole community, including all the guests, met together to eat in silence, the rule was allowed to lapse only in very special circumstances. The other children he had seen at the meal always behaved impeccably, and as George-Louis appeared to act no differently from them, John began to think that perhaps the current principles and techniques of upbringing and education were effective but benign too. Children seemed not to be oppressed by requirements such as this (and even appeared to be listening to the reading). They might look solemn during the meal but were their usual open cheerful selves afterwards. Immediately it was over, most of them, and George-Louis with them, ran off to play in the adventure playground. John, Marianne and Ambrose went for coffee. They were joined by Michael who had a printout of a route he had prepared for their journey. No leg was longer than fifteen miles, many were shorter, and all followed country lanes as much as possible. In two days Michael, and one or two of his fellow Irish monks, had worked wonders arranging not only overnight stopping places but also lunchtime calls at the homes of their relations and friends. That they could not set off immediately after breakfast, because of the need to satisfy George-Louis' curiosity about the cliffs — and this would take them briefly in the opposite direction — caused a hitch. Michael frowned but said there was no problem and he could easily adjust the itinerary.

Because Marianne wanted to attend Mass the next morning, John found himself in two minds. The notion that he had left all this behind was still strong even though he had found his various visits to the church rewarding. However, his desire to be with Marianne as much as was physically possible was a powerful attraction. He had still not committed himself one way or the other to accompanying her next morning when he had walked with her back to her rooms that evening, but he reflected on the dilemma before he went to sleep. If God did exist and if religion had any meaning then it would be hypocritical of him to attend Mass with her and George-Louis: he should attend, not to be with them, but for all the reasons he used to go to Mass before he lost his faith. If God did not exist then it did not matter whether he went or not. So he could go with a clear conscience. But he had his doubts about this: to pretend to be something he was not in order to worm his way into her favour seemed somehow reprehensible too — so the Pascalian line of argument could not be used either. He considered the possibility of telling her his real position as they went into Mass, but George-Louis would be there — what would he think? And what would she think if he were to weaken her son's faith in some way? Bloody hell, he thought, I'm back where I was as a teenager — arguing with myself about sex. He chuckled to himself and then felt more relaxed. Perhaps he had not lost his faith. Perhaps there was still a spark of it hidden under the grey ash of deliberate forgetfulness. Maybe the way out was to claim to be an agnostic rather than an atheist and then he could pray in Mass — God, if you exist, guide us on our journey and make Marianne love me. Aagh! This was even worse! So though he could not work out a satisfactory reason for accompanying her tomorrow, he would go to Mass anyway — and see what happened.

The next morning they knelt together like a little family and John thought that this seemed to be the most natural thing in the world. The cool elegance of the architecture and the gentle ebb and flow of the plain chant did not catch his attention as they usually did because he was so aware of the presence of Marianne next to him. Again, he found this disturbing, not so much because it made his pulse race, but because it seemed somehow improper and unworthy of Marianne who, he was sure, was caught up in the meaning of the ritual. He also reflected that if God did exist then to allow himself to be absorbed by the exhilaration of her nearness was disrespectful to Him too. This notion carried him back, yet again, to his youth when he had believed fervently, and this in turn enabled him to concentrate on the significance of what was being said and done. There were differences, but the ceremony had not changed very much since his day, and as he considered the fact that what was going on had been happening for over four thousand years, through all the vicissitudes of those terrible times, a strange sensation flooded all over him. At first it frightened him because it took him by surprise, but when he tried to analyse it, he found it uplifting. It seemed to be that he had become super conscious of his own existence, and for the first time in his life he was truly aware of his own separateness: he was John More and he was distinct from everybody and everything else, and he alone was responsible for his own actions. Terrifying though this could be he also knew that this was a gift. He did not have to be, but he was: existence had been endowed upon him — by God? he wondered. Then the sensation left him and he heard the words of the Gospel. It was from St John and about the woman taken in adultery, which he had only ever thought of as an example of Jesus' unconditional forgiveness. But on this occasion he became much more fully aware of the predicament of the woman and the complexity of the emotions she must have felt. He could never put Marianne in such a position. He realised then that, up to that point, he had intended to sleep with Marianne at the first opportunity. That no longer seemed possible. She was as distinct a person as he; he must never consider her as an object. His awareness of his own self had made him more completely conscious of the integrity of others and of his responsibility for them. Nevertheless, at the communion he still did not know what he believed, but the old inhibitions were still there. In this state of mind he could not receive communion. George-Louis, however, did not seem to think that this was odd.

At breakfast Michael came in to talk to John about dealing with the horse: how to make her stop, turn right and left and so on. It was decided that he should have a little practice. This meant that he had to forego the pleasure of taking George-Louis to the cliffs, but fortunately Ambrose agreed to take him and Marianne while John and Michael rode, a little jerkily at first, up and down the back lane. It was not so difficult and Michael was right: the old filly knew what to do no matter how stupid her apparent masters might be.

Chapter VIII

There was watery sunshine as they left St Adrienne's, but within half an hour it began to drizzle. They tried to persevere without the hood, but in the end even George-Louis wanted it up. This was not an auspicious start to their adventure and they had to eat a rather damp packed lunch at the side of the road with Sarah the horse looking at them accusingly, as if only lunatics would subject an old lady to such conditions. She did accept a handful of oats. The afternoon journey became something of a gruelling, determined plod and nobody said anything very much. There was no stopping to admire the scenery, the mist was so thick. John also began to wonder what kind of reception they would get at the house of the O'Leary family because they would arrive much earlier than predicted. Marianne told him not to worry: no one would be upset. And, of course, she was right. No sooner had they arrived than they were taken in for warm drinks, showers if they wanted them, and were generally made very welcome.

This was the first time John had been in a real fifth millennium home. He had thought at first that he was arriving at a traditional Irish cottage but, just as with the houses in Jackfield, what he could see was only a facade. Apart from those in the rooms at the front there were no windows, because the rest of the rooms were all 'underground', but they were air-conditioned and so were pleasant to live in no matter what the weather. They were also subtly lit by what appeared to be natural light. This particular house was not built into a hillside but was covered by a mound of earth, which had been put on top of the building to insulate it. This was landscaped: there was a pleasant garden, small enough to be easily kept but big enough to sit in if the weather was mild — which probably happens in Erin more often than most people think. The house also had a rear facade, if that is not a contradiction, and behind it lay a paddock where Sarah, having been rubbed down and watered, now grazed. There were other houses round about and John noticed that they were set in a circle facing away from each other so that their back paddocks all met in the centre, and there a little church had been built. It looked very ancient and, despite its windows, not unlike the Gallarous Oratory he remembered seeing back in the third millennium, but that, he was sure, was much farther south — near the

Dingle, perhaps. He wondered how normal this was and at the first opportunity asked Marianne about it; as she said she had seen nothing like it before, he knew it was safe to raise the matter with the O'Learys. Margaret, the grandmother of the family, told them proudly that the people of Straith, which was the name of the hamlet, had built it themselves and modelled it on the famous oratory.

"And it is built of real stone," she said, "so it's difficult to heat, but lovely for morning Mass in the summer."

"Do you have Mass every day?"

"Most days. You see, two of us are priests — me and Dominic, Dan's eldest son."

This came as an even bigger surprise than married monks, but as there seemed to be no reaction from Marianne, he thought he'd better say nothing till he and she were alone — if ever that should happen.

The evening was regarded as a family occasion because they rarely had visitors and, because they were very fond of cousin Michael and as it was he who had sent them, John, Marianne and George-Louis were looked upon almost as family. The food was good and so was the wine. John was interested to see that the white came from the English Midlands but the red was French. He had never seen the name Brodau before but suspected from its quality that the wine was a good Bordeaux. Perhaps the name was a corruption, but he was too circumspect to ask. After dinner the adults sat around talking while the children played a game on a large monitor. It looked like a board game, the Great Race, which John remembered from his childhood.

He was also given an insight into the working of democracy at a local level. There was a good-humoured family argument about who should attend a meeting of representatives from Straith with those of several other hamlets round about. Any adult O'Leary could act for the rest, but nobody wanted to go because of the visitors. Attendance did not require leaving the house because there was an electronic link-up. In the end, one of the sons, Anthony, who was eighteen and so old enough to vote, agreed to go. John surprised everybody by asking if he could accompany him briefly. They went to what was called the community room and there John saw an array of electronic equipment, which Anthony made no attempt to explain because he thought that John would be well acquainted with it. On a large display of monitors appeared the other members of the meeting and they greeted Anthony and John amicably. Then one of them, a woman of about forty, who was in the chair for that meeting, asked if they could get on quickly. The main item of business was the first on the agenda and was concerned with money for farm equipment, which one of the other communities needed to replace. Everyone seemed well versed in the methods of procedure and it was quickly agreed that the all the pieces of equipment should be purchased, but the amount to be spent was questioned. So every group was then asked for a brief account of their financial situation and, on the basis of this, a sum was suggested and accepted, though this would mean that not all the required equipment could be new: some of it would have to be second-hand, reconditioned. The person acting as secretary for this particular meeting reminded them that each representative would receive a printout of the financial implications and that these should be made available to all the people who were being represented that evening. The rest of the business seemed to be routine and was got through fairly quickly. As they were preparing to return to the family, Anthony wondered aloud how many members of the other communities were linked in tonight and whether there would be any objections to the decisions. If there were and these were serious another meeting would have to be called, but this was very unlikely. On the other hand, he said, they had had discussions on controversial issues that had gone on for months.

"Doesn't that create all sorts of inconvenience?"

"Not really. Does it for you in your community?"

"I suppose not." was the hasty reply.

"Dan always says that when God made time he made plenty of it."

John was worried by all of this. He knew that in his own day interminable discussions were death to efforts at getting democracy to work. There must be a force hidden somewhere that gets these people to work together, he thought, but as yet he had seen no evidence of what it might be.

The next morning they all went to Mass in the Oratory. Margaret was right: the little church was full of light, and this in some way made the meaning of the liturgy transparent. John had often referred to Christian celebrations as gobbledegook when talking to his liberal-minded friends of the twenty-first century, but with the good family O'Leary and their neighbours such a claim would have been wildly inappropriate. He became aware of their entering into the Godhead firstly through the liturgy of the word and then through the sacrifice itself, the forcefulness of which struck him at the words, "the blood of the new and everlasting covenant *shed for you and for all*". Moreover, the work of the rest of the day seemed to be sanctified by being offered at the same time. That this was a meal also became significant, and yet he could not join Marianne and George-Louis when they received communion.

The weather had improved and so the next stage of their journey was better appreciated by all three, except that on several occasions they had to climb quite steep hills and this meant they had to walk because the work would otherwise have been too much of a strain on a horse of Sarah's mature years. When John found this tedious, because the leg which had been broken still bothered him if he walked too far — especially on such ancient trackways — he recalled that they could have had a younger horse but one which might have been bloody-minded. George-Louis seemed to enjoy everything whether he rode or walked, and Marianne was her usual patient and placid self. They stopped for lunch in another little village like the last and with a family related to another of the monks. The hospitality was so overwhelming that they not only ate too much, they also stayed longer than they intended. As the afternoon sun was very warm, they went very slowly and took it in turns to loll and doze on the rear seat.

Their stop for the night was in an interesting building that had begun life centuries before as a lighthouse but had been developed over recent years as a weather station. Again, John was made aware of how the ancient and modern functioned side by side. Apparently, though the navigational aids on the few huge ships that crossed the Atlantic were so sophisticated that they had no need for lighthouses, the local fishermen preferred to keep the lights even though they too had equipment that combined the old techniques of radar, sonar and radio in such a way that the helmsman need never look up from his console. However, they still wanted to see where they were. To fish, they said, you needed to be aware of what was around you, to "feel" the land, the seabed and the sea, not just look at a console.

Though he felt quite tired when they arrived, John climbed uncomplainingly with George-Louis to the top of the lighthouse. A meteorologist who was interested in ancient artefacts and machinery showed them how the lamp worked and pointed out the various mechanisms that came into play in foggy or stormy weather. John realised how useful it was to have George-Louis with them because everyone was keen to explain to him how everything worked and John did not have to appear ignorant. The lad also asked all sorts of naive questions about the complex equipment and displays in the weather station below, and the weathermen responded enthusiastically about how the information from all over the world and from space was co-ordinated, so that weather forecasting was much more accurate than ever before — and for months and even years ahead, so powerful were the computers. Nevertheless, one technician explained that it was still difficult to get very local forecasting right because the astronomical data hardly applied. He also went into what seemed to him to be a simple explanation of chaos theory to show that overall patterns might be discernable but local variations could not be predicted accurately. John and Marianne nodded sagely but understood very little.

Their quarters were as comfortable as John had come to expect. He was a little surprised that he and Marianne were always given separate rooms, but when he thought about it he wondered if this was because of their different surnames, More and Martin. People assumed they were not married. Or perhaps Michael had made this part of what he told his friends and family as he recruited their help. Maybe, the only permanent relationships now were to be found in marriage.

Over the next few days the weather held, though it was not as warm, and they were able to make good but leisurely progress southwards. They always had plenty of time, and one afternoon they found a beautiful beach and so decided to go for a swim. Afterwards, John and Marianne sat on the sand while George-Louis played with part of an abandoned surfboard he had found. John was then able to ask her some of the questions he had been storing up.

He discovered that there had been women priests in all Christian churches since the Dark Times. Because priests had played an important part in what Ambrose had referred to as 'the great underground movement', they had been persecuted severely. In some parts of the world they had been virtually obliterated and it had become almost impossible to replace them. Their oppressors did not expect their place to be taken by women who, because their life styles were different from men, were much more difficult to detect and root out — in fact John remembered some talk of this even in the twenty-first century. The terrible consequences of ordaining women that had been predicted proved unwarranted, and anyway, the opposition to women priests grew less as the church responded to changing times by becoming less hierarchical, less centralised and less authoritarian.

What she had to say about marriage and the relationship between men and women he found less palatable, and she seemed embarrassed to talk about it. She spoke haltingly, but what her roundabout description amounted to was that marriage had become sacrosanct. It was accepted as the norm for the majority of people. Celibacy was still an option but very few people chose it and those who did were usually ones who had difficulty coming to terms with their sexuality for one reason or another — but these people were given as much help as possible so that they could deal with the concomitant frustrations. John was becoming alarmed, but worse was to follow. Courtships were usually long: couples had to be certain of each other because annulment was very rare.

"Annulment …? What about divorce?"

"There's no divorce."

"What! No divorce! How do incompatible people survive if they can't get divorced?"

"That's why courtships are long … and people unhappy with their partners can separate."

"You know, this is beginning to sound like the straitjacket morality of the old Catholic Church. What about people who have no religious belief?"

"There are few of them. Though they do exist," she hastily added.

John was amazed at this answer and it awoke in him once more all the fears and suspicions he had about this society — was it, he asked himself, in thrall to the priests? He wanted to explode, but already he could see that the conversation was making Marianne very anxious. He breathed deeply and looked to the horizon in the hope that this would make him seem calm. He knew that soon George-Louis would join them and the conversation would be at an end, so as gently as he could and in a low, unemotional voice he said, "I suppose sex is confined to marriage too."

He looked at her as affectionately as he could manage, despite the frustration stirring within him. She said nothing but gazed at him almost sorrowfully and nodded gently and apologetically. He was not sure because he looked away again, but he thought her eyes seemed tearful. Along with his dismay he experienced a glimmer of hope: she must feel something more for him other than sympathy. By this time George-Louis was making his way up from the water's edge. She leaned close to John and said softly, "I think you should discuss all this with Ambrose or somebody else at St Adrienne's — someone who knows more about the history. I don't remember much about it, but I think it all goes back to the awful depravity there used to be."

As they continued their journey they were both silent, but George-Louis chatted away and commented on everything they saw. Suddenly, he pointed out to sea.

"Mummy, John, what's that out there?"

They saw an enormously long platform — longer than the one Ambrose had pointed out to John near St Adrienne's — rising and falling with the swell about half a mile off the shore. John realised it was the experiment in power production, which Michael had said his son was working on. When George-Louis asked how it worked, he was able to say, "I'm afraid I don't know because it's very new. There are other platforms, but this one works differently."

After this exchange the tension disappeared and he and Marianne seemed to be back to normal, especially as George-Louis began to sing 'Green Grow the Rushes, O', which John had taught them.

For their accommodation that evening they had been provided with a holiday cottage, so there was only the three of them. On their arrival John felt apprehensive: who would attend to Sarah? However, he need not have worried — George-Louis was very keen to do what was necessary, especially as he had watched their hosts rubbing down, feeding and watering the old horse wherever they had stopped. Marianne, no doubt worrying about the safety of her son as he was really too small, insisted on helping him and found a stool for him to stand on. John offered to get on with preparing a meal, but once in the kitchen he was daunted by the array of modern equipment, none of which he knew how to use. Fortunately, Marianne came back into the house without George-Louis and rescued him, so he stayed there to watch what she did.

Later that evening, he read George-Louis a bedtime story, and when he had finished and was coming quietly out of the child's room, he found that Marianne had been listening outside. They were standing very close to each other and he could not resist putting his arms around her. She responded and kissed him very gently. Then she pulled away slightly and said, "Thank you for trying so hard to understand everything."

George-Louis was fast asleep. They went out on to the verandah and sat there holding hands to watch the sunset, and though John was still aware of his growing desire, he felt that he was about as happy as he could possibly be. Marianne too felt contented and less wary of John who seemed to be learning how to be patient.

The next day they arrived at the Burren quite early in the morning, and as they were about to begin their exploration they saw ahead of them a group of people — mostly children but with several adults, one of whom was calling to them and waving. As they got nearer John recognised Bernard and Abigail, the couple he had met at breakfast back at the monastery.

"My, my, what are you doing here? And in a jaunting car?" said Abigail.

"We're taking a little holiday," said John, "and this is my good friend Marianne and her son George-Louis."

"But why here?"

"Because John said the flowers were very beautiful here," said George-Louis.

"And they are too," said Bernard, "but there's more to it than that."

"We've joined Brigid and Sam and the children they educate — they're doing an investigation of the whole area," said Abigail, "and we're going to help." Then looking at George-Louis, "Would you like to help as well?"

George-Louis had seen that the other children had got all kinds of interesting looking equipment and was already feeling envious.

"May we?" he asked looking towards Brigid and Sam.

"Of course you can," said Sam. "The more help we have the better."

And so they began plotting the geography, the ecology and the micro-climates of a considerable portion of the Burren, and marking on their individual maps where they found particular plants or insects so that later they could see whether variations in temperature, composition and depth of soil and so on could be related to the rich variety of flora and fauna found there.

George-Louis was given a partner to work with so Marianne and John acted as a pair too. John skilfully, he thought, manoeuvred Marianne out of earshot of the others so that he could ask about what was going on.

What he learned was that there were no schools for children under the age of fifteen. When they were five or six — there were no strict rules about this — children would join a group of maybe a dozen others to work with two educators — very often a husband and wife team — who were very highly trained; in fact it took longer to educate them than it did a doctor. The best way to understand what educators were trying to do was to see it as an endeavour by the children, assisted by the educators, to investigate reality. (John wanted to ask what was meant by reality, but thought better of it). This usually began with the immediate environment of the children, but could then be developed on wider lines. To take full advantage of what was going on the educators would have to make sure that the children developed very good skills in reading, writing, information technology and mathematics.

At this point they realised that they had wandered quite a way from the others and were not actually doing the required work. Marianne insisted they should get on with it — as a good example to George-Louis and the other children. They concentrated on the flowers they could match with the beautifully drawn and coloured illustrations that Brigid had prepared. As they did, John insisted on one more question.

"What happens at fifteen?"

"Then college can begin. But there is so much more to say. And as I have said before, I'm not an expert. Why don't you talk to all these teachers about it as you now know them — and they are educators."

Back with the whole group, John and Marianne joined in the animated discussion about what had been found. George-Louis remarked that his mother and John had not discovered as much as he and his partner, Harriet.

"Did you have a patch with not much in it?" he asked.

"No. I don't think so," said John. "It's a long time since me and your mum have done this sort of thing. Maybe we are not as quick with our observations as you and Harriet."

Then Marianne interrupted quickly, "But one flower we did find which I thought rather special. Look. It's this one," and she pulled the picture of the bloody cranesbill out of the set that Brigid had given them.

"Oh," cried Harriet. "We didn't find any as beautiful as that. Can you show me one?"

They set off to find the flower while John and George-Louis continued to compare notes with the other children. The findings were very similar but different enough to see that when all the data was transferred to the large map, which was back at the house the group was using as a centre of operations for the week, there might be some interesting conclusions.

During the morning John took the opportunity to talk to Sam about the overall plan.

"Well, Brigid and I selected four areas to study, each one about a hectare, maybe a bit more or a bit less. This is the second one, which is why the children were able to get on with the work so quickly. And they have already looked at a lot of background material, most of it in our IT packs back at the house. However, we've had to prepare some stuff ourselves — all these lovely pictures of Brigid's, for instance. We had a good idea what kind of information the children would come up with so we were able to plan accordingly. We know the kind of thinking we would like them to do."

"But, for them, that's hardly discovery, is it?"

"Well, no. Not completely. But every generation doesn't have to discover the wheel for itself, does it?"

"I suppose not."

"It's guided discovery, but only up to a point, because, as we both well know, the relationship between the teacher and the pupil and the interaction between them affects how both of them learn. And if the children come up with a new and interesting line of enquiry, we let them get on with it. Often their findings are stimulating for us and affect our perceptions. On the other hand, we have an obligation to them: we can't just let them flounder about, can we?"

"No, I suppose not."

Just then a child came to ask Sam a question, and as John reflected on their conversation he half remembered something he had read about Russian theories of education back in the days of the Soviet Union. Was it something that Vygotsky had said? But no, surely that would be to do with linguistics. So was it social constructionism? It wasn't that either; it was to do with the education of less able children, he thought — something about the child who worked with a teacher making better progress, that really good education requires teaching and learning to function in tandem. It was very annoying not to be able to remember, especially as he had not got his books with him. Perhaps he could find it on the web. Just then, Sam turned back to him saying, "Where had we got to …? Oh, yes. We've still got a lot of work to do here — we want to see if there are any variations in the type of soil to be found in the gullies, 'grikes', as they call them."

" What sort of differences?"

"Well, if some have got more sand or clay or chalk or whatever, and whether the moisture varies, and so on. Oh, and we want to consider depth of soil … Oh … er, I nearly forgot, temperature too. We put thermometers in this morning before you arrived, and they will record changes in temperature over a twenty-four hour period; but that is only a snapshot. We've also got a program that does some very general things about the Burren, like the influence of the sea in some parts, even salt spray, would you believe."

"Won't this become much too complicated for them?"

"No, not really. Many of them, especially those a little older, are used to this and they help the younger ones. Wasn't your education like that? And I'm sure you must use methods similar to ours when you're working with the adolescents."

John felt a little worried by this line but then said, "Oh, yes, but I've never taught about anything like the Burren, and I just wondered ... er ... what you do with all this particular information."

"Actually, what's surprising is that with the right symbols and colours quite a lot is immediately obvious when we plot everything on our large map, so then we can have a brainstorming session before we assign particular features for further study to small groups. At the end we will set all our wall displays and things against the findings of the real experts, and we have those on another program. Usually, we find that the children have got most things right — except for the fauna. They catch sight of some birds and butterflies but they don't see the variety that's actually here. Though I bet young Jamie over there has found all kinds of beetles the others have not spotted ... But we have got a video about the insects and another on when and how the Burren was formed — but we will see what the children come up with on that first."

"It sounds like hard work!"

"It is, but they enjoy it, and on our very last day here we will visit Ailwee Cave."

John must have looked puzzled because Sam went on, "With its stalagmites and stalactites!"

"Oh, yes."

They went back to the house for a lunch, which parents who were accompanying the group had prepared. The data collected that morning were left in a room in which John noticed there was a huge map of the Burren laid out on the floor.

In the afternoon, instead of moving on as they had intended, John, Marianne and George-Louis continued to help with the work. From what he had learned about Sam and Brigid's intentions, John half expected that the children would be using highly technical forty-first century methods of investigation, but was pleased to see that they were fairly simple — though certainly good enough for the task in hand. Sam showed the children how to take a core of soil out of a grike and test it for moisture in a easy way, viz., by squeezing a handful of it to see if it stuck together like clay, broke up into lumps, or fell apart completely. Brigid had a kit not unlike one John remembered from his own school days for testing the pH value of the soil. She showed them how to mix a sample of soil with a little water and an indicator fluid in a test-tube and then establish the alkalinity or acidity by setting the tube against a chart marked with colours ranged to distinguish between variations in pH level. Depths of soil were measured by the only piece of electronic equipment used in the investigation and Abigail and Bernard demonstrated how to use it. As in the morning, everything was carefully recorded and any new flora or fauna observed were added to the lists made earlier. At John's request, he and Marianne were not involved but sat a little way off on a convenient block of limestone and watched. He was surprised by the diligence shown by the children, but he noticed that though they worked hard they still chatted cheerfully, even if more quietly than any pupils he had known. He was also intrigued by the relationship between the teachers and the children: it was friendly but genuine with no trace of patronising on the part of the adults who, nevertheless, seemed to have an air of authority, which he decided must have come from their understanding — not just of the work being done but also of children.

As it was too late to move on, and Sarah seemed to appreciate the attention she was getting from the children, room was made for them at the house. After a good supper they had a sing-song and once again the children surprised John: so many of them could play instruments and they all appeared to be able to read music because Abigail taught them a new song, the notes and words of which she projected on to the wall so that everyone could join in. Though it was in several parts, they sang it as though they were already familiar with it.

The next day, after Mass, they set off on the last leg of their outward journey, which would take them to a holiday cottage near the coast and within reach of the cliffs of Moher, which John wanted George-Louis to see. Saying goodbye to all the people they had met on the Burren was a little sad because they had become such good friends in such a short time and because George-Louis had liked the work the other children were engaged in and wanted to continue with it.

There was no rain but the weather was as misty as on their first day. Because they could see very little as they moved along the lanes on Michael's map, they were not tempted to stop or make any detours and so made good progress. Sarah too, having seemingly gained extra energy, was prepared to trot, i.e. when the road was easy — she still stopped expectantly at the bottom of even any modest hill until the passengers climbed down from the car. As they approached the coast the mist cleared, driven inland, it seemed, by a pleasant onshore breeze.

Michael's directions said they should pick up supplies at a store in a little town near their destination. Neither John nor Marianne were quite sure what the implications of this were until they got to Liscannor, as it was called. Sarah had decided that she had had enough trotting for one day so they went through the town at a very gentle pace with the wheels of the jaunting car making virtually no noise on the smooth tarmac of the main street. They looked around in wonder because the whole place was a reconstruction of an ancient small country town not unlike those John could remember from his youth. It had an authentic air about it, which the museum house where John lived could never match. George-Louis commented enthusiastically on every house and shop they passed; Marianne smiled with pleasure at the thought of what this might all mean to John; and he stared around wondering whether or not he were dreaming, so real did it feel.

Without being requested to, Sarah stopped outside a double-fronted shop, a little larger than the others and marked by a sign that said 'Twentieth Century Stores'. Underneath in red were the words, "Try the Authentic Life of your Ancestors'. They got down and went inside to be met by a tall, thin man wearing a long white apron down nearly to his feet who, on seeing them, came forward and said, "Mr More and party?"

"Yes …"

"Ah, good. Everything is ready for you," and he pointed to several boxes on a table by the door. He continued, "I'd better show you one or two things though," and he opened the first box.

It contained nothing that surprised John, but Marianne looked mystified because it contained candles, two storm lamps and what John recognised as a Tilley lamp. He was pleased to see a can of paraffin oil and even a bottle of methylated spirits. There were also boxes of matches. The grocer said, "Do you want me to show you how to use any of these?"

"No," said John, "I'm well acquainted with them all."

"Are you a museum keeper, then?"

"Sort of," said John, thinking of his 1940s house in Blists Hill.

"Only sort of?"

"Yes, but I teach history too."

"Ah, I see … and you know how they work?"

"I do, indeed."

"In that case I probably don't need to come up to the cottage with you … There's wood, tinder and some coal up there already. Oh, and turf too, if you want to be really authentic."

In the other boxes, besides bread and milk, there were fresh vegetables, old-fashioned tins of meat and all sorts of other things, such as beans. There was rice, pasta and lentils — Marianne looked more at ease when she saw these, but in the next box there were blocks of soap, detergents, disinfectants, etc., things she had never had to use because technology had long since gone beyond them.

"What about Sarah?" broke in George-Louis.

"Sarah?" said the grocer.

"Our horse!" said Marianne.

"Oh, everything you need for her is in the stable. There's plenty of fodder and a paddock to graze in."

When they arrived at the cottage, which was about a mile beyond the town, they realised fully why they had been given these ancient artefacts and provisions: it was a true replica of an old Irish cottage, not just a facade. The inside too was authentic, and when he saw it John felt elated, transformed almost. Positions had been reversed. At last he was useful to, not dependent upon, Marianne.

Chapter IX

They looked into the kitchen first. For cooking, it had a wood burning stove not unlike an Aga, but cruder, which John had had to light in a cottage he and Dorothea had stayed in while on a walking holiday in Yorkshire. There was a large, deep, square sink with only a cold tap. There were cupboards with pots, pans, dishes, plates and so on, as well as drawers full of all sorts of ancient utensils: everything they needed mostly — but new to Marianne. There were several tables with scrubbed wooden tops, all except one of which were placed next to walls. The other, standing in the middle of the room, was larger and obviously for meals; there did not seem to be a dining room. In the living room there was a wide fireplace with a couple of trivets, and on one of them stood a large iron kettle. The easy chairs and sofa looked comfortable. There were books, board games, packs of cards and dominoes but, to George-Louis' consternation, no communicator.

"It's because there's no electricity," John pointed out.

"Is that why no lights came on as we came in?" asked George-Louis.

"I'm afraid so … We've only got these lamps and candles.… Though there could be other lamps elsewhere — in other rooms."

Both Marianne and her son looked crestfallen, so John said, "It'll be fun … won't it?" And they stared at him as though he were mad. He in turn looked dejected at which they both laughed spontaneously. She hugged George-Louis and said, "Let's hope so."

"Right, then," said John, brightening, "Who's going to do what?" But Marianne replied, "Er … I don't know what to do — it all looks a bit strange to me."

"I'll feed Sarah." said George-Louis, making for the door.

"OK," said John, "I'll light the stove and the fire so we can cook."

Then he added, smiling at Marianne, "Why don't you investigate the sleeping arrangements upstairs?"

"That seems a good idea. I can't do much down here — but I'd better "help" George-Louis first, he's still too small to deal with Sarah."

She lowered her voice even though George-Louis was probably out of earshot, and continued, "Beds and bed linen can't have changed that much even in two thousand years, but you never can tell and they'll have to wait a minute."

"Take my word for it — they haven't changed that much. But tell you what; when I've got the stove going, we'll have a hot drink and sit down for a council of war."

Her look of consternation warned him of her fifth millennium sensibilities, so he said, "I mean we'll review the situation."

An hour later they were in front of the fire drinking tea and nibbling biscuits when Marianne said, "The beds are now made but I'm not sure how warm they'll be: everything feels cold … I hope they are just cold and not damp."

"Ah now, just a minute," said John going into the kitchen. "I thought so — firebricks," they heard him say.

"What are firebricks?" said George-Louis.

"I don't know," said his mother as John returned.

"It'll be OK," he said, "We can put them on top of the stove to get hot and then we can wrap them up and put them in the beds sometime before we are ready to go to sleep."

"But what are they?"

John pointed to the fireplace. "You see those bricks there. They get very hot and could crack, so they are made out of a special substance called fireclay which won't crack when it gets hot: they are firebricks." Then he turned to Marianne. "Did you see any old blankets — or towels or that sort of thing that we could wrap them in?"

"Yes, I did. There's plenty in the chest at the top of the stairs."

Marianne was surprised at how hot the stove was when she came to do the cooking, but it had only two hotplates, so John suggested that the third pan could go on the spare trivet next to the kettle on the living room fire. In the meantime he showed George-Louis how to light the storm lamps and two other small lamps, which worked on the same principle. They put the latter in the bedrooms in the hope they would warm them a little. John thought George-Louis was probably still too young to light them himself, but he did let the little boy have a go at turning one of them out.

By that time it was getting quite dark and Marianne was complaining that the candles didn't really give enough light in the kitchen. John took the Tilley lamp in and set about lighting it. He was pleased to be able to explain that whereas the storm lamps burnt the paraffin directly as it climbed up the wick, the Tilley lamp depended on paraffin vapour. Then he filled the lamp and explained why he had to pump it so that the increased pressure would create vapour in the tube going up to the mantle when he turned it on. He told George-Louis what the mantle was and why it improved the light. But when he set the swabs of methylated spirit under the mantle and lit them he said nothing.

"What's that for?"

"What do you think?"

"Er … I don't know."

"Well, what will it do to the mantle?"

"Er … well … I think … I think … it'll make it hot!"

"Yes, that's right. 'Cos if it isn't hot when the vapour gets on to that part it will turn back to paraffin oil and make smelly black smoke."

"Is it ready yet?"

"No, I don't think so."

By now Marianne had left the stove and she too was looking and listening.

After a while John said, "OK. Let's try it now," and he opened the valve, praying that it would light first time … It did and the little kitchen was filled with a light seemingly so bright that it brought a joyous, "Hooray," from all three.

By the time they were ready to eat it seemed that the stove had made the kitchen very warm, but it was probably not very different from what Marianne and George-Louis were used to. Anyway, John was glad because it meant that he could place the firebricks on top of it so that they would be plenty hot enough to warm the beds well before George-Louis' bedtime. At the table they sat in shirtsleeves and ate a meal that was novel to Marianne and George-Louis, but was the sort which John could remember as a veritable feast when he was a boy. They had boiled potatoes and fresh peas and what, according to the tin, were meatballs in gravy, the latter being to John and George-Louis' taste because it was thick and the potatoes could be mashed into it. Afterwards they had tinned mandarin oranges with what he recalled as Carnation Milk. Marianne complained it had a synthetic taste, but both George-Louis and John had second helpings.

For the first time ever, mother and son were confronted with the need to wash up, but John pointed out that at least they had hot water available in the big kettle. It might not be instant and endless, he said, but it was fairly regular as long as you remembered to fill the kettle up and put it back on the trivet each time you used it. Of course you needed a fire too, and he promised that, before they went out to investigate the cliffs of Moher the next day, he would show them how to back up the fire so that it would stay lit all day. After he had been out to check that Sarah was comfortable, he came into the living room to see that they had got out the dominoes, the principle of which they understood from the picture cards from George-Louis' infancy, but they were playing chips out.

"Do you know how to play fives and threes?" he said.

"No, I don't think so," said Marianne.

"Have we got a crib board?"

"A what?"

"It's a cribbage score board, really. Ah yes, would you believe it — we have, and we've got lots of matchsticks to use as markers."

So he explained how you added the number of dots at the very ends of the line of dominoes to score using multiples of five and three. By chance, in the game they were already playing, there was a five at one end and a four at the other and because these added to nine, he was able to demonstrate that three points had been scored. By quickly changing the four for another five, adding to ten, he showed that 2 points would be scored. Then he said, "Just before we leave this, let me show you something. Don't set up a five at each end like this if you can help it because the next person to play might drop a double five — and look what happens."

He picked up the double five that had been played earlier and placed it at one end and said, "What does it add up to, George-Louis?"

"There must be ... errr ... fifteen."

"And how many fives in that?"

"Errerm ...three!"

"And how many threes?"

"Oh ...yes ... there are five!"

"Agreed — so that scores eight points. The most you can score."

However, he did not warn them that the same result would occur if there were a double six at one end and a three at the other.

"Shall we play when you have finished this game?"

"Yes, why not," said Marianne, but as George-Louis seemed uncertain, she went on, "Mummy will help you with the sums."

"OK."

With Marianne helping him, George-Louis won the first game and by then he was already getting used to the figures. In the second game John kept picking up high scoring dominoes but managed to avoid playing them. Marianne was either doing the same thing or not very apt and George-Louis won again. Then in the third game the boy needed only seven points to win again, so John dropped a double six. George-Louis played a two-six at the other end giving him six points. Then John played the six-three and the eight points gave him the game. The child was quite upset and looked as though he were ready to cry.

John had not expected this reaction: George-Louis seemed such a well balanced little boy. Indeed, there had been times when he had thought the child wise beyond his years and almost too much in control of his emotions. He had even wondered whether there was something sinister about this:

was it symptomatic of the whole society? He had also found himself thinking of a science fiction film he had seen when he was young — it portrayed an alien force, the leaders of which transplanted small electronic devices into people's skulls so that they could control human behaviour. Yet, considered seriously, this was nonsense. Hadn't Marianne, and even Ambrose on occasion, been very close to losing control — usually because of something provocative or just plain crass that John had said or done? Now here was George-Louis behaving as you would expect a eight-year-old to behave — John had to remind himself that this was just a little kid. Even so, he felt a glimmer of annoyance with the lad. He had won two games out of three. Why should he not expect others to win? Or did he believe that the adults, John and Marianne, were there simply to ensure that his life ran along smoothly? He wanted to reprimand the boy — albeit gently. However, he looked at Marianne at this point and decided to remain silent because he could see from her frown the concern she felt at George-Louis being upset over such a trivial matter. He wondered how she would deal with it.

George-Louis could look at neither of them: he seemed to be engrossed in the surface of the coffee table. Marianne put her hand on to his shoulder and then, as he turned towards her a little, she moved it to his head, which she stroked gently. Suddenly the boy turned towards her completely and hid his head in her bosom. She held him then in both arms and John could see that this was done both firmly and gently. In a very quiet voice she said, "George-Louis, sweetheart, why are you upset?"

There was no answer.

"Was is because you lost?"

He nodded his head against her and John thought he might be crying.

"Was it also because John won?"

Again, no reaction.

"Was it?" very gently.

There was another nod.

"Why should that upset you?"

There was silence, but she waited patiently, and finally in a very small voice he said, "John didn't tell me about the double six."

She looked at John who, with a shrug, pulled a face that could have meant, "so what?" She continued to look at him and he realised that she expected him to say something. What he felt was annoyance that he should be accused of a kind of cheating — and by an eight-year-old. But Marianne kept looking at him, not glaring but very evenly. And he knew she wanted him to help. He also knew that any assistance he might offer would have to be in the same vein as hers: he would have to be gentle. So, though it irked him, he said, "I'm sorry, George-Louis, it wasn't to gain a secret weapon that I didn't tell you about the double six … I was hoping that you would see for yourself that the double six was dangerous … Also, I wanted you to learn from your mistakes … But I should have realised that because you and your mummy had not played before, it did give me an unfair advantage."

There was silence. Neither Marianne nor George-Louis moved. John began to wonder whether he should say more.

"I'm sorry," he repeated.

Marianne held her son closer and said, "Are you still upset even though John has explained?"

He nodded.

"Why is that?"

Then he did sob and John heard his muffled, "I wanted to win again."

"And do you think you should win every time?"

Silence.

"Well, do you?" sotto voce.

"No."

Momentarily, John thought, why not clip him round the ear. It's better than all this long drawn out soul searching. But he knew that was not sensible. Then it occurred to him that there might be a way to move on … perhaps.

"Tell you what. Let's go back to the place where I played the double six. Now that you know the danger, you can do something different … Shall we try that?"

There was a moment's silence, but Marianne smiled at John and he felt so glad he had not shown annoyance. Then George-Louis looked up sheepishly and said, "OK."

So they played out the end of the game again, and this time because of some very skilful manipulation on John's part, Marianne won — at which George-Louis smiled and then suddenly kissed his mother.

John wondered if the child would now be less friendly and George-Louis did seem a little shy of him, but when John suggested that they read another of the *Naughty Nigel* stories the child's enthusiasm was obvious, and he wanted to go upstairs immediately — especially as he remembered the bricks and wanted to see if they had warmed the beds. Marianne wanted to know too. As George-Louis ran ahead of them she asked John about the stories he was reading, but he was able to assure her that though Nigel could be naughty, his misdemeanours were minor and never paid off: there was always a moral to the tale — and her son did find them funny.

"Oh, it's lovely and warm in my bed," they heard him call.

"Good," replied Marianne, and she went into the other two rooms to try the beds there. As she walked past George-Louis' room she said, "Remember to clean your teeth."

"Yes, Mummy, but where?"

"Where?"

"I can't find a saniroom."

"There isn't one," said John.

"Oh dear," she said. "What do we do? There isn't one outside, is there, like that awful toilet?"

"Not really, but we can wash hands and faces and clean teeth in the sink downstairs," said John.

"Is there no epurifier?"

"Fraid not."

"Nor even a shower?"

"No."

"So how do we keep clean?"

"Ah, now," said John, "there's a large zinc bath in the wash-house."

"The wash house? What does that mean?"

"It's that outhouse next to the stable. It has a big boiler — for washing clothes in."

"Do you have to boil them, then?" she said with astonishment.

"Well, at one time you did, but the box of detergent in the supplies means we just have to have the water hot — not boiling. And we can heat water in it to use in the bath, but we will have to ladle it."

"Oh," she said looking very thoughtful. Then she continued, "I'm glad we're here only two nights."

Later, as she tucked George-Louis into bed, John heard him say, "Doesn't John know a lot about everything. And he can do everything."

"Yes, and I'm very glad — in this very funny house."

"Has he been here before?"

"I don't think so, but he must have been in one like this — perhaps somewhere else."

"Yes," John chipped in as he came in to read the story, "many years ago in Yorkshire."

"Where's Yorkshire?" said George-Louis, and his mother replied, "Oh, it's not very far from where we live," and she looked at John for confirmation.

"No, it's not very far."

"Can we go there too?" said George-Louis.

"We'll see."

"I like the places John takes us to."

When they were sitting side by side on the sofa, after the child had gone to sleep, Marianne said that she now realised that life could be quite difficult in John's time, but he explained that it was not so bad if you were used to it.

"And anyway, what we have here is even earlier — a hundred years before my time. I remember it being like this only in out of the way places and in the countryside during the war, and even then there were some people with electricity, hot water, bathrooms and even cars and telephones."

"Only some people?"

"Yes. Well, a few, really. But it was a very bad war and things had been better for most people before that and it got a lot better afterwards."

"But didn't you all share?"

"Some things we did."

"Now we share everything."

"Do you mean there is complete equality?"

"I suppose so, but we don't call it that — it sounds too legalistic. People's houses are all different. But everyone has an epurifier to keep themselves clean — and all their clothes and things."

"But are there very rich people who have more money and possessions than others?"

She thought for a while and then said, "I don't really know. It depends on what you choose. Some people have bigger houses and more clothes or jewellery or whatever, but that's how they want to spend their money. Others have more audio books and music and things like that. Others travel more, I suppose."

"So you can all be different then, if you want?"

"Well, yes, of course … But everybody has enough to eat and drink. They can all keep clean. No one is without living accommodation. And I don't know of anyone without a communicator: you can't be part of things without one."

"What about us now …? We haven't got one."

"No, but it's only for two days. And I've got my mini-communicator."

"Have you? Can I see it?"

She rummaged in her bag and brought out a mobile phone. John laughed and said, "Wow, it's not very different from my time! It's just as Lien Chou said."

"What did he say?"

"That no matter how old the technology is, if it works you use it."

"Oh, I thought it was something important. And I think I prefer modern technology. I'm still concerned that George-Louis went to bed mucky."

"He can't be that mucky: it's only one day."

"Yes, but by tomorrow evening we will all smell."

"Never mind. I'll light the boiler in the wash-house tomorrow evening and we can all get in that old fashioned bath before bed — but not together!"

She gave him a look of pretended shock and he added, "We wouldn't all fit and...."

"And what?"

"It wouldn't be proper ... especially in the forty-first century, it seems."

She smiled and chuckled in such an intimate way that he felt he could put his arm around her shoulders. He pulled her towards him saying, "Anyway, you don't need a bath: you smell nice. You always do."

He wanted very much to sleep with her, but was afraid to even hint at it even though he was so very close to her. She did not pull away but sighed contentedly and said, "I'm seeing a different side to you on this holiday."

"How do you mean?"

"You used to seem so lost and confused ... and angry."

"But now?"

"Perhaps it's because you are nearer to your own time — not just in this funny old house, but also in the jaunting car — you're so much more confident. And George-Louis now thinks you must be an expert in everything."

"Well, I'm not. And all this, the cottage and everything, is just luck. I'm amazed it's here, but I'm very glad it is."

Is that because it's like home?"

He did not reply immediately and she looked at him intently. She wanted an answer and he thought that this was another sign that their relationship was on firmer ground. He felt could be honest, so he said, "No, not really. It's because I can look after you and George-Louis ... instead of just being a nuisance."

"I never did think you were a nuisance ... but you have to admit the situation was scary and you did frighten me at times ..."

"And yet you took responsibility for me. Why was that?"

There was another pause and she was obviously thinking. He knew he should not press her for an answer. In her own time she said, "I was the one on the spot. I was the one who was there when you regained consciousness. Who else would do it? Everyone has to respond to what happens around them, don't they?"

"Not in my world they don't ... but I'm very glad they do now and that you were the first person I saw when I came round."

"I think now that I'm very glad too," and she leaned forward unexpectedly and kissed him very gently on the corner of the mouth.

Later, when the fire had burnt low, he said he would have to go out to see that Sarah was secure in the stable. She waited for him and they went upstairs together and stood on the landing for some time. Though they kissed passionately they then went off to their separate beds.

The next day John had to get up early to light the fire. He wanted it to be going well by the time the others came down so that they could make toast and a hot drink for breakfast, but also so that he could back it up before they went out. He was glad when they did get up that George-Louis enjoyed the same cereals as him: cornflakes and crunchy oats mixed together. Just to make it all perfect, Marianne said that she had never tasted such good toast even though she had to make it herself with a toasting fork held in front of the hot bars of the fire.

While she and her son got ready for the hike to the cliffs — they had decided to give Sarah a holiday — John filled the boiler and laid the fire in the wash house so that they could light it as soon as they got back. While he was there he checked the windows. They did have hooks for curtain rails but no curtains, so he looked for things he could hang over them so that Marianne would have privacy if she decided to bathe. He found some old sheets in the chest on the stairs. While he was looking for them Marianne presented him with a tin of corned beef.

"How do you get into this?"

"Look. There's a key on the side. Put that bit of raised metal — that sort of lip — into the slot in the key and turn."

She did this very gingerly and then looked very pleased with herself when it worked. It was only half-past nine but he felt he'd done a day's work already.

With just one knapsack containing their lunch and a few necessaries, they set off to walk the couple of miles to the cliffs. The weather was good, in fact quite warm compared to the previous days, and John, carrying the knapsack, soon felt uncomfortable, even though their lunch was not heavy. His leg did not feel right; everything began to seem irksome and, as he grew silent, the other two chatted away even more light-heartedly, which for some inexplicable reason made him feel cut off from them. After half an hour or so he wanted to stop and sit down, but felt that if he did George-Louis might see him as something other than superman. The difficulty he had keeping up made him feel more morose and this turned to annoyance, first with himself but then inevitably with them. No matter how hard he tried to quell his anger it seemed to grow and feed on itself and on the fact that neither Marianne nor George-Louis appeared to notice. But the bitterest feeling came from the thought in the back of his mind that there was absolutely no justification for his anger.

They were coming towards their destination and were walking up a slope. George-Louis had run on ahead. To keep nearer to him Marianne had moved forward from John who, in his sullen determination to not fall too far behind, had put his head down and his hands behind his back in support of the knapsack. He was plodding automatically when he heard

Marianne scream out, "No! George-Louis!" When he looked up the little boy had vanished — he assumed over the cliff. His anger gave way to terror and he was galvanised into a crazy dash for the cliff edge where he arrived at the same time as Marianne. However, both of them had been deceived: they were not at a precipice. The grass now sloped downwards, but beyond it there was a flat platform of rock about ten metres wide and George-Louis was approaching both it and the sheer drop beyond. He was trotting and had not heard his mother's anguished cry. Afraid that the boy would now stumble over the real edge, John ran down the grass, but was so afraid that he might not get to him in time that he rugby tackled him, bringing both of them down violently a yard away from the brim. George-Louis yelled with fright and John swore, "What the bloody hell do you think you are doing?!"

They pulled away from each other — George-Louis sitting on his haunches, John lying on his side. He looked at the boy and saw that his face had turned ashen and his features were distorted with the shock. He was pressing his hands against his sides underneath his armpits as boys used to in John's schooldays when they had been beaten with the ferula. He must have put out his hands to save himself when they fell and they had been grazed by the rough surface of the rock. His knees were cut too. He seemed to be holding his breath; then he did several silent sobs. Finally, he began to cry loudly as Marianne reached him and folded him in her arms saying, "Never mind, sweetheart. Mummy has got you. You are safe now," and she rocked him as though he were a baby.

It was at this point that John realised that he had hurt the bad leg. He stretched it out. It did not look as though it had been broken again. He felt it; it seemed no different so he got awkwardly to his feet and tested it. He could walk — but painfully and only with a limp, which he knew he would have difficulty in disguising. He sat down again on the grassy bank and realised that he no longer felt angry, but now he was afraid. Afraid that through this silly little incident he had lost Marianne because he had frightened her son so much. All that he could do was to wait and see what would transpire. After a while, George-Louis became quiet, but his mother continued to rock him gently and John became aware that she was singing quietly to him as though she were lulling him to sleep. With her son's head pressed against her breast she at last looked at John, but her face was expressionless and his heart sank. However, Marianne could see this, so harrowed was his face, and a great sense of pity for him welled up within her: what he had done had seemed rash — there was no knowing whether George-Louis would have stopped before he got to the edge — but the consequences of what might have happened were unthinkable. She forced herself to smile and then stretched her hand out to him. He got up painfully, went over to them and sat down on the hard cold stone next to her. She put her free hand around his shoulders. There were tears in her eyes and she said, "George-Louis, I think John has got something to say to you."

The child raised his head, his face lined with tears, and looked resentfully at John who, to begin with, felt he had been struck dumb. Where should I begin, he thought — because this conversation could be very important to his future. Begin at the beginning.

"When you ran down the bank, neither your mother nor I could see you. We thought you had fallen over the edge. I panicked and ran after you. Then I could see that you really were near the edge, but if I had shouted I might have caused you to stumble, so I stopped you from getting to the edge in the only way I could."

The child looked at him but did not seem to understand what he was saying. He began again, "Sometimes things happen which mean we have to take drastic action — we just have to or the consequences would be very bad. I thought you were going to fall over the cliff and I tried to stop you."

George-Louis turned his head away again and pressed his face into his mother who stroked his head and said, "Never mind, never mind, it's all over now."

She looked again at John and smiled sympathetically. Then she said to him, "Look in the haversack. I found a first aid kit in the house and I put in just in case, but I've no idea what's in it."

When John found it and opened it he discovered bandages and plasters but nothing to use as an antiseptic except iodine, which he remembered with distaste from his childhood.

"Oh dear," he said, "this will hurt!"

"What is it?"

"Iodine."

"I've never heard of it."

"It's an old-fashioned antiseptic, but it stings when you put it on cuts."

At this George-Louis looked up and said, "Are you going to put it on me?"

Before Marianne could answer, John interposed, "Look, my knees are cut too. Mummy can put some on me first," and he rolled up his trouser leg to show that his knees were even worse than the lad's.

Not far from them along the cliff there was a hide for watching the sea birds on the crags, so they decided to use it as their first aid station. And, as agreed, Marianne saw to John first. Having washed his cuts with some of their drinking water she applied the iodine, and though he tried hard not to show it, he could not help wincing even though he knew that George-Louis was watching. Marianne, sensibly, waited a while before dealing with her son so, after a few minutes, John felt able to say, quite truthfully, that the sting had gone. Yet when she approached George-Louis with only the water, he began to whimper.

"You know that Mummy will be very gentle," she said and John added, "Let's see you be a brave boy. It'll hurt a bit now, but Mummy has to make sure you don't get an infection — that would hurt a lot more."

Marianne did not know if she approved of this approach, but the boy let her wash his knees and his hands. He cried when she put on the iodine, but she did it very quickly and efficiently and by the time she had all his wounds covered up, he had calmed down. John remembered his own childhood: though he knew his mother cared for him he could never remember her treating him as gently as Marianne treated her son. He also suddenly recalled outings that he had looked forward to only to have them spoilt by the weather or some accident — like the time he had been with his cousins in an open cast clay pit riding the trucks when he had been ejected and had his front teeth knocked out. His cousins did not even bother to take him home: he had to go by himself. His aunt took him to the clinic because his mother was at work and there no one was as gentle as Marianne. His badly cut lips were even more swollen after the nurses had seen to him. But he kept all this to himself.

The two of them sat side by side like wounded soldiers while Marianne got them a drink and a biscuit from the haversack. John decided to say nothing — as he did not know what to say anyway. After a while George-Louis got up and began to watch the birds on the cliff, so John went and stood just behind him to see if there was anything interesting he could point out. Unfortunately, though he could distinguish between the various species, he was not sure of the names. Then he noticed some rather stubby birds with a very rapid wing movement and wondered if they were puffins. He fetched the binoculars and on a more careful inspection of their nesting site he decided that they were. He was thinking of a way to call George-Louis' attention to them when the boy said, "What are you looking at, John?"

"Oh, just some puffins."

"Puffins! That's a funny name."

"Well, they are rather comical looking birds."

"Are they? Can I see?"

John handed him the glasses and showed him where to look. However, he also had to adjust the binoculars and show George-Louis how to focus them. Though the child had difficulty finding the birds, when he did he was so obviously delighted that John thought he must be returning to his usual winsome self.

"Mummy, come and look at the puffins — they've got such funny faces."

The rest of the day progressed more or less as expected, yet somehow the edge had been taken off the experience. George-Louis never quite returned to his affable self and neither did John, who also felt that though he and George-Louis were still friends, an invisible barrier had come down between them.

As they made their way back to the cottage, George-Louis again ran on ahead, his grazes and bruises momentarily forgotten. John and Marianne walked behind together but rather more slowly because of John's limp. As this was the first time they had been out of the boy's earshot since the incident, he took the opportunity to say, "Why did he look so shocked when I brought him down with that tackle?"

She frowned, thought for a moment and then said, "I think it might have been because he had never been treated with such violence before."

John himself now felt shocked and for a while was silent. At last he said, "Has he never tripped over, fallen off a bike or been knocked down playing whatever games children play nowadays?"

"Oh, probably, but he has never been attacked by an adult."

"Attacked! I would hardly call it that!"

"You might not, but that is how it appeared to him."

"Do you really think so?"

"I'm sure. I've never seen him look like that before."

"But have you never had to chastise him?"

"Chastise him? That's an antiquated way of putting it."

"Why antiquated? Don't you correct children anymore?"

"Of course we do, but we never use violence."

"Well, I don't mean violence exactly, but you must have to use force, especially with young children who don't understand."

"I suppose we do, but the maxim is always 'with gentle firmness'."

John thought for a while and then said, "As you did over the fives and threes?"

"Yes. As you saw, he came to me because that's how we have always dealt with such situations — you hold the child gently and you talk to him quietly — and it works."

John was silent again and puzzled over whether this could all be true. Surely, there must be times when some children would simply refuse to respond to such gentle treatment. And what about when they are very small and cry for you know not what — and they can be so bad tempered. He remembered his sister's baby on the last of his very rare visits to her getting into a terrible state. So he decided to pursue the matter further with Marianne and raised this very question. She admitted that this did happen but pointed out that it was just a question of finding the cause and removing it. When John said that that was the problem — young children can be so unfathomable — she explained to him that understanding the behaviour of babies had been regarded as one of the most important areas of research and that paediatrics was probably the leading discipline within medicine. So much emphasis had been put upon childhood for the last five hundred years because the whole social and political structure of the modern world was predicated upon children growing up to be well balanced. Everything about growth and development had to be studied. She agreed that very often in the past the unhappiness of babies and young children had not been understood because, as John had said, it seemed unfathomable, but now almost all child behaviour could be explained and the explanations acted upon, so there was far less chance that children would be fractious. Of course, all children would experience unhappiness and frustration but not to the extent where they would be permanently damaged. When John protested that this all assumed that everyone was the same and that the brief introduction she had given him into the methods of upbringing seemed like naked behaviourism — which surely must conflict with Marianne's religious beliefs — she countered that she firmly accepted that each individual is unique, i.e. genetically distinct, so that even if everyone were treated exactly the same — which they were not — they would all still be different. This was not a problem. No one was trying to regiment children; the aim was to try to ensure that children grew up into adults who were at war neither with themselves nor with other people and this could never be done by repressing them. No one would say that this was easy. It's like holding an injured bird; if you hold it too tightly you crush it to death; if you do not hold it tightly enough, it struggles free and further damages itself. What the forms of upbringing tried to do was ensure that the human capacity to love was nurtured to the full. The ideal, and this could probably never be achieved, was that everyone should find fulfilment in caring for everybody else.

"But surely there must be people who simply take advantage of this and lead self-centred lives knowing that everybody else will cater for their needs. Don't you have layabouts and malingerers who lead entirely parasitical lives?"

"I don't think so, and if they do exist I've never met one and wouldn't know how to recognise one."

"But how can you trust each other to be altruistic so consistently? And is it like this everywhere in the world?"

"I must admit I don't really know. You'll have to ask Ambrose or one of the others at St Adrienne's who has studied these things. But you're right about one thing: it's all about trust."

At this point the discussion came to an end. They had reached the gate to the cottage and George-Louis was already feeding Sarah a clutch of luscious grass he had found growing just outside her paddock. In so far as *her* expression seemed fathomable, she seemed pleased to see them. Once in the house John stirred the fire to make it blaze up and then lit the stove in the kitchen. He next went to the outbuildings to light the fire under the boiler, and when he got back he found Marianne and her son discussing what to do about having a bath in the primitive conditions. It was clear that George-Louis was making his various wounds an excuse for remaining mucky, but his mother was insisting, very gently, that he should have a bath, especially as she wanted to have another look at his cuts and bruises and put on them some different antiseptic which she had in her luggage. She assured him it would not hurt and would in fact soothe his injuries. She also used this last point to argue him out of bathing himself: she insisted that in the circumstances she wanted to make sure he was really clean.

By the time the water in the wash house was warm enough, the whole building was too. George-Louis wanted to help John ladle the water into the zinc bath and John decided to let him, because the water was, as yet, not too hot. Unfortunately, the bowl on the ladle was big and the handle long so George-Louis had to abandon "helping John" as the floor was getting very wet. After his bath he allowed John to give him a piggy-back across to the living room and there set himself up in a comfortable armchair with comics he had found there: they looked very like the Tintin and Asterix strip cartoons that John remembered from his childhood. He was amazed at the authenticity of this house, but then recalled how Ambrose had told him that despite all the vicissitudes, very little had been lost.

John had next to prepare the wash house for Marianne and he did this willingly, even though his leg now ached and he did find the mopping up after George-Louis quite irksome. He covered virtually the whole floor with the cloths they had found, and he not only blocked the window, he also rigged up a line across one corner of the room on which she could hang her clean clothes in readiness. He ladled the hot water into the bath and, not knowing how warm she preferred it, he put two large jugs of cold water ready at the side. Then he called to her. When she came in looking rather sheepish, he asked if she needed any help.

"I think I can manage, thank you."

"OK then. I'll just take a jug of hot water for a shave: I can use the mirror in the kitchen." At this she frowned, but he simply grinned and went on, "I'll leave you to it. Don't try to empty the bath — it's very awkward and has to be run down that drain over in the corner."

"Won't the floor get wet?"

"Well, after George-Louis' attempts to help, it's wet already. In the old days they would wash the floor with the water as they flushed it away."

"Oh."

"Right then, I'll leave you. Give me a shout when you are ready."

Half an hour later she came into the house and John went off for his bath. He took a long time because he had to clear up afterwards so that they could leave the wash house as they found it. While he was away, Marianne cooked a meal. In the evening they played fives and threes again — this time without tears.

Their journey back to St Adrienne's was not eventful, but when they stopped again at the O'Leary's he got another taste of modern democracy because a further meeting had had to be called to finalise the business he had witnessed on the outward journey. This time several members of the family went to the community room because their interest had been aroused by certain objections that had been made to the providing of machinery to the needy farming community. Another community reckoned that their need was just as great. John stayed for the whole of the discussion, though there were times when he felt annoyed with some of those attending: they seemed to prolong the proceedings unnecessarily. He thought that the woman who was acting as chair was either stupid or a saint: she was so patient and accommodating. He could see the way the meeting was moving, i.e. to a situation where the required machinery, whether new or reconditioned, would be made available to the objectors too and he wondered why she did not intervene and suggest this. The outcome was the same in the long run.

Later, when George-Louis had gone to bed and he and Marianne were sitting together on a bench in the orchard as the sun disappeared, he spoke about it. She pointed out to him that the people themselves, all of them, had made the final decision. Nobody foisted anything on them and nobody felt pressurised; everything was transparently open.

"That all may be true, but the whole thing could have been tied up so much sooner if that dozy chairperson had done her job efficiently and directed matters a little more."

"But why should she want to direct matters? Isn't it better to let the solution emerge for itself? That's her job — and you are unkind to call her dozy."

"Well, OK, maybe 'dozy' is a bit strong, but couldn't she see the answer?"

"Perhaps she could, but she wouldn't want to force the issue."

"Why not if she knew she was right?"

"But she might not be right: things could turn out differently later."

John found this exasperating: she seemed to have shifted the direction of the argument, but he suppressed the expletive forming in his mind. He was silent for a minute or two and then went on, "Look, it's all very well to say she might not be right, but any decision could be wrong in the long run."

"But it's less likely to be wrong if it emerges rather than is imposed."

"You're not serious!"

"I am! That's our experience of organising things. I don't remember the history as well as I should — you'll have to discuss it with Ambrose — but I do know that that was the lesson we learned from the early communes. When they had forceful leaders, in the long run they failed. When they learned to let things emerge, they survived."

"Marianne, I'm finding this incredible."

She looked at him in the half-light; he was quite obviously dumbfounded, speechless even. Suddenly, she became aware of how difficult all this was for him. It also explained much about what she had thought of as his cynicism, his suspicion of everything. Of course he would find it difficult to see things as she and everybody else did. There really was a chasm between them, and not only a deep divide of time, but also one of understanding, of hundreds of years of inherited experience. He came from a time that had accepted leadership as important. The words of Christ came to her.

"The kings of the Gentiles lord it over them, and those in authority over them are called benefactors. But not so with you."

And she remembered that in John's time the impact of that lesson had hardly been felt. Though he lived two thousand years after Jesus, the message still had not been grasped.

A feeling of pity for him swept over her, not because of his ignorance but because of his confusion. On the other hand, she thought, he must be trying very hard to understand, and maybe in part that effort was motivated by his love for her. Tenderly, she put her hands either side of his face and kissed him very gently, almost reverently. He sat very still. He had no idea why she had done this and felt even more confused. She said, "Let's return quickly so that you can learn from Ambrose how all this came about."

During the journey back to the monastery, he often caught her looking at him surreptitiously. He could not help but smile broadly each time it happened. Also, good relations were re-established between John and George-Louis, though they were never quite as comfortable with each other as before. When they all said goodbye at the Clifden bus-station, George-Louis seemed genuinely sorry that his holiday with John had come to an end and he did not seem to mind when his mother kissed John lovingly before they got on the bus.

Chapter X

John had driven Marianne and George-Louis to the bus station himself because Michael now thought of him as an experienced driver, and he also did not want to be an embarrassment as they made their farewells. This meant that John had time alone on the way back to think about the holiday and also to consider how he and Ambrose might again pick up their work together. He felt he needed to reflect on how the expedition had affected his relationships with both Marianne and her son — there was no point in looking at them separately. Once he had articulated this notion to himself he felt both elated and disturbed. He thought he ought to try to work out why. He knew that his relationship with Marianne was now on a firmer footing: the way she looked at him, responded to him and kissed him all indicated that she had real affection for him. She was no longer simply caring for him out of a sense of duty. He was sure too that she knew full well that for him, if anything, the commitment was even stronger. Then the only reason for the sense of unease must be to do with George-Louis. Unsurprisingly, his thoughts went back to the incident on the cliff. He still felt resentful about it: his response to the danger had been automatic, unthinkingly selfless; he had had no time to reflect because the threat to George-Louis had been so imminent. But you couldn't blame the boy for his response either; that would be ridiculous: his reaction had been as automatic, and as honest, as John's had been in the first place — he recalled the child's look of shock and fear. Perhaps, he thought, Marianne's explanation, which he had been tempted to dismiss as the over-reaction of a loving mother, was correct. George-Louis had never experienced anything so violent before. Could it be that no child did in this supposed utopia? Maybe children never were threatened but corrected (if even that were not too strong a word) by gentle firmness only. Perhaps he would have to accept the notion — unimaginable though it seemed to him. Then again, he reflected, he had now come across so many incredible things: women priests; married monks; and what seemed to him to be hopelessly reactionary (and probably unhealthy) restraints on sexual activity; but most amazing of all, "emergence" as a political principle. What could be more inconceivable? This would have to be the starting point of his discussions with Ambrose.

However, on his arrival at St Adrienne's he could not find his mentor. He was not in his cell, nor at John's study-bedroom, nor the library. He went back to the ancient doorkeeper and asked if she knew of Ambrose's whereabouts.

"What's the date?"

"The date?! It's the twelfth."

"Then it must be the second Tuesday of the month, so he's in the chicken pens."

"The chicken pens?!"

"Oh yes. It's the day each month when he cleans them out."

"I didn't even know there were chicken pens. And I thought you were all vegetarian."

"Ah, but we like eggs!"

"Well, where are the pens?"

"Out beyond the vegetable gardens."

John finally found Ambrose hot and sweaty and covered in a white unspeakable dust. He greeted John very affectionately and then said, "Am I glad to see you … I can now stop …" And he sat down on an old rickety chair with his back against the high chicken-wire fence.

"I'm always glad to begin this job, but I'm even more pleased when I finish."

"How come you never mentioned this work?"

"I didn't even think about it."

"But why are you doing it?"

"Why shouldn't I?"

"Well, you're a history teacher."

"Ah, John. All the more reason for doing such mundane tasks — it keeps your feet on the ground."

"Did the Abbot set you on this, then?"

"Indeed not, I chose it myself after brother Manfred died … The Abbot never tells anybody what to do."

"He doesn't? Then how does anything ever get done?"

"Someone sees a job needs to be done and does it — that's all."

There was a long pause but all John could think of to say was, "I find this so difficult to believe!"

Ambrose chuckled. "Oh, John. Now I know you're back. But before we have our first argument, let me clean up. I'll see you for a coffee in about fifteen minutes — er, not in the refec, in the guest sitting room. It's quiet there at this time of day and I've got a lot I want to discuss with you."

Though Ambrose did not ask any direct questions he was obviously interested in how the holiday had gone, and at first John, because of his own preoccupation with it, thought this was to do with how he had got on with

Marianne and George-Louis, but then he realised that Ambrose was concerned with John's understanding of how society functioned, how politics worked. Here was an opportunity to broach the aspect that interested him most, but he decided to take an oblique approach to the question, so he did not mention the conversation he had had with Marianne but told Ambrose about the two meetings he had attended in the O'Leary household. He was as honest as he had been with Marianne and so talked about his impatience with the procedure because, as he explained once more, any fool could see the solution towards which the discussion was heading. He was not surprised that Ambrose agreed with Marianne, but he thought it odd that he did not use the word 'emergence' as she had done. He seemed to be concerned instead with what he called John's false notion of efficiency, which, he said, seemed to mean saving time, whereas in fact, it had little to do with how quickly decisions were made or work was done. Time was of the essence, yes, but always in terms of the long run. John had to admit, when Ambrose put it to him, that in the institutions in which he had worked, decisions that had seemed expeditious sometimes caused long-term problems — but not always, he added. Moreover, there were times when matters were so urgent that things had to be done as quickly as possible. Here the argument became heated because Ambrose claimed that usually, apparently urgent situations arose because earlier decisions had not been thought through in a way that took into account the needs of everyone who might be affected by them. John maintained that if you considered everyone in this way and it was painfully slow, you might be overtaken by events. For instance, he had had no time to discuss with Marianne whether or not he should rugby tackle George-Louis to prevent him falling over the cliff edge: he had had to act. He knew that the consequences of what he did were serious, but not to have acted would very probably have been worse. He thought that this example, so relevant to his own life, would clinch the argument, but Ambrose responded firstly by saying that he thought there was a significant difference between John's tackling George-Louis and the purchase of machinery for a whole community, and secondly, that if his line that urgent situations required quick decisions because earlier decisions had been taken without adequate consideration of all the facts, then what happened on the cliff was a case in point.

"Oh, you imply that it was negligent of me not to have reconnoitred the cliff beforehand?"

"No, I'm not saying that you were negligent, but you have to admit that had all the facts been known, the dilemma you faced might have been avoided."

"Might, yes, but in such circumstances we can never be sure. None of us is that good at predicting the future."

"I agree. We can never be absolutely certain of anything, but we have to use all our knowledge — of the world out there, of how human beings, young and old, are likely to behave — and all our skills in order to avoid disaster."

"But if we tried to allow for every contingency there'd be no spontaneity in life, no room for the joy of the unexpected. How deadly dull!"

"But our lives are no duller now than they were in your time, but they're a lot less deadly. I admit that there may be occasions when we have to make the best assumptions we can and then act, but that is not the same as always behaving as though everything occurs by chance."

Though John understood what Ambrose was saying there was something about it that did not ring true. He was nonplussed; there still seemed to be a chasm between his assumptions and predilections about life and those of Ambrose. The annoyance he had felt at the supposed accusation of negligence was now replaced by a feeling that there was nowhere to go from here, and once more the sense of being marooned engulfed him. Was this despair, he thought? Both were silent. At last Ambrose said, "John, can we be completely honest with each other?"

"Aren't we always?"

" Yes and no."

"What's that supposed to mean? Yes and no."

"Well, I think you think you are being honest but there are times when you play intellectual games with me."

"I what?"

"Sorry. I don't mean to be offensive, you play games and you don't always realise you are doing it. Now, I am not denying that I might do it too, but one of the things education now tries to do is to make people aware of their propensity to do this and then try to avoid it."

John felt the annoyance mounting again at what seemed to be the arrogance of this statement — the assumption that somehow the people of the fifth millennium were morally and intellectually superior to those of his generation. He was about to explode when unaccountably in his mind's eye he saw the very games that Ambrose referred to being played in the debating society of his university days, and this took him to the adversarial shenanigans he had seen when he had served on a jury. And lastly, he remembered his only visit to the Stranger's Gallery in the House of Commons when he had witnessed the same behaviour. He felt calmer, then said, "OK. What's the point of all this?"

Ambrose put on his serious face and replied, "What I have to be brutally frank about is that, unlike times past, there are now no wars. There is no serious poverty and virtually no crime. And when you and I argue about how decisions are taken, how matters are organised, I am not playing a game. I'm trying to explain how all this happens. You, on the other hand, always seem to be looking for the flaws in my explanations. It's as though you see them not as explanations but as proposals, and you want to put forward counter proposals."

He paused, expecting a reply — John could tell. However, though he saw clearly what Ambrose meant, he was not so sure his own arguments were as spurious as Ambrose seemed to be suggesting. Nevertheless, he replied, "Maybe you are right, but remember, I'm trying to make sense of what you are saying. If I think your explanations are specious I must in all honesty say so. It's got to make sense to me, and there are times when your explanations are so incredible to me that I must wonder whether there is a hidden agenda — well, that something is hidden from me."

"But what on earth can I be hiding from you?"

"I don't bloody know, do I … It's as though there is some form of coercion that no one will tell me about!"

"There isn't, John. Honest, there isn't … You'll have to go on looking, but you won't find it. Or rather, what you will find is that the coercion, though that's totally the wrong word, comes from within each person."

"I can see the sense of that … But there's a contradiction somewhere … I can't …"

"A contradiction? Where?"

"I'm not sure … But look … You and Marianne between you have got me confused."

"Me and Marianne? How can that be?"

"Well, when I was telling her what I told you about the meetings at the O'Leary's, her argument was that the slowness of the process was due to allowing the decision to emerge, and she didn't mean just by not forcing it. She stressed the importance, almost as a political principle, of emergence."

"Seems like a sensible principle to me."

"Oh, does it? Well, to me it doesn't fit with not leaving everything to chance — having everything cut and dried beforehand, as you have been saying."

"But I don't agree that that's what I'm saying."

"Then, what are you saying?"

"Well, if I went to a meeting where everything had been decided beforehand — say, by the chairman and secretary, and I know that this used to happen in the past — then that would be having everything cut and dried. However, if I go to a meeting now I know that no one can be certain of the decisions, but what I also know is that previous meetings of this particular group would have reached conclusions that every member had willingly concurred with. No one would have any hang-ups about the past. There is a difference."

John, somewhat chastened, reluctantly agreed, but then asked if they might discuss how the communities had actually developed. Ambrose looked pleased because, he said, they could now go back to where they had left off before the holiday. He then went on to explain that the emergence of groups into something like those to be found in existence now had taken over four hundred, in fact nearly five hundred, years. There were many failures — though that was perhaps doing an injustice to more than a few of them because they provided useful examples of what not to do — others simply changed out of all recognition. He also described the wide variety of organisation that they adopted: from those at one extreme, which were highly authoritarian and bureaucratic, to those at the other, which were so loosely organised, concerned as they were for individual freedom, that they could scarcely justify the name group. Some became federated, others remained fiercely separate, but they were all linked to each other — in the sense that they communicated with each other, informed each other about developments. Their mutual interest grew as they argued over the values and drawbacks of their various ways and means of organisation, especially as so many of them eschewed leadership.

John expressed his doubts about this, despite Ambrose's earlier admonition about game playing. He could not see why men (in particular) who were interested in power, and especially those who did not recognise this in themselves, did not try to take control. Ambrose admitted that in many cases this happened, but in the long run such groups failed or had to change in order to survive. He talked about how in the very early days, when the groups were first taking shape out of the chaos of the Dark Times, warlords had asserted command over some groups, but this threat lessened as time went on because such usurpers found that the people they tried to exploit either faded away or, in the saddest cases, simply died off.

Still John maintained that he found the story difficult to accept: it did not fit his understanding of people and their social and political forms of co-operation. Ambrose again asked him to look at the facts and provided him with access to information on hundreds and hundreds of communities over several centuries and suggested he look for the variables that correlated with failure on the one hand and success on the other. To his consternation, John found that the former correlated with hierarchy and clearly defined leadership and the latter with flexibility, virtual equality — and certain educational factors. However, a factor leading to success that really surprised him was that such communities all had some sort of religious commitment. This, he knew, he would have to take up with Ambrose.

When they met the next day, John immediately initiated a discussion.

"Ambrose, I find this program very suspicious. Is it arranged so that it provides fixed answers?"

"What do you mean, fixed?" Ambrose looked genuinely shocked.

"Well, so that if I ask the computer to give the factors which correlate highly with say, continuity, it's bound to come up with the answers you want me to get."

"Answers? Answers? That's an odd word to use. The correlations it will come up with, it will come up with! I'm flummoxed by the way you put it. What is it that you find disconcerting?"

John thought for a moment and recalled that he had decided on direct confrontation and so he said, "Well, the factor that surprised me most, the one I find most difficulty in accepting, is that some sort of religious commitment seems important in the successful communities."

"Aha, John. Now why should that surprise you?"

John felt disconcerted by this response and was not sure how to proceed, but Ambrose remained silent and attentive, so he had to say something.

"I suppose it's because in my day religion was one of the main causes of discord — the antipathy between the major religions was so fierce and the fanaticism so implacable."

"But that doesn't have to be the case. The basic tenets of all religions, almost without exception, are about peace and justice and concern for fellow men and women."

"In theory, I suppose, yes — but in practice I found little love for others ... Oh, and another thing; the equality, which according to the program is supposed to be found in successful communities, does not ring true for the hierarchies found in some of the most important religions."

"Ah, now that I cannot deny and my own church used to be hierarchical in the way you imply. But it had to change. It was the only way it could survive."

"Used to be? You mean it isn't anymore? There are no bishops or cardinals? That the Curia has disappeared? That there is no pope?"

"Er, not quite."

"Aha! Now we come to the point. What do you mean, not quite?"

"Well, we do have bishops, but they are there purely as administrators. They do not have the powers they used to have. Also, they are men and women of great learning and I would say holiness — any authority they have comes because of those two factors."

"Men AND women? There are women bishops?!"

"Of course; they even existed in your day."

"Not in the Roman Church."

"Admittedly, but long before the Dark Times the Church was in such a serious crisis that it had to change — and it did. In fact you could argue that since then it has been crucial to the survival of humankind because of its teaching — like that of all the churches whether Christian or not — that we should love one another."

John found all this information as shocking as anything he had heard since his arrival in 4048. It was like Marianne and Sanjit's claim that there was no government, or Michael's revelation about married monks. It was even more disturbing than learning that grandma O'Leary was a priest. It was all so unlikely. Almost without realising it, he said quietly to himself, "And there's no pope."

"Oh, there is, but he's not the powerful central figure he used to be," said Ambrose just as quietly and gently, and he continued, "There is no Curia or College of Cardinals, and though he is honoured as the successor of St Peter and the Bishop of Rome, the Pope has no see. Rome, like London, Paris or Moscow, ceased to exist long ago. As we have said before, there are no cities. The Pope, like any other bishop, travels from community to community."

"You mean as in the old-fashioned visitation?"

"No, not really. It's to show solidarity and continuity. Indeed, Pope Eusebius is due here some time this year, but he won't be inspecting us."

"And what about his claim to infallibility? Has that gone too?"

"Well, I don't really know. It just doesn't seem appropriate to worry about it. Nobody talks about it anymore. Maybe, in certain circumstances, he is, but I don't know what they would be."

Neither of them said anything for a while. John stared in front of him and wondered if Ambrose perhaps thought that he was simply trying to absorb all this information, but in fact he could organise no constructive thoughts. That is until he came to himself and once more tried to think about the whole situation. At last he said, "Look, Ambrose, can you explain to me fairly concisely how communities became the norm? And can you explain, at the same time, the importance of education and religious commitment?"

Ambrose sighed. He suspected that this was the moment he had been waiting for — when John would be really receptive at last.

Over the next two days Ambrose talked and John listened. He explained how, as dislocation became more widespread and the power bases crumbled, people were obliged to find protection wherever they could. This was very often in the form of small groups, which sometimes exhibited signs of ancient feudalism. However, what occurred was not the development of a military form of organisation based on land tenure in which the strong were supposed to protect the weak, as had happened during the period when the very ancient Roman Empire had been in decline: certain factors were different.

Firstly, there was a long and very well documented history of experimental cooperatives going way back beyond John's time — and John himself knew of some of them, and especially the ones like Robert Owen's New Harmony, which had failed. He also knew of others that existed in his day, for example, Mondragon in northern Spain, which was very successful even though in the end it became so huge it lost its original sense of purpose. Also, he had direct experience of the workings of an anarchist commune in southern France, Longo Mai, which he had visited. However, many such experiments were short-lived usually because of internal conflict but also because they existed within relatively prosperous (in comparison with the Dark Times) larger forms of social and political organisation. There were always relatively safe alternatives for members should their communities collapse. However, as times got worse this was not always so easy, and on occasions impossible. People found more and more that they had no alternative but to make their small groups work. Ambrose reminded John at this point that the communities were always in touch with each other and, moreover, that they saw themselves as subversive of the more regular forms of organisation, whether political or economic, which they portrayed as responsible, in part at least, for the descent into the maelstrom. So there was virtually a science of small community organisation available to anyone obliged to set about organising some cooperative means of survival — and cooperation was the watch word.

A second factor that was different was the way in which the churches, or rather groups with a religious commitment, played a part. Here Ambrose went off down another track in order to discuss the Christian Church at the time of the fall of the Roman Empire, when it had filled part of the power vacuum left by the collapse of the state. Indeed, he said, its former politically based hierarchical structure had developed as a response to that collapse of authority. However, in the fourth millennium, its intentions were almost wholly in the opposite direction: it shunned political power; it preached (truer to the words of St Paul than ever before) the equality of all mankind and the need for every person to not only be responsible for every other person but also to be willing to share that responsibility and not fob it off onto someone else. He spoke at first about his own church, but described how others pursued similar objectives. Furthermore, priests, pastors, imams and rabbis conferred with each other more extensively than ever before, and all of them realised, at last, that non-violence was much more important than any of the distinctions between the doctrines that traditionally they thought had separated them, and they looked instead for common ground.

When John yet again expressed his incredulity, Ambrose embarked upon a long argument that attempted to show that it was only through a combination of non-violence and mutual responsibility that the communities could survive and finally prosper. But they also had to cure themselves of the disease of leadership. In the words of the Sermon on the

Mount, the meek had inherited the Earth. However, he went on to suggest that two other factors underpinned all of this. The first was the influence of a commitment to a religious belief, where that belief concentrated on concern for other people rather than self. He agreed that a person does not have to have a religious belief in order to have such concern, but it helps. When John queried this, Ambrose used his own faith as an example: trying to be Christ-like meant forgetting yourself and always behaving out of love.

The other factor was one John had raised a question about and that was education.

"Don't you remember Cromwell's instruction to his troops?" asked Ambrose.

"Which one was that?"

"Trust in God and keep your powder dry."

"And what's the significance of that in this context?"

"Well, Christians may believe that all people are made in the image of God, but they also know, as you and I discussed on the cliff, that they are inherently selfish. We have to learn how to be concerned for others and that process goes right back to babyhood. That's why paediatrics is so important today, and why we invest so much time and energy in education. We would like to make sure that children learn to care for themselves by caring for others first. I know that you think that some of the techniques we use are indoctrination or conditioning, but if you look carefully at them you will see that they are not. Indeed, we know from experience in the early years of the communities that both of those are counterproductive. What we also now know is that people have to be taught meekness — but a meekness that is constructive."

"So how does Cromwell fit into all that?"

"Oh, c'mon, John. You can see surely that we have faith in God, but we are not taking any chances."

"Doesn't that mean that faith is not worth the candle?"

"Not at all. Loving till it hurts — even when it seems contradictory — comes from our religious beliefs: they inform everything we try to do."

"Yes, but couldn't children learn that without all the mumbo- jumbo?"

" Ha! Mumbo-jumbo! John, you are incorrigible. But look … look at the way people treat each other in this society, and then look at the words used in, say, the Mass, and you'll see the consistency — and that coming together of the people, as a community, is important, but what is even more so is that they are celebrating the most amazing sacrifice ever … and … and at the same time joining together in the Agape, the love feast."

John was about to interrupt, but Ambrose went on, "And anyway, look at the facts again — these are the communities that survived and prospered."

"So you say."

"But they are! You'll have to go and look at more of them, but as yet, have you seen anything that contradicts what I am saying?"

"Well, no. But on the other hand, I've seen hardly anything."

"Then go and look some more."

"Don't you worry — I fully intend to. However, there's lots of questions I still want to ask you."

"Fire away, that's what I'm here for."

"Ah, now. To go back to your communities. Something I've been pondering — how can they remain economically viable?"

"Good question — but one that I'd rather not answer."

"Oh, and why not?!"

"Well, hold on to your hat for a minute — I've got not just one, but two people who have made a study of just such questions, and they've agreed to talk to you."

"And are they members of this community? Are they here?"

"One is. That's Father Ernst. The other is his brother, Friedrich, and he arrives tomorrow on a visit from his community in Hansea."

Ambrose was about to say more but a novice came into the guests' sitting room to tell him that there was a problem in the hen house. Thinking he may have left the door open, he was keen to dash straight off to check and so asked John if he could look after his books and papers until he got back.

As John sat mulling over their conversation he idly picked up the book that happened to be on the top of Ambrose's pile. He was hardly aware of what he was doing, but out of habit he looked at the date of publication: it was 1974! Only then did it dawn on him that it was a facsimile — so artfully produced that it was almost indistinguishable from books of his own time. When he looked at the title his immediate reaction was to put the book down: it was *Jesus the Christ*. However, he then noticed that it had originally been written in German and had been published by Matthias-Grunewald-Verlag. Why this should interest him he did not know, but he looked for the author's name. It was Walter Kasper who he discovered was, at the time of writing, a theologian at the University of Tubingen. He riffled through some of the pages — towards the back of the book — and came across passages that Ambrose had highlighted. He read one of them:

"This situation of disaster consists in the fact that in practice men do not accept one another as men and do not grant one another living space, but cut themselves off from and use one another as means to secure their own existence. Order is imposed, not by human solidarity, but by selfishness and self-interest. When human beings use each other like that as means, as commodities, as man-power and numbers, then anonymous factors like money, power, personal and national prestige become ultimate values to which man is subordinated as a means, and on which in the last resort he is dependent. Since the time of Hegel and Marx particularly, this reversal of the relationship between person and thing has been described by what was originally an economic-legal term: 'alienation'. This concept expresses the fact that men become strangers to one another under conditions, which, as anonymous objective factors, themselves gain power over men. Joint involvement helps decide a situation in which we have always been 'sold' to 'powers' and 'authorities', so that we no longer belong to ourselves."

Several pages away he came across another:

"Our freedom is possible only insofar as others grant us space for freedom and respect it. Actual freedom, therefore, as Hegel showed, is based on mutual affirmation and acceptance in love. Hence concrete freedom is ultimately possible only within a joint system of freedom where everyone has through everyone else his concrete scope for living and freedom. Within this scheme the individual again becomes aware of himself only in encounter with others who are significant (Peter Berger) Thus we are defined in our existence by what others are; our existence is essentially co-existence."

He was about to put the book down when he noticed another passage highlighted in a different colour. It said:

"… but also a mental unpretentiousness: refraining from self assertion, from seeking to establish oneself and one's own claims. Non-violence and powerlessness, modesty and straightforwardness, ability to criticize and ability to hear are forms of expression of humanity as Jesus lived and taught them."

He re-read all three passages several times: they seemed to epitomize Ambrose's philosophy and all that he had been trying to teach John, because the first described the underlying cause (as he saw it) of the descent into chaos; the second described the basic tenet upon which the present society depended; and the third made clear why, for Ambrose, the person of Christ was of crucial significance. He felt that he really understood, for the first time, what Ambrose was getting at — and yet it had been written before even John had been born. He began to read other parts of the book, and by the time Ambrose had returned he knew he wanted to read all of it. Ambrose was obviously pleased by John's request to borrow it.

Chapter XI

Ernst looked like Karl Marx, but he wasn't in the least grumpy. Ambrose arranged for him to come to John's room after Compline one evening, and he arrived bearing coffee for them both. It was clear that he did not know where John had come from and it seemed that Ambrose had told him only as much as he had told the Abbot. Nevertheless, John felt very wary of him: he was afraid that his questions would be so basic, even naive, that Ernst would suspect that his provenance was even odder than it really was. If this was the case, Ernst did not show it, and fortunately for John, began the discussion by asking about the work he was doing with Ambrose, which meant that they could concentrate on the early history of the communities; this gave John the opportunity to ask how they became economically viable in the first place.

"Ah well, as you know, the earliest objective of all of them, no matter what their particular genesis, had to be survival and that meant they had to provide enough food to sustain themselves from one year to the next."

"Couldn't that be precarious?"

"Oh yes, and some of the early ones did not survive."

"Do we know why they failed?"

"For the reasons you would expect — they were poorly sited, or tried inappropriate crops, or simply they did not know enough about farming organically and were reluctant to accept advice from the communes that did."

"But I thought that communication was good from the beginning."

"Well, the technology was there, but if people don't use it, there's not a lot you can do to help them."

"Why do you think they were reluctant?"

"For reasons I'm sure you've already discussed with Ambrose. They were to do with their organisational structures — convinced leaders nearly always think they know what's best; hierarchies suffer from sclerosis; libertarians ... well, what can you say?"

He sighed and for a while stared into space. John felt bemused and not a little embarrassed, that is until Ernst woke up again, and apologising for his reverie said, "Sorry, I was just thinking about the libertarians — at least they taught us about the inviolability of the individual. But no matter. What were we talking about?"

"Of the early communes being self-sufficient."

"Oh yes, but in food. That was important, and still is. However, for so many of the things they needed they had to be in touch with others."

John was about to intervene with a question about self-sufficiency in food now, but Ernst, like the teacher he was, went on, "There are two points to remember here about what those early experiences led to. The first is that as far as possible, communes have tried — largely successfully — to remain self-sufficient in food production. Which is why, as you know, everybody, almost without exception, works for some of the time in the fields or in the greenhouses or in the coppices or wherever, so that everyone is involved in what the earth produces. The other is that from the beginning the communes have traded with each other — at first in information and then in goods."

"But what if they were situated in not so fertile land? Wouldn't they need to rely mostly on trade?"

"But they all had to be on fertile land; that was their first priority. There are a few exceptional ones now, but they are rare and their members have to be constantly on their guard to avoid the consequences of not producing a sufficiently wide variety of goods, as you well know."

John did not know but he felt that asking a further question might make him vulnerable, so he decided to reserve this particular query for Ambrose. Instead, he asked, "Why did they not try to become completely self sufficient? Wasn't there an ancient system called autarky in the time of the great dictators in the twentieth century?"

"I have only the vaguest of notions about that. Did it work?"

"No. I don't think so."

"Well, there you are then ... But to go back to your question, I don't think they ever wanted to be completely independent — firstly because it's too difficult, and secondly because there something in us that wants to trade."

"But if the early communes traded out of necessity might it not be that we learned to like it?"

"Oh yes, of course. But I was thinking of something I came across recently about the origins of very early cities."

"Do you mean places like Manchester and London?"

"Oh no, much earlier than that: places like Uruk and Tell Brak."

"I've heard of Uruk ... and Ur of the Chaldees ... but not the other one you mentioned."

"Well, excavation began there as early as the twentieth century, but the wars in what used to be called Mesopotamia brought them to a halt and they've never been resumed. Perhaps someone should start again there."

"And what do you think they'd find?"

"Evidence of very early trade, and evidence of the skilful production of artefacts to trade with."

"So?"

"I would say that's pretty conclusive evidence that humankind has always traded — and there's evidence of even earlier trading in Africa."

"OK then, if trading is so natural to us and if cities are linked so firmly with trading, why don't you … er … sorry … why don't we have cities now?"

"Ah well, you have to consider what awful monsters the cities became — and monsters that were in the end both unsustainable and hopelessly vulnerable to attack, which is why most of them were destroyed: very few were intact when they were deserted."

"But we still engage in trade."

"Yes. It's part of our mutual dependability."

"And yet we have no cities."

"No. We don't because we try not to allow them to develop."

"But doesn't that restrict freedom?"

"Well, yes. In a sense it does, but it's a freedom we agree to forgo … in the long term interests of all, because we know what cities can lead to."

"But are the consequences of living in cities always evil?"

"Ah, I see what you're getting at, and I think we could be drifting into the area of moral philosophy — you'll have to talk to someone like Justin about that — but suffice it to say at this point that cities did lead to good developments for humankind, but that was not the case once they had become enormous: their disadvantages outgrew, I could almost say grew out of, their advantages — at least judging by the examples we know of. Also, if you can have the advantages of cities without having cities, have you lost anything?"

John had to accept this because of the way the question was put, though he felt that somehow Ernst had sidestepped his query about freedom. Perhaps this would have to be taken up with Justin — whoever he was; he could only assume he was another member of the community. However, he now wanted to know what Ernst thought these city-less advantages were, but he wondered if this would reveal his ignorance in a dangerous way. It was safer to keep the discussion academic sounding by concentrating on the early history, and he did have a real problem with this — it was for this reason the Ambrose had suggested consulting Ernst. It dawned on him that the reason he found it difficult to imagine what had happened was because, whatever way he tried to think about it, he always came back to a model of development that could only be described as free market capitalism. Luckily, Ernst seemed to have slipped off into another reverie, thus allowing him plenty of time to formulate his next question. He realised that he could do this if he contrasted pre-Dark Times economic philosophy with post-Dark Times and then ask Ernst for the reasons for the change. The answer he got when he put the question was that whereas in earlier millennia economics had been concerned with the production of goods, in the communities people came first. John immediately remembered the highlighted passages in the book he had recently borrowed from Ambrose.

"But what does that mean for economic activity?"

"Isn't it obvious?"

"I suppose it is, but I would still like to hear it spelt out — especially in terms of early developments in the communities."

Ernst thought for a while and John began to wonder if he had gone off into another dream, but then he went on to explain that the groups that survived had to concentrate on producing enough food while at the same time keeping their means of information technology working. They also had to find ways of building shelters, keeping warm and clothed; but even from their origins in the Dark Times, their basic philosophy held that they must not exploit each other; that could only lead in the long run to the sort of conditions that had produced the cataclysm in the first place. This meant that they functioned cooperatively both internally and externally. They saw to each other's needs within each community, but every community was prepared to help any other community that might be experiencing some difficulty. They also advised each other, encouraged each other and supplied each other if need be.

John could still not see why some community members, and indeed some communities, did not try to behave out of self-interest, and Ernst had to admit they did. But then he reminded John that human knowledge of communities actually went back to the very beginnings of living in groups, and the history of cooperation was actually a very long one.

Most of the communities in existence now, he said, went back in most cases five hundred years. They had not ironed out all the difficulties, and he hoped they never would, but they had learned an enormous amount. Ernst then surprised him by asking, "What sort of activities does your commune engage in?"

John was taken aback, but realising that he needed time to think, he answered, "Well," then picked up the coffee pot and said, "May I have some more?"

As they fussed with their drinks he tried to remember as much as he could about Marianne's commune and was surprised at what he knew. He then described the crops he had seen in the local fields, the tile factory, the pottery, the open-air museum in which he actually lived, and he even remembered to include the hospital in which Marianne worked.

"And how many people live in this community?"

"About 4000," he guessed, remembering a village he lived in at one time.

"Ah, so a bit above average."

"I could be wrong about the numbers."

"Doesn't your commune publish its statistics?"

"Yes, but ..."

"You don't pay much attention," and before John could answer he went on, "You're a bit of a wanderer, then?"

"Ahuh ..."

"Ah well, I was at your age ... That's how I came here in the first place ... I thought I'd try the Celtic monks' wandering in reverse — from Hansea to Eire. Little did I think I'd finish up as a Celtic monk, but here I've been for thirty years."

"What made you stay?"

"Oh, the place and then the lifestyle. What could be better than the balance we have here between physical work, worship and intellectual endeavour? Some communities find it difficult to maintain such a balance, but here it's almost perfect ... Except that now I find Matins a chore, so I'd better get some sleep."

"Will the coffee keep you awake?"

"Naa ... I shouldn't think so — these days nothing keeps me awake. So goodnight and God bless ... I'll see you in the morning with that daft brother of mine." Then, when John looked at him quizzically, he added, "I don't really mean that — he's OK."

As soon as he'd gone John opened a line to Marianne on the communicator.

"Good. I haven't disturbed you? I thought I might have woken you up.... How are you?"

"I'm very well. How are you ...? I was beginning to wonder if there might be something amiss as you had not been through earlier."

John explained about Brother Ernst's visit and his questions on the community, which he wanted now to ask her, but first he wanted to know about George-Louis.

"He was disappointed that you hadn't been in touch earlier. He's got a question about Amerindians: did some of them live in caves or did they all live in tepees? I think that's what he said."

"Err ... perhaps there was one tribe that did. Tell him I'll talk to him tomorrow evening about it.... And I've got all sorts of questions for you."

"Oh dear, are they difficult?"

"No, they are all about the Jackfield Community, or is it the Ironbridge Community?"

"It's both really — and Coalport too. Originally, there were three, but they joined together to make a viable unit."

"So how many people are now in the community?"

"About 3500, just over 1000 in each of the three parts, but the Ironbridge section is bigger because of the steel works."

"Oh my goodness! I knew nothing about that. Are there any other enterprises besides the tiles, the pottery, the museum and the hospital?"

"There are some quite small ones — one family makes furniture and another musical instruments — but the only other sizeable one is the research institute, but then nearly every community has one of them."

"How many people work there?"

"It's difficult to say: sometimes a few; sometimes a lot."

"Why's that?"

"Oh well, anybody can engage in research."

"Anybody? What about qualifications?"

"Qualifications? We don't have them anymore."

"Oh, Marianne, you're kidding, surely?"

"No, I'm not."

"I don't understand how you can … I mean … how … what if someone is a charlatan?"

"A charlatan?"

"Yes. Someone pretending to be what they are not or to do something they can't … don't know how to … whatever."

"But why should they do that?"

"For money … or prestige … all sorts of reasons."

"But no one would do that, surely?"

They were both silent for a moment, she because she was waiting for an answer, he because she had once again surprised him with what she had just announced in her deadpan way. She looked at him intently and said, "Well, would they?" But his only reply was, "Marianne, you never cease to amaze me … But I know there's no point in arguing … I'll just accept what you say … and anyway, it's getting late. I'd better let you get some sleep.… Oh, just one thing before you go. What do they actually make at Coalbrookdale?"

"I'm not really sure: it's one of the few places I've not worked, but I think it's steel rails and things like that."

"And where do they sell them?"

"Wherever they are needed, I suppose. As long as it's not too far away."

"What do you mean … if it's not too far away?"

"Well, someone nearer would supply them, wouldn't they?"

"I see," said John, but doubtfully.

The next morning he was introduced to Friedrich who, facially, was recognizably Ernst's brother, but he was much taller and thinner. John found himself thinking about an illustration of Jack Sprat and his wife in a book of nursery rhymes he'd had as a child, so that during the introductions he could not help grinning. Happily, this meant they got off to a friendly start.

"As I explained to you, the economic viability of the early communes is what John is interested in," said Ernst to his brother.

Deciding to take a chance, John added quickly, "Economic viability any time in their history, really, i.e. how did they get to be as they are now? You see I've looked at the work of very ancient economists like Adam Smith, Ricardo and Marx right through to Keynes and Hayek. They all, even Marx, seem to be saying that what matters most in the long run is the market, and that the market in turn functions as it does because of supply and demand and the consequent competition."

Ernst and Friedrich looked at each other in amazement. Then they both said together, "Have you never read Schumacher?!"

"Well, yes, as a matter of fact I have."

"And ...?"

"Er ... I thought ... he had had little ... er ... that he would be out of date."

"Out of date?" said Friedrich, "He's the most important, more important than even the founder of the science, Adam Smith."

John realised that from the conversations he had with Ambrose and Ernst that he should have seen this coming, but he remembered only vaguely what Schumacher had said and that this had now left him exposed. Fortunately, the panic seemed to inspire him and, in an attempt to recover his position, he said, "I know that he said people are more important than goods and that he was in favour of enterprises remaining small, but in some ways his book *Small is Beautiful* accepts market forces."

As this seemed to mollify Ernst and Friedrich, he thought the best thing he could do would be to shut up, but when he looked up at the pair of them he realised something he should have seen when Ambrose first told him of them: they had Schumacher's names! He could not help smiling and said, "Are you sure you two aren't prejudiced in his favour?"

They too smiled and Ernst said, "Well, perhaps my brother exaggerates a little our namesake's importance, but you have to look at the people he influenced."

"If you mean the Greens, how much effect did they have?" was the reply, but then Friedrich answered, "Immediately, not very much, but they left a body of writing and experience that has been very valuable to later generations and which has formed the basis of work of very influential people like Hundsecher and Li Yu Sen."

As he had heard of neither of these and could only assume that they were from the fourth millennium, John smiled as broadly as he could and nodded his head.

"Anyway," said Ernst, "how did we get on to that? What was your question again?"

"I don't think I ever asked it, but what interests me is how the early communities did not succumb to the attractions of market forces."

"Oh, that is down to the rediscovery of Schumacher and those who followed his line — like those my brother mentioned, but also many others who warned of the dangers. What was crucial, though, was the discovery, through experience, that he was right and that you can have an economic system that puts people first."

"Give me a concrete early example."

Ernst beamed, turned towards his brother and pointed an open hand at him, as though presenting him to a large audience, but said nothing. Friedrich responded appropriately and then looked very serious for quite a long time. At last he said, "I suppose one of the most influential early communes was that at Quevedo in South America; in its earliest form it was one of those that helped to set up the short-lived confederation of Pachacamac at the beginning of the fourth millennium, which, as you no doubt remember, ended in disaster for many of the members when the dictator Manuel took over."

"So, what happened?"

"Oh, like so many of the others, it struggled free, though with reduced numbers. From then on its members were determined to stay independent and, in fact, it was fortunate that Manuel's attention was elsewhere: they were mostly left alone to grow potatoes and so survive. It attracted other members from all over South America, so it had skilful and knowledgeable people, and because it kept good communication links with others it began to diversify both its agriculture and to develop small-scale industry — for its own needs and for whatever others requested from it."

"But what did they make?"

"Woollen clothes first — because they needed them — but what was more important was that their clever engineers were able to use cannibalised parts from machinery from earlier industry to make spinning wheels and weaving looms. They were so successful that they expanded into the production of cotton goods, but they first had to grow the cotton, so they needed to extend their farming — and at the same time they experimented with different forms of power production to drive their machines. So they were diversifying all the time."

"Surely, this meant they grew larger — didn't that become a problem? And what about increasing complexity?"

"Ah, now that's why they are such a good example of what's possible — and also what can go wrong. Once its numbers passed 1000 it began to plan an offshoot and another commune was set up about twenty miles away — again on fertile land so that it had a chance to survive. It too became independent."

"Did this follow the same pattern of development as its mother commune?"

"Only up to a point. The people there found that the new terrain was not the same and so they had to grow different crops, but they wanted to keep physical links with Quevedo as well as the electronic connection. After various attempts they came to the conclusion that the best way of doing this was by a cable car, as it seemed to disturb the environment less than any other system. They had to develop the technologies to do this and so their industries were different from those of Quevedo. On the other hand, this meant that the two communities could cater for each other's needs. Yet, though their economies were interlinked, you could even say complementary, they remained independent politically. In fact, their constitutions, i.e. their decision-making processes, varied considerably."

"How?"

"Well, the engineers at Quevedo formed an elite group and were always dominant, even though there was a grand council to which all subgroups sent representatives. The overall system looked democratic, but it was a kind of corporatism. Mirador, maybe because the original settlers were dissatisfied with the arrangements in their mother commune, set up what they called the Arizmendiarietta system, named after a very ancient form of co-operatism in northern Spain."

"Would that have been at Mondragon?"

"Ah, you know about that?" said Friedrich with a look of surprise.

"Doesn't everyone?" replied John as disconcertingly as he could.

"Only those interested in very ancient history would know the details. So, correct me if I'm wrong, but from what I know, all participants in Mondragon had to have a financial stake in whatever enterprise they joined, and if they left they withdrew the stake. Mirador had no means of exchange at first but members were expected to commit themselves in the same way as Mondragon — and everyone shared administrative responsibility. Later offshoots followed the same pattern. Oh, and by the way, when Quevedo began to decline, which almost inevitably it did, its progeny (so to speak) returned to revive its fortunes."

John was busy formulating another question, but he never got the chance to ask it because Ernst launched into a lecture on the dangers of bureaucracy, claiming that this was the perennial problem faced by all communities: it was necessary but it had to be watched and this was something that economically successful communes were likely to neglect. Quevedo itself was such an example. Friedrich intervened with a host of schemes used by early communities to deal with the problem. He showed how subsidiarity had to be maintained, but also how education, particularly of children, could help in developing each member's sense of responsibility to all other members. An argument, or rather a heated discussion, followed in which John took no part, as they seemed to have forgotten him. However, he was very impressed with the knowledge displayed by both of them as they put forward the relative merits of devising administrative mechanisms as opposed to social and personal education. They came to an amicable conclusion: it was difficult to give priority to either. A watchful eye had to kept on both. John could only agree, though some of the technicalities they had discussed were beyond him. They went off to lunch. In the afternoon John returned to his work with Ambrose and Ernst and Friedrich to discuss their complementary sets of research.

Chapter XII

As his stay at St Adrienne's lengthened, John began to find himself gradually falling into its rhythms. This was partly because he spent so much time with Ambrose who, though at first he seemed prepared to forego some of the services for the sake of the work with John, proved to be a very conscientious monk. John could have used his free time, when Ambrose was attending his offices, reading or at his computer, but sometimes he revolted against the idea of study. He tried walking in the grounds of the monastery instead, and he found this very agreeable. However, he could often hear the singing of the monks and he felt drawn to this. So he began to attend the services more often. Moreover, John found himself waking early in the morning. Yet he always felt refreshed because he had slept well. Perhaps, he thought, it was the wholesome food, or the freshness of the air, or simply everything about the way of life. Whatever it was, by six o'clock he was always wide awake — and looking forward to breakfast, which, of course, was after Mass. Attending seemed a sensible idea: he liked the music, the architecture, the ambience, and he always thought about how happy he had been at Mass with Marianne — and George-Louis too — beside him. They were a family, or so it seemed to him, and he liked that.

Sitting at the rear of the church where he hoped no one could see him, he leaned back and looked up at the tracery in the roof. It would always remind him of the canopy of a tropical forest, and he thought too of the music drifting up towards it where he imagined it wafting through the leaves and the delicate top-most branches. Yet the words being sung so clearly by this fraternity, this collectivity, this fellowship, also took him back to his childhood when all of this had real meaning for him. '*Blessed is he who comes in the name of the Lord*'. What does it mean? "Blessed" — that's an odd word. He'd seen the Latin — *benedictus* — translated as "happy', but that, he felt sure, was not what the word meant. He supposed you would have to go back to the Hebrew or the Aramaic, or whatever the original was written in, to find out. He became aware then that he was not interested in only the aesthetics of the experience: he could not stop himself paying attention to the words — more and more each day. There was always something striking that he would remember for a long time afterwards. The Testaments both

Old and New were quite different from how he had considered them during his childhood — or adult years, for that matter — so much so that he began to wonder if he had ever really listened to the readings before. Intellectually they were more seductive than he had thought.

However, he decided that their effect was insidious: he had begun to feel vulnerable. This was why he had never wanted to come here in the first place — or so he told himself. For several mornings he stayed away, though he attended evensong because, he said to himself, the music was nice. Nice! This was the word his old friends from the college of art had used to condemn anything they thought kitsch. He knew this was unfair and continued to attend — but he also found he wanted to go to Mass too. Then, once again, the process began.

One morning there was a reading from St Luke, which he had heard before but to which he had never really listened:

'Love your enemies, do good to those who hate you, bless those who curse you, pray for those who treat you badly. To the man who slaps you on the cheek, turn the other one too; to the man who takes your cloak, present your tunic ...'

And so it went on. How could anyone be that virtuous? It even said that we should be compassionate because God the Father is compassionate, and also that we should not judge 'that you be not judged'. This was not how John had been taught about God: he saw him as a judge, yes, but a thoroughly rational one from whom you got exactly what you deserved. This text, on the other hand, implied that God forgave us even when we did not deserve it. Perhaps he was an indulgent father (like the father in the story of the prodigal son) who always forgave, no matter what we had done or what our state of mind.

A few days later it was words from the first letter of St Paul to the Corinthians, which stayed with him:

'Love is always patient and kind; it is never jealous; love is never boastful or conceited; it is never rude or selfish; it does not take offence, and is not resentful. Love takes no pleasure in other people's sins but delights in the truth; it is always ready to excuse, to trust, to hope, and to endure whatever comes.'

He thought about his relationship with Dorothea: it had been exciting in its early months, but selfish in its pleasure-seeking. It had never been as Paul described love. He had not been patient, rarely kind and had taken offence very easily. In the end he could never have made excuses for her and had looked for every opportunity to make out that she was at fault. He wondered if it would be different with Marianne, or was he simply, for the present, in awe of her? Would familiarity one day result in him feeling towards her as he had towards Dorothea? As he sat at his window watching

Michael deadhead his roses, he thought not. No, not now. What about later? The notion that one day they might not love each other he found almost unbearable, and as though he had been stricken with a powerful cramp he lurched forward: he wanted to pray that this would never happen. Instead, he promised himself that he would always behave towards Marianne as Paul said you should. But then another thought came to him: he should treat George-Louis in the same way — and not just to please Marianne. But it ought not to be only them. What about Ambrose? And Michael? And everybody else? He felt disturbed by this, but why should this idea make him fearful? "Come on now. Think! What are you afraid of?" he said to himself. It then became clear: he was afraid that others would take advantage of his 'softness' (yes, the very word and one that his mother had used), and he would always be at a disadvantage. Unless, that is, everybody else practised Pauline love! Now that would be better. There would be no reason to be afraid — and he remembered from his early childhood when his mother had read him *The Water Babies* that Mrs Do-as-you-would-be-done-by was really the same person as Mrs Be-done-by-as-you-did. And yet even in the smugness he felt at having worked this out, he knew that it was not quite what St Paul meant. The man who stole your cloak had to be given your waistcoat. John knew that he could never do that naturally. Perhaps Ambrose was right — though you couldn't do it *naturally*, you could do it, perhaps, if you had a religious commitment.

The next morning, as he pondered these notions during Mass, he envied the certainty of the other people about him, and as he watched an old lady who seemed particularly devout, the words of the communion prayer came through to him quite clearly:

'Lord, may the Eucharist you have given us influence our thoughts and actions. May your Spirit guide and direct us in your way.'

The desire to receive communion began to grow in him from then on. Every day he found himself thinking about it at some time or another. However, he felt unworthy, and wondered why. What came to mind was the clear memory of the times in his adolescence when he had avoided receiving communion — because he believed he was in mortal sin. And even though now he was almost certain that however he had transgressed it had not been mortally, the feeling that he was guilty in some way was still strong. Of course, he knew that in those days there had been a straightforward way out of the dilemma and that was to go to confession. Ah, now! There was a hurdle! It seemed that to go to confession, if such a rite still existed, would imply that he was accepting — and it would have to be unreservedly — the discipline. The discipline! Of what? And did he really mean discipline? Maybe, maybe not. Was he afraid that it implied unquestioning obedience? Because what would he be obedient to? The

Church — of his day? Or today? Or was it God? And how did you know what God wanted of you? Was it in the Bible? Did the Church know? Did he want to be obedient to anyone or anything? No! He did not!

These thoughts were going through his mind one afternoon as he sat on a bench next to the path that ran towards the cliff over which he and Ambrose had peered several weeks (or was it months?) ago. The ideas were not running helter-skelter but slowly. He felt he could savour them, inspect them; this was something he had become more aware of in himself and he wondered whether this could be an effect of the more leisurely pace at which people seemed to lead their lives in the fifth millennium. But he dismissed this as fantasy and got back to his earlier train of thought, which, he realised to his surprise, he was enjoying.

To say that he did not want to be obedient might mean that morally he was still a child, and a petulant one at that. Well, he was sometimes — but not very often and hardly ever now, though there might be occasions when he was petulant without being aware of it, but he did not think so. This did not seem to be a profitable line of thought, so he tried another. What had he got that he thought he might lose if he were obedient? Suddenly, it was clear to him and he realised he had thought of it before, quite often: it was freedom, and intellectual freedom especially. Wouldn't that be circum-scribed by any thoroughgoing religious belief? His mind went blank. As on several occasions before, it had stopped working. He reflected on this: yes, there was nothing there except the thought that there was nothing there! However, this was not disturbing — as it had been formerly. Indeed, for the moment he was glad. He stared out across the sea and thought about the beauty of the place, though the waves were high and the wind strong. Then he became aware of a yacht that, though it seemed a long way off, was struggling to keep away from the shore towards which the wind was blowing; there were no cliffs at this point but the rocks could still be dangerous. The yachtsmen had to tack backwards and forwards across the bay in order to move slowly and painfully away from the land. He stared hard to try to gauge if they were succeeding. He decided that they were, but he knew that they were in for some hard, continuous work. He studied their technique: they quite obviously knew what they were doing and worked well together. Of course, they were assisted by the ingenious design of the sail which allowed them to progress, if slowly, against the wind, but they had to be disciplined and work together. The discipline gave them the freedom to sail against the wind. Ah yes, discipline and freedom again. He then remembered a true story he used to tell youngsters to try to teach them, he thought at the time, the value of hard work.

It was about one of his art school friends, who being older than his fellow students came in for very little praise from his tutors. This irked him because so often his meticulous and precise way of drawing seemed to him to produce work of greater merit than the hurried, if inspired, scratchings of his younger fellows. Yet they got the praise and not he. One of his specialities was lithography, which suited his careful approach, and towards the end of his course when he was preparing his final exhibition, he was working in the lithography room on a particularly intricate piece when he felt the need to move, to stretch, to open up his shoulders. He went upstairs to the first year life drawing class, took a large piece of paper, a flow-master pen with a broad felt head and began, with bold open strokes, to sketch the rather fat model, the folds of whose flesh lent themselves to the expansive kind of drawing he felt the need for. As he drew he laughed and joked with the students, many of whom were four years younger than he. They saw him, with his ample beard and twinkling eyes, as one of their more charismatic seniors. Suddenly, the solution to the lithographic problem he had been struggling with came to him and he knew he would have to attend to it immediately, so off he ran. When he returned he found his drawing had gone.

"Who's had my bloody masterpiece?" he said to the youngsters with a chuckle. To his surprise one of them replied, "The principal has taken it. He wants to put it in the summer exhibition."

"Yer what? C'mon, don't mess about. Now I know you've hidden it. What have you done with it?" And he began to search the waste paper bins for his drawing. Finally, however, they convinced him it was not a trick. The principal had taken it. So he went down to the main hall and sure enough, there was the principal and his deputy trying to decide where to hang it to the best advantage. When they saw him they both smiled broadly.

"Look," he said to them, "this does not make sense. For two years I draw carefully, and I believe well, and all that you say is that my work is OK, but you are never really enthusiastic about it. And now I dash something off, as some of these young prats do, and you are overjoyed. It's enough to make you spit!"

"Ah now, Russell, that's where you are wrong: we have always admired your very steady progress — and that's what it has been. And now, my friend, let me tell you that you can draw and, what's more, it's a skill you will never lose. What you have been practising for the last two years is the co-ordination of hand and eye, and now they work so well together that you could never draw badly even if you wanted to. It's a skill — a freedom — that some artists would sell their souls for."

Yes, that was the story and he remembered why he used to tell it; but now there was more to it. He recognised that it would help the children to see that self-discipline, taking pains, could lead to a freedom — the ability to do something that, without the discipline, you would never be able to do well.

But was that the same as obedience? He could see a link, but did not know how to articulate the connection in words that would give it substance. Perhaps he would have to add this as well to the list of things he wanted to discuss with Ambrose.

However, when they met again his mentor responded to his request by suggesting that he might like to talk to another colleague.

"Would this other colleague be called Justin?"

"Yes! How did you know? Have you met him before?"

"No, but his name has been mentioned."

"By me?"

"Maybe. I don't remember. But he was certainly mentioned by Ernst."

Several days later, on a pleasant afternoon when the weather was warm, Ambrose took John to a walled orchard beyond Michael's rose garden. On their way, as they went along shady pathways, Ambrose explained that Justin was very old and spent much of his time in a little grotto (with a heater if need be) in prayer and meditation — and sleep. But usually by this time he would be awake and sitting in the sun. He went on to explain that when he was younger, Justin had been one of their more noteworthy preachers. When John baulked at this Ambrose reassured him that despite his preconceptions, he would not find the old man threatening.

Before Ambrose went off back to the monastery he had explained briefly that John was studying History with him. He had also hinted that John, for perfectly good reasons, was not as well acquainted with the ways of the world in the fifth millennium and had one or two matters that he, Ambrose, thought might be profitably discussed with Justin. John was not quite sure of the common sense of this introduction, but Justin's reaction was merely to smile and nod. Indeed, momentarily, John wondered whether perhaps the old chap was so far gone in his dotage that he would be of little use. He soon discovered how wrong he was, for though Justin was the mildest person John had ever met, and rarely was there a time when half a smile was not playing on his lips, he was intelligent — but surprisingly easy to talk to, even though, unless you sat up close, you had difficulty in hearing him. And John did not find this forced intimacy in any way embarrassing: it seemed perfectly natural.

Their conversation began in a mundane way — the mildness of the weather being an obvious starting point. However, soon John was telling him about his loss of faith once he had left school, and how he had thought for a long time that religious belief was simply a way of avoiding reality because it provided a comfort cushion against the harsh, hard facts that science had uncovered about the universe in which we lived.

"Did you feel guilty when you were going through this process of … this process of … well, abandoning your faith?"

"I suppose I did really."

"And can you remember why that was?"

"Well, looking back now, though I didn't see it then, it was because I had other motivations."

"And can you remember what they were?"

"Oh yes, they were to do with girls mostly ... but other things as well."

"Ah, so religious beliefs were inconvenient."

"Yes, I suppose so, but it was not only that. The hypocrisy of so many people, especially the clergy ..."

Then John realised what he had said. Justin was not smiling any longer. After a while he said, "How long ago was this ...? And where was it?"

There was an even longer pause. John felt exposed. He looked wistfully over Justin's shoulder into the distance and said quietly, "Long ago and far away."

"John?"

"Yes."

"Do you come from another planet?"

The only possible response was to laugh, and to laugh heartily, but when he had recovered his composure he saw that Justin was still looking at him quizzically, but calmly — waiting for an answer.

"No, I don't, but I might as well." And he laughed again.

He did not know what to do. He could tell this gentle old man the truth about himself, and he almost did, but then thought that he would say nothing. He would just sit and see what happened. That seemed like a good fifth millennium thing to do, though after five minutes he began to wonder. But at last Justin said, "Then tell me simply ... what's your problem now?"

John thought it would be politic to think carefully before he answered, and Justin seemed to understand his need. He sat quietly waiting, but when John spoke it came tumbling out.

"Since I've been at St Adrienne's I've attended Mass lots of times ... and now I feel I want to go to communion, but that would mean I would have to go to confession, and if I go to confession it means I have to do so with conviction, and if I have conviction I lose my freedom because I have to be obedient ..."

"Just a minute," interrupted Justin, "you're going so fast and there are so many ... er ... But I do remember the last one. What's so awful about being obedient?"

John took a while to answer but then he said, "What if I thought that what I was being asked to do, or perhaps not to do, was silly or unimportant or pointless?"

"Pointless?"

"Yes, like Jesus being prepared to die," and though he realised immediately that he had chosen a poor example to explain what he meant, he went on, "because his Father wanted him to — but what good did it do? Millions of people had no idea what he had done. Most people were unchanged by it."

"Were they unchanged? Didn't they have their sins forgiven — all of them, whether they had heard of him or not?" Justin paused and then went on. "Look, Jesus knew what his Father wanted and loved him so much that he wanted his actions and thoughts to be in keeping with those of his Father. That's why he was obedient. In fact, that is what obedience means. And what it doesn't mean is simply following slavishly the wishes of another."

John had never quite thought of it like this before, but though he could see that Justin had made what seemed to be an important distinction, he wondered if this were not merely semantic sleight of hand, so he said, " But in the here and now, what if everybody has their own notion of what's right or wrong — of what it means to be obedient to the will of God?"

"So what? Haven't we got just that?"

"Well no, because as far as I can see, people here all behave in the same way. No one ever seems to kick over the traces or, to put it in a good old-fashioned way, to commit sin!"

Justin's shoulders shook with silent laughter, then he spluttered out, "You're wrong there. I hear confessions AND I need to go myself occasionally!" Then he tapped John lightly on the knee and said, "Ah John, you're doing me a power of good."

However, it was now John who felt disgruntled: he found Justin's laughter disconcerting. He sat stony-faced while the old man recovered his composure. When at last he did, he too sat in silence for a while, then said, "I'm sorry that I appeared to mock you. I think it might be best if I were straightforward with you. It seems to me that wherever you are from must be different from here if you think we are all conformist. Really, there is only one rule and that is Jesus' own commandment, 'that ye love one another'. And I think the vast majority of people try to abide by it — we don't always succeed, as you will have gathered, but most of us keep on trying. What we all find difficult is seeing things from the other's point of view, because we find it so hard not to be self-centred, and so, for that reason, we have to try to teach each other and help each other — and, of course, we all remember the Dark Times; we know we don't want to go back to them. Moreover, what is even more important is that because of the message of Jesus or Moses or Mohammed or Buddha or whoever, we know that God loves us so we want to live lives which exemplify love because that is the essence of the Blessed Trinity."

"The Blessed Trinity?"

"For Christians, that is, but for others, who may see the Divine differently, love is still the essence — so how else can we respond to God, or Allah, or Jehovah except by loving Him and each other?"

"That's easy to say, but does it happen in practice? Doesn't there have to be the rule of law or coercion, because we are all self-centred?"

"Well, there's coercion and coercion, isn't there?"

He again looked quizzically at John, who did not know how to respond because once more he suspected that this mentor too was cleverer at playing with words than he, but in the end he said, "OK then. Tell me what you mean by that enigmatic statement."

"Ah, you think I'm equivocating. Tell me, what do you mean by coerce?"

"It means, er, to use force, to impel."

"Yes, I agree that's a meaning. Now, though it's seemingly off the point, can you give me an example of you yourself deciding to act not in your own interests, but in the interests of someone else? Can you?"

John began to feel annoyed again. Was he being led by the nose? At first, he did not want to think of an example — not because there weren't any, but because he felt so resentful. However, in face of the silence, which once more ensued, he began to feel foolish, even childish. There seemed to be no way out: he would have to think of an incident and the one that presented itself almost immediately was his decision not to try to persuade Marianne to sleep with him. He did not know whether he could discuss something so personal with anyone, let alone this old and no doubt holy man, but it was a situation in which he remembered he had had to be very firm with himself.

"Do I have to spell out the details?"

"Only if you want to." There was a pause. Then, "OK, I'm thinking of a situation of the kind you suggest."

"Ah, now. Can you remember why you behaved as you did?"

John considered this for a long time because it seemed to him that he ought to be as honest as he could. He knew that one reason for his reticence with Marianne was fear — or rather apprehension — that she might be so shocked that she would want to end the relationship, even though he suspected that she might not. However, he also remembered that the day he had heard the reading about the woman taken in adultery he had realised in a particularly poignant way that he loved Marianne so much that he did not want her to be put in a situation which might make her unhappy or feel guilty, or put her in any danger. So he tried to explain.

" Well, I was afraid, but also I did not want to hurt someone I loved. Now, behaving as I did might have been to my advantage in the long run, but I could not be sure of that at the time. In fact, I don't think I even considered it, and in the short term I found I had to suppress urgent selfish desires."

"Which was the more important — the fear or the love?"

"I can't be absolutely certain, but I think it was the love."

"And wasn't that a kind of coercion?"

"Well, yes. I suppose you could interpret it that way but ..."

"The fact of the matter is that this is the kind of coercion at work in our communities. It is within ourselves." He reached for his Bible and found Ezekiel, and then read: "I will give you a new heart and a new mind. I will take away your stubborn heart of stone and will give you an obedient heart." He looked at John and said, "We like to think that we help each other to behave as though we had those new hearts. However, we are far from perfect, so I'm not saying the other kind of coercion is never used: we do have what you might call laws, but they are rarely needed, and just occasionally restraint has to be used, but it is always applied with love and not resentment or hate or fear."

As usual, John's reaction to this sort of statement was to feel cynical about it all. On the other hand, he knew his experience of fifth millennium living was limited, and also that he had neither seen nor heard of anything that would contradict Justin's claim.

At this point it occurred to him that the conversation had taken off in a different direction from the one in which it had begun, and he remarked on this. Justin, however, said that he thought the topic had not changed: John's concern about obedience was at the root of the problem. The human dilemma had always been how to serve the interests of others and preserve one's own integrity, i.e. at the same time be obedient to Christ's admonition that we love one other. But preserving one's integrity did not mean that one acted only in one's own interests. Paradoxically, it could be preserved only by serving others. John then remembered words from the passage in Kasper's book: 'existence is essentially co-existence'. But he was not quite sure what was meant by this.

"But how can I be myself if I'm always thinking of other people?"

"On the other hand, how can you be anything if you are concerned only with yourself?"

John thought about this and could see that a life of self-absorption would probably be miserable, but that was not what he meant and he said so.

"Then what do you mean?"

"I'm not sure what I mean, nor what I want to be, but I know what I don't want to be and that's like patient Griselda who, if you've not read Chaucer, was so completely subservient to her husband Walter, that she not only let him take her beloved children away but also subject her to ignominy."

"Yes, but your story requires Walter to be selfish or at least not to be capable of perceiving the pain he is causing his wife."

"So?"

"What if Walter were loving and understanding and if one of his aims in life was to see that she was happy and fulfilled?"

"Then there'd be no story."

"Not in the form written by ... what did you say his name was?"

"Geoffrey Chaucer."

"Wouldn't a different story be possible? She could still be patient but so could he."

John could see the drift of Justin's argument, but he still felt there was something unreal about it. Knowing that he was being awkward and almost to sound as obtuse as possible he said, "So what are you trying to tell me?"

"Don't you see ...? In a society such as ours your fears are unfounded. Nobody wants to exploit you or hurt you."

"Maybe not, but what if I feel discontented because in caring for others I deprive myself of things I want or things I want to do?"

"I'm not denying that that can occur. Indeed, it's bound to happen to all of us at some time or another — to a greater or lesser extent. But that is part of the human condition; we all have to learn to live with it. What is important is how you do it. In former times people either suffered in silence or, more likely, gave vent to their feelings, often to the detriment of their fellows. We can only hope that the prophesy of Ezekiel comes about, but we have to respond to that and we cannot do it alone. We have to try to help each other, not only to bear our burdens but also to find fulfilment. But it's not easy. The alternative, remember, is worse — which is why we ought never to forget the Dark Times and what led to them, i.e. when people believed they were free but in fact were slaves — to their own desires but also, in the long run, to each other. There is no such thing as complete freedom, as used to be preached by libertarians: the freedom to follow your whims iş a luxury we have long since realised we can't afford."

John did not want to accept this, because he did not feel he could be so optimistic about people, but he did not want to argue with it either. Not only did he not know how to, but also, paradoxically, he felt in that instant a resolution forming within him: he must try to live like Justin, Ambrose and Marianne. Consequently, he did not know what to say. Again there was silence until, almost like when as a child he had found himself having to accept arguments put forward by adults, he complied. Nevertheless, what he did say surprised him.

"I suppose the best thing would be to go to confession."

"If you think that would help."

"Well, I do feel the need to commit myself to something — and I might feel I can receive communion … I'm sure I'd feel a more complete part of the community if I did."

"Ah, yes, now … Well … Would you like me to hear your confession?"

John must have looked shocked because Justin quickly added, "You won't have to go into details. Just sit quietly for a moment and think about the underlying causes of what you consider to be your sins — and we'll go from there. Could you do that, do you think?"

"Er … I could try."

At first, when he tried to think of his besetting sins, the only thought he could muster was what an old-fashioned word 'besetting' was. It was old fashioned even in his day, but then so was the notion of sin. What had two thousand years achieved? They had revived the notion of sin! Two thousand years! He smiled to himself as he remembered the words of the ancient ritual. Could he say to Justin, 'Bless me, Father, for I have sinned. It is over two thousand years since my last confession.' He looked at the old priest. His face carried its usual trace of a smile as he waited patiently. 'Come on, More. Concentrate,' he told himself — and was glad he did not have to think of individual sins.

However, when he tried to look into his own soul he did not like what he saw, because he realised something he already knew but had never fully articulated: he was selfish. No, that was the wrong word — self-regarding, concerned for himself. But wouldn't everybody's besetting sin be selfishness, concern for self? He supposed so but knew that this in no way lessened his own guilt. For a moment he reflected on his attitudes to other people. Some, he thought, were morally stronger than he — Marianne, for instance — but he knew he had uncharitable thoughts about his fellow men and women. He rarely gave them the benefit of the doubt or was prepared to consider the sort of extenuating circumstances that he allowed for himself. And he was so often angry with them, impatient and inconsiderate. Even so, his own cowardice meant he lied about these feelings because he feared repercussions — and he thought of the many times his pusillanimity led him to run away from responsibility. And couldn't he too often be a slave to his own appetites? He tried to explain all these thoughts to Justin, expecting he knew not what, but the old man merely nodded sagely and pronounced the words of absolution.

Soon after, Ambrose arrived and Justin retired to his grotto. As the two younger men made their way back to the monastery they discussed the possibility of John bringing his period of study to an end, though there were one or two more questions that he wanted to ask Ambrose. They decided to leave these until the next day.

That evening when John talked to Marianne, after George-Louis had gone to bed, he told her of his intention to receive communion. The smile with which she responded to this convinced him that all the confusion, uncertainty and heartache that had gone into the decision to go to confession had been worth it. Moreover, the officiating priest the next morning was Ambrose. John's arrival in front of him to receive the host obviously came as a great surprise, because, as he pronounced the words 'The Body of Christ', he smiled almost as broadly as Marianne had done. When John got back to his pew he realised that though he had not forgotten how to pray, nothing seemed appropriate. Instead, he considered what all this was supposed to mean: he had received the Son of God into his own body, and if God existed — and in the form that Christians believed — then he had also received God the Father and God the Holy Spirit. As it happened the organ was playing, very gently and quietly, a Bach fugue. John thought that each interweaving line of the music represented a person of the Trinity. There they were, each one distinct, yet each one so intimately and beautifully related to the others. And he had joined them. He closed his eyes and in the darkness of own mind he rested with — what? His maker? He could not be certain, but that did not matter, because what he felt was a peace he had never experienced before. He seemed to be where he ought to be; this is what he was made for: to be with God. Time and place were irrelevant. He could be in outer space, rolling gently with the persons of the Trinity and whether it was 2058 or 4058 did not matter.

Ambrose joined him for breakfast in the guests' refectory, but he did not make a fuss because he realised that John did not wish to draw the attention of the others to what had happened at Mass that morning. Indeed, he did not even mention it — though his joy was obvious to John. What he did say was, "Can we begin discussing these important questions here or do you want to leave them till later?"

"Ah, I think later; they are a little personal."

"That's OK, just as you please. Tell you what, it looks like a nice autumn day and the leaves are beginning to turn. Let's go and sit in the garden — if it's not too cold."

They found it a little chilly for sitting, in fact, so they decided to walk out once more towards the cliffs.

"OK, shoot!" said Ambrose. John could not help but laugh. Ambrose looked bemused. John then added, "That seems such an unlikely phrase to be coming from you."

"Well, it's from your century and it comes from watching old films to try and get the feel of the time."

"Oh, I see."

"Then shoot!"

"I'd better try to explain first. One of my queries is moral and I suppose I should have raised it with Justin, but somehow I found I couldn't: he is so old and benign. Also, I realised that there must be an historical explanation for why fifth millennium attitudes differ from those of my time."

"An historical angle on something you could not discuss with Justin? This is intriguing."

"Well, I'm afraid it's boring old sex."

"Ah, I wondered when this would raise its head … erem … So, what's the problem?"

John tried to put his thoughts in order while Ambrose waited a little more impatiently than usual.

"It seems to me, from conversations that I have had with Marianne, that sexual mores are now quite narrow, especially compared with the twenty-first century. It was she who hinted that there were historical reasons for this … but just let me explain … You see, in my own day, people may have gone over the top in their liberality, but in many ways this was a reaction to the repression that had gone on earlier — what has sometimes been referred to as Victorian morality, though in the reign of that particular queen there was much hypocrisy.… Yes, I know you want to comment, but let me finish … After Freud, much was written about the psychology of sex, some of it rubbish, but one thing that emerged was that repression could be as dangerous as … well, for want of a better word, promiscuity. Furthermore, not allowing people to give expression to their personal sexual preferences was seen as an infringement of not only their personal liberty but even of their political rights … Now, just a minute. I've nearly finished …You talk a good deal about the importance of the individual, but as far as sex is concerned, this seems to have been forgotten in what appears to me to be the tyranny of an old-fashioned folk morality … OK, I'm sure I could say more but I'd better finish there for now."

"Very interesting, but there are a number of assumptions in what you have just said. To deal quickly with an easy one first. No one would dream of trying to tell anyone else what their personal preferences should be, as far as sex is concerned anyway. That is the private concern of the individual. What I can say, though, is that most people are heterosexual, but don't ask for a number or a percentage because nobody knows and nobody counts — and we don't make assumptions about people. If two men or two women, or whatever number, live together, no one will assume they are homosexual. What they do in private is their concern — and not something they are likely to broadcast. No one today would want to tie their identity to their sexual activities — which is something I know happened in the past."

"How can you say most people are heterosexual if you don't know the numbers?"

"Simply because the vast majority of adults are married — and apparently happily — or they have chosen to be celibate."

"But that doesn't mean that there is no hidden homosexuality — the scientists of my day were discovering all sorts of genetic factors that had a bearing on sexual inclinations."

"Yes, and the evidence was conflicting. There's nothing to stop you looking at the whole history of genetics if you want to, but I think you will find that the incidence of, what shall we say, those with unconventional inclinations was less than people thought."

"Well, I can't argue with that, can I? Because I don't know the facts."

"They are available, if you want them. But very few people are concerned about them. There are more important things to worry about."

"Ha! I don't want to get into an argie-bargie about that just now, because there are other aspects of your folk morality that I want to ask about."

"Er … just a minute. Can you explain what you mean by 'folk morality'?"

"Are you serious?"

"Certainly I am. It's an expression I find ambiguous: I'm not sure what it means."

"Oh, it refers to the sort of enforced conventionality that prevails, or used to, mostly in villages and small towns — where gossip could ruin a reputation. The worst thing that could happen to a girl, say, would be pregnancy before marriage. Whether they liked it or not, people's sexual activities were limited by puritanical conventions, unwritten rules that most people were afraid to breach, unless furtively. Yet most people were hardly aware of it. Was it any wonder that most people wanted to get out of such a straitjacket?"

"No, it was perfectly understandable, but what happened when all of that broke down? I don't need to tell you because you know already: the anything goes attitude didn't result in people being any happier. In fact, it led to massive exploitation. To take just one example, pornography became a huge worldwide industry — even in your day it was causing great unhappiness — and it became more and more extreme. What occurred later was even worse as societies broke down completely and we headed towards the Dark Times. Remember that the films you saw were looking mostly at starvation, slavery and unbelievable cruelty, but I can show you others, if you like, of the consequences of having no sexual mores at all. "

"OK, OK. But still … Why go so far in the opposite direction and run all the risks that come from repression?"

"But there isn't any repression."

"How can you say that? From what I'm told, sex is virtually confined to marriage."

"But that doesn't mean people are repressed: they choose to confine it and are happy to do so."

"I can hardly believe this!"

"As I've said to you so often before, it's all due to upbringing and education."

"And as I have said to you: it's conditioning not education. It sounds as bad as *Brave New World*!"

"And what might that be?"

"Oh, it was a book from the twentieth century written by a man called Aldous Huxley."

"Huxley. I've come across the surname but no one with that first name."

"There was a whole family of them; they were all clever. However, we are getting off the point."

"Well, the last point was conditioning, as you call it. I don't think there's anything to be gained from further discussion. Again, you are going to have to live in the real world and see for yourself, but at least you know from our arguments that you'll have to be circumspect."

"On that score, I have had to be circumspect already."

"I know that, John, but I think that now it would be appropriate for you to try some of the full submersion experiences. If you are leaving soon, it had better be tomorrow." Though John felt very apprehensive, he reluctantly agreed.

Chapter XIII

He was quite surprised by the technology involved. He had not expected that there would be a special room for this: he thought there would be a machine about the size of a video player and maybe a set of earphones and not much else. Instead, the room they entered reminded him of a small compact television studio and control room he had used in his student days. There were wires and cables running everywhere and strange looking electronic machines and equipment. At the centre of this clutter stood a black chair with a high back, the sort in which dentists accommodate their patients. This factor alone was alarming enough for John to wish he had never embarked on this exercise, but there was no natural source of light either. Ambrose's explanation was that the room had to be insulated from all outside influences. John found this disturbing too.

The next surprise was that Ambrose asked him to don what looked like a wetsuit, and as John struggled into it he was asked whether he had any preference for the kind of experience he would like. He nearly gave a smutty, laddish answer, but thought better of it and said, "Oh, I have a choice then?"

"Well, of course you do … Er … but might I give you some advice?"

"Always willing to listen to the expert — but what's the catch?"

"O, John, there is no catch. It's just that you're going to find the experience more real than I think you imagine and so I want to suggest that you pick something to begin with that is not completely outside your ken, and one that is not too harrowing. So … er … take a look at these," and he handed John what looked like a set of small DVDs.

All the titles looked disturbing, but amongst them he saw one that was simply called 'Concentration Camp' and, as he had read *Ivan Denisovich* and also of Victor Frankl's experiences, that is what he chose. Ambrose then handed him what, at first, he took to be one of those crash helmets that cover the head completely, but when he laughed at this Ambrose said, "You're going to need help getting that on and then adjusting it."

"Do I have to wear it?"

"I'm afraid so — it's probably the most important item."

As usual, he was right: John had a considerable struggle getting into the helmet and Ambrose seemed to take an age adjusting it so that, as he explained, all the electrodes were in the right place. But once satisfied he said, "Now listen carefully, John. Once you are into the program, you can't come out until it has finished. I think you might find, even with this one, that you do want stop, especially if you come to yourself."

"If I come to myself? What do you mean?"

"Well, the program and the equipment are constructed in a way which will very probably make you believe you are a different person, one for whom these experiences are real. However, if there is a serious clash of personalities — say, where deep moral convictions play a part — your own character may reassert itself, and this will be very unpleasant, I can assure you. I know from my own experience that it's like the worst sort of nightmare … er … and that's why I have to strap you in."

"Strap me in?!"

"Yes. Because some people struggle violently in that chair. So are you sure you want to do this now?"

"I suppose I have no choice."

"But you do. We allow this only for people who are free to choose."

"Sorry, I didn't mean that quite as it sounded. I meant that it's best to get it over with. And I can see that I've got to do this some time or another."

"Right, I'll zip your helmet to the suit and then strap you in, and when I think all is ready I'll touch you on the arm and switch on."

John felt the touch and then …

It seemed that he was awakening, but he soon became aware of his whole body: he ached all over. Then he realised why he was so very uncomfortable. It was the bed. It seemed to be as hard as, as … he felt beneath him …it was made of wooden slats. Slowly, as he got used to the gloom, his surroundings took shape. He was in a bunk in a large, unpleasant hut and he then realised that the smell was dreadful, almost palpable. It was of dirty and very unhappy people, many of whom were ill. He did not know which emotion was the stronger — fear or disgust. He listened to the sounds of this overcrowded midden: men groaning, coughing, spitting; one uttering the suppressed scream of a nightmare; another repeating seemingly pointless words of the first line of a prayer; someone farting openly; yet others already moving, pulling on broken down boots; scratching.

Though it was still dark, the door crashed open, the dim lights came on and there stood two guards, truncheons swinging carelessly from their wrists. One stepped forward and struck the nearest of the wooden pillars supporting the roof. The whole rotten edifice seemed to shake and the noise echoed ominously throughout the hut.

"Get out of here NOW!" the other yelled, and everybody began to move frantically, some in a half-crouched position as they tried to get into their boots. Most, he realised, like him apparently, had slept in whatever footwear and ragged

clothes they possessed, though this meant, for John, that the frosty air pierced him immediately to his very core as soon as he stepped out into the rutted but bone hard clearing to line up untidily with his fellow sufferers. Then other guards appeared as though from nowhere to beat them with their truncheons into more or less straight lines.

The order, "Forward march," was given and the first of the four lines proceeded towards the tall gate in the barbed wire fence; each man was scrutinised by guards placed either side of the line as he went out and John realised in time that it was politic not to glance at any of them but to keep your head up and your eyes to the front. Outside they reassembled into four columns and then began to walk — it was more like a hobble than a march — towards their place of work. It was only then that he became fully aware of the state of his feet: every step was painful and before long he felt that he could not carry on. However, at the first sign of hesitation from him, the men either side grabbed his elbows to support him. He soon knew why: a man several rows in front stumbled and brought down a number of others. They were all beaten indiscriminately and severely by the guards and one of the prisoners could not get up. Two guards dragged him to one side and just as John passed they shot him in the head. He saw the blood and brains spatter the frozen grass and he baulked to try to avoid vomiting though there was nothing in his stomach, not even bile.

This long, agonising march ended near a half dug ditch where not very adequate tools were distributed. Work then began even though the ground was still frozen, the sun only just beginning to rise. John worked in a team of three; they took turns in using the shovel, the pick and the wheelbarrow, but John found all three difficult: the jarring of the pick hurt his wrists, the shovel strained his back, and when he struggled up the make-shift ramp to the rackety lorry to tip his first barrow, it took on a life of its own, twisting when he least expected it, throwing him down to the ground and hitting him in the face with one of its handles. Fortunately, there was no guard nearby to beat him while he tidied up the mess. He found that the shovel caused him the fewest problems because when it was his turn to use it, the man on the pick, the biggest of the three, was able to loosen lots of earth, so there was plenty to get the shovel into. However, you did get respite as only one of the team could work at a time. This, on the other hand, became a problem if a guard came by and more than once in the day John was struck on the arm with a truncheon and told to 'work, you idle bastard' as he waited either to get to use the spade or for the barrow to be filled.

The day was endless and John felt not only tired but also ill. He dearly wanted to sit down, but quite early in the day he saw what happened to prisoners who tried it. He watched the sun's progress across the sky as never before, trying to work out the time. At what seemed about mid-day work stopped for half an hour and they were each given half a turnip to munch, but you had to clean hardened earth off it first. Water was provided, but this you obtained by scooping an old tin can into a not very clean container of brackish-looking water. In the afternoon John felt even sicker and his head ached, but he had to carry on even though he now seemed to be almost in a trance and merely going through the motions of working.

If anything, the return journey was worse than the outward one: he was so tired and his feet hurt dreadfully. Though he wanted to climb into his bunk and sleep, and though he felt nauseous, he knew he had to eat. He got his discoloured mess tin and his bent spoon from under the bundle of old paper that served as his pillow and joined the shambling queue of prisoners processing towards the trolley where a fat, dyspeptic harridan dished out watery gruel and a piece of cardboard-like bread. John had to force himself to eat, whereas others devoured their meagre ration quickly. Several stood around his bunk watching him eat slowly and one even picked up crumbs that he had dropped. He fell asleep soon after eating but woke with griping pains in his stomach. He almost defecated where he lay, but he struggled to the revoltingly smelly latrines just in time. When he got back to his bunk he could not sleep. He then became overwhelmed with the blackest despair: this could go on forever, he thought. He had not been given a fixed term sentence. He would stay here till he died — or 'it' ended! What ended? He did not even know why he was in the camp.

Then he heard Ambrose say his name and he felt the monk's hands taking off the helmet. John felt intense relief … and yet the gloom stayed with him.

"How was it?"

"Awful."

"I did try to warn you."

"Yes, I know. But that despair at the end … How on earth can this electronic paraphernalia produce that?"

"Ah well, I don't know precisely how it's done but I'm reliably informed that it employs actual electrical pulses from the brain of someone suffering from serious clinical depression."

"Well, I found it all harrowing, but that last part — and the incipient dysentery — was the worst."

"Well, now you have some inkling of what people suffered — and remember that this is what happened as we slid into the Dark Times. Worse was to come."

"So where and when was this supposed reality set?"

"Oh, there's very little suppose about it: it's based on real experiences."

"OK. But when?"

Ambrose looked again at the cassette and said, "Er …it's England … towards the end of the third millennium."

"That's difficult to imagine!"

"It's true! It would be in, let me see now … probably the Marlborough Dictatorship … that's when there was an attempt to restore your country to those who were supposed to have 'pure' Anglo-Saxon blood. Did you see lots of brown or black people in the camp?"

"Come to think of it, yes I did, but the person who seemed to take me over was white."

"Then he must have been a dissident: probably someone who stood up to the regime. But you saw what happened — standards got worse and worse as political expediency took over and individual human rights were forgotten."

They went to lunch and once more John was glad that it was a silent meal because he could not get the sense of depression out of his mind and he did not want to talk to anybody. Ambrose rejoined him after they had eaten and said they should not continue with the submersion until the next day. Experience over the years had shown that it was better to limit exposure to the horrors of the Dark Times to one session per day.

Nevertheless, over the next week John experienced the terror of blanket bombing; the deprivations of a nuclear winter; the hunger and thirst of desertification; and an experience that he found even more difficult to cope with — torture, something that he had always been afraid of, but thought he ought to face.

Martin considered himself as a humble technician. Political activity was not for him: it was too dangerous and he only wanted to look after his wife and children as best he could. It was difficult to survive, but they did — just. He knew that life was as hard for her as it was for him because she had to spend long weary hours queuing for food every day, often with little success, and she had to be obsequious to people she really despised. He, on the other hand, did not have to endure the hungry accusing looks of the children because for twelve hours every nine days out of ten he was in the workshop. The job was tedious as well as intricate and rubber gloves on cold hands and fingers meant there could be mistakes and so docked wages. He was unsure of the morality of the work: he suspected that he was producing electronic control mechanisms for instruments of torture. Never mind. Keep your head down. Don't ask questions. Draw your wages — docked or not — and say nothing. Look forward to each Quinling Day, when you could stay at home, when, at least on that day, there would probably be enough food to keep the kids from whining. Enjoy the few rewards as much as possible. Hope there would be no bombs.

Then one Halberd (the last of the nine days), there were no wages. No wages! He was not the only one to protest, but Drury had come out of his sanctum and scowled at them with his heavy brows, sleeked back, pitch black hair and widow's peak: that had been enough. However, matters were even worse than he expected, because when he got home his wife told him tearfully that she had been able to find only cabbage to eat though she had traipsed through the town all day: there was a rumour that there would be a real famine. The children began to cry.

After they had finished their thin cabbage soup and, still hungry and disgruntled, were sitting around the rapidly cooling stove, a knock came at the door. It was a neighbour, who whispered,"There'll be a meeting on the roof tonight of those who think something ought to be done."

"Done about what?"

"Have you been asleep all day?" angrily. "About the wages and the food shortage!"

"Well, what can be done?" hopelessly.

"Come to the meeting and find out!" and he strode off.

He was afraid to go, but his wife said he should. Perhaps somebody did have some ideas on what to do. And even when he had reminded her of the secret police and their informers, she still insisted. So he went — as furtively as he could — and he stayed for the whole meeting, even though there was only a handful of people there. However, as he knew all of them, and some who were even more timid than he, he grew more confident. There was no call for revolution and not even a revolt, but what the invited 'expert', in his incongruous leather jacket, was suggesting was that they should establish contact with like-minded people in other communes either by stealing a computer or making one of their own to do this. Unfortunately, most people thought this might be too difficult or too risky. Messages could be so easily intercepted. However, the expert always seemed to have ready answers to their objections and said he would teach them a secret code, which would enable them to talk to other dissidents without any suspicion. So, it was decided that a computer should be built even though this meant that risks would have to be taken, because the various parts would have to be stolen from the state workshops and bureaux in which they were employed.

He had agreed to help: small electronic components could easily be concealed, or so he thought. On the very first occasion, when he had screwed up his courage enough to take the chance and tried to smuggle stuff out of the workshop, he was searched and it was discovered. He was told that he would be taken to police headquarters — but just for a routine enquiry — there was no need to inform his family. However, the journey in the large car was longer than he expected, and instead of going down town, they seemed to be driving out into the country. He was already sweating with apprehension when he and the two plain clothes police mounted the steps of a large country house and entered an atrium dominated by a huge picture of Quinling (the shit, Martin thought). As he was taken into an interrogation room he noticed, down the corridor, the back of someone in a leather jacket, which he was certain he had seen before. This person was smoking and talking in a casual way to someone inside an office.

The first interview was friendly enough to begin with and he was even offered a cigarette, a good one too, with real tobacco. The tiny components he had stolen were put on the table before him and he was asked to explain what they were doing in the turn-up of his trousers. He maintained that they must have fallen there by accident.

It was suggested to him that he had therefore been careless in how he had handled precious government property. Perhaps that was true, but it was cold in the workshop and his rubber gloves ...But he had been properly trained, hadn't he? And so it went on, over and over again until a big man who had been sitting partly in shadow came and stood next to him. Then he sat down, smiling affably. A few minutes later, half way through a reply to a repeated question, this man suddenly struck him violently on the ear, knocking him to the ground. As he struggled to his feet, dazed and bewildered, this man yelled at him, "Stop telling such bloody lies and tell us why you stole the parts!"

Too stunned to reply, he stood, bent as an old man, feeling sick.

"Take him to the cells; let him think about it for a while."

He was then pushed roughly along the corridor, down slimy steps into a damp passage and shoved into a cell that had no window but a bright, single electric bulb, the light from which showed the remains on the floor of vomit, excrement and blood. There was no furniture. Though he felt ill and indescribably weary he could not bring himself to sit on that terrible floor. At first, he leaned against the wall and knew that he had never, ever felt so frightened. His legs grew so tired they ached.

Crouching down with his back to the wall he tried not to think of what might happen to him, but his mind kept returning to rumours he had heard about how the secret police treated their victims: stories about electrodes on genitals, heads being plunged into baths of excrement, and electric soldering irons on faces. He began to shudder and shake and not only because it was cold and damp. He heard footsteps outside in the passage and almost stopped breathing at the thought that guards were coming for him, but the footsteps were quite slow and he could hear the sounds of something being dragged along. After the footsteps halted he heard a door being slammed shut and then what seemed like another being opened. This was followed by pleading from a whining voice, "Please, no, no. I don't know anything. I don't know the man! Oh, please don't do those things to me again. Please, no, no ..." and the voice faded as the hapless creature was dragged up the stairs. Then they came for him.

He was taken into a room, which was very hot. Two men stripped to the waist stood grinning at him, their livid white skins shining with sweat. The smaller, more wiry of the two said to the guards, "Sit our dear friend in that chair ...No, friend, don't get too comfortable: we have some questions we want to ask you, haven't we?"

The second one, a really burly one, slowly walked towards the chair, bent to put his face so close to Martin that he could smell the garlic on his breath and shouted, "And we expect the truth, do you hear?"

He was already breathing so fast and heavily that he thought he might hyperventilate, but the wiry man said in a pretend calm voice, "Just relax. We only want the truth, and if you tell us what you know, we won't use the hot irons on you ...Oh, just show him, Bill."

Bill went over to a brazier, and putting on a thick glove pulled a steel needle, glowing white, from coals and said, "Can't I push this down his finger nail before you ask him? Just to soften him up a bit."

"Oh, there's no need for that yet. Martin will tell us, I'm sure …You see, Martin, we just want to know the names of the people at the meeting the other night, and, of course, why you've been pinching government property."

"But I haven't been pin …Aaah!" and he felt a searing pain on his arm where Bill had placed the needle.

"Now you see what happens when you tell lies?"

Then Bill yelled, "Now tell us or this one goes up your arse!" And he pulled a poker out of the fire.

He told them all the names and about the plan to make the computer. They listened to him attentively, the wiry one smiling and Bill frowning.

When he had finished, Bill said, "Now that's very good, but you see, Martin, now it's all over we have to put you in the same cell as your friends. And some of them were very slow to tell us the truth. Now you wouldn't want them to think you a coward who told us more than he had to, would you? So, I think it would be best if I put a few marks on you …Now, now, now, it's no good objecting. It's for your own good."

By the time Bill had put the second burn on his face, Martin had lost consciousness. When he came round he was in a crowded cell of dejected men and women. He could not recognise his disfigured neighbours until one of them crawled across to speak to him and told him that this was where they put those who were to be executed.

He found Ambrose looking at him quite anxiously when the helmet was taken off.

"You were struggling a lot during the last few minutes of that. Are you all right?"

"Er, no. I don't think I'll ever be the same again … That one was worse than all the others," and he looked at his arm to see if it had the marks of the burn.

"Oh, well. If that's the case we could perhaps make that do … or at least give you a rest from it."

However, the very next day when they were discussing changing attitudes to women and when John was querying the sense of having absolute equality, Ambrose mentioned submersion experiences that dealt with female horrors. Because the argument had become fairly vehement, and out of bravado as much as anything else, John had said he would like to try one.

Jemima crouched in the few blighted bushes, which lay away from the road on the other side of a ditch, and hoped that the rebel soldiers would pass her and her baby by. Though she had had little to eat or drink that day, there still seemed to be enough

*milk in her breasts to satisfy the six-month-old Philippa, and now she was asleep.
Jemima watched the road anxiously. It looked as though she could stay hidden from
the scruffy soldiers, but the last of them stopped to urinate in the ditch. Jemima
looked away: the only man she had ever seen was her husband. She now thought
about him and felt even more helpless and defenceless, because she had no idea
where he was. Just as the man was about to finish, Philippa began to squirm in her
arms. She watched in horror as the child's bottom lip stuck out: she was going to cry
and Jemima even wondered about putting her hand over the baby's mouth, but
couldn't. Then the little face relaxed again; the man had fastened up his trousers
and she was about to relax a little when the child wailed. As though the cry were a
shot from a starting gun, Jemima took off across the scrub. The startled soldier
called out, "Stop, or I'll fire!"*

*But she ran on, clutching her howling baby tightly. He did fire, but not directly
at her. The shot hit the ground behind her throwing up a shower of grit, which
struck her legs painfully. She fell into the dust and only just managed not to squash
the child beneath her. Before long, as she squatted on the ground, she was
surrounded by the whole troop, brought back by the sound of the shot. One of them,
who could have been a leader, stepped forward.*

"Well, you're the lucky one, Silas. You found her, so you can have the first shag."

*She drew her legs up tight to her body, held Philippa more closely and began to
cry.*

*"You can stop that, you cow. We know you country girls like it, so that's what
you're gonna get."*

*One of them dragged the baby from her and two others tore off her clothes and
pulled her legs apart. Her screams and the wailing of the child had no effect on these
beasts who were by now driven crazy by their all-consuming lust. Because her
attention was on Philippa, she was hardly aware at first of the approach of Silas
until he had pushed himself brutally inside her, the pain made worse by her vain
attempt to keep herself closed. Her screams became even more desperate when she
saw that the other soldiers were throwing her baby from one to another. One of them
ran off some distance with her and, shouting something incoherent, kicked the child
high into the air and back to his buddies. This then became the game, and after a
while the infant became just a silent bundle of bloody, fluttering rags. Jemima could
not believe this was happening: it had to be a nightmare! Why can't I wake up, she
thought. Or why can't I faint if this is real. Or die. She became completely passive.
She was hardly aware of what they did to her, each in turn. That is until the very
last one who, even through her numbness and terror, she saw was a mere boy. He at
least was gentle, but to her horror, despite the terrible pain in her loins and her
stomach, she felt just the slightest hint of pleasure.*

It was at this point that John's character began to assert itself. It was not
Jemima lying in the dust, suffocating under the weight of this unwashed,
acrid-smelling youth, but him. He was trapped. Trapped! He thought, this is

what it is like to go mad, to be paralysed, to be locked into your own prison of a body, and he struggled to throw the lad off.

Then Jemima took over again. The boy lay beside her, whimpering. The others gathered round her as she lay. One of them dropped Philippa's lifeless body on to her and said, "You can have your little bastard back now."

She held the little body close and rocked backwards and forwards with her and wept bitterly. The soldiers began to move away and then one of them said to the leader, "Eh, boss. What are we gonna do if we want a shag tomorrow?"

They stopped on the road and looked at her. He said, "OK then. You'd better bring her with us. Get her."

Two of them pulled her roughly to her feet, still weeping, still holding her dead daughter. The boss said, "You can leave that carcase there."

"Oh no! Oh no!" she screamed, "at least let me bury her!"

"Bury her? Why? The jackals will tidy up the mess."

As the body of the child was hurled into the bushes, John became aware of Ambrose touching his arm. As he helped John to get the helmet off he said, "You struggled even more than last time."

"My God, Ambrose, that was revolting … I began to come to myself at one point near the end … I feel as though I've been violated … But you know, all this has happened right through time. And I've only just realised how ghastly it is for women."

"But do you also realise why we use these techniques?"

"I can see that they would be effective, but it still seems like brainwashing — or worse still, aversion therapy."

"Oh, John, don't you see? It's no good just telling people about the horrors we are trying to avoid; they have to experience them."

"Look, Ambrose, I can see that, but how do you know what the effect will be — some people might like the experiences, so how can you be certain of the effects?"

Ambrose thought for a while and then said, "Well, of course, you can never be absolutely certain. On the other hand, we do have considerable evidence of the effects. The ones you are afraid of certainly occurred with some criminals on whom the techniques were tried long ago. That's why we never force people to undergo the experiences. You also have to know that people are psychologically stable as well as willing. And, as I've pointed out to you before, they are part of a well tried education programme for older children only."

John sighed by way of reluctant acceptance.

Chapter XIV

Ambrose and John agreed that not much more could be done, so over the next couple of days they tried to tie up the ends as far as this was possible and John let Marianne and George-Louis know that he would soon be back at Blists Hill. Just before he made his final farewells to all the friends he had made in the monastery, he was surprised to receive an invitation from Abigail and Bernard to visit them in the Soar Valley, where they were about to begin work with a new group of children.

His journey back was uneventful, but when he got to his 1940s house he was surprised to find Marianne already there; they greeted each other warmly. Then she made him some instant coffee and when they were sitting in his living room, she asked him what he thought about teaching in a local college.

"But what would I teach?"

"What did you teach before?"

"When I was a probationary teacher I taught history — to all forms, from the eleven-year-olds upwards. And as the total course was organised on a strictly chronological basis, that meant everything from the ancient Sumerians, Egyptians and Greeks up to the causes of the Third World War. The trouble is that I know the ancient history, say, only to the level required of an eleven-year-old — except for odd bits that I've read about since out of interest."

"What about later on? I thought you said you taught at a higher level."

"I did, but only part-time — and that was fairly specialised: it was the history of industrialisation, with special reference to education. And about the same time I was teaching senior forms in school. That was general twentieth and early twenty-first century."

"Well, could you teach any of that?"

"I suppose so, but I'm sure you use very different methods now. Ambrose had me using all sorts of electronic gear to research what I needed to know, so I assume there would be more of that. Anyway, what's this all this about?"

"Oh, the group from the hospital that interviewed you in those early days after your arrival met and asked me what was happening. Radah — do you remember him?"

"Yes, I remember him … He grilled me more than the others."

"Well, he has only your interests at heart and he suggested that if you did decide to come back here, after St Adrienne's, it might be best if you had some sort of position. He wondered if through your experience of teaching history something could be sorted. And as one of the people you saw at that time organises history in the college, you should perhaps talk it over with her."

"That sounds like a good idea — but I really would have to have a long talk with her about methods … and I'd need time to prepare. That's if we agreed I should teach."

The next day John made his way to the college in Ironbridge, carefully following Marianne's instructions because, as she had explained, a stranger would have difficulty knowing where the other facilities ended and the college began. Though he felt very self-conscious, he kept reminding himself that he did not look noticeably different from the people around him, and that he knew enough about life in the fifth millennium to bluff his way through any chance encounter. Not that he expected there to be one: nobody took much notice of him, and everyone seemed very relaxed. Indeed, the easy pace at which most people seemed to lead their lives, though it still surprised him, was very useful on this occasion because he could take his time, look around, make sure he was going in the right direction and also savour the taste — the feel — of life in 4058.

Only the bridge itself and the wharfage, as it was called in his day, were the same. There was no market square and no Tontine, as he seemed to remember the hotel/pub had been called. However, there were shops of every description, but they all seemed to be small — at least from their fronts, which was all that could be seen of most of them. How far back they ran into the hillside he did not know, but he suspected not very far because there was an arcade that also ran into the hillside, and in this the shop and café fronts were small too. Down this he made his way, as Marianne had said he should, and found he had come into an amazingly large atrium, which, when he looked up, he realised was surmounted by a huge dome that he took to be made of glass or some modern safer equivalent. At first, he thought he was in the most elegant shopping mall he had ever seen. And there was so much greenery: shrubs, flowers and trees everywhere on each of the four wide balconies. Then he saw that there were no shops. This was where people worked.

There were stairs, escalators and lifts going up to the various levels. As he was early, he decided to go up a floor at a time so that he could look at everything. Though there were no notices on any of the doors, he could get a good idea of what was going on inside the different sections because they all had glass fronts. One he took to be a library because it had what looked like books, another he thought must be some sort of information centre. Yet another seemed to be a drawing office of some kind. However, most places were like offices and several had what could be reception desks. There was also, on the second floor, a large café, or maybe it was a restaurant. Another area looked just like an old-fashioned post office, but next to it was what had to be a machine shop, though he could not tell what kind of work was going on in it. There was even a gym and a swimming pool, as well as an auditorium — or would you say it was a theatre? He realised he was in the very heart of the community.

As he made his way up the escalator to the top floor where he knew he would find an entrance to the college, he recognised a woman who was coming down the other way carrying a small child. He smiled at her and saw that she recognised him too.

"Ah, Mr More … Myrna Strashevska!" she said as she went by, "Just wait for me at the top. I'll be with you in a minute."

He watched her descend to the next floor and there she met a man to whom she passed the baby. She gave him a quick peck of a kiss and then ran to the up escalator, talking over her shoulder to him as she went. She seemed to be the only person in a hurry. When she joined John at the top, she explained that normally this would be her day for looking after the baby, but today her husband would look after him while she talked to John.

They made their way to a very ordinary-looking swing door and down a corridor lined with what seemed to be seminar rooms: there were small groups meeting in each of them. However, as John looked through the clear glass partitions he noticed that many of the people in them were adult.

"Would you like a coffee?"

"Oh, yes please."

"We can get one on our way to my room."

As they waited at the dispenser she said, "So you found us OK? Marianne no doubt gave you good directions: you need them if you have never been here before. There are so many things going on because it is the centre … and there are no nameplates. No one needs them: everybody knows where everything is. And everyone uses the facilities all the time."

"I didn't mind really, and I could see into all the offices to get an idea of what was going on."

Once in her comfortable study they got down to business straight away. It soon became clear that he could become a useful member of the teaching staff: she was impressed with his knowledge, especially as they decided early in the discussion that he need not cover anything after the Third

World War, which was now part of what was called the Middle Period. Anything before that was referred to as Ancient History.

"Of course, you'd have to make reference to the Dark Times and you'd have to show how the period you are covering in some way contained the seeds of later development."

"I can see that, but don't we, as historians, have to be careful not to be too Whiggish?"

"Whiggish? You'll have to remind me of the meaning of that."

"Sorry, I'm afraid that some of my expressions maybe sound antiquated. I had the same difficulty over this with Ambrose Ryan. I'll have to be careful. It means seeing history as a natural progression towards the present, which in its turn is seen as the best of all possible worlds."

"Well, it's not difficult to see why some people nowadays might think that."

"Then beware, because Whiggish attitudes prevailed in parts of Europe during that optimistic period before the First World War. By 1918 they had given way to pessimism."

"The implication being that even now we could still decline into chaos again?"

"I suppose so."

"Then, there's a motive for teaching the history well."

"Yes, and for getting it right — warts and all, even if they are embarrassing to any lesson we might want the history to serve."

"You sound a little sceptical. Do you really want to teach history in this college, given what I assume you now know about our general aims of education?"

"Oh yes, the history I did with Ambrose Ryan was very good — as history — and it was educative in the way history ought to be. Do you know his book, by the way?"

"Which one?"

"The one on the rise and fall of empires is the only one I've read."

"Yes, we do use it from time to time."

"Thinking about Ambrose reminds me. He and I had lots of arguments about conditioning, and now that I think about it, it seems to me that my worries stemmed from the use of evidence in the various electronic media you use nowadays."

"Why should that be? Surely any form is open to distortion."

"Agreed, but in my day there was a lot of tampering with films and videos, and especially photographs. So I'm very wary of these and tend to want to go for documentary evidence whenever I can. And I like to make sure there's variety."

Myrna clearly saw this as a serious point and she thought for a while before she answered. Then she said, "I understand your concerns, but I think you'll agree that, in the first place, it is difficult to get it right — but we have tried very hard over the years to avoid the kind of problems you refer to. The academic checks and balances are as strong as ever they were. Also, our students have worked in all these media since their early days. They know how things can be tampered with. So we use a variety of sources and you can rest assured that documentary evidence is important ... Look, I've got a group to see in a few minutes. They've been looking at industrial relations in twentieth century Britain. You can see how we work if you like, and the very point you have made will be part of our discussion." Despite a sudden surge of apprehension, John agreed.

The group, which included one or two older students, was small, but what became obvious quite quickly was that they were already acquainted with the salient facts, probably from reading a good textbook. So John felt wary even though he himself had direct experience of life only half a century after the events they were looking at. Myrna did a rapid review of earlier work on a period when unions had been portrayed, though not necessarily accurately, as over-mighty, and then went on to show how this had helped to bring about a change of government to one that was determined to challenge the unions. She pinpointed a strike by miners. (John had read about it, but he could also remember having heard people talk about it.) She said that this was the crucial event and then asked the students to assemble evidence to show why. She gave them all sorts of facsimiles of documents: from cabinet papers to newspaper reports to diaries and other comments from contemporaries. Then there were videos and audiotapes of newscasts. She used excerpts from these to illustrate her claims and, probably for John's sake, drew attention to how some of the television broadcasts in particular had been tampered with. However, she also asked them to think about why this had been done and to consider the sort of effects it might have had. The students then organised themselves: it became a co-operative effort, and in pairs they began to sift through all the information that they had been given. Myrna and John moved from pair to pair giving help and advice wherever they might be needed — he could hear that the questions she was putting to them were quite open, even Socratic, and he made a mental note of this. When it was time to go to lunch she called them together and negotiated a date when they could meet again to discuss what they had discovered. They could then also agree a time for the presentation they would do on this topic. However, what impressed John was that she gave them yet more library and information centre reference numbers so they could look for more evidence, which, she said, might challenge the line she had put so tentatively. Then they all went to lunch together.

In the afternoon Myrna showed him their resources centre and how to access the material he would need. They then went through the period of history he would teach and they even worked out a timetable. This was not straightforward because his work in the fields had to be taken into account, and to some extent this was an unknown quantity, if only because of the vagaries of the weather (and some of his work time was sure to be in food production). So they agreed that the final details of all this could be worked out when he met the students later because they would have other commitments too. This, she said, was normal. When he expressed concern about this, because he remembered how some of his twenty-first century students would have used such a situation to avoid lectures or seminars, she assured him that he would find that the first priority of these students would be their education.

John then mentioned the invitation he had had from Bernard and Abigail to visit them in the Soar Valley. If he did this before Christmas it would take up some of his preparation time and he knew he would have to prepare even more carefully than usual. Then there was the question of access to the material he would need. He said he knew that books were still used and he could take some with him, but his real concern was the electronic stuff that he needed to familiarise himself with, especially as some of it, he knew, would be in forms he had never used before.

"Well, books are no problem; we can pick some up today. How soon will you go?"

"To make it worthwhile, within the next couple of days."

"Then there is no problem: you can look through the relevant stuff before you go — and I'll give you all the help I can so that you know what to ask for on the Internet to use while you are there."

"Will I be able to access it there?"

She stared at him and then she smiled, put her hand on his arm and said, "Do you know, as we've been talking here today, I'd forgotten where you came from until you asked me that question. Of course you can get at the material anywhere in the world, and I'd even say anywhere in the universe if there's a means of retrieval."

Armed with a number of textbooks, John made his way back to his museum house. As he walked he wondered about means of transport: there were trains and the little taxis he and Sanjit had used; there were buses (and jaunting cars — in Eire), but what else, he wondered. Everyone walked or cycled, it seemed. Now, that did not bother him: the leg he had broken gave him very little trouble anymore and the geographical extent of this whole community was not so great. Moreover, the distances did not seem as far as they had when he was a boy and had to walk from Jackfield to Ironbridge to go to school. But what about old people? They must have difficulties, especially as some of the roads were quite hilly. At this point he happened to be trudging up what he knew as Dabley Lane, and because it was steep and he felt warm, he had not noticed the increasing autumn chill in the air.

His preoccupation with the means of transport meant that he had not thought about his destination either, until he had opened his front door and breathed in the authentic cold, damp atmosphere of his forties house. In true Proustian fashion he remembered his childhood — times when the family had arrived home to find the fire out. There would always be the smell of coal dust, which, paradoxically, was stronger when the house was cold. He plugged in an ancient single bar electric heater and sat on the settee in his living room and felt sorry for himself: to be marooned in the future with none of its advanced technological comforts and to be stuck in a cold, damp house was depressing. He refused to think of Marianne and George-Louis and wallowed in his misery. He recalled a cold attic flat in which he had once lived in London, before he had met Dorothea, where the cost of lighting the gas fire for a whole evening had meant that it was cheaper to go to the cinema. Do they have cinemas now, he wondered?

There was a knock on the door: it was Marianne and her son. She wanted to know what had happened in his interview, but once she was inside and experienced the chill, she immediately asked John if he would like to eat with them that evening. He accepted the invitation only too willingly, but then said that, surprisingly, he did not know how to get to their house. It was then agreed that they should go straight away.

As they made their way the short distance to what he knew as the Lloyds, John told her about the day's events and how he was now set to teach history in the college. He also mentioned the invitation he had had from Abigail and was gratified to notice that she frowned when he said he was going in two days time.

"It will be only for a couple of weeks, if that. And I'll have a much better idea of how the education of younger children works before I begin my teaching."

She and George-Louis knew that this made sense, but the boy spoke for his mother when he said, "But you've only just got back."

"I know, but it's an opportunity I can't miss, and I will be back again well before Christmas."

"But you said you would take us to Yorkshire," said George-Louis.

"Well, there's nothing to stop us doing that, but I think your mummy might like it better when the weather is warmer — what would it be like if the house was the same as the one in Erin?"

"Oh no, I don't think I'd like that," shivered Marianne, "and your house here is bad enough, even today — and it's not that cold yet. Thank goodness we've got a warm home to go to."

They had arrived. It was a house with two very large ground floor windows either side of a heavy oak door, and three windows up above. As with other houses, most of the living quarters were underground: cut into the hillside, so to speak, and obscured by the impressive frontage. When they entered a wide windowless lobby with a tiled floor, the lights came on and John noticed that the atmosphere was pleasant — not too hot and certainly not dry and prickly as he had found air-conditioned buildings in his own time. They hung their topcoats on hangers and shook off their shoes into a boot rack.

"What time would you like to eat?" said Marianne.

"What time do you usually eat?"

"About six o'clock, to fit with George-Louis' bed-time, but we can leave it a bit later if you like."

"OK, whatever suits you."

Then George-Louis said, "But I'm hungry now."

"But you always are … Let's have a drink and a biscuit now … Then you can show John around the house while I cook something."

So for the next twenty minutes they sat in very comfortable armchairs in Marianne's sitting room. It seemed very spacious to John. It was also very light, not just because of the large window, but also because of the light oak woodblock floor and the delicate pastel colouring of the walls. There was not a great deal of furniture but what there was, was low and expensive looking. There was a large communicator in one corner.

Once they had finished their snack, George-Louis was impatient to show John around because he knew his favourite programme would soon be on. John was glad, because, though he wanted to see around the house, he disliked guided tours. He knew that this one would be quick. Everywhere was as he expected it, really: living and sleeping arrangements were not that different, except that everything appeared opulent to him. What was interesting was George-Louis' suite of rooms at the very top of the house: he had a bedroom, a workroom or study and a playroom. It was in this last that John saw the elegant spiral staircase.

"Where does that go?"

"Out into the garden. Do you want to look? Haven't you got one in your real home?"

"Err … no … I'm afraid I haven't?"

"Look, I'll show you," and he ran up the stairs and pressed a switch that opened an airlock.

John followed him into this circular, small room. The opening they had just used closed and then silently another slid open in the wall. They walked up a set of steps and emerged in a roof garden. What struck John immediately were the three structures at its centre. They looked like even taller and wider versions of the chimneys he had seen many years before on the Pedrera in Barcelona, whose decorated cowls always reminded him of the robot soldiers in the Star Wars series — old films that had been repeated endlessly on TV in his day. However, he knew these could not be chimneys in the ordinary sense. They must have been for ventilation, and he surmised that each of the three probably had a different purpose, but he could not ask George-Louis to explain any of this. The garden sloped gently down towards the hillside and he realised that the front of the house was much taller than the rear, which led him to suppose that maybe the back section of the structure contained only the machinery that kept the house heated, ventilated and lit. The boy ran down to the very bottom of the garden through a small orchard to a well-used lawn where he began to dribble a football about. John joined him, and as they kicked the ball to each other, he noticed that there was a vegetable garden too. As he looked back up the garden towards the beautifully constructed ventilating shafts he could see three grills set in the bank and wondered if these were the outlet points of what he was sure was a complex system of air conditioning. However, he could have been mistaken about the whole lay-out because when George-Louis remembered the programme he wanted to see and took John down a set of almost hidden steps into a back door to the house, he found there was much more to it underground than he expected.

When they were eating their evening meal Marianne asked John if he wanted to continue living in the museum.

"Not really: it's not very comfortable now that the autumn is setting in … But where else can I live?"

"Oh, there are apartments about the place but …"

George-Louis interrupted.

"He could live in our grandad flat." He paused and then said quietly, "Couldn't he, Mummy?"

"That's what I was going to suggest."

"Where is it?" said John. "I didn't notice it in our grand tour."

"You wouldn't see it the way George-Louis took you. It's sort of at the side … but it's got its own outside door and is completely self-contained, though there is a passage that links with the main house. My father uses it when he comes to stay. I'll show you later and you can see what you think."

"But what if he wants to visit you?"

"Oh, we have enough room for him here … and I'm sure he won't mind."

After they had finished their meal all three went to the grandad flat. It was very much more comfortable than the forties house and once more John was struck by what appeared to him as the sumptuousness of the place — it made him realise how difficult it had been for Marianne and George-Louis in the house in Erin. The only aspect he did not like was that only the living room had windows and they were rather small. However, the flat had everything he needed and he was particularly pleased with the large study — and all its electronic equipment. Later, when George-Louis had gone to bed and they were relaxing in Marianne's elegant sitting room John asked if all the houses in the commune were as luxurious as hers.

"I wouldn't say this was luxurious."

"Well, it is to me … Are they similar, then? Do they have the same facilities? And the same kind of furniture and decoration?"

"More or less, I think. Or the ones I know of do … and those other than my friends' that I've been in seem to be like this. The furniture is different, of course, but that depends on what people like."

"But you'd say that the standard is similar?"

"Oh, probably. I should think that most of the furniture would be made here in the commune … unless people come from outside, and then they'd bring their own, wouldn't they?"

"Do many come from outside, then?"

"Not very many."

"Why not?"

"Why should they? Most people want to stay in their own community."

"Then why should anyone ever come?"

"Oh, I don't know really — perhaps for a job … or to be with someone they love …" she smiled shyly and then added, "… for lots of reasons."

"I would have thought that you never needed to advertise a job: there'd be people here already who could do any of the jobs that needed to be done."

"Well, mostly that's the case, but sometimes you need a specialist."

"But I thought everybody can do everything in the super-organised fifth millennium."

"Oh, John, that's silly. Sometimes you need an expert — er, like our community treasurer. He came from Apulia."

"But from all the stuff I did with Ambrose, I thought you all believed that experts are dangerous."

"Why?!"

"Because they can use their expertise to gain control."

"I suppose that could be true in a way. But our treasurer could never do that!"

"But how can you be sure?"

"Well, for one thing, he's not like that, and for another, he works with a committee who know about finance."

"But couldn't he and that committee take control?"

"Oh, no!"

"Why not?"

"Because anyone can scrutinise the accounts — and lots of people do."

"And do they understand them?"

"Of course they do: it's all part of what we learn when we are young. And everybody knows everybody. I know the treasurer very well because he comes to clean in the hospital. You have to remember that nobody ever has only one job — and we all have to share the really unpleasant ones."

"Like what?" said John warily.

"Oh, there are all sorts. But the one I like least is cleaning up the old and incontinent."

Later, when he thought about this, John decided he wouldn't like this either, and as he made his way back to his cold, damp house, he hoped he would never be asked to. However, he also wondered what other unpleasant jobs there could be.

The next day he moved his few possessions into the grandad flat and began gathering the sources of information he needed to take with him to the Soar Valley. Two days later, Marianne went with him to the station to see him off. Her farewell made him wish he were not going.

Chapter XV

Fortunately, his two weeks with Bernard and Abigail went very quickly because he found their work with the children so stimulating and so very different from the education of young children in his own time. He already had some notion of what it would be like from what he had seen on the visit he had made with Marianne and George-Louis to the Burren.

All that she had said at that time was true: there were no schools as such for children under the age of about sixteen. They, and usually there would be about a dozen of them, met with their teachers wherever it seemed appropriate, and during his fortnight in the Soar valley this meant in the house of Bernard and Abigail. However, they all spent as much time outside as possible because they were investigating the shape of the valley, how it had come into existence and taken on its present form, what it was made of, and what the properties of the materials were from which it was made. Bernard explained how the work done during the two weeks formed the basis of much that was to follow over the next year, when the children would be introduced to science in all its forms, as it would help them to understand not only the geology, but also the climate, the biology and the botany of their immediate surroundings. In this way it was hoped that they would not see science in the old-fashioned sense, i.e. as something dangerous and arcane carried out by strange men (usually) in white coats, but as the ways in which all people not only find out about the reality that lies about them, but learn to deal with it too. Learning, he said, has to begin with the learner and his or her immediate environment and then go out from there to embrace — well, everything! The concepts and skills to be grasped by the child need to be in fairly simple forms to begin with; they can become more complex later. Indeed, they will anyway.

When John homed in on this question of the skills involved (because he remembered how obsessed governments had become with mathematics in particular in the third millennium) Bernard explained that the curriculum he and Abigail were trying to operate would not succeed if the children did not have very good skills in numeracy and literacy. From what John could see, the children did have very good skills, and not only in maths and English: they all seemed to be able to draw and paint, and their information technology skills amazed him. It turned out that they had developed the rudiments of all of these before they ever came to work with Abigail and Bernard. It was not really true to say they had been taught by their parents; they had been taught by their families, in fact by the whole community in which they were growing up.

Further careful probing on his part in the discussions he had with these admirable teachers, when the children had gone home, helped him to understand some of what Marianne had said about bringing up very young children. Not only did adults try to avoid exposing their children to negative experiences, they also tried to sequence what happened to them in ways that encouraged the extensive development of all these skills. On this particular topic he and Abigail had a conversation on the origins of this approach. It went back, she said, even as far as very ancient people like Jan Kominski, but others such as Maria Montessori, who came a little later, were even more important. Nevertheless, it was only with the rapid development of neuroscience that the functioning and growth of the young brain was really understood. Children, he discovered, were much more able than they had been in his day, because their early activities had been tailored to the growth of their intelligence. Though this was alarming, and he was very suspicious of it, he was somewhat mollified to learn that history was central to this curriculum, which Abigail described as 'interrelated' (not 'integrated', he was gratified to hear). History, she said, was like a vertical axis underlying everything that was done. Geography formed the horizontal axis. The pupils then had two co-ordinates to help them come to grips with who and where they were. To these, other co-ordinates could be added. There had to be a mathematical dimension to a human being's understanding of reality, a chemical one, a biological one, etc., etc. The more co-ordinates, the better the grasp of reality. However, they have to be interrelated: the various disciplines are each essential in their own right but they also have to discipline each other. When he interjected the notion that perhaps the disciplines were sometimes incompatible (because he remembered some of the confusion that had been caused by trying to make history 'scientific') she reminded him that Newton's Laws of Motion had once upon a time been taught as though they were handed down from on high and that this had given pupils a false view of science: they needed to know that theories, laws, principles, or what have you, can only ever be provisional. They needed to know more about Newton himself and what an odd man he was and how unjustly he had treated other scientists, Flamsteed, for instance; the history was always important.

And yet John also saw that in some ways education never changes. On one very wet day when they had been scheduled to visit an old slate quarry, they had had to stay in. The day before, they had begun to talk about the weather and it had become clear that some of the younger children had no real notion of air pressure. The older ones asked excitedly if they could see again the old experiment with an oilcan. John realised how good a teacher Abigail was when she organised this. At no point did she actually tell them anything, but she elicited the information from them, and from the younger ones at that, though they had never seen the demonstration before. The collapse of the can was as dramatic as when he, as a pupil, had seen it — two thousand years before!

But what John wanted was an overview of the education of young children so that he would have some notion of what they knew and could do before he had to teach them what he was hoping would be 'specialist' history. So his conversations with Abigail, Bernard and Eva, their daughter, especially in the evenings as they sat in the Pugh's pleasant conservatory, became not only one of the most important parts of his stay but also the most enjoyable — even though there were times when they seemed bemused by his ignorance and what they took to be his naivety. However, he realised that they were serious about the way the old subject barriers were well and truly down. For instance, they seemed not to distinguish too finely between science and technology: they taught what was the most appropriate, what was the most educative aspect at that point, and whether it was theoretical or practical did not seem to matter. When he raised this issue, they said that any necessary distinctions between pure science and technology could be made later when they were needed.

If the part of the landscape to be investigated on a particular day was a fair distance away, the 'school' had its own minibus, i.e. a smaller version of the one John had travelled on in Erin. Bernard was very proud of it and was keen to point out how many kilometres it had travelled. This, he said, was because they had used it when the previous group of children had gone on their study trips to Europa. It turned out that the children would spend six months in a French-speaking area and six in either an Italian, German or Spanish area — or they might go further afield. Wherever they went they would use only the language of that area. Abigail and Bernard both spoke several languages and so could prepare the children to some extent beforehand. The idea was to become as fluent as possible in at least one, and possibly two other languages. Abigail told him very forcibly, when he argued with her, that no one could be described as educated unless they knew at least one other culture from the inside, and that required fluency in the language. This was so important to the communication on which world peace depended.

There were times when it seemed to John that there was simply too much to do, but the children were keen and a great deal more could be done with computers, in the use of which the pupils were very accomplished. He tried working through some of the programs. One he looked at dealt with the weather. Level one was concerned with the weather in the immediate locality, and as he opened it up he saw that Bernard was right: the cross section of the area which John had seen the children make was basic to all the work, because the lie of the land was sufficiently varied to affect rainfall, temperature and pressure levels differently in each of the three distinct geographical areas: the hills in the west, the ridge in the east and the valley in between. The computer graphics not only gave him a sense of almost flying low over the actual terrain, they also allowed him to enter deep into the geology and to orient the whole area in any way he wanted. The data (rainfall, etc.) could be accessed in several different forms but could always be referred back to the apparently three-dimensional image of the area. For the younger children all the concepts were illustrated in the form of moving pictures almost like cartoons. Later programs dealt with weather in the wider region, then the national weather and so on right up to global patterns. After that the science was so advanced that he understood little. Yet Bernard led him to believe that most of the programs were rudimentary: the education of older children, he said, was much more sophisticated. Even so, John was convinced that only a very, very highly intelligent sixteen-year-old could have coped with that final program.

On his last evening with the Pugh family, John got into difficulties. Eva, he thought, had always been suspicious of him: she often looked puzzled when he asked his more naïve questions, but on this occasion she was joined by the others. John had been expatiating on what he considered to be the unnecessary extent and complexity of the curriculum.

"Why do they need all this?" he said.

All three looked surprised and then Eva said, "They wouldn't be educated without it, would they?"

John understood what she meant and, in a way, he agreed with her. However, suddenly his mood became … well, bolshie! Though what he told himself was that he was acting as a devil's advocate — for the purposes of his research, of course.

"So, what is education for? Most of them are never going to need this stuff, are they?"

"Aren't they?" said Bernard.

"No. Most of the work they are going to do as adults doesn't require such a depth of knowledge — except for particular professions, of course … such as … such as … well, look at that final program on the weather, you wouldn't need that unless you were a meteorologist — would you?"

"Where have you been, John? Surely you know education has not been so utilitarian, or … or so instrumental for a long time. At least, not directly," said Abigail.

"You are implying that indirectly it is all relevant to jobs."

"And so it is. In the sense that there are very few jobs that everybody does not know something about. Isn't that as it should be? And anyway, most people can do most jobs."

Then Bernard interposed. "But it isn't to do with just work. How can you function in a society and a polity like that of the present day unless you know and can do all the things we teach …? Remember, many of these children will not go to college until later in life when they sense there's a need for it, but they have to play their full part in society from the day they leave us. In fact, they are already playing a part now. But surely you know all this?"

At this point John realised that he had sown a doubt about himself in their minds. He tried to recover as best he could by saying, "Yes, I understand what you are saying, but I just wanted to hear it all spelt out."

Abigail and Bernard both smiled but Eva did not. She looked unconvinced. Nevertheless, John went on, "Let's explore this a bit further … How can you be sure that the children, once they get to sixteen, are ready to play a full part in their communities?"

Again the others looked at each other in a perplexed way. Then Bernard said, "Well, of course you can't really know … But then you can't be absolutely certain about adults, never mind children. But look at almost any community in the world and you'll see that it functions well enough. They all have their difficulties at times, but that's part of life … To go back to the kids: you do your best and you try to practise what you preach and you let your 'school' run like a democracy, and wherever and whenever you can you encourage your charges to engage in the activities of the commune. And you get the children to work together and you remember that their moral development is as important as anything else — or rather that you can't separate the different aspects. The moral, intellectual, social and, of course, religious are all part and parcel of each other. And what's more, you know that parents, relations, friends, everybody is working with the grain like you."

Despite his experiences at St Adrienne's, John found himself bristling at the word 'religious' because he had not lost his suspicion of it and it was then he blurted, "Oh, but it's all too pat!"

Eva looked shocked. "Too pat? Too pat? It's taken generations to develop education as it now works and you say it's too pat!"

John had not heard anybody speak so vehemently even in his arguments with Ambrose. He had got used to the gentleness that everyone habitually displayed, and so his reply was forgetfully sharp.

"Yes, pat. Nothing nowadays ever seems to go wrong and you are all so smug about it!"

There was a long silence. The two adults looked embarrassed, but Eva did not. Then she said, very quietly but intently, "John, I know Mum and Dad met you at St Adrienne's and that you have come from Ironbridge to visit us, but where were you before that?"

John felt all his strength drain away. He became speechless. Weak. Helpless. He did not know what to do. He tried to look pathetic as he had as a child seeking sympathy: it hadn't worked then and it didn't work now. But he knew that the longer they had to wait for an answer the more suspicious they would become. He realised almost instinctively that he could not tell them the bare truth and yet they were such good people that he felt he would be betraying a trust if he lied profoundly to them. What he did mystified them even more. He asked if they would excuse him for a few minutes while he went outside to think. They could only nod silently and they stared at him almost as if they were seeing him differently. So as he went, he mumbled, "I'm not going outside to invent a story. I want to think of the best way to tell you about me."

He sat at the top of their garden with all kinds of thoughts jockeying for position in his head. Should he tell them that he had had an accident and lost his memory? That he had a disease unknown to science that had affected his brain? That he came from a forgotten tribe long lost in the Amazonian jungle? That he had been on a special mission for many years, looking after people who had serious terminal illnesses? That he had been part of a space mission that had gone wrong? That he had come from another planet? That he had crashed on a remote island without means of communication, but the fruit that he had eaten there had prevented him from aging? Each one of these seemed successively more ridiculous and yet no more crazy than the truth. What plausibly could he say?! Then he hit on an idea he thought might work, though it was risky. He would tell them all these tales along with his real story, but point out that only one of them was the truth, though he would not say which: they could choose for themselves. This is what he did. They accepted his ruse, though they laughed very often at what he had to say and he was sure that Eva accepted none of his explanations. He said he knew that special pleading wouldn't necessarily make them trust him, but he asked for their indulgence anyway, because there were good reasons for the secret to be kept. Finally, he said that he hoped that the stories were so daft that they would not tell anyone — or if they did, he said, he hoped they would not mention his real name. He left the next day assured that they would not.

When he emerged from the station at Jackfield he found Marianne and George-Louis waiting to meet him with a taxi. Marianne 'drove' them back to her house, and though the vehicle almost directed itself, John was glad:

the road was frosty and he wondered about skidding — until he remembered that no part of the vehicle actually made contact with the ground unless it had stopped.

Marianne invited him to dinner, even though she had stocked the flat with food ready for his return. As she and George-Louis regarded this as a special occasion, they had wine from her father's vineyard. John tried to place it but all the names had changed over the two thousand years; finally George-Louis brought a map to show him where the vineyard was and he realised he was probably drinking something like a good Gigondas. When George-Louis had gone off to his room, John told her about his gaffe of the final evening at the Pugh's and his ruse for getting out of the dilemma. Marianne was both amused and concerned.

"What if someone here asks you similar questions?"

"Well, perhaps I should think of a story that I can stick to consistently."

She nodded and then looked thoughtful, "Ought it to be one of the alternatives you offered Bernard and Abigail? There's just a chance they might come here."

"Err … one of the possibilities I half considered, but I left it vague — just in case they pushed me — was that I was on a ship engaged in oceanic research."

"But then someone might ask what your job was?"

"Oh, yes. Mmm … er … What about, then, those huge cargo liners that I've heard about? Have you any idea how long they would be at sea? Would the crew have their families with them? Would there be a need for teachers, for instance?"

"There could be. In fact, I'm sure there is. I seem to remember I've got a biography of someone who worked on one of them. This particular ship plied between America and Australia, and the crew was so big that it ran like a community, so they had schools — I think, but you'll have to check."

"Oh, I will. In fact the whole book sounds useful, if you'll lend it me."

"Of course, but let's hope you never have to use it — it makes it seem as though your whole life is built on a lie."

"Well, isn't it?" Then his face dropped. "Aagh! I've already told Tommy Caulfield that I come from the Wirral! I said that was where I'd arrived from the evening he spoke to me and Sanjit."

"That wouldn't matter, would it? You could say you were born there and went back after working on the liner."

"I suppose he might ask me something about the Wirral: perhaps I ought to go and look at that too."

"Oh, I don't think you need to go there: you can get all the information you need off the Internet."

"Can I? Would it be complete enough?"

"I should think so. There's probably a 'reality' on that too: most of the country is covered, because the children need it. Shall we go and look for it now?"

Once in the study of the grandad flat they did not search for the program. They were otherwise engaged.

So John's real life in the fifth millennium began. But though it was what he had been looking forward to for several months, it was not quite the happy experience he thought it would be.

At first, the only serious problem was the teaching, which he found quite difficult, but in ways he had not expected. The students were deferential — in that they seemed to respect him as an adult and as a teacher — and though he followed the approach he had observed Myra using, he was sure that to them he still appeared too didactic, even though he expressed any views of his own very diffidently. From the looks on their faces he could see that they still seemed doubtful about what he had to say, and on one occasion when he began to feel annoyed with them, he almost said, "I do know what I'm talking about: I was there!" but stopped himself just in time.

He had a conversation with Myra in which he touched on this problem — as obliquely as possible. He tentatively suggested that perhaps at their age they would probably display a certain intellectual arrogance, because they were becoming aware of the own real ability and the extent of their knowledge. However, she seemed puzzled by this suggestion, and from the way the discussion progressed, it became clear to him that the real cause of his difficulty was the way they had been taught in the past: they had learned to question everything and to accept nothing at face value. They were putting to him, though not in so many words, what (ironically) he had always put to students in the past, i.e. where's the evidence? He realised that he had to be an expert not only in the history but also as a facilitator — a word he disliked but now had to accept. He also complained to Marianne that he found he was becoming the sort of po-faced teacher he had never liked. This was, he thought, because he was afraid to joke with the students in case he made a slip.

There was, however, a more serious problem, and one that drew attention to him and led people to wonder about him, where he came from and why he was there, though they always treated him amicably. This was the work he did outside college. His academic work had to fit with that of his students and so he found himself working with them on the land. Unfortunately, it soon became clear that not only was he less experienced than they, he also accepted its tedium less willingly. Marianne, Radah and Myra between then managed to get him into other jobs, but the same problem arose whatever he did, whether it were street cleaning or caring for old people. Finally, the problem was partly solved — almost by chance. One evening he met Tommy Caulfield again and the old chap talked about some work he had just been given thinning out the overgrown tangle in a fair sized neglected coppice, which the community had decided should be brought back into use. John expressed interest in this as something he had never done before. And so he found himself working with this garrulous old man for two days each week. Tommy was a good deal older than he appeared and did less and less of the work, but by then John had learned what to do and continued by himself, but this also contributed to the reputation he had developed in the community for being an odd man out.

This might not have mattered too much, but at meetings (of which, he thought, there were too many) the expectation that he could be awkward became well established. At the beginning he tried very hard to say nothing, but he found that everyone was expected to express a view on nearly everything. Marianne had pointed out to him that he had to say something. Though he understood the rationale behind the notion that no one should leave a meeting feeling that they had not been consulted, or had not had their views considered, the length of some of the meetings irked him and, as he had found in Erin, he became disturbed by what he saw as a lack of chairperson skills. Unfortunately, when it was his turn to chair a meeting, his attempt to demonstrate what he meant caused obvious distress amongst the other members. He began to avoid meetings — though this solved nothing.

But what brought matters to a head was his relationship with George-Louis. He had always found it difficult to strike the right balance. There were times when he thought Marianne should be firmer with the boy, even though it was clear that her gentleness achieved far more than his brusqueness. Intellectually, he accepted this and yet still felt a desire to deal with what he saw as intransigence by a sharp word. Though he avoided this he was sure that the boy could feel John becoming distant from him at times. Then, on occasions when John was silent, because he did not know how else to deal with situations, he knew he appeared even more morose than he felt and once more he experienced a sense of helplessness; as at the cliffs of Moher, he thought he was being blamed for something he could not help, and this made him feel an anger that was difficult to hide.

One afternoon he did explode, in a way that was reminiscent of his early relationship with Marianne. It so happened that they were in the bottom garden and he was showing George-Louis how to half-volley a football. After a while he realised that the lad was trying too hard and he knew from his own experience that sometimes it becomes easier to practise a particular skill if it is beset with other problems, so he tried to persuade him to throw the ball over his shoulder and half-volley it as he turned around. This did not work, but he persevered as gently as he could. It was when Marianne said she thought he was patronising the lad that he slammed the ball down and said, "You bloody teach him then!"

Immediately, he knew that this was a serious blunder: George-Louis looked at him in uncomprehending alarm, but Marianne's face set hard. He found himself wishing he could go back in time and live the moment again, differently. His stumbling attempt at apology did not seem to work, and for once he felt that Marianne was not really trying to help him.

Even several hours later she remained obstinately, so it seemed to him, silent.

Alone in his flat he found he could not work because of the turmoil he was experiencing.

"They're not so sodding perfect!" he thought, and if he had had a cigarette he would have smoked, or if he had had a bottle of vodka handy he would have got drunk. And he wondered how they could all remain so calm all the time. Did no one ever act bonkers? Or maybe lots of them were locked in their private rooms kicking the cat. Actually, he realised, he had never noticed a cat or a dog. At home (agh, there was a Freudian slip) you would see them wandering about by themselves, but now that would be too disorderly, wouldn't it? If Marianne ever spoke to him again, he thought, he must ask her about cats and dogs — and horses, for that matter, which he had only ever seen working in the fields. But why am I thinking about stupid animals when I ought to be trying to figure out how to establish better relations with Marianne and George-Louis? And once more the feeling of helplessness swept over him: he had tried so hard to hold his tongue, to look calm when really he was seething with frustrated emotion, to be like them — and yet his true self had come through to take him and them by surprise, and to spoil something that was essentially good. These are just words, John!!! What are you going to do? He did not know, except that he must try harder. Like school, he thought, and the very mundaneness of the notion consoled him a little. Then, once more as so often in the past, his heart lightened as he heard Marianne's gentle knock on his door. But she did not come straight in and he had to open it to her. She smiled her shyest smile and said, "May I come in?"

"Of course, but why ask?"

"I just wondered ..."

"What did you wonder ..."

She was now in the room and he half expected her to put her arms around him as she usually did. But no ... she seemed wary and serious. She looked around as though she were deciding very carefully where to sit — and finally settled for an ordinary straight-backed chair but perched uncomfortably on the edge of it. He could only stand and look perplexed. Then she said, "John, please sit down. I think we need to have a serious talk."

"Ah, about the way I spoke in the garden?"

"More than that … how you spoke was only part of the problem …"

"Now look, Marianne …"

He had been determined to object to whatever she might say, but then he became aware that she had tears in her eyes and all his annoyance with her vanished; he knelt in front of her as she had once done before him. He put his hands on hers as they rested on her knees and said, "Oh Marianne, I've made you so unhappy. I'm very sorry and I will try hard to control my temper and hold my tongue."

Then she began to cry; sobs that shook her right through. He put his arms around her and held her close and it became quite clear to him that this had not been brought on just by his few sharp words. This was not the Marianne who was always so calm. He whispered to her, "Ssh, ssh, then, sweetheart. Tell me, what is the matter …?"

Only very gradually did she become still and all the time he remained silent. At last, she leaned back from him and for once looked almost ugly because her eyes were raw and her face lined and blotchy. Her nose was runny and her mouth twisted. He handed her his handkerchief, which she used noisily and wetly. In that moment he knew he could never love anyone so much.

"Tell me. Tell me what's the matter."

She went on wiping her face and then tried to speak, but almost began to cry again. He waited as calmly as he could and watched his Marianne re-establish her usual self. When she was ready she said, "There are so many things … but what I want to say first of all, because it's the most important … is that I love you, and really that is why I am so unhappy …"

He could not remain silent at this point, no matter how hard he tried.

"But that makes me so happy. Why should it make …?"

"Darling, don't you see? No, you couldn't … You must listen to me … Something important has happened."

He did not understand what she meant and he simply knelt there open-mouthed.

"What on earth can be so important? To make you so …"

"Radah has had a message from Dr James."

"Dr James? Who is he?" (Even though he knew.)

"I told you about him. He's the one leading the team looking at your craft. The one who thought he knew how you had travelled through time."

"So?"

"He wants you to go and see him at his research centre."

"But, sweetheart, why should that make you so unhappy?"

To his surprise she came off the chair, wrapped her arms tightly around him and cried, "But he'll persuade you to go back through time, and I'll never see you again. I couldn't bear that again. Not again. I tried not to feel for you what I felt for George, but when you came back from Erin, you and I and George-Louis seemed so happy!"

And she began to cry again. He held her firmly and breathed as deeply but as surreptitiously as he could and knew that now he had to be the strong one. And he began to fully understand how much strain and responsibility she had borne since his arrival. After a while he felt able to say, "Look, Marianne, you don't know what he wants to see me about. It might be to tell me that I have to stay here forever."

"No, he won't. I know he wants to send you back. I just know and now I feel so guilty."

"You feel guilty? Why should you?"

There was a long pause and then she groaned so feelingly and said, "Because that was what I wanted, I thought, before the news came ... There seemed to be so many problems with your work, with the community and George-Louis. And then when Radah spoke to me I suddenly realised I might lose you ..."

Somewhere, in the dark recesses of his brain, he felt fear, the fear he had experienced when he had first agreed to go to the moon: he was afraid of space, the sensation of having nothing about him. Yet he knew that at this precise moment he must not show the least inkling of it. He had to comfort Marianne instead; he had to try to convince her that her fears were, if not entirely unfounded, at least premature. He continued to hold her until she was quite calm again. Then he said, "Don't feel guilty about me. It's not at all surprising that you thought about the possibility of my going away and leaving you in peace: I've been very difficult to deal with and I know I've caused you heartache. It would be odd if you hadn't found me a nuisance ..."

"But I ..."

"No buts ... You didn't ask to be lumbered with me, now did you?"

"Well no, but ..."

"We agreed, no buts ... Now, let's think of Dr James. You really don't know what he wants me for. And even if he does want to talk about going back in time, he might not want someone as ham-fisted as me to go: I could ruin it! And lastly, even if he does, I can always say no, can't I."

"But will you?"

"Who knows? Until I've seen him and talked to him, the question's academic, isn't it?"

She saw an implication in this that she did not like because her face changed and she looked a little shocked. Her mouth opened and then closed tightly and she said, "That could mean that there might be circumstances in which you would go."

"Well, yes, though I can't imagine what they might be. They'd have to be foolproof and that means I'd have to be sure I could get back here — without risk."

"Oh darling, I can't see how there'd be no risk."

"Perhaps not, but we don't know until I've seen him. That's why it's academic. Look, let's try not to worry about it now. Let's see if I can fit in better here: that's one thing I can do, isn't it?"

She did not answer, so he went on, "Look, Dr James, or whoever he is, has not asked me, has he? I only know because you told me. It could be ages before he gets in touch with me personally. Let's try to forget about him until he does. Eh? What do you think?"

She smiled bravely but weakly and nodded. Half satisfied that he had calmed her fears for the moment, John tried to quell the fear and apprehension that he felt mounting within himself.

Chapter XVI

Despite his anguish, John managed to put thoughts of Dr James to the back of his mind, but even then the news had a strange effect on him: life seemed even more unreal and the expression 'borrowed time' kept occurring to him. Nevertheless, he felt calm: life was good in spite of, or perhaps because of, the notion that this phase would be brief. Furthermore, he found that he did fit in better — though, to begin with, this seemed to him to be mostly fortuitous.

First of all, he lost his classes temporarily because a trip to the Andes had been arranged for his students by their teachers: they were to be away for a couple of months. Not only would they study all aspects of the geography, but also the flora and fauna, and at the same time monitor their own respiratory and cardiac responses to life at high altitude. John himself had to prepare an outline programme of the history for them to consider and this threw him into a panic because, though he knew something of the ancient history — from the early civilisations of South America, through the periods of the Conquistadors and the time of Spanish and Portuguese domination, to the struggle for liberation and so on — he knew very little of the more recent history except what he had picked up from Ernst and Friedrich; he needed an intense seminar with Myra who also provided help with computer programs for the students.

The students themselves surprised him by asking his permission for the trip, and when he told them jokingly that he would now be at a loose end, one of them asked him if he would like to help in his grandfather's carpentry shop, as it would now be shorthanded without him. John was very pleased to agree because, though he thought of himself as not being particularly practical, woodwork was the only craft subject he had ever really enjoyed at school.

And so it was that he found himself one frosty morning cycling across towards a place he had known as the Dingle to work with Byron and Orlando Shuttleworth in their furniture-making business. He was surprised to see power tools he recognised — drills, lathes, band-saws and the like — but of other machines he could only guess at their function: they looked streamlined and were no doubt computer controlled. For the first few days he was simply a labourer, fetching and carrying and cleaning up. But fairly soon Orlando, who was the grandfather, asked him to carry out a simple job on a lathe. He worked slowly and was very careful to check every measurement twice and to double-check the positions he had to use on the lathe. No one seemed to mind that he took so long and at the end of the job he felt great satisfaction. Gradually, he was introduced to most of the tools he had actually worked with before, in his youth.

They seemed to be pleased with him and towards the end of the second week Orlando asked him if he would like to be responsible for a complete piece of work and showed him a design for a small table — what John thought of as a coffee table. There were no complicated joints and the woods to be used — cherry (for the top) and sycamore (for the legs) — were neither too soft nor too hard and so were good to work with. Byron joined in the discussion of the project and told him to take as long as he liked: there was no urgency. He had his own bench in the far corner of the shop, but next to a window from which he had a view of a hazel copse. He got quietly on with the work and nobody bothered him. He did not feel supervised, though Orlando and Byron, or an old man called Mr Davies who did wonderful carvings of all sorts of figures, would come to his bench for a chat at some time most days.

He awoke early each morning, often just before dawn, and usually found that he felt good; he would lie awake and think of what lay ahead of him and all of it seemed blessed. There would be breakfast with Marianne and George-Louis; this meal had always been his favourite of the day anyway, and to share it with two people he always wanted to be with was an especial joy. Then there would be the cycle journey to work; the weather had remained crisp and he never had to struggle with the bike, neither up hill nor against the wind, because as soon as riding became a strain, the tiny motor cut in to give the cyclist just enough help — so that he could continue to pedal easily. The work he enjoyed too, because as time went on he realised that not only could he do it, he could do it well. He looked forward to its challenges and the physicality of his labours. He had had problems putting the legs and their support spindles together, because the joints were tight and he did not want to make them any bigger lest they became sloppy, but Byron had helped him and showed him that the materials were much more robust than he had thought. He liked his lunchtime when he sat with the others in a comfortable room that linked the workshop with the house. Members of the family who worked elsewhere joined them for the mid-day meal and the conversations were varied and interesting without ever being too serious on the one hand, or too silly on the other. The workshop seemed to develop a different atmosphere in the afternoon. Everyone got on with their own work and rarely did they interfere with each other until about four o'clock when they all began to talk again, and Mr Davies on occasions even warbled an old song in a wavery voice.

On two afternoons a week he spent his time continuing to clear the copse. He thought that his arbitrary decision to reduce the amount of time there would lead to some sort of reprimand, but then thought, who would reprimand me? There are no bosses! All that happened was that he and Tommy reported to the committee concerned on the progress they were making. Tommy had taught John how to select the trees to keep and how to prune them in such a way as to help them produce the kind of poles needed, but he expected John to draw up a two-year plan, including maps, to show how they thought everything would work out. John thought that he might have to do the drawings laboriously, but George-Louis showed him how to do this on the computer.

Whether he had spent his afternoon in the carpenter's shop or in the copse, at the end of the working day he rode home knowing that something worthwhile had been achieved. And Marianne always greeted him warmly on his arrival. He would then spend some time with her and George-Louis, talking about the day that each had had and drinking tea. More often than not he had his evening meal with them, but before that he would work on an article that Myra had asked him to write on how in the distant past education systems had evolved under the influence of industrialisation. Once he had found his way into the electronic archive he discovered that almost every document he could think of was easily available — and there were lots of others he had never been aware of which the program suggested he might want to look at. He was contented to spend the rest of the evening with Marianne and he tried to help George-Louis with anything he might be doing. By the time he got to bed he felt pleasantly weary and went to sleep straight away. However, one night he lay awake for a while and thought about his good fortune, and as he reflected on his daily life, he remembered the words of a hymn written by Jan Struther during the Second World War about how blessed an ordinary mundane but well ordered life could be: when he had sung the words at school he had thought them banal, but now their true significance was made clear to him. However, his habitual pessimism inevitably crept back into his consciousness: this was all too good to last. When, he wondered, would the holiday be over? A message from Dr James was inevitable and would have to be answered; John once more felt afraid. If James asked him to travel through time again he might die in a terrible way lost in space, or he might arrive back only as far as the Dark Times, and whatever happened, he might never see Marianne again. The message did come but it merely asked him to visit the research centre.

When the day came for John to leave, he, Marianne and George-Louis were very unhappy. Even though the boy did not know the significance of the visit, he felt the stress that his mother was under. He also sensed that John was afraid and that all his joking was a front. On the other hand, he did understand that what John was about to become engaged in was to do with space. The best fathers were astronauts, he thought, and so John perhaps could become a real father.

Even though John had to change trains in London, his journey to Sarum took only an hour. From there he travelled by bus to what was known in his day as Salisbury Plain. It dropped him outside the centre and he was astonished to see that it was next to Stonehenge, which, from his quick glance, did not seem to have changed since the twenty-first century. He expected the research centre to have a wall or a fence around it, but it was completely open an all sides: anyone could go in and there seemed to be lots of people about, some of whom were in coloured overalls of various designs. He assumed these were researchers. Others were dressed like him, but he had no idea whether they were visitors or not, except that some were children. As in all the community centres he had visited, there were no direction signs. He assumed that everybody knew which building was which. However, on some buildings he did notice small plaques carrying icons, which he supposed indicated the presence of radioactive materials or dangerous chemicals.

The lack of directions was not a problem because, following the instructions in Dr James' letter, he simply made his way to the taxi rank, climbed into one of the now familiar Perspex-domed vehicles and said, "John More to see Dr Alan James, please," and the taxi set off by itself. It took him past what he thought might be laboratories or workshops both large and small, and structures the like of which he had never seen before and which he could only assume were experimental centres whose purposes somehow dictated their shapes. The taxi stopped outside a very impressive building that was much taller and architecturally more traditional than the others. In front of it stood what he was sure must be a V2 rocket. He ascended the marble steps, walked between two sets of Doric pillars and into a busy atrium. He made his way to what could only be a reception desk and said who he was. The receptionist's fingers flicked over a keyboard and she said, "Mr More to see you." At this point John felt something touch his leg, and when he looked down saw what appeared to be a mechanical dog, whose green, glowing eyes were peering up at him expectantly. Then the receptionist, trying to look over the edge of the desk, said, "Is he there?"

"Who?"

"Pointer."

"Do you mean this dog-like thing?"

"Yes. Just follow him. You'll be all right."

"Oh, OK. Thanks."

Pointer had already set off, but John noticed that the dog quickly adjusted its pace to his. Occasionally, as they made their way along several corridors, Pointer looked round to make sure his charge was still with him, wagged his tail, and somehow managed to look pleased.

Finally, they entered a huge hangar, and there amongst other space craft John could see the dreaded capsule; it looked so small and insignificant compared with the other craft, but that was where the mechanical dog headed. Alongside his capsule was a much larger ship, and next to this stood a man dressed in what had once been a green boiler suit but which was now washed out and smeared with oil and grease. He turned and saw John, smiled broadly and held out his hand.

"John More. How I've looked forward to meeting you."

"Dr James, I presume?"

"Oh, call me Al." Then, looking at Pointer, he said. "You'll have to thank him or he will stay with you all day."

"Thank you, Pointer, that was very good of you."

The dog wagged its tail once more, turned round and, presumably, made its way back to the reception desk. And Dr James began, "Now, listen John, this is most important, so let's get straight down to business. I want you to try to remember everything about your journey from the moon, because something odd happened ... Now, I think I know what it might have been, but I still would like to know how you saw it."

John was surprised that there were no further formalities, and being confronted, unexpectedly, with the task of remembering something he had only vague ideas about resulted, as usual, in a mental confusion, which momentarily struck him dumb. Dr James frowned at him and he realised his mouth was open, and no doubt his eyes were goggling.

"Are you all right?"

"Err ... yes ... Your request threw me for a minute ... and I ... err ...don't remember a lot about it, anyway."

"Oh, silly me, jumping straight in. Let's go and have a cuppa and you can relax a bit." Then he shouted, "Eh, Alphonse!"

"Yeah," came a reply, echoing up from the contraption next to the capsule.

"John More is here and we are going for a cup of tea."

"Bien! OK! See you, Merlin!"

"Merlin, who's Merlin?" said John.

"Ah, that's the technicians' joke-name for me: it's because I can never remember the names of chemicals and things and I use old-fashioned terms for them."

"And he's a magician!" Alphonse added, shouting from the rocket.

As they walked across to the canteen, John had an opportunity to put his thinking in order, and as he reflected, he began to realise that he had remembered more than he had first thought about that nightmare journey from the moon, though what he had felt rather than what he had thought was still uppermost in his mind: he recalled that he had had an inflated sense of apprehension from the moment he had climbed into his spacesuit. In particular, there was something about the attitude of the astronauts that had bothered him. They seemed uncharacteristically solicitous — but he could not tell if their concern was genuine or not, and so he had dismissed this fearfulness as part of his usual paranoia: he was very afraid of space travel — but then these temporary colleagues had hardly ceased to rib him for the whole of his week's stay in their base. Would they continue to tease him? 'Surely,' he told himself, 'they would do nothing to jeopardise the flight home.'

Take-off went smoothly: it was just as the astronauts said it would be and the instruments in the vehicle behaved as he expected. He was surprised that the ship went into orbit around the moon, but moon-base assured him that this was normal and necessary, though he could not understand why he did three orbits at what seemed increasing speed. He was even more sure of this when he left the moon's gravitational pull and headed towards Earth; he was travelling faster than on the way out, he was sure, but he wondered if this might be due to the larger size of his target. Once the well-known features of Earth became clearer he was certain he was coming in too fast. Nevertheless, he knew that his oblique angle of entry was correct. But he was terrified and felt sick; realising that he was breathing faster and faster made him feel worse. He began to hyperventilate. Then … nothing; all that he could remember was Marianne's beautiful smile when he at last opened his eyes in the hospital. All this he told to Merlin.

"Aha, just as I suspected, they did play a trick on you but they got more than they bargained for. I've looked at the transcripts of the enquiry and I reckon those lads bamboozled their interrogators as well as you."

"So what do you think happened?" said John, his eyes wide with apprehension.

"Well, we will never know for certain, but I think they wanted to give you a fright, but their plan to speed you up meant that you went into orbit around the Earth in a way that had an effect like a sling shot. You were thrown back to the moon. Fortunately for them, and you, they were able to control the direction if not the speed, so they sent you back to Earth, and maybe the same thing happened again — I don't know, but probably your tremendous speed at the third run in could have meant you went through a wormhole, which would not normally be detectable. That's when you travelled through time."

"I'll have to take your word for it. I understand very little about all this."

"Not to worry. The machine I have devised is simple to operate and I, or rather Alphonse, has reduced the controls and the instruments to a minimum, so I think we can teach you very quickly how to get back to the twenty-first century."

John held his cup half way to his mouth and stared in alarm at Dr James. He could say nothing. He had told himself that this might happen, but now that he was suddenly confronted with the idea of travelling through space, never mind time, he felt as though he had been shoved under a cold shower. Al James, who was just about to say something innocuous, now looked at John and saw the horror on his face. He in turn was shocked.

"No, don't tell me you don't want to go!" Realising the inappropriateness of what he had said, he added quickly, "Oh, John, I should have realised how terrifying this can all be, but I just thought you'd want to get home."

Neither of them spoke; they stared into the bottoms of their cups as though they were searching for an answer in the tea leaves. Dr James felt thwarted and angry. What John did not know about him was that throughout his adult years he had been intrigued by the possibility of time travel and had been working on it for years, but since the arrival of the capsule at the centre he had given up everything else, as he tried to figuring out how John, arriving like a deus ex machina, had travelled through time. At last he thought the solution was within his grasp and so he had then devoted himself to the immense problem of finding a way to get John back to his own century again. Unfortunately, he had immersed himself so thoroughly in the theoretical and technical difficulties that he had not considered the human factors involved. He himself would willingly try out the machine, but he knew that this would only compound the contradictions surrounding John's arrival. The logical solution, indeed the ethical solution, was for John to go. He now feared that persuading him might be more difficult than constructing the machine.

However, John too was thinking about the problem; what had stuck in his mind was Dr James' statement that he had assumed John would want to go home and from there it took only a short mental step to see that he was the only person who could go and in the end he would have to agree to it. He was still very afraid when he thought about it. Moreover, just as disconcerting was the notion that he would have to break the news to Marianne and George-Louis. However, he did not wish to tell Dr James any of this: he had first to acclimatise himself to the idea — now that he knew that it was all too likely. He said, much to his own surprise, "I think I knew even before I set off this morning that if someone had found a way to travel back to my time, I would be the one who would have to go. But at this precise moment I think I need some time to get used to the idea."

Dr James sighed audibly with relief and said, "Well, Alphonse, Ben and I will need several days to teach you what you are going to need to know."

"Who's Ben?"

"The third member of the core team. He'll be with us tomorrow. He's away looking for one or two things we need to complete the work."

"The core team? What does that mean?"

"Ah, now to explain that, I need to tell you that you have caused us a lot of heart searching. Usually, there are no secrets here — anywhere in the research centre. But because your local people thought your origins should be kept secret we had to follow suit — though unwillingly, I might add. Now, large numbers of people have been consulted on, and engaged in, the building of this machine, but only the core team know the full truth, though I think some colleagues are suspicious. And you ought to realise that if you do make the trip, your secret will have to be revealed."

Strangely, this did not bother John. In a way, he thought, it would be a relief. However, he knew that was not the deepest cause of his concern. No. What was uppermost in his mind was not his anonymity, but the now near certainty that he would have to submit himself to whatever terrifying experience James and his team had devised for him. And every time he had that thought it was accompanied by the even more painful idea that he might never see Marianne again. As he accompanied Dr James back to the hangar he tried not to look miserable. He suspected that his smile had become a rictus.

As they neared the machine a door slid open in its side and Alphonse came out grinning. He walked down a flight of steps that emerged silently beneath the door.

"Fixed it," he said. "It slotted in just like you said it would, Merlin."

"Good, now say hello to John More."

The pleasantries observed, the two experts invited John into the time machine.

"Come and see what we've got for the lucky traveller. We'll explain everything as we go along."

John was amazed at what he saw once he got inside, for he realised it was very big — so much of it was below the level of what he had thought of as the floor. However, at first they climbed to the command module, which sat near the top, but to one side. Alphonse explained that as John was coming back to Earth — hopefully, in another century, preferably his own — this would act as a cockpit. There was a daunting array of controls, instruments, dials and levers. However, he had little time to consider them as James hurried them on so that John could see what he referred to as 'the working gubbins', which was a complete misnomer as the various parts looked large and complicated.

Immediately beneath the command module they descended a spiral staircase, which ran around what seemed to John to be a cylinder about six metres in diameter and of similar depth. As they went, Dr James explained, "This is the first of the working parts and we call it the collider — and that is what it is in a way, but the name is taken from a very old text written by an ancient physicist named Paul Davies. I don't think he ever tried to build a time machine, or if he did it wouldn't have worked — not without the miniaturisation techniques available to us. He'd have needed a massive generator to supply it with power."

In the next section John found that the staircase had been transferred to the outer wall, for the next working part was in the shape of a large sphere, which Dr James referred to as the imploder. He was about to launch into an explanation of how it functioned, but a glance at John made him say, "Oh, never mind. Trust me: it works." As they went through a sliding trapdoor he continued, "and this works too. It's an inflator."

This meant nothing to John but it looked to him like the pictures of floating mines he had seen in illustrations from the Second World War: it too was spherical but had spikes protruding from its surface. The last part, the differentiator (according to the doctor), was a flat cylinder surmounted by what John took to be a Perspex dome. One final level further down contained living quarters, but they were very sparse, because, as Al James explained, "I hope you're not going to need them."

Then he sighed contentedly, smiled a smile of deep satisfaction and said, "Well, what do you think of her?"

As so often — in the presence of experts — John's mind went blank. He was so confused that he could think of nothing relevant to say. But Dr James was looking at him with what John could only describe as a sardonic smile. This description of James' expression absorbed him: he had come across it in the romantic stories he had read as a teenager in his sister's magazines and he often wondered what a sardonic smile looked like. Now he knew, he told himself. And it was the sort of smile he would expect a Merlin to wear. Suddenly, the idiocy of this line of thought occurred to him and he at last blurted out, "Look, I have to confess that all this is beyond me! I cannot give you an opinion on your time machine because I've no idea what any of the parts do!"

Merlin did not seem surprised. He said, "That's what I expected."

"What you expected?"

"Yes … you see … as I said, I've read the transcripts of the enquiry. At first I thought the various witnesses from the moon base were trying to blackguard you when they claimed you were ignorant and ham-fisted. But now that I have met you, I've realised that the first part of their accusation was not wholly untrue." Here he paused to see what effect this had on John and then quickly went on, "I hope the second part is completely untrue because you are the one who is going to have to learn to manage this craft, even if you don't understand the principles behind it or the technologies which drive it."

At this point John began to feel annoyed with Merlin who seemed now to be not in the least concerned about what John might feel.

"Look," he said, "I never wanted to go on that bloody stupid space trip in the first place! And I never claimed to have any knowledge of space travel. My technical ability amounted to no more than driving a car."

"Oh, that's OK."

"That's OK? It doesn't sound like that to me!"

"Ah, don't worry. Alphonse and Ben have reduced the technical complexity into a nearly foolproof system that is indeed no more difficult than driving one of your ancient automobiles."

"Ha! I'll believe that when I see it."

"OK. Then we will show you … Alphonse, take us back up to the command module."

The wall moved and Alphonse, with a comic subservient gesture, waved his hand towards the cubicle that was revealed and said, "After you, gentlemen. Lead on, O mighty Merlin …"

They travelled back up to the top of the machine in an instant and stepped out into the command module. At first it did not seem to John that what Merlin James had said about the handiwork of Alphonse and Ben was true because, once more, the display of dials and controls looked extensive. But the technician said, "OK, John, sit in that seat with the joystick in front of it and I'll show you which bits really matter — most of the clocks and dials you can see are there for our benefit — but if you touch that button on your right — yes, that's it next to the arm rest — you'll see …"

John did as he was told and immediately, directly in front of him, a panel glowed green and above it a screen lit up. There were only three dials on the panel: one he could recognise as a pressure gauge; another was for fuel; and the third was a speedometer. John looked hard at this one and was aghast to see that the maximum speed indicated was 200,000 KPH. However, Alphonse continued, "This is your command post for take-off, so look at the row of buttons between the panel and the screen; you'll notice that each one has a letter written on it. It would be best to memorise them, but it's not a matter of life and death, because the computers can, if need be, do everything for you. On the first is a 'T': that means 'Take-off'. Press it."

John hesitated and looked round nervously, but Merlin interrupted rather impatiently and said, "Go ahead, man. We're not yet set up for take-off!"

When John did press it the screen flickered and then a diagram of what looked to him like a runway appeared with the image of a rocket near the bottom edge. He heard Alphonse go on, "If you want to be in control, you are going to have to look at this as you take off and use the joystick to keep that rocket on the centre line. The auxiliary engines are computer controlled from that screen, so you shouldn't have any accidents. Now press the next button, the one that says 'F'."

A similar diagram appeared and John was told that this would help him stay on course, again if the need arose. There were other diagrams for orbiting the moon and the Earth and one for landing.

"That is really all you need, and as you can see, it is quite simple; Merlin has worked out the mathematics and physics and Ben and I have set up the computers accordingly."

Merlin said, "Now let's go to the most important bit." And he led the way to another console on the other side of the cockpit.

The general layout of this second console was similar to the first: there was a screen underneath which ran a row of buttons, and beneath that there were a number of dials. Below all of these there was a joystick. Alphonse explained, "A screen would not necessarily be an astronaut's preferred method of accessing the kind of information needed to manoeuvre a craft like this through a wormhole, but we thought it safest for you ... as it is similar to the screen on the take-off and landing console. All you will need to do is to manipulate the joystick. So press the second button on the left. See ..."

Again, something like a landing strip with a matrix superimposed upon it appeared with the image of a rocket approaching it.

"You just have to keep the rocket on course; the computers will do the rest."

"But how will I know when ...?"

"Don't worry! Press the first button, the one marked RM, A and B, which stands, by the way, for 'Robots Merlin, Alphonse and Ben'."

Then a metallic-sounding version of Al James' voice boomed through a speaker, 'Steady as she goes.'

Then his real voice said, "You see, old pal, I'm going to be with you all the way. All you need to do is listen to me or follow the instructions, which will appear as necessary on the screen. It'll be easy."

John was beginning to be very irritated by Merlin 'bloody' James' manner, but all that he could think of saying was, "It's easy to say here and now, but will it be easy at the time?"

"Aagh, you worry too much. Of course it will be easy, even for you," he added almost as an afterthought, but with that infuriating smile, "And anyway, we have set up a simulator, haven't we, Alphonse?"

"It sounds as though you planned all this just for me."

"Oh, we did!"

John stared at him with distaste because of his presumption. As he struggled to cope with his annoyance he tried to imagine what had gone on in Merlin's head when the capsule had arrived at the research centre. There and then it came to him: just as he'd said, Merlin must have been interested in, and even working on, time travel for a long time before this. No matter how dedicated, how bright, or how technically accomplished, a team as small as this could not have got such a machine to this state or readiness in less than a year. Dr Al 'Merlin' James, Alphonse and Ben must have seen him as a heaven-sent guinea pig — or, more likely, dog or monkey of the kind the Americans and Russians had sent off in rockets in the early days of space travel. Yes, John was perfect: someone whose life they could risk legitimately. Though he was aware that he could not accuse them directly of this — after all, he did not really know the facts — he felt his anger increase because he was being used. He said, "I must have come on the scene at a very opportune time for you."

There was a brief silence and then Al said, "What are you implying?"

John chose his words carefully, "That you were already building this contraption even before I arrived, but you faced a moral and maybe even legal dilemma because of the risks involved — and I don't mean just to the life of whoever was sent, but also of violating the laws of physics."

Alphonse looked sheepish, but James' jawbone set; he looked suddenly older. He sat down on the seat in front of the console. Neither of them spoke for a while. John broke the silence, "Am I right?"

Dr James sighed and said, "In a way, yes. But let me try to explain." He spoke quietly in a tired voice that suggested he'd been over this ground before. "There is throughout the world, and not only in this research centre, a sort of moratorium on time travel. But that has not meant that some of us have not thought about it. Also, there is no actual law on this — it's a kind of gentlemen's agreement. Some of us, half seriously and yet almost as a hobby, have been trying to build a machine that *could* travel through time, but would not necessarily ever be tested. We have debated with like-minded people everywhere the rights and wrongs of it over many years. But the work has been mostly, but by no means completely, theoretical — until out of the blue, so to speak, you came along. And once your capsule came here we could not forgo such an opportunity. The fact that you had no idea how you had done it, i.e. travelled through time, also seemed fortuitous: we assumed you would want to go back. So that's what we worked on, but we have had lots of help from others here."

"And we know it's going to work," added Alphonse.

"But you can't be certain," retorted John.

"No, not absolutely, but as certain as any scientist can be. And that is why we want to encourage you to go," said Merlin.

"And your colleagues all agree?"

"We don't know yet."

"You don't know yet?"

"No, but there's an extraordinary meeting of the moot tomorrow. Alphonse and I are hoping that you will speak up — we have always assumed that you would want to go back and if you say you do, we think the moot will agree to us having a shot at it. We can't do anything without fairly general agreement because so many of our colleagues would have to help us at ground control. And that also means that, one way or another, your secret will be out."

"Oh, I don't think I'm really bothered about that any more … What concerns me is the effect on the people who have virtually become my family here … and (I hate to say this) the fact that the very notion of travelling through space and time terrifies me!"

"But this is no more dangerous than your trip to the moon. In fact, it's probably less so, because we know a lot more and are technically more accomplished."

"No more dangerous than my trip to the moon? Look where that got me!"

"Yes, but you were the victim of a vicious prank — with this trip you will be in safe hands."

"Hah!"

Then Alphonse came in, "Really, this is as safe as it could be: we've been very careful and not only checked everything thoroughly, we've had everything checked by independent assessors too."

"But can you get me back here again?"

Merlin and Alphonse looked at each other and momentarily John thought they would say they couldn't, but then Merlin said, "Technically, yes we can, but …"

"But what?"

"Well, it depends on the circumstances you find yourself in. Remember, once you enter the wormhole we won't be able to help you: you will be on your own. But don't worry, we'll see you are thoroughly briefed on how to handle the craft, and if you do want to come back, once you have taken off — from wherever — the Robots will come into play."

This did little to allay John's doubts, but he tried not to think what Merlin might mean by 'circumstances'. He could not express his fears to them again, so he said nothing but stared at the console instead. Then Merlin said, "Oh, by the way, we have assumed that for the next few days at least, you will stay here and we've set up a room for you. Can I suggest that we do no more today, but that we meet early tomorrow and have a session in the simulator before we meet the moot?"

The room was very comfortable but dominated by the communicator whose single eye, though blank, seemed to accuse him of betraying Marianne and George-Louis. He wondered whether he should talk to them immediately, but felt he could not — just yet. He needed time to think things through even though he feared that this might lead him to assemble arguments for going rather than staying. He had run away from so many things in his life and now he wanted to do the right thing, but he had no notion of what that might be because there were so many contradictions. He wondered about praying about it and the idea was attractive because it might remove some of the responsibility from him: that seemed to be running away again! And when he considered the sort of abject words he might use, he rejected the notion, but that did not help either: it made him feel even more nervous and unsettled.

He could not continue to stare at the communicator any longer, so he decided to go for a walk outside. The night was clear and frosty. The moon was full. No one seemed to take particular notice of him, and in a few minutes he found himself at Stonehenge. In the eerie light it seemed not only bigger than he remembered, but more mysterious. He recalled that when he had visited it in the twenty-first century he had been disappointed because, he had thought then, it was not as grand as in photographs, but maybe it was also because it had been crowded with people. Now he was the only person there and it was not just the arrangement of the blocks of stone that made it seem strange, but also the fact that all the grass around the monument shone silver; he thought his eyes were playing tricks until he remembered that he had witnessed this phenomenon before when he had gone carol singing as a boy. The frost was already forming even though the sun had not long gone down. Once more the sensation he had felt on the edge of the cliffs with Ambrose came back to him: what he could see had gone on happening for thousands, perhaps even millions of years. Time seemed not to exist: was it then merely an illusion?

He found a bench and sat down so that he could contemplate this amazing scene: Stonehenge like a ship sailing smoothly across a lime-lit sea. The beauty of it brought a lump to his throat and he did not know why. However, perhaps (he thought) this was an instance of his human soul longing for the presence of God — which is what mystics had often claimed. Then he remembered his intention to pray, but no words seemed appropriate; so he sat, as he put it to himself, in the presence of his maker.

As in the church of St Adrienne's, he told himself that this was why he existed: to be with the Trinity in peace and calm, in a serenity where time really did not matter. In that instant he made up his mind, once and for all, very firmly, that he would go back to his own century. Though he then felt almost simultaneously, and in a most poignant way, the loss of Marianne, he knew that he had to go because that was where he belonged. Marianne and George-Louis were better off without him. However, he also knew that he could not tell them that. Moreover, the idea of letting them know by means of the communicator was appalling: it would be better face-to-face. So, when he finally called them, he did not tell them everything that had transpired that afternoon. Even so, Marianne was suspicious because, as she told him, he looked awful.

"Are you unwell?" she asked.

"No, but I feel very tired," he replied.

"Did Dr James give you no indication of what is going to happen?"

"Not really. That's in the hands of the centre's moot, which meets tomorrow."

"Will its deliberations be on the Instant News?"

"I don't know — would that be normal for a research centre like this?"

"I should think so. Maybe George-Louis and I will be able to watch."

John's misery increased with the thought of this, but Marianne, who misinterpreted his look, told him he should get some sleep and promised to talk to him tomorrow. In fact, he slept very little.

Early the next morning he looked for a chapel because he felt the need to pray. The only one in the centre was interdenominational and at that time was allocated to the Baptists. When he entered he found that the room was round and already several people were sitting with their backs to the wall. On one side of the circle there stood a small altar and facing it at the opposite side was a lectern. Everyone seemed engaged in their own private meditations: no one looked at him. Then a woman entered wearing what could have been a surplice; the congregation stirred. She went to the lectern and asked if anyone had a particular hymn they would like to sing and someone suggested one that John actually knew and he marvelled that it was still known after so many centuries. It was 'Be still for the presence of the Lord is moving in this place', and he felt it was very appropriate: he needed to feel calm. There followed a reading from Corinthians about how the wisdom of the world is foolishness to God, and how we need to be foolish as He is foolish in order to be truly wise. The celebrant's comment on the reading drew attention to this and she said that we almost need to turn human thinking inside out in order to align it with God's thinking. But all that John could think was that his future was unknowable. He could only put his trust in God. He was very moved by the spontaneous prayers of the various members of the congregation: they each seemed to have a depth of trust that he found unimaginable.

After breakfast he spent an hour on the simulator with Alan and Alphonse hovering over him anxiously as they instructed, or rather cajoled him into learning how to use the controls they had set up for him. What they had claimed the day before he found to be true: everything seemed easy — as long as he did not panic.

At eleven o'clock, Merlin said it was time to go before the moot, and so they made their way to the theatre. This was a building with a dome. It was stepped and John estimated that it had seats for a couple of hundred people set in the round with thirty or so seats at each of several levels. It was nearly full, and there was a murmur of conversation — until the time machine party arrived. James, smiling benignly, led Alphonse and John to the front row where three seats had been left vacant. He did not sit down but stepped into the middle of the arena and said quietly but distinctly and quite audibly, "Comrades, I assume that all interested parties are here, and it certainly looks as though we are quorate, so shall we begin?" And he sat down between Alphonse and John.

There was, for John at least, an uncomfortable silence. Once more the thought came to him that these people took their principle of eschewing leadership to extremes: no one seemed to be prepared to take on the mantle even of primus inter pares. Then a voice from the top row said, "Dr James, have you deceived us?"

"Er … yes … but I think with good reason."

There was a silence and then the same voice asked, "Would you like to explain?"

Alan James now leaned towards John and whispered, "This is it, old chap, I'll have to explain who you are and introduce you." And without giving him a chance to reply he stood up and moved to the centre of the floor once more, looked around confidently and said, "Friends and colleagues, as many of you have suspected, the research team of which I am a member has been planning for several months now to send someone through time."

Immediately there was a buzz of animated comment, but James raised his hand for silence and went on, "But the person about to undertake this journey is someone who has already travelled through time!"

There was now an unrestrained outburst of loud and disbelieving comment. James called John forward and gradually the noise subsided so that he was able to say, "May I introduce Mr John More who comes from the twenty-first century."

Momentarily, the audience was shocked into silence, and then once more there was cacophony, during which John stood up and moved sheepishly to the centre of the theatre. There he waited patiently until he thought he might be heard. He tried to think about what he might say, but in his heightened emotional state he did not find this easy. At last the noise subsided enough for him to be able to say, "Ladies and gentlemen, I think that I should point out first of all that travelling here from the my century was not planned — by me or anybody else. It was a colossal and incredible accident, which I do not claim to understand. Dr James, however, thinks he knows how it happened, and using that information he and the team think they can send me back to my own time."

He wondered if Marianne were watching this and what she might be thinking. However, he was immediately more concerned about what the reaction of the moot might be. It was at first slow in coming. Then there was a confused flood of questions, the general tone of which was indignant. John had no idea of how to deal with the situation: all that he could do was to look towards Dr James for help, hoping that his reputation for magical solutions was justified. Merlin stood up and joined him in the centre of the theatre. Once again, he raised his hand imperiously for silence and gradually the noise subsided.

"Don't blame John for the secrecy," he said, "and that is really what bothers you, I know. I am more to blame than he. But really, I was only doing what was asked of me by the community in Ironbridge, which is where John materialised, so to speak. It seemed to them, at the time, which is now getting on for a year ago, that it was best to keep quiet — for his sake. I think that probably they now believe they made a mistake and I know that John himself no longer wants his origins to be kept secret."

There was another outburst from the audience, but it seemed less vehement, and it very soon sank to a low murmur. Merlin then continued, "Our principle of complete openness has not been too badly damaged because the secret is now out: I notice that the monitors are on as usual so the whole interested world now knows about John ... but what is more important is that he has agreed to be sent back to his own time."

Any concern John might have had for what Marianne might think of this was lost in the cacophony that followed, especially as Dr James sat down making no effort to quell the outburst. After a while an old man came to the front; he seemed to be someone who had the respect of everyone there, and he called for questions to be put one at a time with him acting as chair. John was then treated to a demonstration of fifth millennium democracy at its best.

Through a series of questions and answers the facts of what had gone on at the centre were established: those who had assisted Merlin owned up.

Some admitted that they suspected that he intended somehow to engage in time travel, but maintained that he had kept them guessing — though they pointed out he had never denied it. Others said that they were now realising for the first time that they had assisted unknowingly in building the time machine. Nathaniel, the elderly acting chair, calmly assuaged the fears and the indignation of those who felt most affronted by all this, and pointed out that here was an opportunity for all of them to see why a policy of complete openness with each other had been established at the centre — and also why it should be maintained. He then suggested that despite John's declared intention of travelling back, they should discuss firstly the possible physical consequences of time travel, and then the morality of it. Should they agree that in the circumstances it was permissible, then they should be able to establish who should go.

Though John felt that there was, for him, an inevitability about all this, he was surprised how calmly, thoroughly and comprehensively all of this was discussed. The sense of outrage had disappeared: the deliberations were orderly and everyone displayed a patience that he would not have thought possible at the beginning of the enquiry. After at least two hours, Merlin at last asked if he could speak and was given the floor.

"Colleagues," he said, "I don't wish to shorten unduly our discussion, particularly as I feel that my overweening concern for my own interests is what led to it in the first place. However, it seems to me that all the various angles from which we have approached this question bring us to one clear point, and it is that John, who is from the past, should be allowed to return to it. And really that is the only moral question we need to consider. It is, I believe, within our power to send him and, if he wants to go, then it is our duty to him, as a fellow human being, to send him. If he were marooned on a desert island or in space, we would not think twice about trying to rescue him: we'd do it."

No one seemed to disagree with this. There was silence. Then Nathaniel asked, "What does John think about this?"

He stood up and came to the middle of the theatre. He looked around calmly and said, "In the light of the discussion, I find I have no option but to go." He paused momentarily and then went on, "Because in that way alone can all the anomalies be removed. Moreover, one way or the other, a scientific question can be resolved. However, I must be honest with you and say that I am reluctant to go. My most important reason is that I have established relationships with people of this time. I have a sense of obligation to them. You can see, of course, that this is one of the very anomalies we discussed earlier. Now I can iron out that problem, but I do ask you to let me return, albeit briefly, to Ironbridge to settle my affairs.

However, there is another reason for my reluctance, and I'm sure you will all appreciate this; it is that such a journey will be dangerous and we have no real notion of the outcome."

Once more there was a buzz of comment, but this time Alphonse stood up. He said, "Colleagues, those of you who have worked with Dr James, Benjamin Steinmetz and me know how thoroughly everything has been worked out and checked. There is very little risk involved." To which the voice from the back row responded, "That depends what you mean by very little … and also, does any of that eminent trio, in fact anybody in this place or anywhere else in the world, for that matter, know what the unintended consequences might be? Gentlemen, you are playing with the laws of physics!"

Merlin got back to his feet at this point to say, "Colleagues, we have discussed this already. But look, if time travel did have fundamental effects on the laws of physics, wouldn't we have experienced them already? John More's travelling through time to get here has had effects only on the people he has met — and the consequences, as far as we can see, are social. Has anyone noticed any dire changes? Most people are now only just becoming aware that time travel has happened — and that's because they are watching this debate."

This seemed to settle everything: no one replied. After a short time Nathaniel asked whether there were any further comments and also said that there were no comments from viewers. He then asked if there was a need for a vote, but the resulting murmur indicated that such would be superfluous. He looked around the theatre and finally turned to John, saying, "OK, John, it looks as though you are going." He then smiled at the assembly and said, "Right, colleagues let's prepare!"

As the meeting broke up several people came to John and shook his hand. More often than not their eyes shone in the way that happens when people meet celebrities, but he felt that this was in no way gratifying: he was merely embarrassed. It heightened his feeling of apprehension — their very adulation seemed to him to presage disaster, so unworthy was he of even their attention. Furthermore, at some time he would have to face Marianne and George-Louis.

She was already in tears.

"Oh, Marianne, what can I say? I'm sorry …"

George-Louis interrupted excitedly, "John, are you really going to travel through time?"

"It looks like it, but your mummy is upset. I think you'll have to let me talk to her first."

He looked at his mother, and as she dried her tears she said, "Yes, please, sweetheart, let me talk to John for a few minutes." Then, as he was about to protest, she continued, "I won't be long."

She turned back to John, her face now composed, but her eyes full of sadness, almost resignation. She sighed and said, "Did you know all this, even last night when we spoke?"

It hurt him to lie, because he dearly wanted to be completely truthful with her, and yet at the same time he wanted to soften the blow.

"I must confess, I had a shrewd idea, but it was by no means certain ..."

"Oh, John ..."

"Honestly, darling, I feel like piggy in the middle ... I don't really want to go — as you heard me say in that meeting — and it isn't just that I'm terrified. It's because I don't want to leave you and George-Louis. But everything here is now set up and it is right and proper that it should be me who goes — I'm the one from the past ... it's almost a moral obligation."

"But, Oh, John ..."

Both fell silent. Neither of them could think of what to say. John felt that whatever he might say would sound false — as though he were making excuses. Marianne thought that if she began to express what she really felt she would sound angry, and she did not wish to hurt him, not at a time like this, because she knew that he was very afraid. Also, she did believe him when he said that he did not wish to leave her and George-Louis. When she did speak it was without reflecting on the effect it might have.

"Will you come home again before you go?"

Despite his deep unhappiness, John felt a surge of pleasure at these words. What she had said was so simple and yet the implication was that his life and that of Marianne were one: they were a family.

"Dr James wants me to stay here for a few days to train, but I'm not going to. I'm coming home now — immediately, this very minute."

"Are you sure ...? Can you get here?"

"I'll try, and I'm setting off now!"

What about Merlin, he thought. Confront him! Immediately! And he tried him on the communicator. There he was.

"John ... hello. This is a surprise," then anxiously, "Is there a problem?"

"Not really, but I've got to go back to Ironbridge tonight — now — straight away."

"You've what! Look, John ..."

"Sorry, Merlin, but if you want your guinea pig, you'd better make sure I can go ... If you are worried about the project — don't. I assure you I will go, but if you can't accommodate this one request, I'll be difficult, I promise ..."

"But, John ..."

"I tell you, Merlin, I mean it!"

There was a pause and Merlin suddenly realised he had made some unwarranted assumptions about John: he saw from the set of the jaw that this particular guinea pig could be stubborn. For once less sure of himself he said, "Well, if you put it like that, and then more firmly, "How much time do you want?"

"Two, no, three days at the most."

"And what about the training?"

"We'll have to take a chance on that. But I'll do it and I will be a good pupil. And you yourself said it should be easy."

"Yes, that's true, but you do need more practice in the simulator — and we have to think about the weather. It'll be OK for a few days, but after that we can't be sure."

"Can't be sure? Look, Merlin, I know that long-range forecasting is much more reliable now than in my day, so are you sure it won't hold?"

He could tell from Dr James' face that he did not know, so he continued, "You don't know, do you? Sorry, then it looks as though we've got to take a chance ..."

"Well, I'm not so sure ... and, anyway, what's so urgent in Ironbridge?"

"Ah! One of the anomalies inherent in time travel has come about ... In fact, it's personal, but I've got to go!"

They continued to argue about it for a while but John was determined and stuck to his decision. Finally, when Merlin had clearly given up, John even got him to take him to the station, as he knew there would be no buses. He managed to catch a train almost immediately in Sarum. He did not have to wait long for a connection in London either. It was only when he got to Jackfield that he was held up: there were no taxis. So he set off to walk to the Lloyds. It was late. The moon had not yet set and its light, reflected by the frost, lit his way making everything easy. The whiteness of that light and the clearness with which it endued all that he passed reminded him of his childhood when moonlight had still been mysterious. Such brightness had seemed completely appropriate to that Christmas Eve in the twenty-first century when he had gone carol singing in this very village. That night his immediate childish expectations had been high, but on this night, as he approached Marianne's house, his feelings were apprehensive. However, when she opened her door he had no chance to utter even a single word: she threw her arms around him and held him very tight.

For the next hour there were tears and recriminations, and yet unaccountably, there were also smiles and even laughter: they were so pleased to be with each other. Though they kept telling themselves that what he had to do was dangerous and that they both had to prepare for the worst, neither of them really believed that they would not see each other again. The sun was already lighting the sky when, exhausted, they both fell into Marianne's bed together.

They did not sleep for long because George-Louis, as soon as he had woken up, had gone first to John's room and then, not being able to find him, had run, puzzled, to his mother's room. He burst in and at first seemed surprised to find John there. Then he climbed in between them and again asked his question.

"John, are you really going to travel through time?"

"I'm going to try — and Merlin James says that he's certain I can do it, with his help."

"Why is he called Merlin? Is he a magician?"

"Well, he thinks he is, but really he's crackers!"

"Tell me about the time you come from. Was it like in Erin?"

"Yes and no …"

And so it went on: question after eager question, while Marianne made the breakfast.

After they had eaten, John went to his own apartment. Shortly, he was joined by Marianne who looked very serious.

"John, I've been thinking."

"Yes …"

She sat down with her hands folded in her lap. Her frown deepened.

"Er … I don't quite know how to put this … but our relationship is sort of disjointed … No … that's the wrong word … What I mean is … would it be crazy if it were permanent, but you were in one century and me in another?"

"I'm not sure what you mean. But I know that wherever I am I will always be committed to you and George-Louis and …"

"Yes, but should we be married?!"

He was taken aback. Then, when he realised fully what she had said, he threw back his head and laughed and laughed. Calming down, he grabbed the bewildered Marianne and lifted her out of the chair and into the air and said, "Oh, yes, yes, yes!"

So when he arrived back in the Research Centre he was accompanied by his new wife and stepson. They had left behind in Ironbridge a community in festive mood. Everyone there who could had congratulated John. No one saw him anymore as an interloper: he was regarded as a hero. Only the journey into time past seemed important and where he had come from in the first place seemed forgotten.

Chapter XVII

The next few days were very busy, but when John was not in the simulator or visiting the launching site with Merlin, Alphonse, Ben and other experts he was with Marianne and George-Louis. There were times when she seemed preoccupied, but John, not wishing to increase her stress, did not draw attention to this. George-Louis, on the other hand, was excited by everything. Nevertheless, all too soon for all three the time for take-off arrived.

At least, John thought, this space suit is less cumbersome than the one I arrived in. But this in no way eased his almost choking apprehension — and he was sweating profusely. Merlin could not help noticing this, but though he occasionally smiled at John and even made clucking noises of encouragement, he got on with the preparation of the ship and the checking of the instruments. Alphonse and Ben seemed more concerned about John's mental state, but they too were busy. One of Alphonse's tasks was to go over with John, for one final rehearsal, all that John had to do, but though John kept saying, "Yes, yes," he could not be sure he was listening. As he helped to strap the unwilling time-traveller into his seat, he looked intently into his eyes and said, "Now, are you all right?"

"Yes."

"Are you sure?"

John managed a smile, but really he felt as though he were about to be executed and just wanted to get it over with. He said, "If you are all ready, let's go. It's the suspense that's the killer."

He watched them leave and saw the wheel on the airlock turn. Then he was on his own. Entombed, he thought. But then, don't be so bloody daft; you missed your calling, boy: you should have been an actor ... or a dramatist ... A dramatist? Yes, a dramatist, or a bloody scriptwriter ... You saw too many B films on the bloody television when you should have been studying ...

Then, on the tiny plug in his ear, he heard Merlin's voice as he checked with everybody at ground control that all was ready. This procedure complete, there was one last check with John, and then he was off.

The ascent was quite unlike that on his original trip to the moon because it was surprisingly gentle. He was not affected by g forces as he had been on that occasion. He did pick up speed, but so very gradually that he was hardly aware of any acceleration at all. Nevertheless, he knew from the instruments that he was travelling even faster than he ever had before and yet keeping the craft on line by means of the screen in front of him was easy — as easy as if he were in the simulator. He felt encouraged and thought that perhaps Merlin was right: the technology was now so advanced that all would be well. Into this reverie came Alphonse's voice, "OK, John, all is looking good. You are on track and you have done well. There's nothing else for you to do just now. Why don't you try to get some rest? And we'll call you when you are needed."

He used the high-speed lift to go down to the living quarters and lay down on the bunk. It was comfortable so he closed his eyes, even though he knew full well that he would not be able to sleep. He began to consider what was ahead of him, but he deliberately rejected this line of thought and decided to think about Marianne instead: he tried to remember everything he could about her and began with their very first meeting; he had thought he was dead and she must be an angel. Would he ever see her again? Even if he did not, he had been with her for nearly a year and nothing could ever change that. The trip in the jaunting car; the Burren; living in her house with her and George-Louis; everything had been much more wonderful than he had thought at the time. Why had he been so silly and spoilt things so often with his temper and his ignorance and his self-centredness? And always there had been her benign smile … He fell asleep … and dreamt he was running with his childhood friends, but so smoothly and effortlessly, through the coppice behind the house, down the path that slanted through the trees where he had pretended he was one of Robin Hood's merry men riding to rescue the peasants oppressed by the wicked sheriff. Then he heard someone call his name from afar … more and more insistently. It was Alphonse telling him to go back to the controls. He was about to travel through time.

He went to the time travel console and switched on. The screen glowed green and unearthly. 'It's because I'm never going to be on Earth ever again,' he told himself glumly. 'I'm marooned in space, Jim lad! Oo aagh! Many's the night I dreamt of cheese! Oh, shut up — acting again — now concentrate! Listen to Merlin — Aagh, sod Merlin.' Then that very voice broke in and John wondered if he had been talking aloud to himself and Merlin had heard. If he had he did not show it.

"John, did you enjoy your sleep?"

"I don't remember — I was asleep!"

"Eh! Oh, yes. Now listen, John. As we said, the next bit should be easy, but it could get a little tricky."

After a pause John replied, under his breath, "What's new?" Then aloud, "OK, tell me."

"Right! On your screen you should be seeing what looks like a matrix — or ... or ... a mesh."

"Yes."

"And there's a red area in the middle."

"Yes, but it's not very clear — it's sort of muzzy."

"That doesn't matter — just keep moving towards it — right for the centre of it. Have you got that? It's just as in the simulator."

"Well, yes. I suppose so, but it's not quite the same."

There was what seemed to be an impatient pause and the Merlin said, "OK, is it near enough?"

"Er, yes. I think so — and I am steering towards it."

Then, before Merlin could speak again, John said, "It's becoming clearer ... sort of more defined ... and much smaller. Eerr! I think it's drawing me in. Is it supposed ...?"

But before he could finish he felt the ship surge forward. Everything began to quiver and then to shake. Merlin's voice was chattering, getting higher and higher in pitch. John could not decipher what was being said. But that only added to his growing terror. The craft was being sucked into a hole and it seemed to become thinner and thinner — and so did he! The pressure on his whole body became heavier and heavier. The last thought he was aware of was a memory of reading a description of a deep sea diver, who descended to a depth where the pressure pushed the whole of his body up into the helmet. The reverse was happening to John: he was being sucked out. He lost consciousness.

When he had arrived in the future he had been injured and it was only gradually that his memory of what preceded his crash had come to him. This time he knew exactly who he was and that he was in the space-cum-time ship, but of where he might be, and when, he had no idea. His immediate surroundings seemed not to have changed despite what he had thought had been the complete squashing of him and his vehicle. The time travel console was blank. He made his way to the other and squinted at the various dials he had gone through with Alphonse. One gauge told him he was still moving in space and another that the date was Friday 13th March, 3006. He was somewhere above the Earth in the middle of the Dark Times! The shock was such that he sat down involuntarily. He felt his energy drain away and he stared ahead unseeingly. Little by little he became aware of a voice, to which he began to pay attention, slowly and reluctantly. It was Alphonse telling him over and over again to press the switch marked 'On Arrival'. Merlin, Alphonse and Ben appeared together: they were congratulating him on his having travelled through time. It was a recording. Even through his anguish he thought, how presumptuous of that bastard, Merlin! But he threw the switch.

Immediately, screens lit up all around him, just as in the simulator. One showed the Earth as a sphere with the image of his craft moving around it; the orbit was shallower than he expected, and though he knew that some dial or screen or monitor somewhere could tell him his actual height, the array was so extensive that he could remember little. Another screen captured his interest because on it the pictures were moving. He remembered what it did — he was looking at the Earth below, precisely beneath the ship; at that very moment he was moving across central Russia. He now felt it imperative that he discover his height. First he found a dial showing the outside temperature and knew that next to it would be his height: fifty kilometres! At first this piece of information frightened him — that is until he noticed that the figure remained steady. He thought that being in orbit meant that he had time to consider what to do next: 'Remember your training, you idiot!' It was simple enough as it merely required him to throw another switch, and flashing on a third screen he saw his instructions for landing. However, he did not want to take the risk of doing that because he was too afraid of what he might find down there. He reasoned with himself that because he had now travelled through time he had covered any bargain he might have made with the people of the fifth millennium, so he could now go back — if that was at all possible. Guiltily, he moved back towards the time travelling console, but when he switched on nothing happened for a very long time. Then a doleful message chattered across the screen: 'Available only after take-off.'

'Am I marooned again?' he said to himself. 'No, no, of course you are not. Think, man, think.' And he walked back across the cockpit and stared at nothing in particular until after a while he became aware of a screen set above the others, and on this was an image of Alphonse making a 'listen to me' gesture over and over again. John touched the correct button and Alphonse's dour face looked at him accusingly.

"What took you so long? Where've you been?" he said. Then he smiled so broadly that John thought fleetingly he might be real. This, as well as the rhetorical questions, annoyed him.

"Where you bloody sent me!" he replied.

At this Alphonse's head shuddered, his mouth opened and shut repeatedly and his eyes blinked. John realised that he had given an unexpected reply to the interactive video. He sighed — he was still all alone in space.

"OK," he said, "What do I do next?" Alphonse's image beamed at him once more.

"The first thing to decide is where you want to land. We reckon you have about three orbits. Any more and you might not have enough fuel should you ever want to take off again. Do you know where you are now?"

"Yes, I'm somewhere over Russia, but what exercises my mind is that it is 3006!"

The image seized up again. Then came back to life and Alphonse said, "Oh."

"Oh? Is that all you have to say?"

Once more the image froze. Then it suddenly sprang to life and said in a much more mechanical tone of voice, "Better not land there … Er …er … choose somewhere you know … where there's some chance you at least speak the language."

"That's bloody comforting, Alphonse!"

"Reply not understood … Choose area for landing …"

John put the screen on hold and began to think seriously about his landing spot. Clearly the best place would be England, which he knew. He was familiar with some remote bits of France, such as the Grands Causses — mostly flat, but they could be rocky. He could think of a particular outcrop of limestone pillars with a central clear space in the middle, but you couldn't hide a spaceship there. No, that was no good and his French was poor. What about Merseyside? In times of trouble? No bloody fear — any time could spell trouble there. And anyway, did it still exist? Was there any part of the country that would be recognisable? What about his beloved Severn Valley — where Marianne was? He remembered that there had been a monstrous raid there in his own day but what would it be like in 3006? The only information he had was 1000 years too late. Even so, it was as near as he could get. Sod it! It would have to do. He turned again to the screen with his instructions and he re-activated Alphonse for company. It was a pleasant surprise to discover the two were synchronised. And anyway, the ship's computers did all the work. All that he had to do was to press a few buttons and feed in the co-ordinates. Those he decided upon would, he hoped, bring him down in the woods of his childhood — those in his dream. He returned to his bunk and waited. Initially, he felt calm, but then, as he became aware that the spaceship was manoeuvring itself, he became anxious and wondered if he should go back to the control room. He told himself that even if he did there was nothing he could do: Merlin, Alphonse and Ben had worked everything out — and if they had got it wrong! Well, what could you do? Nothing! Nevertheless, he decided to go; that way he would not be acting like an ostrich and he might feel better if he had some idea of what was happening. He didn't on either count. The screens were changing rapidly, the noise of the engines was loud — for the first time in the whole journey — and all the clocks and dials were spinning crazily. But then, gradually, everything seemed to slow down. There was almost silence, then a gentle bump, a slight recoil — and he knew he had landed.

Now, he thought, the real nightmare will begin. He looked at the screens, which he had remembered would give him all round vision, and was amazed to see that although he was surrounded by trees he was actually in a clearing. What comforted him most, however, was that he could see no people. Was he hidden? The only way to find out was by going outside, but the thought of that was very frightening. Better to wait awhile and see if anything or anybody turned up. Perhaps he should try to get some sleep — but what if a warlord, or somebody worse, were to arrive with his band of desperados to capture him while he was asleep? No, that couldn't happen — but could he really believe Merlin that the outer shell of the ship was impenetrable? He decided to wait in the control room and keep an eye on the screens. It got dark and that meant he had at least twelve hours before he needed to venture out, so he returned to the cramped living quarters, ate some of the very black chocolate that was amongst the food he had found earlier, and lay once more on the bunk. He drifted off into an uneasy sleep. When he awoke he felt apprehensive but did not know why until he began to recognise the main features of his living space: When reality hit him, he wanted to curl up on his bed, go back to sleep and wake up in his own room in the twenty-first century to discover that everything that had happened in the last year had been a bad dream. His eyes were screwed up tight, but they opened wide suddenly because he was certain he could hear tapping somewhere on the ship. He jumped from the bunk and began to make his way through the craft, looking intently but nervously and carefully in every nook and cranny as he went. Half way up he stopped and listened to see if he could locate exactly where the noise was coming from: it was on the outer wall. Already his heart was racing, but he ran the rest of the way to the control room and switched on the screens. Slowly, he traced every inch of his surroundings until his picture showed a group of ragged and very skinny people. They looked small. He wondered about this and then realised that they were children. As they were unaware that he was watching them he was able to scrutinise them very thoroughly. They had no weapons, he was sure. He decided to go out, but first searched for something to carry with him; something which would at least look like a weapon. He remembered that Ben had once mentioned that somewhere on the ship there was a stun gun. A panel in the airlock was marked with the letters 'ST.G.' Perhaps this stood for stun gun. There was only one way to find out. He pushed gently on the panel itself and it opened to reveal something that looked to him like a toy tommy gun. He felt he had plenty of time, so he read the instructions carefully. Then, convinced that he could defend himself without actually killing anybody, he tapped in the code and set in motion the mechanism that operated the outer door, which slid open silently. So did the landing platform.

He stepped out expecting to see the children, but there was no sign of them. He hesitated then looked around carefully. There was a slight flutter in the trees opposite his exit and then he saw a face — long and thin with doleful eyes. The creature, for it seemed hardly human, was observing him apprehensively. Slowly, a pitiful band of half-starved waifs emerged into the clearing. Common sense told him to smile and he did so, but with difficulty. One of them said, "Eh, mister, are you from America? Have you come to save us?"

John was so surprised by this that he really did smile quite spontaneously. He began to walk down the platform but stopped when the children stepped back nervously. He said, "No. I'm not American. I'm English and ... and I've ... arrived here by accident ..."

"Have you come from the moon, then?"

"No ... I've ..."

"You're from Mars!"

"No, I'm from England."

"Where, then, in England?" This was no child's voice but an adult's — firm and strong. John looked at the group intently and could see only children. Then a tall figure stepped from the trees.

My God, thought John, it's Don Quixote! His hair and beard were long, not out of some misguided desire to play a part, but simply because, of necessity, they had not been cut for a very long time. As he hobbled towards the craft, he leaned heavily and awkwardly on a long staff. He looked ill and his thinness was only partly hidden by a ragged poncho. But his voice was strong, "Which side of the Severn do you come from?"

Not understanding the significance of the question, John felt perplexed, but thought that he should answer as straightforwardly as he could, "This side ... the west."

There was a sigh from the children and then the old man said, "Friend, have you any food for these poor children?"

Again, John did not know what to say, but when he looked again at the painfully thin unfortunates below him, he felt that what little he had he must give to them. However, what could he do? He knew that, though he felt very sorry for them, he should not allow them on board. He must go back inside and close the exit securely while he looked through the food Merlin and the others had provided.

"Wait here," he said and stepped backwards through the exit and into the airlock. Once he heard the door and the landing platform click into place he put down the gun and leaned against the wall breathing heavily. The temptation to try to take off straight away while he was safe was very strong, but the pity he felt for the old man and his pathetic charges was stronger. He went down to the living quarters.

There was more food than he had at first suspected, but the chocolate, which he had already tried and which he thought would probably make the starving children sick, he knew he should not offer them. What he did take for them was the vegetable powders, which, according to the instructions, could be reconstituted into quite large quantities. Cradling the heavy tins over his left arm by means of a thick plastic-like sheet he found with the food and carrying the stun gun in his right, he went out onto the platform again.

His concern that the hungry children might simply grab what they could was unfounded: they obeyed the old man — who organised them to carry the food back to their camp. But he warned them, before they set off, to remain alert. He and John brought up the rear, with John remaining half a pace behind, just in case. Their camp, which consisted of rusty pieces of corrugated iron, plastic sheeting and old carpets, all supported on whatever lay at hand, consisted of about ten 'dwellings' on a piece of level ground which John remembered had been called 'the flats' when he was a boy. He realised that they all lay a good way back from the edge — probably so that they could not be seen from the river. Indeed, Piper, as the old man was called by the children, set a lookout lying in the long grass to watch to see if anyone approached from below.

However, the children were more concerned about another problem: the powder had to be mixed with hot water and that meant making a fire which might be seen from the other side of the river. Piper assembled them around him and asked, "How many communicators that are still working have we got?"

Two children put up their hands.

"Have you seen or heard anything on them to make you think Trelawney and his gang are near us?"

"No …" said a wisp of a girl, "and I don't think they could have observed the landing of the spacecraft. I've hacked into their messages all day. No one has mentioned it; they seem to be attacking a village a long way away."

"Good, but even so we'll take no chances. Some of us can go back into the woods to boil water — and hope the smoke is not seen."

Later, when they had all eaten and the children had gone to their makeshift beds, having, each one of them, come up and gently touched John first, he and Piper talked, the old man keeping watch for any lights on the river. John knew what the first question would be and had already decided to be completely honest. There seemed to be no point in lying: anything he made up would sound even more ridiculous than the truth.

"Where are you really from, John?"

"I'm from both the past and the future." There was enough light from the stars for John to see the amazement on the usually impassive face.

"No! I can't believe it."

"It's true, but I don't know what I could say to convince you … I'm not a very likely space traveller … It's a long story of improbable, seemingly implausible occurrences …" John then went on to tell the story of how he got from the third millennium to the fifth and back to the beginning of the fourth. When he had finished Piper said, "Then it's most important that Trelawney does not even suspect that someone like you is about. I only hope the top of your spaceship does not protrude through the trees or he'll be over here like a flash. And though he might have been busy today murdering and stealing, he'll be back tomorrow and one of his men might look this way. If they do, and see that spacesuit you've got on, we'll all be in trouble. I'll send Sansom and Singh down to the ruined house by the river as soon as it is light to see if they can find you something else to wear."

"Do we just stay here? What are you trying to do? Just survive?"

"For the present, yes. That's all we can do. However, we've picked up information about a community to the west of here and I'm trying to get the children there. But it's not easy, and because we had had no food for days they were beginning to give up hope — some of the more wayward ones were even talking about joining Trelawney, though they know they'll be mistreated in his camp. Some of them have been badly abused in every way — physically and sexually — before they joined me."

"How did such a strange bunch come to be together?"

"Ah, that's a long story too. But briefly, when London was last hit, life there became so miserable that I decided to get out and my daughter persuaded me to take her little girl, Lizzie, with me. She's the one you would have seen in that rickety old pram … We travelled by night and I had no idea where we were going. We slept in ditches and one day ended up in the same ditch as two half-starved kids who tried to steal our food, and then when I got a bit rough with them pleaded to come with us.". He sighed and went on, "Since then the band as grown. Some of the older ones, like Sansom and Angharad, that's the hacker, are more worldly-wise than me. They are the ones who vet any newcomers — it's a good job you had food, by the way — and they can be ruthless. Mostly the kids help each other, but if one of them threatens the group in any way they'll be abandoned."

"Wouldn't they just keep on following you?"

"Well, the last one was left tied to a tree for Trelawney, or some other bastard warlord, to have fun with!"

"What about this community you are headed for?"

"That's something the hackers have picked up, but the information is vague. We don't really know, but now we've got the food you gave us, we might get there — if we are sparing with it. That's why Fred seemed so mean when he dished it out tonight. But they all know what's what."

They talked long into the night and the very last part of their conversation John found very disturbing. He was asked whether his craft could take the whole band when he took off. And though he told Piper that there was hardly enough room even for him and that most of the giant size was needed to house all the machinery to travel through time, he could tell that the old man did not really believe him. He also pointed out that time travel was hazardous.

"Look where I've ended up — because the clever clogs who sent me here think they know how to control what happens. But obviously they don't."

"Yes, John, but any time, any place would be better than this, as you'll find out if you hang around long enough."

"Well, I don't intend to. I'm going to set off as soon as I can."

Piper looked disappointed at this but he said nothing. Neither did John for a while. Then he said, "You look upset, but I can't see how my staying here can achieve anything."

"I was hoping that you might help me to get the kids to this camp — they are such a pitiful lot and some of them are sick, but with two adults there is some chance we can make it."

John did not reply, but already his conscience was beginning to bother him. When he left the camp to sleep in the craft he made sure he was not followed. When he arrived he tapped the digits of his mother's birthday with his knuckles on the outer shell, pausing appropriately between each set of taps — and all the time wondering if this device, the brainchild of Alphonse, would actually work. He was relieved when it did and he got inside. However, he slept badly, so concerned was he for what might happen at the camp. A loud banging on the wall woke him early and outside he found Sansom with some very tatty and smelly clothes; they felt as uncomfortable as they looked when John got into them. Then, having stowed his shiny silvery suit under the bed in his living quarters, he accompanied this wild-looking youth back to the camp.

Everything was in turmoil: Angharad had picked up information that could mean that Trelawney would soon be looking for them. The children had already stripped their shacks of whatever could be carried and having tried to make the rest look uninhabitable, were ready to move. Piper presented him with a fait accompli by leading the group off and calling to John.

"Would you bring up the rear as you have a weapon?" John had no time to think of an answer.

They struggled through the trees and John was surprised at how little noise they made. They had not gone far when Piper signalled them to halt. The ground had been steadily rising but they had arrived at what appeared to be a shallow ditch. The children got down in it and Piper made his way towards John saying, "The next bit is easy, but we had better make sure that it's the camp that Trelawney is looking for and not your ship. If you go back down a little way with Sansom and Singh you should be able to see what they want — if they come."

John said nothing but felt that he wanted to run back to his ship and take off anywhere, just to be out of this situation that seemed to be developing beyond his control. But he was not sure he could even find it after the scramble through the trees, so he simply followed the boys who must have chosen their vantage point earlier because they went straight to a spot where they could see both the camp and the overgrown path that led to the clearing with the craft. Though John was impatient and wanted to squirm with apprehension and fear, Sansom and Singh were good at waiting and very relaxed as they lay on their bellies to watch. He tried, for shame's sake, to be like them, but more than once he thought he was about to scream with anguish. Then after about an hour, Trelawney arrived.

The gang, for there was no better description, looked rough, but they were disciplined and approached the now forsaken camp very carefully. Amongst them were some women, but they seemed to John to be just as menacingly punk as the men, even though they were dressed slightly less outrageously. They all, men and women, moved around the camp silently and as though every object, no matter how commonplace, might be booby-trapped, until a red-haired giant, who John thought must be Trelawney himself, waved his arm dismissively and growled, "We are too late. Whatever miserable miscreants lived here have flown and taken anything worth having with them … Where's that misbegotten little bastard who suggested coming here?"

There was a little laughter and murmurings from the brigands and a skinny youth was pitched in front of this hirsute leader. He crouched cringing in front of the chief who kicked him, seemingly as a matter of course, in the midriff and said, "Right, you little sod, tell us why we are here?"

He was just about to kick him again when a wavering female voice cried out, "OK, son, so he made a mistake … but leave the poor little bugger alone. I need him all in one piece."

An old hag stepped up to the boss and looked him fearlessly in the eye; as his mother she was able to draw a least a little respect from him, but the rest of the gang guffawed lasciviously, knowing why she needed him. She lifted the lad up, but the look he gave her was one of both subservience and hate. Sansom and Singh looked at each other and Sansom whispered, "My God, it's Bowden. I always thought he was a shithouse, but you can't help but feel sorry for him now."

"Don't worry about him. He'll not last long with that lot," was the reply.

The gang slowly began to drift back towards the river and as they had shown no interest in the path that ran towards the ship, John was able to conclude that they knew nothing about it. The three spies began to make their way back to the rest of the group, and when they were well out of earshot of the Trelawney gang, Sansom brought up the question of Bowden again.

"But when you think what that old bag wants him for … uugh … and I don't think we had any right to abandon him to them in the first place."

"You what?"

"And I was not the only one. Piper said we shouldn't, because we would be no better than Trelawney, and Angharad and some of the other girls almost went back for him … but Piper said it was too dangerous."

"Look, Sansom, he was trouble from the very start and some of the lads could have easily been led by him, and then where would we be, eh?"

"Yes, but even so …"

"When we get back I'm going to make sure those lads know exactly what's in store for him … we gotta use him as an example … if we don't stick together, we'll all end up in the hands of Trelawney or one of the other gangs … Do you want to go back to the lot we escaped from?"

"You know I don't."

"Well then."

As the group made their way through the rest of the wood, quickly across a stretch of open ground, and to the high woods they could just make out ahead of them, John could hear Singh as he moved from one member of the group to the next whispering about the fate he believed was in store for Bowden. At least one of the boys began to whimper, and Piper put his arm around him and said, "Never mind, you'll be safe with us, and now we've got an astronaut to help us, and he's got a stun gun."

John did not welcome this remark: he knew he was not the kind of hero Piper was trying to make him out to be, but he kept quiet … And admired the efficiency with which all the children established their new camp … and posted guards.

After they had eaten, again sparingly, of the reconstituted food John had provided, they were called together by Piper in order to review their situation and decide how they should proceed. The first thing they did was to put together all they knew, and for this those who had communicators were all important. Angharad and Sebastian created a model from soil in the middle of the group and explained to the others the lie of the land between them and the community they hoped to join. They also pointed out where they suspected marauding gangs might be located, but Piper warned everyone that there could be others who for one reason or another were keeping radio silence — so everyone should keep watching for signs of other people. Because the group kept together there was no need for them to send each other messages and so they hoped that no one could use electronic means to locate them. There was just a slight risk that very clever hackers could trace them when they eavesdropped on the gangs or used their communicators to receive messages from satellites to locate their position or to obtain contour maps of the areas they had moved, or hoped to move, through. Once, as far as possible, their situation was known, Piper asked for ideas on how they should proceed. John was amazed how democratic the process was and how even the youngest child's suggestions were patiently listened to by all. Piper's influence only came into its own when he summarised what had been said in such a way as to make decisions possible. Just as they were about to break up there was a warning whistle from one of the guards. Everyone fell silent and all moved to the perimeter. What was coming towards them was a pack of wild dogs and they had picked up the scent of the children; the animals knew such groups to be vulnerable, but they had not reckoned with John and his stun gun. When the dogs were about fifty yards off he fired, and was surprised to discover that the gun was silent. At first he thought it had failed to go off but then saw the havoc that his shots caused among the animals: they howled in pain and several of them fell to the ground temporarily paralysed; the rest scattered. Piper and the children moved to surround the fallen ones; as they began to revive, the kids kicked them until Piper told them that that was enough. As the dogs revived and staggered off, John asked what this was all about and Piper explained that the hope was that the dogs would now remember them and leave them alone. He said that for these kids, packs of wandering animals were as dangerous as people.

The plan for the next day was that they should move further west as unobtrusively as possible, and for this they had pored over the contour maps trying to work out which would be the safest way. Where they had knowledge of cover from trees and shrubs, they could also use these too — but carefully because such places could conceal dangers. They were ready at first light, and again John was impressed by the discipline, especially of the very young children. Even Lizzie, the smallest of them all, only ever whispered when she spoke. Progress was slow as the route was somewhat tortuous and the various woods that were used were all scouted first. Then, at about midday, they had some luck: they came across the remains of a fortified camp. There were signs that it had been set on fire, but not even Piper knew whether this had been the work of marauders or an accident. Once the site had been searched by older, reliable children, more of them moved in to see what they could find — but not all of them went in. Most of the children, and particularly the younger ones, moved beyond the settlement and lay almost hidden in the long grass near by. Piper stayed with them; John joined the others in the disused camp. It looked as though it had accommodated about thirty people who seemed to have lived communally. There were rooms that had obviously housed electronic equipment, but nothing worth keeping was found amongst the wreckage. Then he became aware of a commotion outside in the compound. It turned out that, quite by accident, one of the boys had uncovered a trapdoor, which had been hidden by a layer of earth — to conceal it where marauders would least likely look, i.e. right in the middle of an open space. What they found in there was a portable generator and what smelt like diesel oil to run it. They carried their find out to Piper who, to the chagrin of Singh, did not seem impressed. He saw it as a mixed blessing for though they could now recharge their run down communicators, it had to be carried and so did the diesel, and the noise and fumes, should they operate it, might give them away. Sansom was of the opinion that they should keep it and so was John, who agreed to carry it. As it happened, he did not have to: the generator was carried in Lizzie's pram, which meant it was also concealed. Of course, John had to agree to push the pram. He did not mind because he could put the rest of his pack in with the child, and she was an engaging little girl, anyway. Moreover, when they ran it they discovered it was almost silent and the exhaust gases were negligible. John, however, had not bargained for the difficulty of pushing the pram over rough ground. For the next few days he earned his keep.

Fortunately, the weather was good and this meant that hiding in ditches, or in long grass, or in shrubbery was not too uncomfortable. They had to do this quite often because Piper wanted them to avoid all the people they met. The older children were very good at warning of the approach of strangers in plenty of time. Sometimes, however, John felt sorry for those who passed by. A group of young children, following a woman so haggard he could not tell her age, wandered past them; they looked as though they were desperately hungry, but Piper had warned him that no one they met was to be trusted. This worried John: if the people in the community for which they were heading were as suspicious as Piper, then their reception there could be unpleasant. Several attempts had been made to reach them by communicator, but replies had been ambiguous, which made John even more uneasy. Piper, despite his habitual pessimism, remained non-committal when John tried to discover what he thought the prospects of a frosty reception were. What happened next surprised him and everybody else.

They had found a secluded place to camp for the night and Piper had said he thought they were as safe as they could be. The first watch of guards had been posted and most of the younger children were asleep. Piper and John were talking quietly under a sort of lean-to when suddenly the whole of the clearing was filled with bright light, and, most alarming, massed choirs singing the 'Hallelujah Chorus'! Crazily, momentarily, John wondered if he had travelled through time again and had arrived at the Nativity! Then he heard a voice as though through a very large loudspeaker. It was in no way angelic.

"We want you all to remain very still. Do not try to run away or escape: you are surrounded and there is nowhere to run. If you try to leave the area you will find the consequences painful."

The speaking ceased but the music, now soft and gentle, even soothing, continued. Piper spoke, "Who are you and what do you want with us?"

"We are the Caer Caradoc Community and we believe you and your group are searching for us. We have been monitoring your progress towards us for several weeks, but we also know that you have recently been joined by a spaceman and we wish to speak to him before we decide whether to admit any of you."

John was about to speak but Piper motioned to him to be silent. Then he said, "What makes you think we have such a person in our group?"

"Piper, we know more about you than you think and we have access to technology that you could only dream of. We tracked the spaceman from the moment he appeared in the Earth's atmosphere and we know that he landed near your camp by the River Severn. He could be even more dangerous than that scoundrel Trelawney whom you have been avoiding. Though we are peaceful, we will not take any risks that might jeopardise our freedom; you have no alternative but to allow us to speak with him."

Without even looking at Piper, John stepped out into the clearing, but he took the stun gun with him.

"Mr More, put down the weapon and move to your right — into the woods — and you will find our control module."

John had no choice but to obey. When he arrived at what looked like a plastic cabin, a door opened and he went in. Inside there was a table at which sat two women and a man. After spending a week with Piper's rather mucky group, John was struck by how clean and beautifully dressed they were. They all smiled affably at him and the man motioned him to sit down on a seat in front of the table. One of the women spoke, "Tell us who you are and where you have come from … and what you want with Piper and the children."

John took a deep breath and began, "As you seem to know already, my name is John More. I am English, peace-loving and have travelled here through time." He paused and looked at them. He was gratified to see that two of them at least, the women, seemed suitably shocked. The man smiled — as John remembered Merlin smiling. John continued, "I don't expect you to believe me. I can hardly believe it myself …" and he told them his story from the time of his first journey to the moon to his landing near Piper's camp.

The man spoke first, "Have you any way to prove your incredible story?"

"Only through the time machine. If your technology is as good as you have hinted, then you may have scientists and technologists who can confirm that that is what it is. I myself do not understand the technology. As I explained, I was the one sent back from the future only because I was in the wrong time anyway. Given the contradictions to which time travel might give rise, morally there was only one choice and that was me. The aim was to put me back in my own time. That I am here is an accident — and one I wish I was not part of, believe me."

The three looked at each other and then the man said, "Can you speak Welsh?"

Surprised by this question, John laughed and said he couldn't. They seemed to take his response as genuine and began to converse earnestly in what John was certain really was Welsh. After about five minutes their discussion came to an end and one of the women said, "Very well, John More, we are going to allow all of you into our community — provisionally, of course. Whether Piper and the children remain with us depends on how they behave, but we do have considerable knowledge of all of them. Of you we are not so certain, so we want to visit your ship as soon as possible to confirm what you have told us. Do you agree to allowing us to inspect it?" And before he could answer she went on, "You really have no alternative, because unless you agree, none of Piper's party will be permitted either."

John thought for a moment and then replied, "These children are in dire need — of proper food, of medical care, of education — of everything, really. I couldn't be responsible for them being sent back out into what seems to me to be a terrifying world." Then he paused for a second and added, "I hope you really can look after them … that you are not as vulnerable as everybody else seems to be in this country."

" Not just this country, Mr More, but the whole world … I'm afraid we can give you no absolute guarantee of safety. Nobody could. But you will all be safer with us than with anybody else. That is as much as we can offer."

When John emerged from the cabin he found Piper and all the children clustered round the entrance looking very anxious. They broke out into cheering when he told them all was well and they would be going to the Caer Caradoc Community. Then the three interrogators came out. The man spoke, "I am Howard. This is Ruth and this is Esther. We welcome you all to Caer Caradoc."

He stepped forward and shook hands with Piper and said, "We have followed your progress with great interest. We congratulate you personally because we think you have done a marvellous job for these youngsters. Please follow us to the road and we will take you all to safety."

John, Piper and the children were ushered on to what looked like amphibious vehicles, which drove off at great speed, even though they had no lights and the night was pitch black. The children expected to pass through some sort of palisade, like those that surrounded the various gang camps they had come from, but when they approached Caer Caradoc nothing of the kind appeared. Instead, they heard strange electronic noises as the speed of the vehicles dropped to a crawl. Piper told John that at that point they were probably passing through some sort of electronic defence shield, and once they were through they heard the same sounds again as the vehicles picked up speed.

Even though the children were tired, they had to pass through a delousing and disinfecting area and their clothes were taken from them and burnt. One or two of the little ones were upset by this, but they quietened down when they were all given beautifully clean cotton nightshirts and sat down to hot soup before being taken into a warm dormitory with comfortable beds. Piper was asked to tell them that this was only a temporary arrangement and matters would be sorted out properly the next day.

Early the next morning Piper and John were taken to another reception room where, over breakfast, they were introduced to other members of the community by Howard, Ruth and Esther. Many of these people greeted Piper very warmly as they saw him as a kind of folk hero. John they treated courteously, it seemed, but with a deference that was disturbing. Piper was asked how he thought the children would take to joining families. Siblings and special friends would be kept together and none of the group would be far from the others, he was told. While he was discussing this, John was invited to meet with other members of the community who, so they said, would like to talk to him. As he expected, it was the future they wanted to know about. He tried to reassure them that better conditions would emerge — everywhere, as far as he knew — but that this would take centuries. He also thought of saying that from his brief acquaintance with their community, he thought they were probably moving on the right lines, but he had learned to be circumspect and said as little as possible.

As he became more acquainted with the community over the next few days he realised that it was a much more extensive organisation than he had expected. Though the 'village' where he and Piper's children were accommodated amounted to only about one hundred families, it was linked with several other villages of about the same size; there was extensive land under cultivation in-between. The community also had small factories, schools and hospitals. When he asked how it was that they seemed to be left unmolested by the gangs of marauders, he was told that the electronic shield kept them out. However, this was probably not so important. The crucial fact was that the community was too useful to the gangs, who not only bartered for food but also used the medical services that the community could offer. This had not always been the case and the community still felt vulnerable, hence the shield and the precautions taken over new recruits. Nevertheless, security was improving and the community had attracted men and women who had outstanding technical skills and scientific knowledge. Moreover, they were in constant touch with other such communities throughout the world. The true danger, he was informed, came not from the gangs, which were dwindling anyway, but from the dictators who, through their vast conquered territories in parts of Europe, Asia, Africa and America, still dominated the world and had the military might to crush Caer Caradoc easily — and other communities like it, shield or no shield. Indeed, they knew of sister communities that had been crushed. Fortunately, the dictators seemed to be obsessed with fighting each other. But unfortunately, they seemed to care little about the misery they inflicted on the world's unhappy population. The horrific conditions in some places — which people insisted on telling him about — confirmed everything he had seen on Ambrose's virtual reality videos, and even the full submersion experiences.

Chapter XVIII

Once the children had settled in, were beginning to put on weight and look generally healthier, Howard approached John and told him it was time to inspect the ship.

"You still don't trust me, then?"

"Oh, yes. I think most people here do. But they are intrigued. Nothing like this has happened before. They are really excited."

"Who's coming? The whole community?"

"Of course not! Only seven of us will fit in the helicopter."

"So, we are going by helicopter? I didn't know you had such things."

"Well, we use them only when we have to and we want a quick get-in and out because of Trelawney, even though our intelligence tells us that he's busy elsewhere. You never know with him: he's crafty."

"Then I'd better take the stun gun."

"I'm afraid you can't: it's community rules. But don't worry, it will be with us — along with several others that our technicians have copied from yours."

"That's comforting." But John did not feel comfortable.

When it was time to board the helicopter there was a great kerfuffle: the whole community seemed to be milling about despite the whirling of the blades. Lizzie was crying and calling to John. She had become quite attached to him and wanted to be wherever he was. People were getting on and off the craft as though it where an ancient cruise ship. In the confusion, she remained on board when it finally took off and they could not go back to drop her because the shield had to be shut off when they climbed out of the village, and this had to be as brief as possible. John tried to re-assure everyone that he could look after her, but he did not know quite how.

It was obvious from the air where the boundary of the community lay because once beyond it, the land could be seen to be reverting almost to the way it had been in pre-historic times: it was wild, but even so had about it a disorganised lushness. Very soon they were over the clearing, and there stood the spaceship — glistening in the sunlight, though more dully than when John had landed. They came to earth quite near it and got out, the members of the community rather gingerly and carrying their stun guns.

They looked at the craft in awe, hesitating to approach it. John, however, walked quickly towards it and was followed closely by Lizzie. He was appalled by what he could see. It was obvious that someone had tried to get in: it had, near the base, what looked like burns from an acetylene cutter. There were also dents that could have been caused by bullets — or even shells, some were so large. Yet whoever it was had not succeeded and he knew that Merlin had been right — no ancient technology was capable of penetrating the outer skin. The rest of the party stood some way off when he rapped the code with his knuckles. The door slid open and the platform came down to the ground as smoothly and silently as ever it had. He picked up Lizzie to carry her in and called to the others to follow.

It was then that a shot rang out and Howard fell forward in a heap without even raising his gun. Immediately, the rest of the community party fired into the undergrowth indiscriminately, but effectively. There were yells of pain and cries of anguish. The bushes and shrubbery seemed to come alive as the brigands of Trelawney's gang fell out into the clearing writhing in agony. But some had not been hit and began to fire their more conventional weapons at the Caer Caradoc people. John did not even think about what he was doing: he ran up the platform into the ship and locked the door behind him. It was only then that he realised what he had done: he had deserted his friends. Telling Lizzie to follow him, he ran up to the command module and sat down at the console that controlled the monitors for looking at his immediate surroundings. There seemed to be fighting going on all around the ship. At first, he thought his friends had dealt effectively with the gang, but he had not reckoned with the reinforcements, which Trelawney could draw on. He watched in horror as the Caer Caradoc members were disposed of one by one. In the close hand to hand fighting that ended the skirmish they were no match for Trelawney's ruffians.

The gang then gathered round the ship and the chief stepped forward and cried out, "Right, louse of a spaceman, if that's what you are, now we are going to get you — even if we have to destroy your ship. So you think you are clever with your impenetrable shield. Well, let's see how you do with a nuclear shell."

His companions guffawed and out of the woods rolled what looked to John like a piece of complex artillery. He now knew he had no choice. He sat in the command seat, pulled Lizzie onto his lap and fastened her along with himself into the safety harness. Then he prayed that everything would work. His mind felt sharp; he knew, almost instinctively, the switches to throw and the buttons to press. There was a slight heart-wrenching pause and then he heard the engines roar and felt the ship lift off gently but majestically. On this occasion he felt impatient about the slowness of the initial ascent, because Trelawney could still blast him out of existence, but nothing happened; he did not know that his pursuers had been scorched to a cinder. He and Lizzie had escaped and that was all that mattered. It was only then that he fully realised the consequences of having taken Lizzie with him. But the worry was brief because there was work to do. He got the ship into orbit and then used the monitors again to try to see what had happened to the clearing. When he finally found it, he saw that the take-off had incinerated most of the wood — and he hoped all of Trelawney's gang with it.

He tried to remember what Alphonse had said about the number of orbits he could afford, and as he sat there he realised that Lizzie was asleep. She had whimpered once or twice but on the whole seemed undaunted by what had happened and he wondered if this was because of all the horrors she must have already seen before he had met her and her grandfather. Her grandfather! He'll be devastated! He looked frantically at all the instruments and dials to see if he could find some way to make at least radio contact with Caer Caradoc. On what he thought would be the relevant parts of the console, he threw switches and turned knobs more or less indiscriminately until at last he got a sound; it seemed like static at first, but then he heard human voices. He swore and was amazed to hear his own voice coming back to him. Whatever he had hit upon must have been two-way, so as he twiddled with various knobs he kept repeating, "Hello, Caer Caradoc. Come in, Caer Caradoc." Nothing seemed to work. Despair overwhelmed him and he was about to fall on his knees and sob when he noticed the child; she was sleeping peacefully, so beautiful — but so vulnerable … and he had become responsible for her. 'Bloody try again,' he told himself. And this time he got a reply.

"Hello, John More. Hello, John More."

"Hello, Caradoc."

"John, Are you OK?"

"Yes."

"What happened? We lost touch with the group just as you landed."

"We were attacked by Trelawney and I fear most of the group are dead."

There was a silence of disbelief, then a gabble of voices from which John could not get any sense, and then one anguished voice above the others. It was Piper's, who cried out, "Where's Lizzie?"

John was about to say that she was safe, but the little girl woke up and shouted, "Hello, Grandad, I can hear you."

"Lizzie, Oh, Lizzie. Where are you?"

"I'm in a nice aeroplane with John. It's lovely, Grandad. I like it here."

Again there was a silence and then Piper said more calmly, "John, what has happened?"

And John told the story of their escape and included his view of the devastated wood.

"I don't think much could have lived in there. I don't know if any of the Caradoc people were still alive before I went, but when that nuclear gun rolled out I just had to go!"

"And?"

"Well. We are now in orbit."

Again cacophony and then someone said, "Then you must be the spacecraft we've just picked up on our monitors. You're miles away. How are you going to get back?"

"I don't know, but let me try to open up my interactive instructions to see if Alphonse can tell me what to do — and never mind who Alphonse is — I'll tell you when I see you."

Though there were protests, John persuaded them to close the channel so that he could try to figure out what to do next, and once on his own he tried to raise Alphonse. This time the screen that had told him it could only be operated after take off came alive and the wonderman technician appeared, smiling as usual. After some friendly banter, John explained that he had to land again. Alphonse's head shivered and shook and then in a voice like a robot it said, "Impossible! Impossible!"

"Why impossible? I've got a three-year-old child here with me ... She belongs here, now!"

Alphonse's image jerked backwards and forwards and then in a stutter he said, "Fuel levels critical. You must go into time mode travel immediately."

John froze and looked at Lizzie, "My God! What have I done ...? Look, Alphonse, can I crash land?"

"Not advisable," said the robot. "Levels critical ... er ... er ... computer taking over."

"You bastard, Merlin, you didn't tell me that could happen!"

But he could tell from the screens and the behaviour of the ship that protest was useless. The ship was about to take him and Lizzie where it would. He said, "Come and sit on John's knee, sweetheart, because I think it might be a bit bumpy."

He fastened her in his harness as before and tried to think of a way to occupy her. He noticed that one of the screens was of the stars. There was one especially bright one.

"Oh, Lizzie, look at that bright star."

"Ah, yes."

"Do you know that song about the little star?" And he began to sing, "Twinkle, Twinkle, Little star ..."and Lizzie joined in ... just as they entered the wormhole. At first she did not seem alarmed, but then as the pressure began to build she clung on to John and began to cry and then to scream in terror. John heard his own voice get higher and higher as he said, "It's all right, sweetheart, Joh ..." and then oblivion.

Slowly, John came to. Lizzie was still on his knee. She was wakening too and she smiled at him beatifically. He knew he ought to be worried, but he was not. He felt a warm calmness: it was not just in his mind but coursed through his whole body. There was peace, and he knew it was everywhere.

"Come on, Lizzie, let's find out where we are."

They rose and went towards the door. John was about to press the numbers for the code when the door opened of its own accord. But what was stranger still was that he was not surprised by this. Hand in hand they walked down the platform, and there standing at the end of it was Piper. John knew who it was even though the person was much younger. Standing next to him was a young woman. Lizzie let go of his hand and ran forwards.

"Mummy! Grandad!" she shouted.

John looked around. Everything seemed real and yet was suffused with a golden light.

'Where is this wonderful place?' he wondered. Then he heard Marianne calling to him.